1

Never Enough

A Matt Teeson Western – Book no 1

By AC Craft

First published June 2022.

I hope you enjoy reading *Never Enough, A Matt Teeson Western, Book no 1*. If you do enjoy reading it, at the end of the book, there is a link for reviews. Please tell your friends and post a review or rating.

I aim to write four books a year.

If you wish to send me further comments, my email address is: accraft@iafrica.com

AC Craft

———

Other books by AC Craft:

Follow the author for notification of new books:

Please go to my author page by clicking this link and then click follow, and you will be notified when my next book comes out, which should be every three to four months: Author page to click follow for notification when next book comes out

Also, to see a list of all books by AC Craft and about the author.

Westerns.

A Matt Teeson Western, Book no 2 - Teeson's Creek

A Matt Teeson Western, Book no 3 - Teeson's Creek Justice

Africa, Action, Aviation, Romance Series.

4

Table of Contents

Chapter 1

Life should be easier. Why can't everyone get along and not be so greedy? Matt thought as he looked for movement in the sparse yellow grass over the sights of his Winchester. "How're you doing there, Tate?" He asked of his friend and partner without taking his eyes off where he had last seen the Apache. "I would help you stop the blood flowing if I thought the Apache had gone."

Tate grunted. "I'm going to be no help to you. You keep doing your job, and I'll sort this wound out. If you don't do your job, I'll lose my golden locks, and there goes my chance with the pretty ladies of Willow Creek."

Matt squeezed the trigger and was rewarded with a yelp. "I winged one. I only had a glimpse of him."

"You need to do better than that if I'm going to get to see that new doctor. I think she might fall in love with me. There's an upside to this," Tate said.

Matt squeezed another shot off and was rewarded with nothing other than a puff of dust. "I think you're getting ahead of yourself on a number of fronts. Firstly, no woman can possibly be a competent doctor, so you're done for anyway. Secondly, I'll have to take you to her, and once she's met me, she'll fall in love."

Tate laughed and then grunted in pain. "I look forward to seeing her reaction when I tell her you said no woman can possibly be a competent doctor."

Matt almost turned his head to look at his partner, but movement to his left and right prevented him. He squeezed off another shot, the distraction of two movements causing him to miss again.

"Since she won't be able to save you anyway, I might as well leave you here. That way, you won't be able to tell her anything. The problem with that plan is, to build this ranch into something, I need you."

There was no answer from Tate. Matt risked a glance and saw his friend slumped on his side, eyes closed. The arrow was buried deep in his left shoulder. He felt nauseous, his heart raced as he thought of a future without his friend and partner. He turned his attention to the seemingly empty space in front. He wondered if the arrow was poisoned. A group of arrows arced into the air from his left. There were no Apache to their left a few moments ago. The rocks were no protection against arrows. They would have worked fine against rifles. Another batch of arrows arced up from their right this time. Matt kept his head down and hoped his Stetson would protect him from the arrows. He didn't look up. He had sent his other three hands to another section of the ranch. The arid New Mexico landscape meant that the grazing land for his 200 head of cattle was extensive. He couldn't rely on the other hands to hear the rifle shots and come to his rescue. His neighbor, George Hamilton, was also far away, and even if he did hear the shots, he would be more likely to help the Apache than Matt. Matt looked around. He needed to get further up the slope before the Indians made the high ground. Matt looked across at Tate. His friend wasn't moving. Matt crept up the hill further through the rocks. The arrows continued to rain down on where he had been. He crawled into another set of rocks, took his Stetson off, and laid it down next to him. He peeped around one of the rocks. He could see there appeared to be eight Apache, split into two groups, each working to surround his previous position. He guessed that wasn't all of them, as he didn't see an obvious leader. He lined up one of the Indians on the right and squeezed the trigger. The Indian threw his bow up in the air and tumbled onto his back with a yelp. Matt swept the rifle to the left and squeezed a shot off at the next one with a similar result. The balance of the Indians on that side retreated a few paces behind some rocks. Matt swung to the group on the left, who were still visible, moving up the slope. He squeezed the trigger again and missed. The Apache zig-zagged up the slope. Matt sighted on another target, squeezed the trigger, and was rewarded with another yelp. The group of Indians on the left retreated behind some rocks. There were no further Indians in sight. Matt rested on his elbow on his side and took the opportunity to replace the bullets in his Winchester. He glanced at the sun. There was no cloud to be seen. He guessed it was about 9 am. He still had his sheepskin jacket on. He looked around. He could not see any of the Apache now, he worried when he could see them, and he worried when he couldn't see them. Matt had seen a group of Apache on the ranch before. There had been twelve of them. If it was the same group, there were four unaccounted for, which was worrisome. He needed to end this soon and patch Tate up. Building the ranch without Tate would lose its appeal. He turned and climbed further up the rocks. He stopped at another bunch of rocks and turned to look down. He now had a clear view of the group on the left and fired off two shots eliciting more cries. They ducked out of sight. Matt turned toward where he had left Tate. He could see one of the Indians from the group on the right getting close to where Tate was. He fired three rounds at him, but he was partially obscured and made a poor target. It did stop his progress and caused him to move into deeper cover. The rest of the Indians on the right were nowhere to be seen. Matt scampered back down the slope to where Tate was. He saw a route where he could possibly sneak up on the Indian who was stalking Tate. Matt moved further right and down toward the Indian. He remained hidden in a shallow gully until he was at the position where he last saw the Apache.

———————

Chapter 2

Matt came up to where he had last seen the Indian and leaped out at what he thought would be the Indian's back. There were only rocks and grass. Matt swung around, his heart racing. No one. Maybe the Apache had got to Tate while Matt had been moving down the gully.

Matt raced toward where he had left Tate. He didn't mind who saw him. His only goal was to save Tate. He leaped into the circle of rocks where he had left Tate. The warrior swung his hatchet at Tate. Matt threw himself off the rock, landing on the Indian's back. Matt knocked the air out of the warrior, the hatchet buried into the ground next to Tate's head. Matt swung a roundhouse punch at the warrior's temple. It connected with a bone-jarring thump, shooting pain up Matt's right arm. The Indian slumped to the ground, his eyes turned toward Matt. Matt grabbed the hatchet and pulled his arm back for the Coup de Grace. The warrior's eyes widened, but he appeared too stunned to move. Matt started his swing and then stopped. He dropped the hatchet and picked up his rifle. He turned it toward the warrior whose eyes widened for the second time in as many seconds. Matt gestured with the rifle for the Indian to get out of there. As Matt did that, there was a volley of shots from behind the

Indians. The Indian pulled himself up, a puzzled look on his face, and dragged himself toward his companions, only to see his companions had leaped on their horses and were disappearing in a cloud of dust. Matt followed him.

"Do you speak English?" Matt asked.

The Indian turned. "Yes." He touched the lump that had formed on his temple.

"Looks like your companions have left you. My other ranch hands have arrived. Put your hands up so that they can see you've surrendered, and once they understand the situation, you can be on your way," Matt said.

"Why would you spare me?" The warrior asked.

"I cannot kill a defenseless person, and I want to live in peace with you. There's space for us all. I want this area to be one big community living in harmony."

"I will not forget this." The warrior said. "I will repay you, but I don't think our people will be able to live in peace."

"You'll see, we'll be able to live in peace," Matt said.

Three cowhands rode up to them, their rifles pointed at the Indian.

Matt said. "What's your name?"

"Nitis." The warrior replied.

"This is my friend Nitis." Matt introduced him.

"It didn't look like he was much of a friend when we arrived." One of the hands said.

"Misunderstanding," Matt replied.

The hand grunted.

"Are you alright to walk?" Matt asked the Apache.

Nitis grinned. He again touched the lump on his head. "I am an Apache warrior. I can walk forever, not like you white boys."

Matt grinned at him. "You better get walking then. You're in no position to throw out insults."

Nitis grinned again, raised his hand in thanks, and set off after his companions, who were long gone.

———

Chapter 3

Matt turned to the hands. "Am I pleased to see you, boys. We were on a hiding to nothing there. I thought I sent you to the opposite end of the ranch. I'm going to have to make my instructions clearer in future." He grimaced as he turned to Tate. "Tate is badly hurt. We need to get him to the house and tend to his wound."

One of the hands turned his horse and went to fetch Matt and Tate's horses from where they'd tied them in a clump of Pinyon-juniper.

Matt squatted next to Tate and felt for a pulse. "Pulse feels good. We need to make a Travois to get him back to the house."

"Shouldn't we take him into town to that new Doctor?" One of the hands said.

"A woman can't possibly be a doctor," Matt said.

The hand shrugged. "You have a point there."

When the other hand came back with the horses, Matt pulled an axe from his saddle bag and hacked four poles from the pinyon-juniper trees. They used a slicker and rope to fashion a travois and hitched it behind Matt's horse.

Matt took his shirt off and put his jacket back on. He ripped the shirt up and bound the wound leaving the arrow where it was, embedded in the shoulder.

They eased Tate onto the travois. Matt tied rope around him to keep him still. Matt swung into the saddle. His horse humped his back and bounced. The travois was something unfamiliar trailing behind him. Matt talked to the horse and patted him. "Easy, Sox." Sox settled down and set off at a walk toward the house. His name was imaginative. Sox was a chestnut whose coat gleamed in the sun, four white socks adorned his legs up to his fetlocks. Matt had owned sox for three years now, and they had an understanding. In the beginning, Sox was the winner of their various battles and seemed to find amusement every time he caught Matt unawares and managed to deposit him on the ground. It appeared that now he had shown Matt who the boss was; he only needed to deposit Matt occasionally as a reminder. Matt would not swap Sox for any other horses. He liked his sense of humor. He did have other work horses that he rode. At 18 hands, Sox was not the ideal cow pony. Matt had not seen a horse his size anywhere else.

As they got closer to the house, it was more like a cabin, Tate groaned. Matt turned around and saw that Tate still had his eyes closed, but his face was screwed up in pain.

With the help of the other hands, Matt got Tate onto his bed in the main house and got to work on him. Tate cried out as Matt removed the arrow and then again as he poured whiskey into the wound. One of the hands had coaxed the fire in the fireplace back to life and laid a knife in the flames.

Tate yelled and passed out as Matt used the knife to check there was nothing else left in the wound and then cauterized the wound before pouring another helping of whiskey into the wound.

"There's nothing else we can do for Tate now. We'll wait and see what happens. You can head out and carry on with the chores, except you, Patrick. You can stay and keep an eye on Tate. I want to go back to the site where the Indians attacked us and get a feel for how many there were and where they came from." He turned back to the other two hands. "First though, you better check and see the Indians have left the ranch." Matt looked down at Tate and frowned.

"Okay, boss, we'll see you back here this evening." The hands turned and walked toward their horses.

Patrick said. "I'll get to work on some fixing of the barn and corrals. I'll check in on Tate from time to time."

The April sun was now as high as it was going to get. Matt had put a blanket on Tate. The cabin was about 60 Fahrenheit. Outside, Matt guessed it was closer to 70. He Climbed back onto Sox and headed back the way they had come. He scanned around for any sign of the Indians, at the same time taking in the surroundings. The grassy plains stretched far to his left, rising to his right into shales and tougher rock intrusions with woodlands and forests. A saw-whet-owl called to his left, ignoring the birds that were mobbing it.

He reached the site of the attack and scanned around before climbing off Sox. He walked around the site checking prints and particularly where the horses had been tied. It appeared there were twelve Apache, including Nitis. He collected some of the arrows and two bows that had been left behind, stuffing the ends of the arrows into his saddle bag and tying the bows to his saddle. He turned and followed the tracks. He didn't have to look hard for the tracks in the sandy soil, given the pace the Indians had taken off at. They had headed straight out across the grassy plains. Matt continued following them, looking down at the tracks and then up into the distance for possible ambush sites.

The hands arrived back at six that evening and Matt shortly after them. The sun still had half an hour more before it dipped below the horizon. Tate was awake this time when Matt wandered in with the hands.

"How're you feeling, Tate," Matt asked.

"In agony," Tate said. "I don't know what kind of doctor hacked away at me. I'm sure it wasn't the beautiful Julia Hamilton. If it had been, I would be up and about by now and planning my wedding to her."

"We'll see how you are tomorrow and then decide what to do. I don't think Dr. Julia will be of any help." Matt put his hand on Tate's forehead. He could feel the heat radiating from Tate's forehead. "That George Hamilton sent her off to medical school to make her happy and, more to the point, to find herself a Dr. Husband who could fit in with George Hamilton's inflated opinion of himself."

Tate laughed and then grimaced. "You hear that, boys? You're my witnesses when Dr. Julia wants to verify what Matt has been saying about her."

The other hands said. "We heard Tate."

Matt said. "I'm only speaking the truth. I'm not worried what you tell her."

"We've been friends since we were knee-high to a grasshopper, and how often have I been right," Tate said. "Particularly when you're running your mouth off about something."

Matt frowned and said nothing.

"Exactly," Tate said.

"You seem full of yourself," Matt said. "Which tells me that you're on the mend and your current doctor has done a good job."

Tate shut his eyes and grimaced.

Matt sighed and turned away. "I don't need to put up with this nonsense from someone whose life I've saved." He was tempted to turn back and check on Tate but decided not to give Tate the satisfaction.

He could only stay turned away for a couple of minutes before coming back to the bed to check on Tate. Tate had closed his eyes. His breathing was rapid and shallow. Matt was having second thoughts about not taking him to the doctor.

He turned to the hands, "let's get something to eat. We'll need our strength for whatever tomorrow might bring." He raised his hand and cocked an ear toward the door. He could hear what sounded like a great horned owl. In normal times he would relish the sound, but he was now trying to figure out whether it was the Indians returning or an actual owl. "What do you think?" He looked toward his hands.

The hands turned their ears toward the door, checking the sound of the owl. "It sounds genuine to me," Patrick said. "I think you're right," Matt said.

Patrick walked outside with a sharp knife to cut some meat off the pronghorn he had shot yesterday. Hugh Thompson walked across to the fireplace. He spread the coals out and moved the logs that were still burning to the side. Hugh placed a grate across the fire. Patrick walked in the door carrying four chunks of meat. He threw the meat on the fire. Matt walked out the door ducking to the side as he exited. He listened again. The owl was still hooting. He listened a bit longer and then walked inside, minimizing his silhouette as he went through the door.

"Keep your guns ready, boys. I think we're safe, but rather be ready," Matt said. "We'll have to go without whiskey tonight. I need to keep our supply in case we need to use it on Tate's wound again."

Chapter 4

"I think we can survive without it, boss," Patrick said as he turned the sizzling meat on the fire. "I'm going to pay that Melissa Hamilton a visit tomorrow. She's a beauty. I'm going to ask her to supper in town on Saturday night."

"That's a bad idea," Matt said. "George Hamilton will not allow you anywhere near his daughters."

"That's Melissa's choice," Patrick said. "I've had coffee with her in town a couple of times, and I know she likes me. What's not to like?"

"I agree with you, Patrick, but George doesn't think anyone is good enough for his daughters. Plus, he's pissed with Tate and me owning this ranch. We registered the title to it under his nose. He was going on the basis that possession is nine-tenths of the law. You being associated with us makes you the enemy." Matt leaned back in his chair, watching Patrick cook the meat.

"I'll take my chances." Patrick flicked the meat off the fire onto a tin plate. "What's the worst he can do? He can only send me packing, but at least Melissa will know my feelings for her. I'll win her over in the end."

"Be careful, don't get yourself into a corner," Matt said. "George Hamilton thinks he's the law around here. He'll realize too late that sheriff John Gamble is no pushover, and although George Hamilton put him in, he'll do what's right. Unfortunately, by that stage, George will probably have killed someone, and it had better not be you."

"I think you're wrong about Julia Hamilton," Patrick said. "From what I've seen of her, she's a sharp lady, and I'm sure she's a good doctor. Not that I have any reason to say that."

"George sent her off to medical school to keep her happy," Matt said. "He probably thought she would find a wealthy husband at medical school. He thinks all women are good for is cooking and making babies."

"It sounds like you think the same as George," Patrick said.

Matt shifted in his chair but didn't reply. *Patrick may have a point*, he thought. Matt said. "You be careful. I'm lucky to have such good hands, and I don't want to lose any of you."

The four of them were silent as they tore into the steaks.

"Good job with the steaks, Patrick." Geoff Barrett said. "I'm with Matt here. You be careful. None of us cook such good steaks."

"You're right there," Patrick said. "I'm probably best at everything, so you guys would be totally lost without me. Melissa is getting the bargain of the century."

They finished their meal and piled the tin plates in a corner. Patrick pulled out a battered deck of cards. "Anyone for a game of poker before bed."

Everyone was in. They pulled the chairs around the table. After a few hands, Patrick said. "This is too easy. I feel embarrassed taking your money. I'm off to bed."

Matt checked on Tate before turning in. He seemed to be sleeping easier. Although when Matt felt his forehead, it was still burning.

They all turned in. Matt thought about whether they should be keeping watch, he decided that it wasn't necessary. The Apache, when he had followed the tracks, seemed intent on getting out of the area. Matt listened to the night noises as he fell asleep. The horned owl hooted, it was joined by a coyote howling in the distance. He sighed. *This would be bliss without George and the Apache.*

Patrick, as always, was up first, lighting the fire. Matt stretched and climbed out of bed. "Morning Patrick, I thought you would still be fast asleep dreaming of Melissa." "Nope, times a'wastin. Got to get on with the day and off to see Melissa," Patrick said.

The others rolled out of bed. Geoff collected the plates from last night and wandered down to the stream to clean them. By the time he came back, Patrick had eggs and bacon in the pan over the fire. The others carried out various tasks, ready for the day. Matt checked on Tate, who seemed no worse but no better. Matt issued instructions while they ate breakfast. "Patrick, you can go out with Geoff and Hugh. I'll keep a watch on Tate and continue fixing up around the barn and

25

corral. I may have to eat my words and get Dr. Julia out here. From now on, you three need to stick together and be alert. I'm worried about the Apache and even more so about George."

The hands were back by three in the afternoon. They had an early supper, Geoff taking on the cooking duties while Patrick jumped in the stream and cleaned himself up. When he came back, his hair was brushed back, and his skin glowing from the icy water. Matt said to him, "you screamed like a girl when you dived into the water. It's lucky Melissa didn't hear that. I don't think it would've impressed her."

"I'm sure she would overlook the screaming like a girl for me braving the water to get clean for her," Patrick replied.

"You're probably right there," Matt said. "You weren't smelling too good."

"Grub's up," Geoff said.

They made short work of the meal. Hugh said. "I prefer Patrick's cooking."

"So do I," Matt said. "But I don't think he would have been focused on the task at hand today. Geoff's cooking is not bad, though."

"I was hoping I had done a bad enough job not to have to cook ever again," Geoff replied.

"We're not stupid enough to say that," Matt said.

"I'm on my way." Patrick got to his feet and dumped his plate in the corner. "I can't have Melissa pining for me any longer."

"Remember what I said," Matt said. "Don't trust George or his men. Play it low-key, and don't push."

"Yes, boss." Patrick grinned, saluted, turned, and marched off to his horse, waving as he went.

Matt watched him and frowned.

———

Chapter 5

Patrick climbed on his horse, wheeled it around, and set off at a walk, whistling as he went. He headed down a path next to the creek running out of the mountains toward the plains. He crossed the creek, where it widened out onto the plains. He urged the horse into a trot after crossing the creek. An hour later, he passed through the archway onto George Hamilton's ranch. He was now on a smooth cart track that went straight for a mile up to an ostentatious ranch house. Patrick saw that most of the hands were returning to the ranch house. Some of the hands stopped to see who was riding up the track. *This looks like it could be trouble,* Patrick thought.

He rode into the ranch yard. George's ranch hands spread out in front of him, some of them he recognized. The slim weedy -looking man asked, "what are you here for?"

"I'm here to see Melissa," Patrick said.

The man stared at him a moment. Patrick noticed his light blue eyes held no feeling. "She's not seeing anyone."

"Tell her Patrick O'Hagan is here to see her. She'll definitely want to see me."

"I don't think she will." The man moved his feet so that his right side was now facing Patrick, his body making a slim target, his right hand close to his gun. He eased the loop off the hammer of his gun.

Patrick realized his loop was still over the hammer of his gun. He wasn't going to remove it now. That would be asking for trouble.

"Tell her Patrick O'Hagan is here to see her. Let her make the decision," Patrick said.

"I know her answer already." The man said.

Matt's warning replayed in Patrick's mind. He now remembered that someone had mentioned to him that George Hamilton had hired a gunman by the name of Peter Knox. That person had mentioned that he was a weedy-looking fellow with piercing blue eyes and long blonde hair. This man fit that description. Patrick was in two minds. His Irish heritage told him there was no way he could back down. Good sense said he should back down and live another day.

"Patrick O'Hagan, what are you doing here? It's good to see you. Peter, I know Patrick, and I want to see him." Melissa had seen Patrick coming up the road and was now walking out of the front door of the ranch house. She had anticipated Peter Knox's actions.

"You see, I told you she would want to see me." The words were out of Patrick's mouth before his brain engaged. He saw a flash of anger in Knox's eyes and saw his hand twitch toward his gun. Patrick held his breath and didn't move. Knox stopped moving, but the anger was still in his eyes. He turned and walked away, stopped again, and turned to watch Patrick.

"I was hoping I would have the pleasure of your company at supper on Saturday night at your diner. I would take you somewhere else if there was somewhere else, but only the best is fit for you," Patrick said.

"Patrick O'Hagan, you have a smooth tongue. Who could resist that? I'll meet you at the diner at six o'clock Saturday evening, and you can escort me home after supper."

Patrick grinned. "I can't wait. See you Saturday evening." He waved at Melissa and glanced at Knox, he didn't like what he saw in those eyes, but all that mattered was Melissa had said yes.

———

Chapter 6

At supper that night, George Hamilton was holding court at the family table.

"Melissa, Knox tells me that Patrick O'Hagan was here, and you agreed to meet him for supper on Saturday night. That's not going to happen. You're not going to see that boy again. He is not in your class," George said.

"I have agreed to see him, and I'm not going to let him down. When I say I'll do something, I do it," Melissa said.

"You will not. That is the end of the conversation." George glared at her.

Melissa said nothing and carried on eating.

George looked at Julia, his younger daughter. "I hear you didn't have any patients today. I'm not surprised. No one wants to go to a woman doctor. I told you that before you went to medical school. I thought at least you'd find a suitable man to marry there." George looked at Julia.

Julia's face flushed red. She glared at George. "I went to medical school because I wanted to become a doctor and heal people. With all the diseases around, everyone needs a doctor, and there's a shortage of doctors. Eventually, some people will come to me, and then word-of-mouth will ensure that more patients come. I know why you sent me to medical school, and it's a lot of nonsense. It's your bigoted view."

31

George's face flushed, although it wasn't as obvious under his tan. "I will not have you speak to me like that."

"You opened the topic. I told you why I was going to medical school when I went. You chose to ignore my opinion," Julia said.

Melissa looked ready to jump in and support her sister. George's wife, Amy, kept her head down, tension etched on her face. Jim Davies, the foreman, also kept his head down, the corners of his mouth threatening to twitch up in a smile. He shoved some more food in his mouth in the hopes that he wouldn't be caught out by George Hamilton in finding this conversation amusing. That could be the end of his job or worse. Julia caught Melissa's eyes and gave a small shake of her head.

"Then why are you paying the rent for my offices if you think I'm not going to have any customers." Julia immediately regretted her comment.

"I'm happy to pay the rent so that you understand no one is interested in going to a woman doctor," George replied.

George turned to Jim Davies. Apparently, discussions about women being doctors and Melissa seeing ranch hands were over. "Things seem to be going well on the ranch. What d'you think, Jim?"

"They are, but we need more land. We've got too many cattle for the land we have. I reckon we need about forty acres per cow." Jim said.

"Don't worry. The shortage of land is temporary. If I can't buy Matt Teeson out, I'll find some way of getting hold of his land." George replied.

Julia sighed. George glanced at her but said nothing.

The only sounds were knives and forks clinking on the plates.

The hammering on the door drowned out the noise of the knives and forks. One of the hands barged into the room without waiting for permission to come in. "You need to come quickly, boss, or you'll be a hand short. Peter Knox is about to make Adam Carter an ex-hand."

George sighed and stood up, "come, Jim." He turned to the hand, "what's the problem?"

"We were playing poker, and Adam accused Knox of cheating." The hand said.

The three men raced across to the bunkhouse. When they arrived, Knox and Carter were standing on opposite sides of the table, side on to each other ready to draw their weapons.

"What's going on?" George asked.

"Carter called me a cheat. No one calls me a cheat and lives," Knox said. "But he's too scared to draw. I like to give people a fair chance to back up their accusations."

Adam Carter opened his mouth. George held up his hand.

"Not a word Adam. Unless it is to apologize to Knox."

Adam frowned and pursed his lips but said nothing.

"Apologize," George said.

Adam's frown deepened. "I'm sorry." He mumbled.

"Now, shake hands, both of you," George said. Neither Knox nor Adam moved. "That's an order. Otherwise, you can draw your pay and be on your way."

No one was sure whether he was addressing Knox or Adam when he said they could draw their pay. Jim was certain he was addressing Adam. There was no way George had any intention of getting rid of Knox. He had hired Knox as a henchman with the intention of growing his empire. Jim suspected that Matt Teeson would be the first person that George would sick Knox onto.

George turned and walked out. Jim followed. As George reached the door, he turned and said. "I don't want any more trouble from you lot tonight. Make that any time." Partway across the yard, he turned back. Jim stopped, "do you want me to come back with you, boss?"

"No, you go on into the house," George said. He turned, checking Jim was out of earshot. "Knox, come here a moment."

Knox came out of the bunkhouse. George could see in the moonlight he was still scowling. "I need you to do a job for me, don't mention it to anyone."

Knox said nothing. He continued to scowl.

"I want you to deal with that, Patrick O'Hagan. I leave it up to you. You know what to do," George said.

Knox replaced the scowl with a smile. "It'll be a pleasure, boss."

"We didn't have this conversation," George said.

"That's what I'm employed for, boss. I know how this works."

George turned and walked off toward the house.

———

Chapter 7

Patrick O'Hagan was on his way back to Matt's cabin. From time to time, he whistled, and when he was tired of whistling, he would listen to the owls and the coyotes, occasionally dreaming of having his own ranch and sitting on the porch with Melissa.

He dismounted next to the corral, unsaddled his horse, rubbed it down, and turned it into the corral, checking there was food and water for it. He took his saddle and bridle, stored them in the barn, and then walked toward the house whistling. He stopped whistling as he got closer, thinking maybe everyone was asleep. Then he saw Matt sitting on the porch in the dark.

"Glad to see you back," Matt said.

"Were you worried about me, boss? Did you think I wouldn't listen to you?" Patrick said.

"It did cross my mind," Matt said. "I'm relieved to see you back. How did it go?"

"It was tense for a moment that hired gunman Knox, who Hamilton recently employed, met me as I came into the yard at the ranch. He asked me what I wanted. When I said I wanted to talk to Melissa, he said Melissa didn't want to talk to me. At that moment, your warning popped into my head.

Knox had removed the loop on his gun, and looked like he wanted to draw on me. I hope you're proud of me."

"I am," Matt said. "It must be the first time you've listened to me. Then what happened?"

"Melissa arrived on the scene and said she did want to see me. I nearly undid my good work by gloating and saying, *see, she did want to see me*. I could see in Knox's eyes that I'd annoyed him. I don't think he's going to forget," Patrick said.

"So, is Melissa going to go to supper with you?"

"Yup, all set up for Saturday night. What did you expect? This is me we're talking about," Patrick said.

"You be careful. I would hate you not to make Saturday night," Matt said.

Patrick headed off to bed. "Good night, boss. I'd better get a good night's sleep. I have a tough boss who seems to expect us to get up before the first birds and go to sleep after the birds have gone to sleep."

"I don't think your boss works you hard enough. I seem to remember him letting you go off early chasing some girl or other," Matt said.

"That's not some girl. That's the gorgeous Melissa," Patrick said.

Matt checked on Tate before he turned in. There was no change in his condition. He was restless and running a temperature. Matt fell asleep, the last thought in his mind being, *I hope I don't have to take Tate in to see that woman doctor. She'll be asking me what took me so long to bring him in.*

Matt checked on Tate again the next morning while Patrick made breakfast and the other hands cleaned and tidied up. Matt changed the bandages and poured the last of the whiskey into the wound.

"Patrick, I want you to go to town today and pick up some more bandages and two bottles of whiskey," Matt said.

"You want me to get that new doctor to come out here?" Patrick asked. "It can't do any harm. In fact, it can only help."

"No, I think Tate will be fine after a few more days. Maybe there was some poison on the arrow that is working its way out of his system," Matt said.

Patrick sighed, "I think you don't want that woman doctor to prove you wrong, and no doubt she'll give you an ear-bashing for not calling her earlier."

Matt turned away, trying to cover his discomfort. Patrick grinned.

While they ate breakfast, Matt issued instructions to the other two hands. "I want you two to go out and check on the cattle. Make sure that we're not losing any, do a rough count of each area, make a note so that you can count the areas you don't get to today, tomorrow. I'm worried about Tate, so I'm going to stay here and look after him."

They finished breakfast and headed out for their chores.
Patrick whistled as normal. He relished the crisp blue New
Mexico sky. Despite there being no clouds, the temperature
was comfortable. He smiled to himself as he thought. *Maybe
I can even sneak a cup of coffee with Melissa at her diner
before heading back.*

An hour later, Patrick rode into Willow Creek, his horse
kicking up puffs of dust as it walked down the main street.
He noticed a couple of George Hamilton's hands coming out
of Melissa's diner and decided to avoid them. He turned back
toward the doctor's office. As he turned back toward the
doctor's office, he noticed one of George's hands pull himself
up into the saddle of his horse, wheel around and head off at
a canter toward George's ranch. *I wonder why he's in such a
hurry*, Patrick thought. Patrick stepped off his horse and tied
it to the hitching rail outside the doctor's office. He walked
into the office, there was no one in the front room. "Anyone
here?" He said.

Julia walked out. "Hello, can I help you?"

"I don't know who I should choose," Patrick said. "I can't
make up my mind. Who is more beautiful, Melissa or you."

Julia stared at Patrick, waiting for him to continue.

I think I'll stick to Melissa, Patrick thought, intimidated by
Julia's stare.

"Err, sorry about that. Sometimes I open my mouth before
my brain has time to engage," Patrick said.

The corners of Julia's mouth twitched up momentarily, and then she waited for Patrick to continue.

"I've come to buy some bandages," Patrick said.

"What do you need the bandages for?" Julia asked.

"Err, we like to keep bandages on the ranch. There's always someone getting injured," Patrick said.

Julia raised one eyebrow. "Or is it that you think a woman can't be a doctor?"

Patrick looked down and shifted from foot to foot.

"I thought so," Julia said. "Well, I hope whoever needs the bandages doesn't die in the meantime because of you men's bigotry."

"Can I buy some bandages from you?" Patrick said.

"You can, but bring the person in before he dies. I can assure you I'll do a better job than you and your friends of fixing him up." Julia said as she turned and went back to her surgery.

Patrick stood, twisting his hat in his hands.

Julia came out of the surgery with a pack of bandages and handed it to Patrick. "These are on the house," Julia said. "To show I'm not holding your bigotry against you. In any case, I'm sure you'll be back here with your friend, assuming he doesn't die before you come to your senses."

"Thank you, ma'am," Patrick said, looking down.

———

Chapter 8

Patrick walked out, pushed the bandages into his saddlebags, climbed on his horse, and headed off to the saloon. He hitched his horse outside the saloon and walked in, the batwing doors squeaking and clanking behind him. The saloon was empty other than a skinny boy mopping the floors and the owner polishing the bar counter. The saloon still stunk of cigar smoke, stale beer, and sweat from the night before.

"Patrick O'Hagan, what can I do for you today? It's early for you to be having a drink." The owner said.

"I've come to town for some supplies. We've run out of whiskey at the ranch," Patrick said.

"That's a bad state of affairs." The owner said.

"It is. It's even worse because the Apache attacked us the other day, and Tate was wounded. We've been using the whiskey to sterilize his wound," Patrick said.

"That's a waste of good whiskey." The owner said.

"I wouldn't call your rot gut good whiskey, but I'm sure no bug will survive that stuff," Patrick said. "You might as well give me a shot while I'm here."

"If it's such bad whiskey, I'm surprised you want to drink any." The owner said.

"Well, there's not much choice around here. In fact, there's no choice at all," Patrick said.

"That's the best type of business to have." The owner smiled at him. "You can do what you like when there's no competition."

"I suppose so," Patrick said. "It only needs to be drinkable."

"Tell me about this attack by the Apache. We haven't seen that around here recently."

"There were twelve of them. We think it was Mangas Mescal's tribe. I don't think they're happy with us taking over their hunting grounds. Matt reckons we should be able to live in peace, and they hunt on the ranches. We could even agree that they can take a limited number of cattle over a year. But Matt hasn't had a chance to put this suggestion to Chief Mescal," Patrick said.

"I can't see the other ranchers agreeing to that, particularly George Hamilton." The saloon keeper said.

"I think I'll have another one of those," Patrick said, tapping his finger on the bar.

"The whiskey can't be too bad." The owner said.

Patrick didn't have an answer to that. He finished his second drink and placed money on the bar for the drinks and the bottles of whiskey. "I better be going, the boss is a slave driver, and I want to pop in and see the gorgeous Melissa Hamilton before I head back."

"I don't think that's a good idea." The saloon owner said. "George is not going to be happy with the likes of you calling on his daughter."

"What do you mean by the likes of me?" Patrick said.

"You're a good kid, Patrick. If I had a daughter, I'd be happy to have the likes of you calling on her." The owner polished a glass while he looked at Patrick. "But I don't think that's the way George Hamilton looks at it. He looks at his daughters as goods to be traded. He'll only be happy if he can trade his daughters for some business deal or other."

"At least someone in this town understands what a fine person I am." Patrick grinned, touched his hand to his hat, scooped up the bottles of whiskey, and headed toward the door.

"Good to see you, Patrick. Watch out for George Hamilton." The owner said.

Patrick raised a hand in acknowledgment as he walked toward the door.

Patrick pushed the whiskey bottles into his saddlebags, left his horse hitched outside the saloon, and wandered down to Melissa's diner.

He walked in the door, a young girl with red hair was rushing around, supplying coffees and breakfasts to the various tables. Melissa was nowhere to be seen. Patrick sat down at one of the tables. The young girl waved acknowledgment to him and carried on with her rushing. Eventually, she came across to Patrick's table.

"Good morning, Patrick. What can I get you this morning?"

"A cup of coffee, please. Is Melissa here?" Patrick said.

"Cup of coffee coming up, Melissa is here, but she's busy at the moment." The girl raced away and came back with a cup and a pot of coffee. "There you go. I'll tell Melissa you're here and see if she can spare a moment to say hello to you."

The young girl disappeared into the back. A moment later, she came rushing out to one of the other tables with a breakfast. Shortly afterward, Melissa came out and beamed at Patrick as she walked toward his table. "You're a bit early for our Saturday evening date." Melissa smiled at him.

"I had to come in and get some supplies for Matt. We had an Apache attack the other day, and Tate was wounded, so we need some bandages and some whiskey to sterilize the wound," Patrick said.

"Is he badly wounded?" Melissa asked. "If he is, you should get Julia to come out and see him."

"Julia has already given me that lecture, and I've already given Matt that lecture," Patrick said. "Between you and me, Matt has this idea that a woman can't be a doctor. There I go again, opening my mouth before engaging my brain. Don't mention this to Julia. She's already guessed that and looked angry. But if you confirm it, she'll have words with Matt, and then I'll be in trouble with my boss."

"Matt's not the only one who thinks like that. I think all the men do. I know my father does," Melissa said. "Sorry, Patrick, I need to get back to work, I'm looking forward to seeing you on Saturday evening, and I hope you don't share your boss's views. I'm tempted to tell Julia what your boss thinks. It would be entertaining to see him cowering under Julia's wrath."

"I can't wait to see you either. That's why I'm now drinking a cup of coffee that I didn't need," Patrick said.

"See you Saturday," Melissa said as she waved a hand and turned back to the kitchen. As she walked through the door, she turned once more and smiled at Patrick.

Patrick finished his coffee and left money on the table for the coffee and tip. *I better get back to the ranch; otherwise, Matt is going to think I'm taking advantage of him.*

Patrick walked out of the diner and headed off back to the saloon and his horse.

He took the reins off the hitching rack and flipped them over his horse's head, putting his foot in the stirrup. As he was about to pull himself up, Knox called out to him. "O'Hagan, I thought I told you to stay away from Melissa."

Patrick turned and looked at Knox. Knox was in the middle of the street to Patrick's left. The sun was directly behind him, making it difficult for Patrick to see him properly. "You might have told me that, but Melissa said she wanted to see me, and what Melissa thinks is far more important than what you think," Patrick said. *I need to start thinking before I speak,* Patrick thought.

"I'm tired of your lip, boy," Knox said. "I'm going to put an end to your lip now. Move away from your horse. I'll give you a chance to draw first."

Patrick's brain was now working. He was trying to figure out a way of getting out of this fight. He knew he couldn't beat Knox. He squinted through the sun and could see that Knox had taken the loop off his gun. *Note to self, always take the loop off your gun when you are likely to meet any of Hamilton's hands. I wonder if he'll draw on me even though he can see the loop's still on my gun. I don't think that'll worry him.*

"Can I take the loop off my weapon without you drawing on me? Although, that's the sort of cowardly thing you'd do." *There I go again, speaking without thinking.* Patrick thought.

"You can take the loop off your gun," Knox said.

Patrick reached toward the loop, and as he did so, there was an explosion and a sharp pain in his chest. He looked down and saw blood coming from his chest on the left side. As he looked up toward Knox, there was another explosion. Patrick dropped onto his back, creating a cloud of dust. His eyes stared sightlessly at the clear blue New Mexico sky.

The two George Hamilton hands with Knox stared at him, mouths open. Knox said. "You saw him draw on me."

46

The hands hesitated and then said, "yes, we saw that."

———————

Chapter 9

Knox holstered his gun and kicked his horse into a walk pulling it to stop next to Patrick. Jumped off the horse, leaned down, and slipped the loop off Patrick's gun. He glanced at Patrick, "good riddance, I had enough of your nonsense."

He climbed back onto his horse. He turned his horse, joined the other two hands, and said, "we'd better go and tell the sheriff what happened. Then we can head back and tell the boss he has one less problem to think about." Knox kicked his horse into a canter. The other two followed.

As they left toward the sheriff's building in a cloud of dust, people walked out onto the street to see what had happened. Melissa had a sick feeling as she walked onto the sidewalk. She looked down the street toward where the shots had come from and saw a body lying out on one side of the street.

"Nooo." She wailed. She recognized the clothes Patrick had been wearing that morning.

She pulled up her skirt and ran down the street to Patrick. She knelt beside him and looked at his sightless eyes. She sobbed, tears running down her cheeks. She was still sobbing five minutes later when she felt a hand round her shoulder, looked up, it was Julia. Julia helped her up. Melissa turned to Julia. They wrapped their arms around each other. "I'm sorry, Melissa," Julia said.

They stood there a while longer. Once Melissa's sobs had died down, Julia turned to the small crowd that had formed. "Did anyone see what happened?"

No one answered. Julia looked around the crowd.

Eventually, one of the onlookers said. "I don't think anyone was looking this way. I did see Knox and two of your father's other hands riding toward the sheriff's office after the shooting."

Julia turned toward the sheriff's office. She saw that Knox and the two hands had left their horses outside the sheriff's office and were now heading back toward them.

Knox talked to the sheriff as they walked. "I don't know what got into that boy's head. I think he wanted to make a name for himself. He was always a hothead. He called me out and was going for his gun. I had no option but to draw on him."

Everyone had turned and were watching the four walk toward them. They cleared a space to let the sheriff view the body.

The sheriff said. "Step back, please, ladies."

Julia helped Melissa out of the way. Melissa looked up at Knox. "This is murder." She said.

"I was doing what any man would do. Defend himself. He was crazy, I was minding my own business, and he called me out and went for his gun." Knox shrugged.

"You're lying," Melissa said.

The sheriff looked around at the bystanders and asked. "Did anyone witness the shooting?" The people stared at him. Sheriff John Gamble sighed. "Well, I guess then it happened, as Knox said."

The sheriff squatted down next to the body. He noted the two shots in the front. He noted the loop was off Patrick's gun. He stood up and saw little Johnny Harlow. He handed Johnny a coin and said. "Johnny, run and fetch Bones."

"Sure will," Johnny said as he scampered off down the street toward the undertaker's premises. It was actually the general dealer store. Bones Chapman acted as the Town's undertaker. There wasn't enough business to support a full-time undertaker.

"Can we go now, sheriff?" Knox asked.

"Yes." The sheriff replied.

Knox urged his horse into a walk skirting around the small group of people. The other two hands followed him,

"You don't believe his story, do you?" Melissa glared at the sheriff, tears running down her cheeks.

"I have no choice. There are no witnesses to the shooting other than Knox and your father's hands. They're all telling the same story. When I look at the scene, it ties in with what they say." The sheriff replied.

"Come," Julia said and led Melissa away, down the street toward her office.

As they walked, Melissa said. "Knox is lying, and those other two are backing him up because they're scared of him. Patrick didn't deserve that. I haven't spent much time with Patrick, but I couldn't help but like him."

"You're right. I don't believe them at all," Julia said. "But there's no way of proving otherwise."

"Do you think Pa put Knox up to this?" Melissa said.

"No, Pa may have his faults, but he would never do that," Julia said.

Back at Julia's offices, Julia sat Melissa down and poured her a cup of coffee from the coffee pot kept warm on the stove.

"I can't go back to the ranch at the moment. Seeing Knox again will make me angry," Melissa said. "Once I've finished my coffee, I'm going to go back to the diner and work. What'll happen to Patrick's horse, and who'll tell Matt Teeson?" Melissa asked.

"The sheriff will attend to all of that, I'm sure," Julia said.

———

The hands rode into George's yard. George was at the corral watching a hand breaking in a mustang. Knox rode up to him with the two hands following him. George turned around.

"Hi, Knox." He turned back to the goings on in the corral.

"I'm afraid I shot Patrick O'Hagan in town, boss," Knox said.

George turned around. "What happened?"

Knox told the same story as he had told the sheriff.

George shrugged. "That boy was trouble. He had it coming." He turned back to watch the proceedings in the corral. "Was Melissa there?"

"She came out afterward and accused me of murdering Patrick. She had no reason to say that. She didn't see the shooting," Knox said.

"She's going to be pissed at you for a long time Knox," George said. "But, no matter, you'll have to ignore her. Julia will take her side as well. But they're just women."

"I'm sorry I had to do that, boss," Knox said.

George shrugged. "You can all get back to work now, boys. Patrick was not important. Melissa will get over it. Knox, you'd better stay out of Melissa and Julia's sight for a couple of days."

———

Chapter 10

Matt checked on Tate. He seemed to be getting worse. *Where has Patrick got to? He thought. I need to change the bandages and pour some more whiskey on the wound.* He sighed. *I suppose he's got distracted and gone to see Melissa.*

An hour later, he saw someone heading up the trail. It looked like the sheriff's horse. He was leading another horse that looked mighty like Patrick's horse. *I wonder what's happened. This doesn't look good.* Matt thought. He could only think of one reason that the sheriff could be heading to the ranch with Patrick's horse in tow.

The sheriff rode up to Matt. "Morning, Matt."

Matt said. "Do you want a cup of coffee?"

"Yes, that would be good." The sheriff said and stepped off his horse.

"What brings you here? It's a long way out of your way. I see you've brought Patrick's horse," Matt said.

"Not good news." The sheriff said. "Let's get that coffee first, and then I'll get into it." The sheriff said.

"I'm guessing either Patrick is dead or badly injured," Matt said.

The sheriff sighed and sat on a chair on the veranda. "He's dead, I'm sorry to tell you."

Matt said nothing. He poured two cups of coffee. "Do you take sugar?" He looked at the sheriff.

"Three spoons, thanks." The sheriff said.

Matt ladled three spoons in, handed the cup to the sheriff, and sat down opposite the sheriff. He looked at the sheriff. "What happened?

"Patrick was shot and killed in front of the saloon." The sheriff said.

"What! But he's not a big drinker, and certainly not at that time of day," Matt said. "I sent him to get whiskey. Tate was wounded by Apache, and we have used all the whiskey cleaning his wounds."

"I heard about that." The sheriff said.

The sheriff took his hat off and held it in his two hands fiddling with the rim. "Knox, he's a new hand of George Hamilton's, shot him."

"That bastard, George Hamilton, he sent Knox after Patrick because he doesn't want, didn't want, Patrick seeing Melissa. He knew Melissa couldn't resist Patrick's charm."

Matt stared at the sheriff. "I hope you've arrested Knox and put him in jail until he hangs for this."

"Can't." The sheriff said.

"What d'you mean, can't?" Matt asked.

"The only two witnesses were two of George's hands. They both swear. Patrick drew on Knox, un-provoked. The bullet holes are in Patrick's chest, and the loop was off his gun." On that basis, there is nothing else I can do. I asked for other witnesses, and there are none."

"You can be sure that's a bullshit story," Matt said.

"Yes, I agree, but we're stuck unless we have a witness come forward."

Matt sighed. "Somehow, I'm going to get revenge for this. I realize the law can't do it for me."

"My official line is, don't take the law into your own hands. But we both know the story here, so the unofficial line is, be careful. I don't want to be arresting you when I know all you're doing is getting the justice that the law cannot give Patrick." The sheriff said.

"I understand," Matt said. "He was my best hand, not that I would tell the other two that. Patrick was always busy. By choice, he ended up as unofficial cook. He always had some smart comment. Where's the body?"

"Bones has collected him." The sheriff said.

"I'll get him buried out here and pay for a proper burial," Matt said. "He had no family that he was close to. We were his family."

The sheriff finished his coffee and stood up. "I'll be on my way. Sorry to be the bearer of bad news."

"That George Hamilton is trouble," Matt said. "He's going to meet with a bad end, and not necessarily from me. Things always catch up with those people. Didn't he get you elected?"

The sheriff stared at Matt. "That doesn't mean he owns me. I do what's right."

"Thanks for coming out, sheriff," Matt said.

The sheriff touched his hand to his hat, turned his horse around, and headed down the trail.

Matt sat a while longer, trying to come to terms with the fact that Patrick was not coming back. He sighed and stood up, realizing he would never come to terms with it. He took Patrick's horse to the corral. He checked the saddlebags and found the whiskey and bandages. He unsaddled the horse and parked the tack on the corral rail. He turned the horse into the corral and checked there was food and water for him.

He went back and checked on Tate, causing him more distress. He wondered whether he was bad luck. Tate did not look good. He cleaned the wound again, poured some of the whiskey on it, and re-bandaged it.

When Hugh and Geoff came back to the ranch house in the evening, Matt filled them in on Patrick's death.

Hugh said, "That was George Hamilton's doing. He didn't want Melissa hooking up with Patrick. Anyone with any sense would be happy to have Patrick as a son-in-law. What are we going to do about it?"

"We can't do anything about it," Matt said. "There's no proof, and we'll end up in jail, which will make matters worse for no benefit."

Hugh frowned and grunted. "I suppose you're right. I'm not happy, though."

Geoff said. "I'm not happy either. If I get a chance, I'm going to get even for Patrick."

"Don't do anything silly," Matt said.

"I won't, but I'll keep my eyes open," Geoff said.

———

Chapter 11

"I'm going to town to fetch the doctor tomorrow. After she's seen Tate, I might escort her back and ask around about the shooting. I wonder where she and Melissa are on this," Matt said.

"They probably believe the story, I'm sure Melissa is upset about Patrick, but I guess she will have a blind spot where her father is concerned," Geoff said.

"I'm glad you've decided to fetch the doctor. That's a good idea," Hugh said. "I think even though she's a woman doctor, she at least has had training, and I'm sure will do a better job than us. It would be interesting to get her take on Patrick's shooting."

"I don't think I'll get into that until she's attended to Tate, in case she thinks I'm accusing her father of having Patrick shot, which I will be. It's bad enough she's a woman doctor," Matt said.

"My advice to you would be to change that attitude," Hugh said. "I've heard she's a feisty lady.

Matt frowned at Hugh but said nothing.

Matt checked in on Tate again at midnight. Tate was drenched with sweat, tossing, turning, and muttering. Matt wiped his forehead with a cold cloth. "Tate, you've got to hang in there. I can't possibly run this ranch without you.

We've always done everything together. Tomorrow morning first thing, I'm going to fetch the doctor out here."

Matt went back to his bed. Sleep eluded him. He could hear a great horned owl and some coyotes howling. They didn't bring the sense of peace they normally did. After an hour, he got up again and checked on Tate. There was no change. Matt could see the first slivers of dawn creeping under the door. All he wanted to do now was fall asleep. He dragged himself to a sitting position on the edge of the bed, rubbed his eyes, and stretched. He went over to Tate with a sense of dread. He was relieved to find that Tate was still breathing, he seemed to have quietened down, and the sweat was gone. *Maybe I don't need to fetch the doctor.* Matt thought. *I'm being dumb. I'll be back where I was. This is probably a lull in the fever.*

Matt kept himself busy, lighting the fire, starting breakfast, and putting some coffee on. This brought his thoughts to Patrick. He walked to Patrick's bed and stared at it for a while as if staring at the bed would bring Patrick back. He turned back to the fire and continued with breakfast.

He gave Geoff and Hugh their instructions for the day over breakfast. He finished his breakfast, dumped the plate in the corner with the other dirty plates, and headed out to the corral. He collected his saddle and bridle from the barn and walked back out to the corral. He placed the saddle and bridle on the corral rails and called to Sox. Sox turned and raced up to him, sliding to a halt in a cloud of dust, snorting as he did so. "Hello, boy, you're full of yourself this morning." Matt put his hands around Sox's neck and hugged him. Sox gave Matt a push with his head. Matt staggered back, even though that was Sox's normal trick. He bridled and saddled Sox, who accepted it quietly, knowing this meant he was going to have a run. Matt climbed into the saddle. Sox humped his back as normal and skittered to one side before settling down. Matt rode past the cabin, put two fingers to his hat, and said, "see you later, boys."

"Good luck with the doctor." Hugh grinned at him. "I think she's going to give you a lecture."

Matt grimaced as he urged Sox into a ground-eating canter. He let Sox choose the paths and pace. The terrain was uneven, heading down the hill trail to the plains beyond. An hour later, Matt rode into town, a plume of dust following behind him. His heart rate increased as he anticipated the lecture from the doctor.

Matt wasn't sure what time the doctor opened. He looked at the sun and guessed the time now was probably about 7 o'clock. The doctor's office looked closed up. He rapped on the door, there was no answer. He rapped again and then moved to the window next to the door, cupped his hands around his face, and tried to see in. From what he could see, there was no one there. He leaned against the wall next to the door, facing out to the street, his arms folded, and watched the street. He saw a man walk into the general dealer store. He recognized Bones. He would go and talk to Bones afterward about Patrick's burial. The only other person he could see was a man sitting on the sidewalk outside the saloon, his hat was crooked, and his head slumped on his chest. He was about to head across to see Bones. The time was now closer to what he guessed was 8 o'clock when he saw a buggy with a black horse pulling it. The horse was at a leisurely trot and heading toward the doctor's office. Matt saw a woman was driving the buggy. His heart rate again ramped up as he anticipated the conversation with the doctor. The doctor pulled around the back of the offices. The woman was un-hitching the horse as Matt walked up to her. "Can I do that for you?" Matt asked.

"You can, thank you," Julia said, eyeing Matt. "And who might you be?"

"I'm Matt Teeson. I'm here to…."

Julia interrupted him. "You're Patrick O'Hagan's boss." She said.

"Yes, that's right," Matt said.

Matt saw sympathy in her eyes. "Did the sheriff come and see you yesterday about Patrick?" She asked.

"He did," Matt said.

"I'm sorry for your loss." Julia looked at him.

Matt waited, Julia said nothing further about the incident.

"Thanks," Matt said. "He's a big loss. Not only was he a great hand, but he was also good to be around."

Julia unlocked the office and led Matt in.

"I got that impression from Melissa," Julia said. "What can I do for you?"

"I want you to come out and look at my partner and friend. He was wounded in a raid on the ranch by a band of Apache. He's not doing well," Matt said.

"I gather this was a few days back?" Julia raised one eyebrow and stared at him.

"Err, yes," Matt said. Staring at a corner of the ceiling of the room, he wondered if he should point out the cobweb in the corner to her. He kept quiet. Maybe she would forget her line of questioning.

"Well, I'm still wondering why it took you so long to bring him in. It doesn't seem like the sort of thing a good boss would do," Julia said. "I presume since you didn't call me earlier, he can't be that bad."

It crossed Matt's mind to head back to the ranch and get away from this annoying line of questioning. She had no right. His concern for Tate was stronger than his feelings of embarrassment which was saying something.

"Things will be much better if you come clean," Julia said.

"What do you mean?" Matt said, trying to will a fresh rush of blood to the face down.

Julia continued to stare at him. Matt shifted his feet.

He's quite handsome. Julia thought. *A bit of color to his face makes him look more handsome.*

"I doubt we can delay any longer. I'm surprised you didn't come clean and say now can we get on with fixing my worker," Julia said.

"He's not my worker. He's my best friend and partner," Matt said.

"I'm even more surprised you didn't fetch me earlier then."

"I haven't had one customer since I opened. Do you know why that is?" Julia asked.

Matt sighed and said. "Yes."

"I'm pleased to see you're at least somewhat embarrassed, and so you should be. I'm probably better than any man doctor who has recently come out of medical training. I lack experience, yes, but I can't get experience because no one will come to me. If I was a man doctor starting out, no one would worry. My surgery would be full." While she talked, Julia collected some medical items and added them to her doctor's bag.

———

Chapter 12

"We won't be able to take your buggy out there," Matt said.

"Í suppose you think I can't ride," Julia said.

"I'm not saying a word," Matt said. "I'm smarter than that."

"Very wise," Julia said as she headed toward the back. There's my bridle and saddle. Please bring it out for me. I'll let you prove how incompetent women are by allowing you to saddle my horse. That buggy horse doubles as a riding horse.

Matt picked up the saddle and bridle and followed Julia out, "Patrick came by for some bandages and told me what happened. I grilled him on why you were not bringing the injured hand to me. Under pressure, he admitted it was because you didn't think a woman could be a doctor," Julia said. "So, at least you kept silent, probably because you didn't want to annoy me in case I wouldn't then treat your friend."

Matt said not a word in the hopes that that would finish the lecture.

Julia climbed into the saddle, she rode side-saddle. Matt mounted up. Julia said, "Lead on."

"I want to go past Bones' place and arrange for him to bring Patrick's body to the ranch for burial. It'll only take a minute," Matt said.

They rode to the general dealer. Matt stepped off his horse and went inside. Julia waited on her horse outside.

Matt came out a few minutes later. "That's arranged. Let's go."

Matt turned and headed out toward his ranch.

"I might as well get up to date with the patient while we're on the ride. Tell me all you can about the wound and Tate's condition," Julia said.

Matt turned to look at her, which was a mistake. He couldn't think for a moment as he locked eyes with her. Her gaze didn't waver. Matt turned back to the front so his mind would come back from wherever it had gone to.

He cleared his throat and proceeded to tell her of the attack, where and how Tate was wounded, what he had done to the wound, and Tate's condition when he left this morning.

"Sounds like you've done a pretty good job for a man," Julia said.

Matt smiled but didn't turn. He wasn't about to let his mind disappear again.

"Do you think you'll be able to help him?" Matt asked.

"Definitely," Julia said. "From what you say, I can speed his recovery, and he should be fine in a few days. I have some potions to put on the wound and some medicine he should take. I'll also stitch the wound up, depending if I think the infection will need further treatment or not. If you had brought him to me immediately, he'd be back at work by now."

Matt frowned. She wasn't going to let him off the hook easily. Julia looked around as they rode up the trail. They were following a twisty trail through rocks and pine trees. A creek ran down their left side toward the plains. "This is a pretty place." She said. "It doesn't look like suitable land for ranching."

"It is beautiful," Matt said. "I wanted the best of all worlds. I wanted the beauty of the foothills to live in and the plains below for ranching."

"Good choice of land for that," Julia said. "My father's ranch is only on the plains. For him, it's only about wealth."

Matt grunted. He wasn't going to express his thoughts about Julia's father and end up being berated again, certainly not before she had attended to Tate.

"I know you've had some run-ins with my father. He's not a bad man, though," Julia said.

Matt grunted again. *Well, at least that gives me guidance for any further conversation on the topic.* Matt thought.

———

Chapter 13

They arrived at Matt's ranch. Julia looked around. She noted the small house, or rather cabin, the corral, and the barn wasn't much else. Not even a bunkhouse. Matt jumped off his horse and saw Julia looking around.

"There's not quite the money your father has to spend." He said.

Julia climbed off her horse. "Let's have a look at the patient." Matt led her into the house and over to Tate. His eyes were open, his face pale, and sweat ran down his forehead. Even so, he managed a grin.

"Ah," Tate said. "The lovely Julia, do you know Matt sa...."

Matt interrupted him. "Doctor is not here to listen to your nonsense. Keep quiet, and don't distract her while she attends to you."

Julia sat on Tate's bed and looked at him.

"I just want to say that I have every faith in you as a doctor, but my good friend here..."

"The Doctor is not interested in what you have to say." Matt interrupted again.

As Julia took the bandages off, she said. "The Doctor is very interested to hear what you have to say."

"I thought you would be," Tate said.

Matt sighed. "It doesn't matter. The Doctor has already given me a lecture."

"I'm anxious to hear what Matt said, and I promise I won't take it out on you." While she talked, Julia worked on the wound. "Matt didn't admit to anything. He just kept quiet, so I want to hear it from you."

"I'm not feeling well enough to talk anymore," Tate said as he looked at Matt's scowling face.

"Oh, so men do eventually stick together. I can understand why, if you talk, Matt might not look after you properly, and then when you die, he'll blame the woman doctor and say I told you so, to your dead body," Julia said.

Tate's eyes went wide. "I'm going to die?"

"No, unfortunately not, I took the Hippocratic Oath, so I'll have to fix you in spite of you," Julia said.

Tate relaxed.

Julia finished cleaning the wound. Matt watched with admiration as she stitched the wound. Finished stitching, Julia applied some more potions and then re-bandaged the wound. "I think he'll be fine. If the fever is not gone by tomorrow or if it disappears and then comes back, come and fetch me, but I don't think it will be necessary."

"Will you marry me?" Tate said.

Julia smiled. "He still has a fever, it should be gone by tonight, and then he might start talking some sense."

"Believe me, he never talks sense, so it always seems like he has a fever. That's why I didn't think he was bad enough to bring to you," Matt said.

"Oh no, you're not going to wriggle out of your mistakes as easy as that. It'll take a long time before I look at you without thinking, dumb man," Julia said.

Julia got up. "I'll be on my way. Good luck, Tate. You'll need it with a nurse like Matt."

"You forgot to answer my question," Tate said.

Julia waved. "Goodbye, Tate."

"Oh, so it's not a no," Tate said.

Julia smiled as she walked away.

"I'll ride back to town with you," Matt said.

"No need," Julia said. "I know my way."

"I want to ride back with you. Make sure you get back to town safely. I would hate something to happen to the best doctor in the country," Matt said.

"Nice try. You're going to have to do a lot more than that. You can tell that to all the other men, though. If I don't start getting patients, I'll have to close my practice down and move to a town where the men are more intelligent," Julia said.

"Well, I'll definitely do that. I've changed my tune since seeing you at work. It would be a big loss to the town if you closed your practice," Matt said.

"You're so easy," Julia said.

Matt smiled as they turned their horses down the trail toward town. They rode single file, Matt, ahead. The trail was too narrow to ride abreast. Matt would have liked to ride abreast so that he could look at her.

Matt asked about the bill. Julia told him the amount. "I'll draw the money when we get to town," Matt said.

"No rush," Julia said.

"That's not the way to do business," Matt said. "People will take advantage of you. You should get money upfront."

"That would be a great way to do business, all the patients who are too sick to draw money would die, and I would eventually have no population of patients," Julia said. "I can see it's not only women you need to learn about. I'll have to give you some business lessons as well."

Matt didn't want to turn and see a look of sympathy on her face. She had a good point. He continued to stare straight ahead.

Matt changed the topic. "Did your father put Knox up to shooting Patrick?" He asked.

"No, he did not. My father would never do that. He has his faults, but having people murdered is not one of them. How dare you suggest that. You don't seem to have any sense. I think it happened as Knox said it," Julia said.

"Not a chance did it happen as Knox said. I know Patrick, knew Patrick well. He may have been prone to opening his mouth before thinking."

"Like someone else I know." Julia interrupted.

Matt ignored her comment. "But he was too smart to draw on someone like Knox, and he was one of those people who would avoid harming anyone else at all costs, whatever their faults."

"He did seem like that sort of person. It's possible then that Knox decided to do this on his own," Julia said.

"You need to at least get your father to fire Knox. Otherwise, it's going to happen again. He'll think he can kill whoever he wants with no consequences," Matt said.

"My father won't do that. He'll take Knox at his word." Julia said, "That's all he can do. There were two witnesses only, and they back Knox's story."

"The two witnesses also happen to be your father's hands," Matt said.

"I'm not prepared to talk about this anymore," Julia said. "Topic closed."

Matt sighed, but for once, sense prevailed, and he didn't pursue the topic further.

The rest of the journey was carried out in silence. At the surgery, Matt offered to unsaddle Julia's horse.

"No thanks, I can do it myself." She replied and jumped off the horse.

Matt grimaced and turned his horse. "I'll see you back here with your fee shortly."

71

Matt rode down to the bank, drew the money, and walked back to Julia's surgery. He walked in. Julia was sitting at the desk in the front office. There were no patients. Matt paid her the money. "I'm sorry to see there are no patients, I'll put the word out about your skills, and I'll ask my hands to, as well."

"Thanks, Matt. I'm sure you'll find Tate will recover quickly now. See you, bye," Julia said.

"Bye, I'll let you know how it goes with Tate, good luck with the practice," Matt said.

Matt headed off back to the ranch.

———

Chapter 14

The three Apache watched Julia and Matt riding back into town. They hid in a gully near Julia's surgery. One of them said, "we'll move around to the trail to her ranch. She's got to pass that way sometime."

By three in the afternoon, no patients had come to Julia's surgery. She decided there was no point in waiting any longer for patients, and she might as well head back home. She tidied up around the surgery, locked the front door, went out to the horse at the back, gave the horse a hug and a pat, led it over to the buggy, and harnessed it into the buggy. She snapped the reins and guided the horse out into the main street and toward the trail to the ranch. *Well, I suppose at least I got one customer today.* She thought. *I hope my father doesn't stop paying the rent before I have enough income coming in to pay my own rent.*

As she cleared the town, she snapped the reins and eased the horse into a trot. The increased speed kicked up a plume of dust behind her. The Apache focused their eyes on the plume of dust heading down the track toward them.

"This looks like her." One of them said. There were two on one side of the road and one on the other. The one Apache gave the call of a Saw-Whet-Owl. The Apache, on the other side, gave an answering call.

Julia heard a Saw-Whet-Owl calling ahead of her. She hoped she would be able to see it. She slowed as she came to where she thought she heard the owl. As she looked to her right, a brown blur rushed out to the head of her horse. She turned to see what it was. She gasped. The Apache brought the horse to a halt. Another Apache dashed from the right, and then another one from the left. She cracked the reins and urged the horse onwards, but the Apache had a firm grip on the reins, and the horse went nowhere. The two Apache that had run out once the horse had been stopped leaped onto the buggy and pulled her off. She screamed even though she knew it was pointless. There was no one for miles. The Apache at the head of the horse led the horse off the track, pulling the buggy behind it. The other two dragged Julia off the track. She struggled against their hold, eventually relaxing, realizing they were too strong.

Her heart raced as she imagined all sorts of things they might do to her. She had never heard of anything good happening, she was either going to be killed, or she would be forced to become one of the warrior's wives.

The one Apache vaulted onto his horse while one held her and then passed her up to sit in front of the one on the horse. "You struggle, we tie your hands, you come quiet, we no tie your hands." The Apache on the ground said. He waited for her to answer.

"I won't struggle," Julia said. "Why are you doing this? I have done you no harm," Julia said.

"Your people have done us harm. No more talking; otherwise, I put cloth in your mouth." The Apache said.

Julia held her hands up in supplication.

"Good." The Apache said and headed for his horse.

The third Apache came back from somewhere off in the bush. Julia could no longer see the buggy. The Apache was leading her horse and had tied her doctor's bag onto the horse.

I wonder what they want with my bag. She thought.

The Apache were now mounted, and they headed away from the road. The one who had done the talking in the lead. The one with Julia in front of him second and the third bringing up the rear with Julia's horse. They rode at a fast canter. Eventually, the one in the lead dropped back behind them. Julia couldn't see where he had gone. She guessed maybe he'd stayed back and was now wiping out their tracks. One of the others tied a cloth around her eyes.

Julia occupied her time on the ride, trying to come up with an escape plan. Nothing came to mind. The Indian on the horse behind her was far more powerful than she was, and she doubted she could catch him by surprise. She would have to wait for an opportunity to arise later.

"Do you speak English?" She asked of the one she was riding with. There was no answer. Either he wanted to discourage her from talking, or he didn't understand English. She went with he didn't want her talking to him,

"You're making a big mistake," Julia said. "I hope you have lots of warriors to defend your village. My father will be coming for me. And if anything has happened to me, he'll wipe out your whole village."

No reply. They rode on. The sun headed off to the horizon. It would be a while before it set. Julia shivered. She hadn't planned on being outside at this time. Her dress was up around the top of her legs. She was not dressed for riding astride. She saw it was pointless asking for a coat. The Apache had no coats. She wanted to get somewhere warm, but on the other hand, she was not sure what her fate was at the other end.

They camped overnight. The Apache allowed Julia to sleep next to the fire.

The next day after what seemed like a few hours of riding, one of them removed the blindfold.

They were at the top of a hill. Julia saw the village below her. There were women going about their chores, children playing, and men sitting in various groups talking. The two men rode up to the second biggest wikiup. An Apache who had been sitting outside the dwelling stood up and greeted the two warriors. They returned the greeting and jumped off their horses.

———

Chapter 15

He spoke to them in Apache, and they returned answers in the same language. Julia got the impression he was congratulating them. The Apache who had ridden with her pulled her off the horse and held her in front of him.

The chief looked at her and said, "welcome, it is good of you to come."

Julia was surprised at how good his English was. "I didn't have any choice in the matter."

"I like to pretend that you did. I didn't think you would come without a little persuasion." The chief said. "My name is Mangas Mescal. I'm the chief of this tribe. You must refer to me as Chief Mescal. I need your help."

"If that's all you wanted, I'm sure if your men had asked me instead of man-handling me, I would've come," Julia said. "What is it you need my help with?"

"Three of my warriors were wounded in a raid the other day. You are a doctor. I know that. I need you to tend to their wounds and make them better." The chief said.

"I would be honored to attend to their wounds. I can't guarantee that I can cure them, but I will tend to them to the best of my abilities. In fact, happily. I have no patients in my town. None of the men there believe that a woman can be a doctor," Julia said.

"Those white men are stupid. We Apache know that women are good doctors." The chief said. "I've never heard of a white person helping an Apache, so I had no choice other than to order your abduction."

"Take me to these men, and I'll see what I can do. I wondered what your men wanted with my doctor's bag," Julia said.

Most of the village had gathered around and were staring at Julia. An older woman had stepped forward.

"Go with Liluye. She is also a doctor, but I think you can help her." The chief said.

Julia followed the woman. Two of the warriors who had captured her walked close behind. The woman led her into the biggest wikiup. Julia presumed that this was some kind of village meeting place. At the moment, though, it was acting as a hospital. The woman stood aside. Julia glanced at the three wounded warriors and then knelt next to the one that looked the worst. She felt his pulse, then rested her hand on his forehead. His pulse was faint, his forehead hot, and his skin dry. The wound was bandaged with cloth. She moved the cloth aside. There was some sort of paste on the wound. She carried out the same process with the other two. The chief stood inside the door. She presumed the other two warriors were outside.

"What do you think?" The chief asked.

"Hard to say," Julia said. "Two of them seem like they are in quite a good way and should survive. I'm not sure about the third one, though."

"I'll leave you to it." The chief said. "The two warriors who brought you will remain at the door in case you think you can run away. Liluye will stay to help you."

"I have no intention of running away. It is my duty to help these warriors," Julia said.

The chief grunted and walked off.

Julia got to work on the warrior who seemed to be the worst off.

———

Chapter 16

George Hamilton, Jim Davies, and Amy Hamilton sat down to supper.

"Where's Julia?" George asked. "She should be back by now, especially as she wouldn't have any customers."

"She probably stayed to have supper with Melissa," Amy said.

"Probably," George said. He tucked into his steak and then turned to discuss ranch matters with Jim.

George was in his study after supper, having a whiskey and cigar with Jim, when there was a knock on the door. "Come in." He said.

Melissa walked in. "I've asked ma where Julia is. She said you all thought Julia was having supper with me. She didn't have supper with me. I saw her heading out toward the ranch shortly after three this afternoon. Something's happened to her."

"I bet it's something to do with that idiot Matt Teeson. He probably thinks he can get back at me for O'Hagan's death by kidnapping Julia. Well, he's going to learn a lesson now," George said.

"That doesn't seem like Matt Teeson at all," Melissa said. "I'm sure he's not that dumb. What would he have to gain from that."

"He has a lot to gain from it. He'll be getting back at me for O'Hagan's death," George said.

"Are you saying you arranged for Patrick's death?" Melissa said.

"No, I'm not, but I'm sure that's what Teeson thinks, or even if he doesn't think that he's getting back at me because Knox is my employee," George said.

"I'm going to get all the men together now, and we're going to go straight to Teeson's place and get Julia back," George said.

"You can go and look at Matt's place, but I guarantee you won't find Julia there. You will have wasted a whole lot of time. I suggest you don't go in guns blazing and kill Matt Teeson or his hands, or the sheriff will arrest you," Melissa said.

"Don't you tell me what to do. You're my daughter, and you'll do exactly as I say, and I'll do exactly what I think is right. That sheriff can't arrest me. I appointed him," George said.

"That's the end of this conversation." George got up and marched out of the room.

At the bunkhouse, he called all the hands for their attention. He said, "Julia didn't come back from town this afternoon. She left at about three and hasn't been seen since. I think Matt Teeson has kidnapped her in retaliation for O'Hagan's death. So, we're all going to go up to Teeson's place, recover

Julia and hang Teeson and his hands. That'll be a lesson to everyone in this area not to mess with me ever again."

"We're with you, boss, let's go everybody," Knox said.

Jim Davies frowned but said nothing. The hands got busy making sure they were warm enough to ride and had their firearms and ammunition with them. They all headed out to the corrals. Jim Davies hung back. "Do you think this is a good idea, boss? I don't think Matt Teeson would do this. I think we're wasting time going there."

"You're sounding like Melissa now," George said.

"I think our time would be better spent looking for tracks and evidence on the path from town as to what happened," Jim said.

George frowned, what Jim said made sense, but it would mean he'd have to backtrack with his men.

At the corral, when everyone was saddled up and mounted, George said. "I've had a change of plan, we're going to first scour the road from town for evidence as to what has happened, and then we'll take it from there."

Jim arranged for some of the hands to carry lanterns. They set off down the road to town, looking with the light of the lanterns for any tracks and evidence as to what might have happened. It was slow going in the dark.

"I've got something here." One of the hands said.

George and Jim rode up to the hand to have a look at what he was seeing.

"There are bare human footprints here. The road seems to have been turned up as well. It looks like someone grabbed Julia's horse. You can see the cart tracks coming from town, and they end here, except that it looks like the cart then went off into the bush over there." The hand said.

Two of the men and George followed the tracks of the cart off into the bush. They came across the cart in a gully.

"Okay, we know for sure now that Julia has been abducted. We need to figure out by who," George said.

They looked around the scene on the road and saw the horse tracks heading off into the bush on the opposite side of the road to the cart.

"I think Julia has been abducted by Apache." The hand who had initially found the tracks said. "You can see that there were probably three people, and two of them had bare feet and one moccasins. The horses are also un–shod except of course for Julia's."

"It looks like you're right," George said. "Luckily, I thought to do some investigation before we rushed off to Teeson's. Okay, boys, we're going to call it a night. We'll struggle to track them through the bush in the dark."

Jim thought it would be unwise to mention to George that he had pointed out to George that they should do some investigation first. That's probably why George kept Jim on. *Oh well, that's the price to pay to hang on to my job,* Jim thought.

Chapter 17

The next morning George and the hands followed the tracks. "This is easy," George said. "We'll soon catch up to the Apache.

Not long after, the hand leading the tracking said. "The tracks have disappeared." All the other hands had been tagging along, not paying any attention to the tracks.

"They can't have disappeared," George said. "Find them, all of you."

Everyone sprang into action, looking for tracks, all heading off in different directions.

After two hours, George said. "It looks like we've lost the tracks. We need to get back to attending to the ranch. I'll get the sheriff onto this. Time he did his job."

They headed back to the ranch. George peeled off and headed for Town.

The sheriff was not in his office when George got there. He searched the town for him and found him having a coffee in Melissa's diner.

"This is not what I pay you to do." George scowled at John Gamble.

John looked up. "Couple of points. Firstly you don't pay me, the town does. Secondly, I don't work regular hours, and if you paid me by the hour that I work, you'd pay me a lot more. Have a seat and a cup of coffee, and let's hear what's bothering you."

George sat. "I may not pay you directly, but if I was not here, there would be no town money to pay you."

John said nothing. He eyed George thinking. *People like you come and go. Someone will always fill your place.*

"The Apache have kidnapped Julia, we've tried to follow her, but the tracks led us off into the bush and then disappeared. I need you to do your job and find Julia and bring her back," George said.

"I'm sorry to hear that. I'll get on it. If you lost the tracks, I'm going to struggle to find where they've gone. My best bet is to ask around and see what anyone around here might know about the Apache and their whereabouts," John said. "I'll ask around town, then the various ranches, and take it from there. I'll also get some people to help canvas."

"Well, get on it then, don't dawdle around. This is my daughter," George said.

John resisted saying anything further.

"I wouldn't be surprised if that Matt Teeson didn't pay the Apache. I think you should put him in jail anyway," George said.

"I presume you're making conversation while you finish your coffee," John said.

George's face flushed. "I'm tired of you protecting Matt Teeson. What's he got on you?"

John took a sip of coffee and looked at George but said nothing.

George grunted and got up from the table. "You'll see, he'll be involved somewhere, and when we find that, you'll lose your job."

John tipped two fingers to his head as George strode off.

———

Chapter 18

Early that morning, Matt had leaped out of bed to check on Tate.

"Morning, Matt," Tate said as Matt rushed to check on Tate. "Worried about me, were you? You shouldn't have been. Once my future wife attended to me, everything was certain to come right. Now if you hadn't taken me to see her, I would've been a goner. You must stick to ranching. Don't ever think of becoming a doctor."

"You obviously still have a fever, all this nonsense you're spouting," Matt said. "I was never worried about you. I just don't like it when my partner is a malingerer." Matt replied."

"Oh well, I'll let you carry on with your dream world," Tate said. "I think I'll get up once room service has delivered my breakfast."

Matt didn't bother answering. He turned around and started the fire.

Hugh said. "Want me to do the breakfast, boss?"

"That would be great. I'll go and get Sox ready to go into town. I want to update Julia on Tate's condition," Matt said.

Hugh grinned, "Or check up on Julia, more like it."

Matt frowned at Hugh as he went out the door, which wiped the grin off Hugh's face. Hugh thought, *maybe I shouldn't be teasing the boss. It looks like he's not amused.*

Before Matt left, he said to the others, "I don't think anyone needs to watch over Tate today. He's now well on the way to recovery. He's spinning it out, so the less we pander to him, the quicker he'll be up and working."

"Hey, I'm still very sick and weak," Tate said with a grin. "Don't worry though, I'll look after myself."

Matt headed off to town, and the other two out onto the ranch. Matt thought about why he was really going into town, especially since there was a lot to do on the ranch. He realized that Hugh had been right. It was to see Julia again. He tried to convince himself that it was to thank her and apologize for his attitude to women doctors. He knew that was not true and wondered, in fact, if he would be able to apologize.

He arrived at Julia's surgery early again and saw it was locked up. He decided to head down to Melissa's and get a cup of coffee while he waited. He would be able to see down the street when Julia arrived.

He went in and sat down at a table in Melissa's. There were only two other people in there. He knew them both, one worked at the bank, and the other was Bones. Matt nodded to them in greeting. The same girl with red hair came past and asked what she could get him. He ordered a coffee. Melissa came out with his pot of coffee. "I don't suppose you've heard. Julia has been kidnapped by Apache."

"What? No. I hadn't heard. When was this?"

90

"It was last night on her way home," Melissa said. "My father and his hands discovered the buggy in a gully and tracks of the Apache all around. They followed the tracks, and then they disappeared. Pa has asked John Gamble to find her."

"Oh. I came into town especially to see her and thank her. She did a great job with Tate. He's recovering quickly now," Matt said. "I'll join the search."

"You better go and talk to Pa first. He initially thought you had something to do with it. I think he still does. Now he thinks you paid the Apache," Melissa said.

"What an idiot. Does he think I'm friends with the Apache after they nearly killed my partner?" Matt said.

"Well, everyone knows you would like to be friends with the Apache," Melissa said.

"True, because I think we'll all be better off living in peace, and we are encroaching on land they have hunted on for years," Matt said.

"Exactly, so I suggest you talk to my father first," Melissa said.

"Well, I hope he gives me a chance to ask him and doesn't get his henchman, Knox, to gun me down for no reason like he did Patrick," Matt said.

"He says he did not. I accused him of that. But I would still be cautious," Melissa said. "I hope someone finds my sister soon. I'd be happy if I knew you were out looking. Good luck."

"I will be out there looking as long as your father doesn't do something dumb," Matt replied.

————

Chapter 19

Matt finished his coffee and left money on the table for the coffee and a tip, and headed out. He climbed on Sox and rode out toward the Hamilton ranch. He unhooked the loop from his gun. When he arrived at the ranch, there were a couple of hands near the corral but no sign of Knox or George. Matt wondered whether Knox was actually doing some ranch work. He doubted it. He went over to the hands at the corral. "Is George around?" He asked.

"He's inside the house somewhere. "Go and knock on the door. Someone will show you in." One of the hands said.

"And Knox, where's he? I don't want him catching me by surprise and shooting me?" Matt said.

"He's in the bunkhouse, so you better keep an eye out for him." The hand said.

"Thanks," Matt said as he turned and walked toward the house. Matt knocked on the door. A Mexican maid came to the door.

"Yes, who do you want to see?" She asked.

"I've come to see George Hamilton," Matt replied. "I'm Matt Teeson."

"Wait here. I will go and tell him." The maid said.

The maid came back and said. "He'll see you. Follow me."

Matt followed the maid. At the study door, she waved him in.

George stood up. "I suppose you're here to gloat. Your plan of getting the Apache to kidnap Julia worked."

"That's the stupidest thing I've ever heard," Matt said. "Tate was wounded in an attack by the Apache. It's unlikely we would be on good terms to be able to arrange that. I'm grateful that Julia is such a good doctor and was able to fix Tate up."

"You're blowing smoke up my arse. No woman can be a good doctor," George said. "I sent her to medical school to find a suitable husband and indulge her. She came back without a husband and with these highfalutin ideas that she could be a doctor. She'll soon see that she can't get any patients."

"I have no reason to blow smoke up your arse. Julia has had her first patient, and I'll make sure everyone hears what a good doctor she is, and then she'll have too much work. I do admit I had the same attitude as you, that a woman could not be a doctor, but I've changed my mind since I've seen her in action," Matt said. "I came to tell you I'm going to look for her, and I don't want you shooting me by mistake when I find her."

"Everything alright, boss." Knox appeared behind Matt. "Do you want me to shoot him?"

"No, not right now. He says he wants to go and find Julia. He probably knows where she is. So, we'll let him find her, and then you can shoot him," George said.

"I'm going to look for Julia. If I find any of your men trailing me, I'll take them out," Matt said.

"See, boss, he's already threatening you. I should take care of him now," Knox said.

"No, leave him for the moment, he'll give us cause somewhere along the way, and then you'll have your chance," George said.

"We're wasting time talking," Matt said as he turned and brushed past Knox. Knox stared at him as he passed. Matt's back muscles tensed, expecting a shot at any time. He turned the corner, and outside, he heard no footsteps behind him. He mounted Sox and headed back to town at a canter. His back muscles relaxed once he was a few miles from the ranch house.

In town, he went past the sheriff's office. The sheriff wasn't there. It was all locked up. Matt rode up and down the street, asking if anyone had seen the sheriff. As Matt rode back down the street for the third time with the intention of riding back to his ranch, the sheriff came out of the general dealer.

"Hi, sheriff. Been looking for you." Matt said as he dismounted and hitched Sox to one of the hitching rails.

"What can I do for you?" The sheriff asked.

"I believe you're looking for Julia Hamilton, and I'd like to help," Matt said.

"I am, but I'm not having much success. At the moment, I'm asking around to see if anyone has any ideas as to where the

Apache camp might be. George says the tracks disappeared. I figured there was no point in me trying to follow the tracks. I'll do no better. George has a couple of hands who are good trackers." The sheriff said.

"You carry on canvassing the various people. I'll follow the tracks from where I left off when the Apache attacked me," Matt said.

"Okay, we'll try and meet up sometime and update each other." The sheriff said.

Matt rode off directly to where he had left the tracks after the attack. It took him about an hour to get there. When he got there, he realized this might be a futile expedition. The tracks were already dimmed by the New Mexico wind. He followed the tracks, from time to time losing them, and having to circle around to find them again. The plains were not easy to follow tracks on, the hoof prints appeared from time to time between the tufts of grass. After two hours of tracking, the tracks disappeared altogether. Matt made a note of where he had got to in case he decided that he was going to try again from where the tracks had disappeared. He rode back into town and found the sheriff in his office.

"Sit, Matt. What did you find?" The sheriff asked.

"Unfortunately, nothing. The tracks are old now, which makes it difficult to follow them, and as George's hands found, the tracks also disappeared at a certain point," Matt said. "How did you go?"

"No better than you." The sheriff said. "No one around here knows where the Apache camp is. I'm guessing it's quite new because no one seems to have seen the Apache other than yourself." The sheriff said.

"I'm exhausted after the days riding," Matt said. "I'm going to head down to the saloon, have a couple of beers, and then head back to the ranch. I'll keep my eyes open, but I don't hold out much hope. If you want me to do anything more, let me know."

Matt pushed his way through the saloon doors. The saloon was filling up with hands tired from the day's work in the dusty dry conditions. Matt knew everyone there. Quite a few of them greeted him. In fact, the only ones who didn't greet him were three of George Hamilton's hands who were at one of the tables. They looked at him but didn't acknowledge him. Matt sat at the bar and talked to the men on either side of him. After he finished his second drink, he said, "good to talk, fellas. I'm on my way."

———

Chapter 20

Matt mounted Sox, who had clearly been bored waiting. As a result, Sox gave a couple of bucks and then jumped into a gallop. Matt was ready for him. This was his normal trick when he was bored. Even so, Matt only just managed to hang on. After a tussle all the way down the street, Sox settled into a steady canter. Matt arrived at the ranch shortly before the sun disappeared. He saw to Sox and headed into the cabin. Hugh and Geoff were already there.

"That was a long day checking on Julia," Hugh said with a grin.

"Unfortunately, I didn't see Julia. She's been abducted by the Apache, probably the same ones that attacked us. I spent the day trying to find their camp, but no luck. They've hidden their tracks after a certain point," Matt said.

"Oh no." Tate piped up from the corner. "I'm feeling stronger now. Maybe I can help look for her. I think the Apache might be smarter than you, Matt. I think they have realized Julia is a good doctor, and they have taken her to tend to the warriors that we wounded."

"I think you have developed a fever again and are talking nonsense," Matt said. He considered it further. "Maybe you have a point. I hope that is the case. Then she won't be in much danger, as they'll need her."

"Aaah, at last, you realize who is the smart one here," Tate said.

Matt scowled at him.

"I don't think you should be trying to find Julia," Matt said.

"It's fine as long as you don't come upon the Apache. If you do come upon them, you won't be able to get away in your condition."

"You have a point there. I'll start doing some ranch work tomorrow and leave you to go out and look for Julia." Tate said.

———————

Chapter 21

Julia was in a routine in the Apache camp. They had allocated her a wikiup with a young girl by the name of Nascha. Julia noticed that Nitis, one of the other young warriors, and Nascha seemed to be an item. The Apache fed Julia three meals a day consisting of mostly meat and mescal cactus. Julia would check on the wounded Apache before breakfast and then two or three times during the day. They were making a good recovery.

Today Julia had a look at the three patients before breakfast. She was certain now that they would not experience any complications and would make a full recovery in the not-too-distant future. Nitis came by to speak to Nascha while they were eating breakfast.

"Nitis, do you think you could organize for me to speak to chief Mescal?" Julia asked.

"What do you want to talk to him about?" Nitis asked.

"My job is done. The three warriors will make a full recovery now. I want to ask him if I can go back to my people," Julia said.

"I will ask him, but I don't think he will let you go back. You can be of use to us here. If we let you go, you will tell your people where we live, and they will come and attack us," Nitis said.

"No, I won't do that. I have come to like your people, and I understand you. I will work with my people to have peace with you. Any time you need me, you can come and fetch me," Julia said.

Nitis loitered and talked to Nascha and then wandered off.

Two hours later, Nitis came back and said, "Chief Mescal will see you now. Follow me."

Julia stood up and followed Nitis to the chief's wikiup. The chief was sitting outside his wikiup talking to one of the other warriors. The chief waved the warrior away and beckoned Julia to come and sit in front of him.

"So, Nitis tells me you want to leave us." The chief said.

"Yes," Julia said. "It's not that I don't like you, I've got to know your people over the last few days, and I understand why you don't like my people. I'm happy to help your people any time. If you need me, come and fetch me. But before that happens, I'll need to make sure that our people can live in peace together. I think I can make them understand it is to their benefit," Julia said.

"But you might lead your people to us. They will attack us and wipe us out. I cannot risk that." Mescal said.

"I understand that it is a risk for you. But you have my word that I will not disclose where your camp is. I was blindfolded when I came here. Your warriors only took the blindfold off at the top of the hill over your camp. If they blindfold me and take me to where they blindfolded me, then I won't be able to tell anyone where your camp is," Julia said.

The chief sat staring off toward the hill. He turned to Julia. "You have done good work with my warriors. We are too few to fight with your people for the long term. So, it is better if we can live in peace. But until your people allow us to hunt on the land, then we can never live in peace. I will let you go back to your people and hope that you can persuade them to live in peace with us and allow us to continue hunting on the land. I say *the* land, not *their* land."

"You have my word that I will do my best to persuade my people to allow this so that we can live in peace. If you ever need me as a doctor, come and fetch me," Julia said. "Those men you attacked the other day, their leader could be an ally to you. I know that he wants to live in peace with you and allow you to hunt on his land. I will talk further with him."

"Until we have come to some sort of agreement, you must understand we are all enemies, and we will continue to fight. If we stop fighting, your people will think they can run over us. I will arrange for my warriors to take you back." The chief said.

Julia was escorted back to Nascha's wikiup by Nitis. Julia explained to Nitis and Nascha what chief Mescal had said.

"Nascha, I want to have one last check on those warriors, and I'll explain to you how to look after them until they are better. I assume the chief will send some warriors to escort me from here after that," Julia said.

Julia took Nascha to the warriors. Two of them did not speak English.

Julia said to the one who spoke English. "Your chief has said I can go now. You should all recover well. I will explain to Nascha what to do until you are fully better."

"Myself and my two companions." The warrior waved to the other two wounded warriors. "Are grateful to you. You are a good doctor. We would not have recovered without you."

"I'm pleased to have helped you. I want our people to live in peace with you. I have promised you're chief I will try and make that happen. Anytime anyone wants me here, I have told your chief he should send someone to fetch me. It may be difficult to fetch me until our people are living in peace. But I'm sure you'll find a way to get word to me," Julia said.

Chapter 22

The same three warriors that had captured Julia came to fetch her. The one said, "we can take you back now."

Julia followed the warriors to where the horses were tethered. Julia vaulted onto her horse like an Apache. Her dress was up around her waist. The Apache paid no attention. Julia tucked her dress down around her legs as best she could. Two rode off. The third one waited behind. He was the one who spoke English. He bound a blindfold around Julia's eyes.

"We can go now." He said. "Get your horse to canter to catch up."

Julia urged the horse into a canter and left it to find its own way. She felt it slow down as it caught up to the other two warriors. The horse settled into a walk. Julia had been uneasy cantering. It was disconcerting with the blindfold on.

Julia sensed that they had been twisting and turning. She suspected it was to disorientate her. It was working. She had no idea in what direction they had gone or were now going.

They again camped overnight.

The next day they rode for a few hours and came to a stop. The Apache removed her blindfold. The Apache, who was proficient in English, said to her, "we leave you here. You see that hill over there with the tree standing on top of it." He extended his arm to point to the tree. "Go straight to that tree, over the hill, keep going straight, and you will find the track to your ranch."

"Thank you," Julia said. "I'm sure I'll see you again. I hope we'll all be able to live in peace."

The Apache waited. "We will wait here until you are out of sight over the hill."

Julia turned and headed for the tree that he had pointed out to her. After another hour, she recognized the scenery around the ranch. When she hit the track to the ranch, she turned left and headed home.

She rode into the ranch yard. The hands were arriving back from their work out on the ranch for the day. One of them shouted, "you're back, Miss Julia. What happened to you?"

"I'll tell you later," Julia said as she slid off the horse. Settling her dress in the proper position once she was on the ground. "Please look after my horse."

"Sure, Miss Julia, good to see you back safe and sound." The hand said as he took the horse from her and led it off toward the corral.

Julia walked into the house. "Hello, anyone here?"

Amy Hamilton came running out of the sitting room and flung her arms around Julia. "You're back safe and sound." She said as she hugged Julia, tears flowing down her cheeks. "Are you alright?"

"I'm absolutely fine. I'm sure you figured out the Apache abducted me. They treated me well, though. They wanted me to look after three wounded warriors from the attack on Matt Teeson's ranch," Julia said.

"I'm glad to see those savages didn't harm you," George said as he came out of the study. "So, I was right. It was Matt Teeson's fault."

"Hardly," Julia said. "You can't blame Matt for defending himself."

"It's Matt now, is it? Don't you go getting ideas about Matt Teeson," George said.

"Or he'll end up like Patrick O'Hagan. Is that what you're saying?" Julia said.

"No, that's not what I'm saying, although I'm sure he'll get what he deserves somewhere along the way," George said.

"I'm glad to see you too, Pa," Julia said.

The sarcasm was lost on George. "I'm glad to see you back too. You're lucky those savages didn't violate you," George said.

"They treated me well," Julia said. "They had no intention of doing anything bad to me. All they wanted was my help. They have more faith in me than my own people and probably treat me better than my own people."

"They're ignorant savages. They know no better," George said.

Julia sighed. "I want to get cleaned up. I'm going to arrange for Maria to heat some water up for a bath for me." Julia turned around and saw Maria in the doorway from the kitchen, beaming at her.

"Hello, Miss Julia. I'm so happy you are back safe and sound. I will organize the hot water for you now and call you when the bath is ready. Can I get you some coffee first?" Maria said.

"That sounds wonderful. Thank you, Maria," Julia said.

Chapter 23

By the time Julia had finished bathing and dressed in clean clothes, it was time for supper.

Melissa walked in shortly before supper. Her face lit up when she saw Julia. "Julia, you're back. Are you alright? Where have you been?"

"I'll give you all the whole story, once, at supper," Julia said.

Jim came in after Melissa and said pretty much the same.

At supper, Julia related the story.

Partway into the story, George interrupted. "Where is this Apache camp? I'm going to get all my hands and as many people as I can get from town, plus the sheriff, and we'll wipe these Apache out. They'll never be a problem to anyone again."

"That's the wrong thing to do," Julia said. "Yes, I'm sure you could eliminate them and make life easy for yourself, but it's not the humane thing to do. I agree they do fight us but with good reason. They have been here, or their people have, for years, and they are hunter-gatherers. We have now taken away their ability to live by claiming their land and trying to chase them off."

"You always look at things with rose-tinted spectacles," George said. "It's like you wanting to be a doctor, no one will ever come to you, but you continue to believe that you can be a doctor."

"That's rubbish. I've already had four customers," Julia said.

"And I bet none of them have paid you a cent," George said.

"Matt has paid me, and he says he'll spread the word about how good I am as a doctor," Julia said.

"Matt's a nobody and is not going to be around for long. I'm going to take his land away from him. It rightfully belongs to me," George said.

"This is going to lead to disaster for you," Melissa said. "All you're doing is making enemies, don't underestimate them."

"They're small fry. I'll sort them out," George said. "So, Julia, where is the Apache camp?"

"I wouldn't tell you even if I knew," Julia said. "And I can't tell you because I don't know where the camp is."

"How can you not know where the camp is?" George said.

"When they took me there, they blindfolded me. They only removed the blindfold when we got to the camp. They did the same when they brought me back," Julia said. "For exactly the reason you want to know where their camp is. They're not stupid."

George abruptly changed the topic and turned to Jim about ranch matters, for which Julia was grateful.

————

Chapter 24

The next morning, Matt sent Geoff into town to pick up some supplies. "While you're there, check around and see if there's news of Julia," Matt said.

"Will do," Geoff said, touching his hand to his hat and turning his horse toward town.

Geoff arrived in town, the sun was well up in the sky. He guessed the temperature was somewhere slightly above 70 degrees Fahrenheit. He decided he would check on Julia first. He jumped off his horse outside the sheriff's office. He walked in, beating his hat against his chaps, creating a cloud of dust.

"Hey, get rid of your dust outside." The sheriff said.

"Sorry, sheriff," Geoff said as he retreated out the door, beat his chaps again to another cloud of dust, and then walked in.

"Sit." The sheriff said. "Can I offer you a cup of coffee?"

"I wouldn't say no to a cup of coffee," Geoff said as he sat.

The sheriff poured him a cup of coffee. As he placed it in front of Geoff, he said, "what can I do for you?"

"Matt asked me to find out if there's any news on Julia," Geoff said.

"You've saved me a trip out to Matt's ranch. One of the hands from George's ranch came in this morning and said she was back safely. She is at her surgery this morning. Maybe you want to stop by there and find out about her time with the Apache." The sheriff said.

"I think I'll do that," Geoff said. "I understand she's not busy."

"I've actually seen a couple of people go in there this morning." The sheriff said. "It's probably out of curiosity to find out what happened to her, but I'm sure they also need some doctoring. I suspect she'll get busier."

Geoff finished his coffee, thanked the sheriff for the coffee and the information, and headed off down the street to Julia's.

At Julia's, he walked into the reception area. The door to the surgery was closed. It had a sign on it saying: *Busy, please take a seat.* Geoff did as the sign said and sat in the reception area, hoping Julia had not gone out and forgotten to change the sign.

Ten minutes later, the door opened, and a rough-looking cowhand walked out, greeted Geoff, and went out onto the street.

Julia came out. "Hello, can I help you?"

"Matt sent me into town to find out whether you had been found yet," Geoff said.

"Well, I would've thought if he was so concerned, he would be out looking for me, or maybe he has been." Julia raised her eyebrows.

"Don't tell him I said so," Geoff said. "But you seem to occupy all his thoughts at the moment. He did try and track the Apache from the attack to see where their camp was. He already knew that your father and his hands had been unable to follow the tracks from where you were abducted. I'm glad to see you weren't injured. Tell me what happened."

Julia said. "It's a long story. Do you want to come into my surgery, and I'll tell you about it, and you can have some coffee?"

"Thanks. But I'll pass on the coffee. I've had a cup with the sheriff." Geoff said. He got up and followed Julia into the surgery.

Once she had told him the story, she said. "Tell Matt I was disappointed that he didn't even bother looking for me, and when he asks you for the story, tell him you were sworn to secrecy and tell him to come and find out for himself."

Geoff finished his chores in town and then headed back to the ranch. He was surprised to see Matt around the ranch house when he got there to drop off the purchases.

"Where have you been? Surely it didn't take that long to get those few things," Matt said.

"No, it didn't. If you remember, you asked me to find out about Julia, which took time. I saw the sheriff first and had a cup of coffee with him, and when he told me Julia was back, I went to see her and find out all about her abduction," Geoff said.

Matt grinned. "She's back, safe and sound?"

"She is," Geoff said.

"Tell me what happened to her. Is she alright?" Matt said.

"She swore me to secrecy. She said I couldn't tell you. She said if you were really concerned, you would come in and see for yourself," Geoff said.

"I'm your boss, and I'm instructing you to tell me," Matt said.

"You can instruct me on work matters but not on non-work matters. Besides, I fear Julia's wrath more than yours," Geoff said.

"You're sounding like Tate. Julia seems to have waived a magic wand over the two of you. She hasn't waived her wand over me," Matt said. "We'll get on with the important work of looking after the ranch. I can't afford the time to be pandering to a woman's wants."

They all headed off to their work on the ranch, including Tate. Matt, though, stayed behind.

"Aren't you coming with us, Boss?" Hugh said.

"No, I've got a few things to do around here," Matt said.

"Yes, boss," Geoff said.

"And what's that meant to mean?" Matt asked Geoff.

"Nothing, boss. I'm acknowledging you've got stuff to do around here." Geoff grinned as he turned his horse to follow Hugh and Tate to the area of the ranch they were working.

Matt frowned at their backs as they departed.

There was little left to do around the yard since one of them had been around all the time while Tate was recovering. After pottering around for a while and achieving exactly nothing, Matt frowned, sighed, and headed to the corral to saddle Sox. They went through the normal battle as Matt turned Sox toward town. Matt was on edge, and Sox noticed the battle continued for longer than normal. Sox only quieted after fifteen minutes when he was bored of messing Matt about. Sox settled into a lazy canter. They were in town in a shorter time than normal. Matt pulled up outside the surgery and dropped Sox's reins over the hitching rail. Matt paused on the sidewalk, dusted himself off with his hat, and ran his hands through his hair. He paused at the reception door and went through the process again. He knocked, there was no answer. The sign on the door said, *open.* He pushed the door open, his heart thudding in his chest. There were two men waiting in reception, and the door to the surgery was closed. *My. Julia's business is picking up quickly.* Matt thought.

The surgery door opened a woman from the saloon walked out, thanking Julia. Matt stood up.

Julia said who's next. Matt walked toward the surgery door.

One of the two men said. "Hey, we were before you. Wait your turn." The other nodded.

"I'm not sick. I'm here to check up on the doctor," Matt said.

"All the more reason to wait." The man said.

"You'll have to take your turn," Julia said. "If more patients come in, you'll have to wait for them. I can't have visitors in front of patients unless, of course, you're paying for a consult." Julia ushered the next patient into the surgery, turned, and closed the door behind her.

Matt frowned at the door as Julia closed it, only managing to get in an, "err..." before the door closed completely. Matt sat down, twisting his Stetson between his knees. The other man in the surgery grinned at him. Matt scowled back. *I'm getting up and leaving,* Matt thought, glued to his seat, frowning at the door. He continued to sit, frowning at the door. Julia came out and called the next person.

She turned as she went back into her surgery. "I see you're still here, Matt. I hope you aren't chasing customers away so you can sneak in to see me." She closed the door as Matt opened his mouth, he closed his mouth.

Fifteen minutes later, Julia ushered the patient out. "Do you want to come through, Matt? Is this a paying visit, or are you here to get a free coffee?"

"No, this is not a paying visit, I'm personally checking up on your well-being, but I will say yes to that cup of coffee. I should get something for all this wasted time. I'm a busy man," Matt said.

"Huh, doesn't seem like it. Geoff will have already told you I'm fine, and yet you've got the time to ride in from the ranch, waste my time shooting the breeze and ride back. I suppose you big-shot ranchers have minions to do all the hard work," Julia said.

"Minions?" Matt said.

"Slaves or whatever you call your ranch workers," Julia replied.

Matt followed her into the surgery, his frown back in place.

Julia smiled at him as she placed a cup of coffee in front of him. "I'm pleased to see you're concerned about me. It makes you human."

"I'm concerned about all the people in this town," Matt said.

"I'm sure you are a model citizen. Geoff mentioned that you were beside yourself with worry for me. Whoops, Geoff said not to tell you," Julia said.

"Well, he's going to be looking for a new job when I get back," Matt said.

Julia smiled, knowing from her short interactions with Matt that he was all bark and no bite when it came to his workers and partner.

"So, tell me about your abduction from start to finish," Matt said.

Julia told him all about it. By the time she had finished the story, Matt had finished his coffee.

"I'm glad you're back safe and sound. You have sown some goodwill between the Apache and us settlers. I hope we're able to make good on it and live in peace, it sounds like we have a way to go, but it's a start.

"Thank you for your concern for me as a citizen in your kingdom," Julia said. "It's touching. I must chase you out now in case other customers come in and think they don't have time to wait."

Matt stood and turned, muttering as he did so. "Well, I'm glad you're alright, and your business is picking up."

Riding back to the ranch, Matt thought. *I could have handled that much better. She seems to bring out the worst in me. Although I guess charming women is not my strong suit.* Sox swung around and accelerated into a gallop heading back the way they had come. Matt grabbed the pommel as he was tipped toward the ground. He managed to right himself. Out of the corner of his eye, he caught a glimpse of a mountain lion slipping into the vegetation at the side of the track. After 500 yards, he got Sox under control, patting and soothing him. After a battle, he had Sox walking back up the trail toward the ranch. His ears were pricked forward, and his nose stretched out toward where the mountain lion had disappeared. As they passed the spot, Sox danced sideways and tried to break into a gallop. Matt kept that from happening and vowed to himself that he would pay more attention in the future. This doctor lady was distracting him.

Matt turned off the trail toward the ranch before he got to the cabin. It was closer to check up on what Tate and the other hands were doing. He rode up to the others. As he got there, Tate asked, "how's my future wife?"

"Your future wife is fine," Matt said.

"I hope you're not thinking of competing for her because if you are, you're wasting your time," Tate said. "Geoff tells me you're a little bit distracted by her."

"Geoff, you and I are going to have to have some words. Julia tells me that you said to her I was beside myself with worry for her and that she shouldn't tell me that you said that."

"These women haven't a clue how to keep a secret," Geoff said.

Matt asked them how the ranching was going.

"Seems to be going well," Tate said. "We've lost the odd cow here and there, but generally, they look in good condition. Hopefully, the Apache don't try and steal any, or George Hamilton cause us trouble. I think that's wishful thinking. I think both will happen. I need to check my shooting since I've been wounded. My arm feels stiff, but it should be fine, I think. Probably not with the rifle, but a pistol will be fine. Maybe, when we get back to the ranch, we can have a competition with our sidearms, see if I can still beat you. I'm sure it'll be as easy as ever."

"I still think that arrow must've damaged your brain somehow. Maybe the poison befuddled your brain. I don't think you'd come close to beating me. But you're on. We'll put some money on it as well to add some pressure. Although it won't be nearly the same pressure as if someone is shooting at you," Matt said.

———

"

Chapter 25

Once back at the ranch and the horses were watered and fed. Matt said. "It's time for the competition. Hugh and Geoff, you can either watch me hand out a crushing defeat to Tate, or you can start getting our evening grub ready. I would imagine you'd prefer to do the latter, as it's a foregone conclusion who's going to win here."

"I think I'd like to watch anyway," Hugh said.

Matt collected some tins they had kept in the cabin for such an occasion. He paced out twenty steps and then added a few more, as there was a convenient log to place them on a bit further out. Behind the log was a bank of mixed earth and some rocks.

"Hugh, you can do something useful. Count to three, and on three, we'll both draw and shoot and carry on shooting until both our lots of four cans are down. Geoff, you make a note of whose are down first and declare the winner. Your word is final. No winging and whining from Tate is allowed to change the verdict," Matt said.

Everyone agreed to the rules. Hugh counted to three. Matt and Tate both drew, firing at their respective cans. Matt noted he got the first shot off before Tate. He saw Tate's shot kick up dust three yards in front of Tate. As Matt downed the rest of his cans, he was surprised to hear no further shots from Tate. Noting all his cans down and none of Tate's, he turned toward Tate, grinning. "See, I told you so..." His voice trailed off as he saw Tate flat on his back, blood pouring from a wound on the top of his head.

He jumped down on the ground next to Tate, almost colliding with Geoff. "What happened?" Matt shouted.

"I think you're first bullet didn't strike the can in the center and ricocheted off the rocks behind and came back and hit Tate," Geoff said.

"No, this can't be happening," Matt said. "Help me get him inside on the bed."

They carried Tate to his bed. "Hugh, heat some water up and bring it across in a bowl when it's ready."

Matt checked for a pulse letting his breath out as he felt Tate's pulse beating. "Hugh and Geoff, do what you can for Tate, bathe the wound, pour some whiskey on it, and bandage it. I'm going to ride to George Hamilton's ranch and fetch Julia."

"Be careful, boss. George Hamilton or one of his hands is likely to shoot you if you go tearing up to the ranch house," Geoff said.

"I'll take my chances. This was dumb. I should've spotted those rocks behind. In fact, I did, but Tate and I never miss, so I didn't think it would matter," Matt said.

Matt raced out the door to the corral. He bridled and saddled Sox, who made it a slow process. He was not used to Matt rushing at him. Matt jumped in the saddle, and as he landed, Sox was off at a gallop. Matt slowed him down to a canter to cater to the rough trail. By the time he arrived at George Hamilton's, the sun had set. There was still enough light for Matt to make out who was in the yard and for them to place who he was. He slowed Sox to a walk and raised his hands to his sides. The loop was still on his sidearm. As he passed the bunkhouse, he saw Knox staring at him. His back muscles tensed as he rode up to the house with Knox behind him. He jumped off Sox and left the reins hanging. He knocked on the door. Maria came to the door.

"Can I help you, sir?" Maria said.

"I'm looking for Miss Julia. Someone is badly injured," Matt said.

Julia appeared behind Maria. "Who's hurt now? You need to take better care of your people."

"It's Tate," Matt said.

"It can't be. Tate was recovering fine," Julia said.

"Different injury," Matt said. "Let's go."

"Amazing how you suddenly have such great faith in my doctoring skills when a while ago you said a woman couldn't be a doctor," Julia said.

"Okay, you've made your point," Matt said. "This is a life-or-death matter. When I left Tate, he was unconscious."

"I'm going to change and get my doctor's bag, Maria. Ask one of the hands to saddle a horse for me. I'll be riding astride. I won't take my side saddle," Julia said.

Maria and Julia rushed off in different directions. George came out of the study. "What are you doing here, Teeson?" George asked.

"I need Julia's doctoring skills," Matt said.

"She can't come," George said. "You need to take better care of your people."

"Julia has already told me that. She's already said she'll come and help," Matt said.

"It's after dark. It'll be dangerous for Julia," George said.

"Don't worry, I'll look after her. She'll need to stay the night, though. She'll be safe. My other two hands are there as well," Matt said.

"The way you look after people and keep needing a doctor, I don't think she'll be safe," George said. "She can go, on condition you take Knox with you."

"That's fine. I'm in no position to argue," Matt said.

George wandered over to the bunkhouse, where Knox was still loitering in the doorway. He instructed Knox to go with Matt and Julia.

"Okay," Knox said without adding his normal *boss* at the end of the sentence. He looked at George without a smile and turned to collect his stuff from the bunkhouse.

———

Chapter 26

By the time they were on their way, daylight had disappeared. The moon had risen and illuminated the trail. It would get brighter as the night went on. Matt couldn't see any clouds around. He led the way, his back muscles tingled with Knox behind him.

"Tell me what happened and what Tate's condition is," Julia said.

Matt vaguely explained how Tate had been hit by a ricochet and then explained the extent of his wound.

"Were you attacked again by the Apache?" Julia asked. "I'd be surprised."

"No, we weren't," Matt said.

"That sounds evasive," Julia said. "Did you and Tate have a fight?"

Matt sighed. "No, we didn't."

"And?" Julia said.

"You don't give up, do you?" Matt said. "We were having a competition, shooting cans off a log, and my first shot skimmed the can and ricocheted off a rock behind."

Knox snorted behind them.

"That sounds careless. I would think anyone with half a brain would think there is a possibility of a ricochet," Julia said.

"Hindsight is always great," Matt said. "We've done this many a time, and neither of us ever misses the cans."

"Overconfidence with no brains is always a bad combination. But, good for business. It sounds like Tate will be all right this time," Julia said.

"You can be sure I'll never make the same mistake again," Matt said. "I hope you can save Tate."

They carried on, the moonlight on the trail illuminating the way. Arriving at the ranch, Matt grabbed Julia's horse and said, "you know the way. I'll look after your horse."

Julia rushed into the cabin with her doctor's bag that Matt had carried on Sox for her. She greeted Hugh and Geoff, knelt beside Tate, and said, "let's see what we've got here."

She eased the bandages off the wound. She checked on Tate's pulse, "that's good. His pulse is strong."

She cleaned the wound and placed some ointment on it from her doctor's bag. Satisfied she'd done all she could, she said to Matt, "there's nothing more I can do here. He'll be fine. It's better if I go back to my ranch tonight. If you're concerned about him tomorrow, come in and see me."

"I prefer it if you stay here. I'm worried about Tate," Matt said.

"I don't think you have anything to worry about, it's a concussion, and there is nothing further I can do. Come, Knox, take me back," Julia said.

"I'll come with you," Matt said.

Julia looked at Matt. Matt could see she didn't entirely trust Knox either.

"Not necessary for you to come," Knox said. "I'm quite capable of looking after Julia without your help."

"It's not a problem. I enjoy riding at night. I like listening to the night sounds," Matt said.

Julia was relieved when Knox shrugged and headed toward his horse. They mounted up and headed back to George Hamilton's ranch. No one said a thing on the ride back. It gave Matt the opportunity to enjoy the night sounds of the owls, whip–poor–wills, and coyotes.

At George Hamilton's ranch, Matt said, "Thanks, Julia, for coming on such short notice. I'll pay your bill in the next week when I come into town to update you on how Tate is doing."

"It's good to be getting work and paying work," Julia said. "And the way you go about your business, I'll be busy. In fact, I can probably survive on you and your ranch hands only."

Matt noticed Knox had disappeared and hadn't put his horse in the corral. Matt turned his horse and headed back the way he'd come. It worried him that he hadn't seen where Knox had gone. He debated about taking a different route back but then decided he was being paranoid. Even so, he kept a sharp eye ahead and to the sides.

Matt breathed a sigh of relief once he had attended to Sox, turned him loose, and settled himself into his bed. He checked on Tate before turning in. There was little change, his breathing was even, and he appeared not to have a temperature.

———

Chapter 27

Knox had watched Matt head back to the ranch. Knox was tempted to disobey George and take Matt out. Three things decided him against that: He was being paid well for a job he liked, and he did not feel like jeopardizing it. He noticed Matt was on high alert, and the only way he could safely dispatch him would be to shoot him in the back, which could get Knox a hanging. Thirdly he was sure he would get a better opportunity with his boss' blessing sooner rather than later. He would raise the matter with George tomorrow.

The next morning Knox saw George riding out on his own to look over the ranch. Knox intercepted him.

"What are you going to do about Teeson?" Knox asked.

"Your daughters seem to be developing an allegiance to him, and he is only going to get stronger as time goes on," Knox said.

"I'm not worried about him, and even if I was, I have a plan," George said.

"Are you going to let me in on that plan?" Knox said.

"I will do when the time is right," George said. "I need to know where the Apache camp is first, though."

"What's your plan with the Apache?" Knox asked.

"You don't need to know yet," George said.

Knox shrugged. "Okay, let me know if you need me to do anything." He turned his horse and headed back to the ranch house.

George carried on to where some of the hands were working. He singled out two of them who were excellent trackers.

"You two, you're now off ranch duty, and I want you to find the Apache camp. Don't come back until you've found it. I'll let Jim know that I have relieved you of ranch duties in the meantime."

The two hands turned to go back to the ranch to pick up supplies for what they thought would be a long trip.

As they departed for the ranch, George shouted after them. "Don't think you can ride around for a few days with no ranch duties and come back and say you can't find the camp. That's exactly what they were thinking. "If you are not back within a week with the location of the camp, you can draw your pay and be gone."

"Noted, boss." Shorty McQueen said.

"He's too smart for us." Curly James said when they were out of earshot. "I had every intention of riding around on a hunting and fishing trip and taking a vacation from ranch work. I guess that's why he's the boss."

"I had the same idea," Shorty replied. "Looking for their campsite is dangerous business. They'll be on the lookout for us and take our scalps before we know it. But not having paying work is as bad for our health."

They collected their supplies from the ranch and headed out. As they were leaving, they bumped into Jim Davies, who asked. "Where are you two off to?"

"The boss has told us to find the Apache camp. He said he would tell you when he sees you." Shorty said.

"Well, don't ride around and come back empty-handed. The boss won't stand for that." Jim said.

"You know the boss well. He said if we came back empty-handed, we could draw our pay." Curly replied.

"Good luck. I think you're on a hiding to nothing. You're either going to lose your scalps or your jobs." Jim said.

The two hands grimaced. "I hope not," Curly said.

They rode to where the tracks left the road, where the Apache had abducted Julia, and followed the tracks until they disappeared. At that point, they had a conflab.

"What do you think is the best way to proceed?" Curly said.

"I think we should ride out ten miles from here together and then split up, ride around in a circle to join up where we saw the last tracks," Shorty replied. "We'll come across the tracks then. We won't be in much danger as the lookouts will be closer to the camp than we'll get to."

Curly agreed. They went straight ahead for ten miles and split off. Curly came upon the tracks after an hour. The tracks were faded from the wind but still visible. There had been no rain since Julia's abduction. Various animals had overridden the tracks. There were coyote tracks and pronghorn tracks. He noted the landmarks around and then rode back toward where the tracks had disappeared. When he got to where the tracks disappeared, he set up camp. It would be a while before Shorty had covered his semi-circle and arrived back. Curly decided he would find a pronghorn or big horn sheep to give them some meat. He wrote a message in a sandy patch and built a pile of stones to attract his partner to the message, that he would be back there with some meat and to wait for him there. He thought it unlikely his partner would be back today as he would have to ride thirty or so miles, half the circle. He rode away from the spot, looking out for a target. After half an hour of riding, he spotted a herd of eight desert big horn sheep. There was a steady wind from the west. He rode around to the east of the herd and jumped off his horse, leaving it to graze on the sparse grass. He crept to within 90 yards of the herd and picked out a ewe. He lay on the ground with a rock to steady his aim and keep him out of sight. He steadied his breathing, sighted behind the sheep's elbow, and squeezed a shot off. The ewe dropped to the ground, and the rest of the herd took off. Curly stayed where he was and watched for a while to see if anyone came to investigate the shot. No one came. The rest of the herd stopped a way off to browse on the bush. Curly walked up to the sheep, checked it was dead, and walked back to his horse. He rode the horse up to the sheep and heaved the sheep onto the horse behind his saddle. The horse danced around for a minute or two and then settled with Curly talking to him and patting him. Once the horse settled, Curly climbed into the saddle and headed back to the meeting spot. Back at the meeting spot, he dressed the sheep and cut some steaks off. He salted other of the meat and hung the salted meat to dry into jerky. He glanced around but saw no coyote yet. He worried that their acute sense of smell would bring them around at some point. He placed the remains of the sheep some way from his camp in the hopes that that would satisfy the coyote and they would leave him and his dressed meat alone.

Curly spent the night half sleeping, half listening. Coyote squabbling in the middle of the night woke him. They had found the meat he had left away from the camp. So far, his plan was working. He built up the fire further. The night air was cold. Curly hoped the bigger fire would keep the coyote away and keep him warm. The next morning, the sun creeping over the horizon woke him. He got up, boosted the fire from ashes back into flames, and threw a steak in the pan. He finished breakfast and then had nothing to do other than sit and wait for Shorty. He sat in the sun to keep himself warm. By about nine thirty, he moved into the shade of a bush. He watched a red-tailed hawk circling overhead and then dip into the scrub, emerging with what looked like a mouse. Mid-morning, Curly saw a horse and rider heading toward him. He guessed it was Shorty but kept his rifle ready until he was certain it was Shorty.

He greeted Shorty with a "What kept you? Have you been out picnicking? I've been waiting here since yesterday. I've found the tracks, and I've bagged us some big horn sheep meat while you've been on your picnic."

"I thought I would take my time so that you would be looking forward to my company by the time I got back to you," Shorty said.

"I've been enjoying the peace and quiet," Curly replied. "Can I cook you a steak for breakfast before we move out?"

"Yeah, that would be great. I'm starving. I've been looking for tracks, not filling my stomach." Shorty replied.

Curly stoked the fire once again and threw a steak on for Shorty.

Done with breakfast, Curly led the way to where he had left the tracks. It didn't take long to reach the tracks. Curly's memory for landmarks was well developed over years of riding on various ranches and trails and all the tracking he had done. Progress slowed once they were following the faded Apache tracks. The tracks were hard to follow, and the further on they went, the more they scanned around for Apache. Toward sunset, Curly noted the direction birds were flying. "We need to find water for our canteen and horses. We'll leave the tracks here. I know where to pick them up again. I see where the birds have been heading, and I'm now seeing some coming back.

"You're the expert." Shorty said, "I'll follow your lead."

Half an hour before sunset, they found a spring that fed a waterhole. There were birds flying in and out. A herd of pronghorn had come down to drink. "Maybe we should live here," Curly said. "We won't need a job, and we won't lose our scalps. This water looks like it's always here, and there's plenty of meat for the taking."

"I'm not sure about not losing our scalps. I'm sure the Apache use this water hole. I'm surprised their tracks didn't come past here." Shorty said.

They lit a fire in the lee of some rocks, ensuring the wind wouldn't interfere with the fire.

"I don't think the Apache will see the fire, they're unlikely to be wandering around at night, but we may be close to their camp. It'll be worth us having a look from some high ground to see if we can see their fires. It might save us some time tomorrow." Curly said.

Shorty placed a griddle over the fire and placed two chunks of meat on it, cooking it for their supper. On finishing eating, Curly said. "Good job with the cooking, Shorty." He poured them each a cup of coffee from the pot hanging over the fire. "We'll head out once we've finished our coffee and see if we can spot the Apache fires."

They finished their coffee and walked over to their horses, saddled them, and headed out of camp, Curly in the lead. They left the camp as it was for their return once they finished the reconnoiter. They pulled on sheepskin jackets. The temperature plummeted with the sun slipping below the horizon. The stars twinkled at them out of a purple night sky. Coyotes and Owls welcomed in the night with their calls.

"Hey, this is a great country," Shorty said. "When you see it like this, it seems like paradise. It's us, humans, that mess it up. We need to learn to get along with each other and not be so greedy."

"Don't go getting all philosophical on me," Curly said. "You know, when we find these Apache and report back to the boss where their camp is, he'll put into action some plan that he has. He isn't wanting to know where they are for interest's sake."

"I know." Shorty sighed. "You and I are just tools for him."

They rode on in silence. Heading for the top of a hill, they could see with the help of the sliver of the moon and the stars. They dismounted before the top of the hill and tethered their horses. They crept up to the crest of the hill, ensuring they did not create silhouettes against the evening sky. They scanned around. "There are some fires." Curly pointed to a spot far in the distance. "It's hard to tell how far away they are with such a clear evening. It can only be the Apache camp with all those fires. They are far away from everything. They wouldn't expect anyone else to be so far out in the desert."

"What do you think we do tomorrow?" Shorty asked.

"We'll ride closer to get a good set of landmarks so we can easily lead the boss here, and then we'll head back, wiping out our tracks as we go. We don't want them following us and wiping us out to protect the whereabouts of their camp or packing up camp and moving." Curly said.

They crept back off the crest of the hill, mounted their horses, and headed back to camp.

Shorty was up first the next morning, coaxing the fire into life, cooking breakfast, and warming up a pot of coffee.

After breakfast, they retraced the previous night's tracks and did the same, searching for the camp from the crest of the hill without showing themselves. In the distance, instead of the pinpricks of the fires, they saw the smoke rising straight up into the air.

They looked around, noting landmarks. "I think I've got it. I can find my way back here." Curly said. "What about you?"

"Yeah, I think I've got it," Shorty said.

They turned to retrace their route back to the ranch. There was a steady wind in their face. They kept their sheep skin jackets on for the first three hours of the ride and then took them off and tied them behind the saddles. They rode for another half hour before dismounting at a spring and allowing the horses to drink. While the horses drank, they filled their canteens. Curly lit a cigarette and sat on a rock, watching the horses eat. The horses had moved off from the spring and were now cropping the sparse green grass a little way from the spring. Shorty sat down next to Curly and lit a cigarette, sucking in and then blowing a cloud of smoke out with a sigh.

"I'm in no hurry to get back," Shorty said, with another suck on his cigarette. "This sure beats chasing cows around."

"We'll reach the ranch sometime tomorrow morning," Curly said, breathing out a cloud of smoke. "We don't want to kill the horses getting back."

They sat for another half hour and then mounted up and continued toward the ranch. Curly scanned around for any signs of Apache. Shorty rode glancing around from time to time to admire some pronghorn, or big horned sheep, or a raptor searching for an unsuspecting mouse or lizard.

"Hey, Shorty, you need to keep a lookout for Apache. We don't want to be losing our scalps." Curly said.

"I'm not worried. I don't think they'll head this way." Shorty said. "Anyway, I'm relying on you. You're doing a thorough job of looking out for them."

Curly sighed. He realized there was no changing Shorty. If someone else was doing the work, Shorty was not going to get involved. Curly had no intention of relying on Shorty. He glanced across at his partner and saw that his eyes were fluttering toward sleep. Curly was tempted to pull his Colt out and fire it next to Shorty's ear, but his fear of the Apache hearing overrode his desire to give Shorty the fright of his life.

They pulled their jackets on and had a break to water the horses and let them at the grass lining a small stream. They took the opportunity to sit on a rock and watch the horses while they had a smoke.

"We've got another hour of riding, and then we'll find somewhere to camp for the night, and you can shoot us some fresh meat to eat," Curly said.

"Sounds right to me," Shorty said.

They found a spring through Curly's tried and trusted method of watching the activities of the birds.

Curly attended to the horses and set about collecting sticks and logs for the fire.

Shorty picked up his Winchester. "Right, let's go find us some supper."

Curly said. "You reckon we're far enough from the Apache not to have to worry about them hearing the shot?"

"Yeah, I think we're safe from them now. We're plenty far enough away." Shorty replied.

Shorty stepped out through the tufty grass, keeping his eyes scanning for snakes on the ground and further afield for something for supper. After fifteen minutes, he spotted a lone prairie chicken scrabbling for food. The shinnery oak gave Shorty cover but also made it difficult to get a clear shot at the bird. Shorty aimed at the bird and then sighed and lowered the rifle as the bird disappeared into the oak. He raised the rifle again and kept the rifle up to his shoulder, ready should the bird present a clear shot. The prairie chicken popped into a small gap in the shinnery oak. Shorty squinted down the sights and squeezed off a shot. The bird dropped. "Got him," Shorty shouted. He walked up to it and picked it up by its feet, holding it away from him, avoiding the blood dripping from the bird. He sized it up. "That should be enough for the two of us." He said a smile on his face.

Shorty held up the prairie chicken to Curly as he walked into camp. "This should do us. What do you think?"

"Good job," Curly said. "It's about time you contributed to this party."

"We've got to work to our strengths." Shorty grinned. He placed his rifle down, picked up a knife, and walked out a way from camp. He squatted down, de-feathered the bird, and cleaned it. He buried the feathers and guts before heading back into the camp. "I'll cook it." He said.

"Thanks," Curly said as he poured himself a cup of coffee and moved away from the fire.

After eating, they cleaned up and sat back, watching the fire and having a last smoke and coffee before bed.

"What do you think the boss will do with the information we bring him?" Shorty asked.

"I think he wants to wipe the Apache out. You know him. He's not about to share any of the land with anyone. I know he also wants Matt Teeson's land. But Teeson is no pushover, and he's registered his land properly." Curly said.

"I heard that Teeson wants to live in peace with the Apache and let them continue to hunt on the ranches. He's a do-gooder." Shorty said. "If the Apache and Teeson tie up, our boss might be in trouble."

"You have a point there. Maybe the boss has thought of that, and he'll try and set the Apache against Teeson." Curly said. "It probably wouldn't be difficult. The Apache and Teeson have already had one run-in."

"I think you might be right there. I'm not eager to get into a fight with the Apache and Teeson. It'll end badly for us. I just want to look after cows, drink whiskey and enjoy the ladies at the saloon." Shorty said.

"You're not thinking of joining Teeson, are you?" Curly asked.

"No, I want away from this whole thing," Shorty said. "When I get back, I think I'll ask for my pay and move on."

"That's not a good idea," Curly said. "I don't think the Boss will let you go. He'll worry that you're going to join Teeson."

"I'll assure him I'm not. What do you think he'll do?" Shorty said.

"He'll set Knox onto you." Curly stared at Shorty.

"Do you really think he'll do that?" Shorty said. "I'm good with this." He tapped the Colt in its holster at his hip.

"You are, but I think the risk of you being killed is much bigger if you say you're leaving than if you stay and take your chances with the Apache and Teeson," Curly said. "That Knox is not averse to shooting someone in the back. I hear tell that he shot O'Hagan when O'Hagan was not looking for a fight and still had the loop over his six-shooter. He told O'Hagan he would let him take the loop off before drawing but drew as soon as O'Hagan moved slowly to the loop to un-hook it. Then he went up to O'Hagan when he was dead and lifted the loop off. I shouldn't be telling you this, but I don't want you to die the same way as O'Hagan."

"Thanks, Curly. Forewarned is forearmed." Shorty said.

"Think hard about it between now and when we reach the ranch," Curly said.

"Nothing to think about," Shorty said.

Curly sighed. "I'm going to turn in."

"Me too," Shorty said.

"I hope this isn't the last time you turn in," Curly said.

Shorty grunted. "Good night, Curly."

They were up at first light, warmed some coffee on the fire, and ate dried pronghorn meat.

"What have you decided, Shorty," Curly asked.

Shorty glanced at him, "I haven't given it any more thought."

"You should do," Curly said.

Shorty glanced at him and said nothing as he lit a cigarette. He stared into the flame of the fire, breathing out the smoke from his cigarette.

There was no talking as they packed up camp, mounted their horses, and headed toward the ranch.

———————

Chapter 28

At ten that morning, they rode into the ranch yard. They dismounted. Shorty unhooked the loop on his sidearm once he was on the ground. They led their horses across to the corral, unsaddled them, and turned them into the corral. Someone must have told George Hamilton they were back. He came out of the house and walked over to the corral.

"So, did you find them, or have you just been on a picnic?" George asked.

"We found them, boss," Curly said. "Shorty has the best idea of where they are and will be able to lead you to them. I'll help. Between us, we can take you there."

Shorty looked at Curly, surprise on his face for a moment. He realized Curly was trying to keep him alive and stop him from following through on drawing his pay.

George glanced at Shorty and raised his eyebrows.

"Err," Shorty hesitated. "Yeah, I can find our way there. Curly should be along as well in case there's anything I forgot."

"How long do you think it'll take us to get there?" George asked.

"It'll take under two days," Curly said.

George furrowed his brows and stared at the ground for a moment. "We'll start early tomorrow morning. We can get everything ready this afternoon."

"What're you going to do?" Curly asked.

"I'll tell you once we're on our way," George said. "I don't want anyone here broadcasting our plans."

Curly shrugged. "Okay, we'll be ready to go first thing tomorrow morning." He turned his horse away and headed toward the corral. Shorty followed him.

"Are you any the wiser?" Shorty said.

Curly glanced around. In a whisper, he said, "I'm guessing that our theory is correct. I think he wants to set the Apache against Matt and or vice versa. That's why he's only going to tell us once we're on our way so that no one can warn Matt Teeson."

They walked toward the cookhouse, where some of the hands were getting something to eat for lunch. As they sat down at the table with their beef and beans, Knox said, "did you two find what you were sent out to look for?"

"We did. We found the Apache camp." Curly replied.

"What did the boss say to that?" Knox asked.

"He wants us to take him out there tomorrow with some of the hands. I'm guessing he'll include you." Curly said.

"That's good news. I need some shooting practice. It's getting boring around here," Knox said.

"The boss wouldn't tell us what his plan was. I don't think it's as straightforward as wiping the Apache out." Curly said.

Knox grunted through a mouthful of beef and beans. Curly looked toward George Hamilton. George was giving Jim Davis instructions and waving his hands around while he was doing it. Curly gathered from the body language that Jim Davis was not happy with the instructions and was arguing about them. Curly guessed that Jim would do exactly what George ordered him to do. Five minutes later, he saw Jim heading toward the cookhouse.

Jim stopped and placed his hands on his hips. "Tomorrow, we head out to the Apache camp at first light. You all will need to be ready at first light. Expect to camp out for a couple of nights. Make sure you have your sidearms and rifles and a stock of ammunition. We'll leave four men here to look after the cattle. I'll let the four know that they're staying. You all here will be going."

"Any questions?" Jim asked.

"Yeah, what are we going to do when we catch up to the Apache?" Knox asked.

"The boss hasn't told me yet. He says he'll tell us on the way out there. But given the instruction on the guns and ammunition, you can be sure there'll be a fight." Jim said.

At supper that night. Melissa said. "I hear you've told the men to be ready in the morning to ride out and find the Apache camp. And they must bring their rifles and sidearms and plenty of ammunition. What's all that about?"

"It's none of your business. It's men's business," George said.

"I think it's foolish to be attacking the Apache. Yes, you might win, but you're going to lose some men. You'd be better off making peace with them. It..." George interrupted her.

George's face flushed red. He hammered his fist on the table and stood up. His chair crashed to the floor. "As I said, you have no say in this. If you're going to keep giving your opinion on the matter, you can take your food and eat elsewhere."

"You would do a whole lot better if you listened to us," Julia said.

"Don't you start now," George said.

Dinner carried on in silence, just the clinking of cutlery on plates.

As they left the table, Julia said. "You're making an enormous mistake. This'll end badly for you. Greed will be the death of you."

George said nothing further. He stomped off to his study. He poured himself a brandy, sat in the chair behind his desk, pulled a cigar out of the top right-hand drawer, clipped the end off the cigar, and lit it. He sucked at it, blew the smoke out, grabbed the glass of brandy, put his feet on the desk, and took a sip of brandy. He stared up at the ceiling, breathing heavily. After fifteen minutes, his breathing slowed. *I don't know why I've been burdened with daughters, they'll never understand me, and we'll never have a relationship,* he thought. He alternately sipped at his brandy and puffed at his cigar while he contemplated his plan for the Apache and Matt Teeson.

———

Chapter 29

The next morning George set off leading a group of twelve men, Curly and Shorty close behind him, giving directions. After half an hour, George dropped back behind Curly and Shorty and said, "you lead the way."

Curly was in front of Shorty. He hoped George had not remembered his comments about Shorty knowing the way better. That evening they camped around one of the springs that Shorty and Curly had camped around on their way back from finding the Apache. George had earlier dispatched Shorty to find some meat for supper. The men were carrying out camp chores when Shorty came into camp with a bighorn sheep tied behind his saddle.

"Good for you, Shorty. That looks like it'll make a good meal for us." One of the hands said.

"It sure will," Shorty said. "I'm showing you what I got so that you can start preparing the fire for it. I'm going to go and skin and gut it now."

Shorty rode off some way from the camp. While gutting and skinning the bighorn sheep, he thought about what he was going to do. He didn't want to be involved in a fight with the Apache. He also didn't want to take his chances with Knox.

He was owed half a month's pay. He came to a decision, if he did nothing, he wouldn't be able to spend the pay anyway. He would sneak off in the middle of the night. It was unlikely that George would send anybody after him. He would need all his men to deal with the Apache. Shorty hoped that he would not take it out on Curly. He figured that George would need Curly to find the Apache and would be so pleased with Curly that he wouldn't take it out on Curly.

Shorty carried the sheep back to the camp, huffing and puffing. He placed the sheep next to the fire and cut steaks off the carcass, enough for all the men.

One of the other men said, "I'll do the cooking, Shorty. You've done all the hard work."

"Thanks, I appreciate that," Shorty said. He grabbed himself a cup of coffee and sat back, and watched the cooking. He wondered if George would put a guard on for the night.

After supper, the hands all turned in. There was nothing else to do, not enough light from the fire to play even a game of cards.

"We need to have someone on guard all night," George said. "We don't want the Apache sneaking up on us during the night."

"I don't think that'll happen," Shorty said. "They don't even know we're coming after them."

"It's not going to do us any harm to post a watch," George said. "I'd rather be safe than sorry."

Shorty turned away so that George wouldn't see the involuntary expression of disappointment on Shorty's face. Shorty turned in. He lay in his bedroll, wondering what to do. He decided he couldn't sneak out in the night. Whoever was on guard would see him go to his horse. The guards would be watching the horses more closely than anything, given the Apache might well want the horses and realize that it would make the group sitting ducks for an attack. He could sneak off during his watch, which would be from 4 to 6 in the morning. He considered this and decided that that would be disloyal to his fellow hands. He thought it was unlikely that the Apache would attack in the night, but if that was his job, he was going to do it. Shorty lay there worrying for a while and eventually fell asleep. Shorty was awakened shortly before four in the morning, enough time for him to grab a cup of coffee and make himself comfortable for his two-hour watch. He sat with his back against a rock, keeping an eye on the camp and the horses, cursing his sense of loyalty, which may well get him killed. He wasn't worried about George and Knox, but the other hands were his friends. He spent the rest of the night worrying about what would happen. He would just have to go along with it and hope for the best. His worrying stopped as the first sliver of dawn crept over the horizon. He had a last scan around the camp, saw nothing, and climbed down from his spot to stoke the fire and get the coffee going. He threw more chunks of meat on the fire for breakfast. The hands stirred one by one and carried out the morning ablutions, splashing water from the cold spring on their faces and then wandering up to the fire to grab a cup of coffee and greet Shorty. Shorty realized at this point he was going nowhere. These were his people. He had no one else in the world. He only wished that George would stick to ranching and not focus on growing his empire at the expense of everyone else.

After breakfast and packing up camp, they all headed out, following Curly. Curly glanced at Shorty as if he could read his mind. Maybe he could, maybe he couldn't, but Shorty got the impression Curly was surprised to see him still there.

At about two that afternoon, Curly stopped and pointed out where the Apache camp was. "What's the plan, boss?" He asked.

Chapter 30

"I want to grab some of their horses but not harm any of them or as few as possible. I want to drop the horses off on Matt Teeson's ranch so that they think it was him that stole the horses, and then they'll wipe Matt Teeson and his crew out. It'll look like Matt Teeson is the bad guy. He'll probably kill a few of the Apache, and then I can chase after the rest and get rid of them." He looked around at his men. He saw mixed reactions on their faces, mostly attempts to disguise their unhappiness. The only one who looked happy about the plan was Knox. "Anyone not happy, they can leave now. When we get back, you can come and collect your pay."

No one was going to take up that offer. They all knew that they would be signing their death warrants. Of course, if they all stuck together, that wouldn't be true, but no one was sure whether they all would stick together.

Someone mumbled, "sounds like a good plan, boss. We're with you." There was a general mumbling of agreement.

"Okay, you all keep an eye on the Apache camp. Knox, Jim, Curly, and Shorty come with me. We'll sit over there and come up with a plan," George said.

Everyone gravitated toward their assigned spots.

Curly opened the discussion. "I don't think we can plan without having reconnoitered the site. I think I should reconnoiter the site on my own, and then we can discuss what to do."

George frowned. "I suppose what you say makes sense." George liked to be seen as a man of action and felt this delay would look like a weakness to his men, but he couldn't fault Curly's logic. "Okay, off you go and check out the scene, and then we'll make a plan."

Curly headed out, keeping to low ground. George and his group moved back to the other men. George explained what was happening.

Curly dismounted some distance from the camp and tied his horse in an arroyo. The arroyo allowed Curly to walk closer to the camp without the Apache seeing him. He crawled up a hill close to the camp and lay on his stomach surveying the camp and its surrounds. The horses were all grouped together near a stream. There was one Apache guarding them. The Apache had his back leaning against a rock and was looking over the horses at the activities in the camp. He didn't look like he was expecting any kind of danger. Looking at the scene, Curly decided it would be easy to execute George's plan. He watched for about an hour longer. Once he saw the guard had changed and that the new guard had taken up the same position as the old one and looked as relaxed, Curly left. He sneaked back down the arroyo, mounted his horse, and, keeping to low ground, made his way back to the group of men. He went back to the spot where he had left George and signaled George to come across. He dismounted and sat on a rock, waiting for George and the two others to get there. When they arrived, he said, "I think it'll be easy to execute your plan, boss. They only have one guard on the horses, and he doesn't look too worried about anything. I think the best thing is, if someone sneaks up on the guard and incapacitates him, we steal some horses, move the other horses away, and then a couple of us fire shots into the camp, and we hightail it out of there. It'll take a while for them to collect their horses. By then, we'll be long gone. We then plant the stolen horses on Teeson's land and let events unfold."

George smiled. "That sounds like a fine plan. Let's go and explain the plan to the men."

They wandered across to the men, and George explained the plan. At the end, he said, "let's move out and get set up."

George selected Curly to incapacitate the guard as he was the most capable in the group at sneaking around, and he had seen the lay of the land. The selected few rode out with Curly in the lead. He placed the men overlooking the camp, out of sight, where they would have a clear shot at the camp. He carried on and tied his horse in the same spot where he had tied him before. He sneaked down the arroyo as close to the guard as possible. He then circled around behind the guard keeping low and out of sight. He crept through the shinnery oak, which provided excellent cover for him. The closer he got to the Apache, the louder and faster his heart beat. He paused as he got closer, took a deep breath, and breathed out silently, hoping to slow his heart down. He crept within striking distance of the Apache and paused. He snaked his right arm around the Apache's neck, cutting off the blood supply to the carotid artery. He closed his left hand over the Apache's mouth. The Apache gave a muffled scream and struggled. His efforts were too little too late. He collapsed. Curly stuffed cloth in his mouth and tied a neckerchief tight over it. He then rolled the Apache onto his front and tied his hands behind his back with piggin strings and then tied his ankles together with another set of piggin strings. He decided to blindfold him as well for good measure. He would soon recover from the carotid artery being blocked. He attached ropes that he had brought with him to four horses and then herded the rest down the arroyo toward the other men. He was joined by four of the men who drove the loose horses ahead of them. One of the men grabbed the ropes of two of the horses that Curly was leading to help him. The men carried on away from the Apache camp. The plan was they would continue as far as possible without making any noise until they heard shots, which would alert them to the fact that the Apache had now noticed the horses had gone. Once Curly figured they were far enough from the camp for the Apache not to hear them, he upped the pace. They were well away from the Apache camp before they heard shots.

George and the rest of the hands watched in admiration as Curly carried out his task. They watched for some time before any of the Apache noticed the horses had gone. The Apache that Curly had tied up had managed to dislodge the gag by rubbing his face on the ground. Once clear of the gag, he shouted for help. Two Apache ran from the camp to him and untied him. George could see him explaining to them what had happened. They ran back to camp shouting and gesticulating. They went straight to the Chief's wikiup. There was more gesticulating and shouting. George wondered whether the chief would execute the guard for not carrying out his duties diligently. It seemed at this point that was not a priority.

"Hold your fire," George said. "I'll tell you when to shoot."

The chief summoned all the warriors around him at his wikiup. George could see he was explaining a plan of action. He led the warriors toward where the horses had been. As he got closer to the edge of the camp, George said. "Right, we need to keep them back from the edge of the camp, don't shoot at anyone. Just keep them in the camp. Open fire now."

The men fired, creating a volley of sound and kicking up dust in front of the warriors heading toward the horses or where the horses had been. The Apache turned and looked toward the ridge. They raced toward a gully at the far edge of the camp. George's hands put up another volley of shots in front of them, turning them back away from the gully. The Apache all disappeared into various wikiups. The hands ceased fire. Every time someone poked their head out of a wikiup, a volley of shots chased the head back in. After two hours of this, the hands mounted up and rode out, being as quiet as possible, in the hope that the Apache would stay hidden for a while longer while they got further from the camp. When George figured they would not be heard by the Apache in the camp, he urged his horse to a canter. The rest of the hands followed. He reckoned they would be well clear by the time the Apache had caught their horses and started a pursuit. To slow the Apache down further, he set up two hands on either side of the trail where high ground flanked the trail. George and his hands were long gone by the time the two left behind open fired on the Apache. The Apache retreated to cover, firing blindly at where they thought their oppressors were. After two hours of this cat-and-mouse game, the two hands left and headed back to the ranch by different routes.

George caught up with Curly and the horses late in the next day when they were nearly at Matt Teeson's. They left the horses on Matt's ranch in a place where he was unlikely to come across them soon. They headed back to George's ranch, leaving two of the hands to clear the tracks back to the ranch.

The hands unsaddled the horses at the ranch and settled in for supper. Pleased to be back with the comforts of the ranch, such as they were.

When the other hands who had been clearing up the tracks arrived back at the ranch, George said, "well, boys, a job well done." He had a bag of cash with him. "To show my appreciation, here's a bonus for all of you."

He called out the hands one by one and handed them their bonus. Their faces brightened at the sight of the bonus. The bonus washed away the concerns over what they were doing.

"Now we wait for the Apache to do their job, and we'll have a much bigger ranch to look after, which means I'll be able to pay you more," George said.

The hands smiled in anticipation. The only one who didn't look overly happy was Knox. He was only happy when there was action, and the action involved killing people.

———

Chapter 31

That same evening Matt was at his ranch with Tate, Geoff, and Hugh. They were sitting around the table outside the cabin, talking while eating supper.

"It seems to be very quiet the last few days," Tate said. "I would've expected more trouble from George."

"If it seems too good to be true, it usually is," Matt said. "I'm sure he's up to something or scheming."

"You're probably right," Tate said. "We'll have to keep a good lookout, and I think we need to check the whole ranch tomorrow."

"You're right. It's annoying that we have to do these things. It takes away from the real business of ranching," Matt said.

Later that evening, when they'd all turned in, Matt was in his bed, doing his normal before he went to sleep, listening to the owls and coyotes and thinking about ranching. Tonight though, he was troubled. He was wondering what he should do about George Hamilton. He couldn't carry on like this forever, and in any event, he was taking a liking to Julia, which made it more difficult when thinking about what to do about George. He fell asleep without having reached any conclusions.

The next morning after breakfast, Matt split them into twos. He was paired with Geoff and Tate with Hugh. They agreed on the areas of the ranch that each would inspect. By 10 o'clock that morning, Matt was beginning to relax. Everything on the ranch looked to be in order, although there was still a lot of the ranch to cover. They stopped next to a stream at midday to water the horses and chew on some jerky. The land around them was flat. The stream meandered across the plains. They sat under a group of pinyon-junipers following the stream. Geoff pointed in the distance. "Are those horses? I think they are, but I don't know whose they would be. They're too far away to identify."

"Good spot," Matt said. "We'll get closer and check them out after we've had a break and a rest. There shouldn't be horses there. It's hard to tell from here, but they look like Apache horses to me."

"You're right. That's worrying," Geoff said. "It's weird that they're running around loose. I can't imagine the Apache camping here. If the Apache were here, I would expect them to be on the warpath."

"Yeah, it's suspicious. We'd better watch ourselves," Matt said.

Once the horses were rested and had had some water and grass, Matt and Geoff mounted up and headed toward the horses. They scanned around for people but couldn't see any.

"If there are Apache around, we wouldn't see them anyway." Matt said, drawing his rifle out of its scabbard."

Geoff followed suit. They rested their rifles across their saddles. They reached the horses with no sign of anyone.

"These are definitely Apache horses," Matt said. "This puts us in a bad position. If we try and return the horses, the Apache will think we are stealing, and if we keep them there, they'll think the same. We're in a no-win position. I think this is George Hamilton's doing."

"I think you're right," Geoff said. "Maybe we should hide the horses, and then one or all of us ride to the Apache camp and tells them the story."

"That's a good idea, but we don't know where the Apache camp is," Matt said.

"Maybe we can track the horses back to the Apache camp," Geoff said, looking at the horses' tracks. "Although these tracks look like the horses have been just wandering around eating grass, so that's not going to be much help."

"Okay, we'll carry out the first part of the plan and take the horses back to the ranch house. They're less likely to be found there. We'll wipe out the tracks as well," Matt said. With that, he shifted the horses toward the ranch house. An hour later, they were back at the ranch house. They tethered the horses in the trees.

"Tomorrow, I'll ride in to see the sheriff and see if he has heard anything further about where the Apache camp is and see if he has any suggestions as to what we do," Matt said. "I'm going to ride back and wipe out the tracks."

Matt headed back to where they had found the horses and methodically wiped out the tracks. It was almost dark by the time he got back to the cabin. Tate and Hugh had arrived while Matt was out. Geoff had explained the situation to them.

"I don't like this," Tate said. "This is a setup."

"You're right," Matt said. "We'll have to keep watch tonight. Although I don't think they'll do anything tonight, it's more likely to be first thing tomorrow morning, but we can't take chances."

They had supper and set up a roster for the night watch. The next morning everything seemed peaceful. It was a clear day. The birds sang with not a care in the world.

"We'll all stick together and work on the ranch. We can't have anyone isolated," Matt said. "I'll be happy if the Apache steal the horses back without bothering us. I think it's a good idea if we all work away from the ranch house today. We'll have to take our chances that they don't burn it down, but if they do, at least we'll all be alive still."

That evening, they approached the cabin warily. "I can't see the horses," Matt said. "Maybe the Apache have stolen the horses back and will leave us in peace. Although I'll be surprised, I think they'll want revenge and to teach us a lesson."

At the cabin, nothing had been disturbed. They were reluctant to go out to where the horses had been and look for tracks. There were too many rocks and trees affording cover in that area.

Matt grabbed a ladder and placed it against the cabin. "I'm going to climb onto the roof and keep a watch while you guys make supper."

"You better make sure you're not a target up there," Tate said.

"Yeah, I'll keep a sharp look out while I'm up here," Matt said.

Matt climbed up and settled himself on the roof at the top. He straddled the apex with his back against the chimney. He stared out into the bush surrounding the cabin, watching for any movement. His eyes jumped to some movement that he caught out of the corner of his eyes. He let out a breath when he realized it was a squirrel foraging. He stared at a shape on the ground. It looked like a foot sticking out beneath a bush. After five minutes of staring at it, he had almost decided it was nothing when it moved. Realizing now that it was a foot, he was able to discern the shape of an Apache behind the bush. Matt didn't move. He scanned around, moving only his eyes. He picked out two other shapes that were Apache. He eased himself off the apex and down to the ladder. He shimmied down the ladder. The rest were sitting on the porch. "Get inside, and between us, we must cover all directions. The Apache are here. They're hiding in the bushes. I'm not sure what they're waiting for."

Matt and Tate covered the side where Matt had seen the Apache. Hugh and Geoff covered the other two sides. The side with the fireplace and chimney had no openings.

"Here they come," Matt said as he pulled the trigger on his Winchester. One of the Apache yelled and dropped. "That's one less."

Tate also squeezed off a shot, and another one dropped. Matt saw one of the Apache drop behind a rock. Matt was surprised to see he had a rifle. "I see one of them at least has a rifle." He said. "That surprises me. When they attacked us, none had rifles."

As he said that, he saw a puff of smoke and heard the shot. Tate shouted and dropped beside Matt. Matt glanced at Tate and saw blood flowing out of his chest. He dragged his eyes away from Tate. He needed to keep the Apache at bay. The Apache who had shot at Tate jumped from behind the rock, and as he did that, Matt fired, hitting the Apache center mass, sending him sprawling backward and throwing the rifle in the air. One of the other Apache jumped from behind cover to recover the rifle. As he did that, Matt took another shot, hitting the Apache under the armpit. The Apache dropped to the ground, not moving again. Hugh and Geoff had maintained their positions but had not fired. It appeared that the Apache had hidden on the one side of the cabin. "Stay where you are," Matt said to them. "I've got this side covered. We don't want them sneaking up on your side. Also, make sure they don't sneak around the fireplace side. As he said that, Geoff poked his head out of the window toward the fireplace side and saw an Apache racing from that side. He swung his rifle and pulled the trigger in one motion. The Apache dropped, arms spread out. A hush formed around the cabin. Not even the birds and squirrels made a noise. No one moved in the cabin.

"Have they gone?" Geoff said.

"They may have," Matt said. "But keep looking out." As he said that, he saw six Apache riding away on their horses, leading the horses that had been behind the cabin. "It looks like they're bugging out. We'll keep watching for a while. Tate's been hit. Hugh, keep a lookout on this side while I attend to Tate."

Hugh moved across to Matt's side and took up the watch on that side. Matt knelt next to Tate. "How're you doing, buddy?"

Tate didn't respond. His eyes were closed. Matt felt for a pulse. He was relieved when he felt a pulse. He eased Tate's shirt away from the wound. There was lots of blood. Matt's heart thundered in his chest, and his stomach churned. This didn't look good. He pulled a clean shirt from a pile of his clothes and ripped the shirt into strips. He pressed a ball of cloth onto the wound and wrapped a strip of cloth around Tate over the wound, pulling it as tight as he could. The bleeding out of Tate's chest eased, but more worrying was the thin stream of blood trickling out of Tate's mouth.

———

Chapter 32

"I'm going to have to get Julia here again. Tate isn't looking good. I can't wait to be sure the Apache have gone. I must go now," Matt said.

Hugh turned to Matt. "Good luck, boss. See you later."

Matt touched his head in acknowledgment and eased out the door, scanning around as he did so. He saddled Sox, his back tense, expecting a shot at any time. None came. He mounted Sox, who for once behaved. He seemed to sense the seriousness of the occasion. He cantered off down the trail, feeling reasonably safe from the Apache as they had headed off in a different direction. As the danger subsided, Matt's anger increased. He was certain this was a setup by George Hamilton, and now he was going to have to ride onto George's ranch to fetch Julia. He suspected Julia couldn't believe that George would set this up. He hoped that Knox or George wouldn't shoot him on sight and come up with some cock and bull story. His priority was for Julia to save Tate. He didn't hold out a lot of hope. He would tackle George once that was done. Matt slowed up as he reached the ranch. He unhooked the loop on his Colt and then moved his hands away from it. He rode up to the porch with his hands half up in the air. He jumped off Sox and hammered on the door. As usual, Maria answered the door.

"I need Julia to come with me. Tate has been badly wounded again," Matt said. Matt saw the expression on Maria's face, saying to him, you really should look after your partners and staff better.

"I'll fetch Julia," Maria said. "Wait here." Maria turned and went in search of Julia. Two minutes later, she was back, with Julia behind her.

"What's happened now?" Julia raised her eyebrows.

"The Apache have attacked us again. Tate has been wounded. It's worse this time," Matt said.

"I'll go and get my stuff and change. Maria, ask one of the hands to saddle my horse," Julia said.

Matt stood waiting at the door. George came out. He walked down the passage toward Matt. "What're you doing here?" George asked.

"I'm sure you can probably guess," Matt said.

"What's that meant to mean?" George said.

"Don't play innocent with me. I know what you did. If Tate dies, I'm coming for you," Matt said.

"I haven't a clue what you're talking about," George said. "I'll ask again, what are you doing here?"

"I've come for Julia. Tate's been wounded by Apache again. I'm sure you know why that is," Matt said.

George shrugged. "Haven't a clue. I can't imagine what you think I have to do with the Apache. You and I don't like them. In fact, you're the one who wants to be close to the Apache."

"So, you know nothing about Apache horses mysteriously appearing on my ranch as if they had been stolen from the Apache?" Matt said.

George smiled. "You're delirious. That's got nothing to do with me. You stole horses, and now you're trying to blame it on me, now that it's all gone wrong for you."

Julia came toward them and saw Matt glaring at George. "Now, what's going on?" Julia asked.

"You better ask your boyfriend. He's making wild nonsensical accusations," George said.

"Come, Matt, let's go. I'm guessing we don't have time to finish this argument," Julia said.

"No, we don't." Matt turned and followed her. He felt safer with Julia there. He didn't think George would do anything with her around. If she hadn't been around, his back would be prickling. He also noticed that Julia didn't comment on the boyfriend part. He guessed that that was because she thought it was ridiculous.

Fifteen minutes after arriving at the ranch, they were on their way.

They rode in silence for 10 minutes, and then Julia said, "so, tell me about Tate's wound."

"It's much worse this time. He was hit in the chest with a rifle bullet, there was a lot of blood, and there was also blood trickling out of his mouth. He did have a pulse, though," Matt said.

"Shew, that doesn't sound good," Julia said.

They were silent for another five minutes, and then Julia said, "what were you and my father arguing about?"

"I'd rather talk about it after you've treated Tate," Matt said.

"If you think that your argument with my father is going to affect my treatment of Tate, you better think a lot more carefully, and you need to get to know me better. When it comes to patients, it doesn't matter who they are. I'm going to do my best for them," Julia said.

"I'm sorry. I do know you better than that," Matt said. "I'll tell you the story. You be the judge. We were checking around the ranch yesterday and came across four Apache horses in a spot that we wouldn't normally check on the ranch. We had decided to check the ranch because things seemed too peaceful. We know we didn't steal the horses. We concluded that your father was trying to set the Apache against us and had stolen the horses and placed them on our ranch so that the Apache and ourselves would wipe each other out, and then your father would have free run of the country. We were between a rock and a hard place. If we took the Apache horses back to them, they would attack us on the way back with their horses and wipe us out. If we took the horses back to my cabin, they would also think that. We took the horses back to my cabin. We were going to go and check with the sheriff what he thought the best plan was, but the Apache attacked us before we had the chance."

"Huum, that seems like a big leap," Julia said.

———————

Chapter 33

They arrived at the cabin. The moon was bright, almost as bright as daytime. There was a lantern on in the cabin. Julia and Matt dismounted and walked onto the porch, Matt carrying Julia's doctor's bag. Matt pushed the door open and allowed Julia in front of him. As Matt walked in the door, he could see from Geoff and Hugh's expressions that there was no good news. He turned toward Tate's bed.

"I'm sorry, Matt, he's gone," Geoff said.

"He can't be." Matt was across the floor to Tate's bed in one stride. He knelt beside Tate's bed, grabbed his arm, and felt for a pulse. They could see him moving his finger around Matt's wrist, hoping that he was feeling the wrong spot. He dropped his head onto the bed and kept it there for 10 minutes. He didn't want anyone to see his tears. No one said a word. Julia had edged in beside him and felt for a pulse. She looked at the other two and shook her head, stepping back. Matt surreptitiously wiped his eyes and stood up.

"We've been friends forever. No one can replace him. We were going to build this ranch into something to be proud of together," Matt said.

Julia stepped forward and rested her hand on Matt's arm. "I'm sorry." She looked up into his eyes and saw tears there and anger burning through. She stepped back involuntarily.

No one said anything or moved for a few minutes. Matt appeared to compose himself. "I'll take you back now. Thank you for coming."

Julia said nothing. She knew what Matt believed, but she didn't believe her father would stoop to that.

"I'll see you later," Matt said as he stood back for Julia to pass.

Neither Julia nor Matt spoke on the ride back.

As they reached the perimeter of the ranch yard, Matt said, "I'll leave you here, but I'll watch you safely into the house."

Julia looked at him. "I'm truly sorry, Matt. I know what Tate meant to you." She turned and headed into the ranch yard. Matt saw her go up to the corrals, dismount, unsaddle her horse, rub it down and then check that it had food and water. He watched her walk into the house. Once she had closed the door, he turned Sox and headed back to the cabin. His mind was numb. He noticed nothing on the ride back. He couldn't believe that Tate was gone. All he wanted now was revenge. He was certain that he had the events correct. He would do some more digging around for further evidence of what had occurred, then he would kill George.

Back at the cabin, he saw a lantern under the lee of the hill and Hugh and Geoff sitting there, shirts off, sweat glistening in the light of the lantern. He rode up to them. "Thanks, boys, I appreciate this." He said as he looked down into the deep grave that Hugh and Geoff had dug.

"We're sorry, boss. He was a great guy. He was our friend, too," Hugh said.

"I know, I attract death, first Patrick, now Tate. If you two want to pull out, I'll pay you for three months to give you time to find another job," Matt said.

"Speaking for myself, I'll stay through thick and thin," Hugh said.

"Me too," Geoff said.

"I appreciate that, boys. Thanks," Matt said. "We'll bury Tate now. I'll say a few words and read a verse from the Bible."

"I'd also like to say a few words," Geoff said.

"Me too," Hugh said.

They walked back to the cabin.

They wrapped Tate in a blanket. Matt handed Hugh a Bible.

"Geoff, help get Tate onto my shoulders. I'll carry him to the grave. Then you can help me lower him into the grave," Matt said.

Geoff helped Matt to get Tate onto his shoulders in a fireman's lift. Matt felt ill. He felt as if he was treating his friend like a bag of flour. There was nothing for it. It had to be done. Hugh led the way back to the grave, holding a lantern. At the grave, Hugh and Geoff helped ease Tate off Matt's shoulders and lay him on the earth next to the grave. The three of them jumped down into the grave and dragged Tate toward the grave, taking his weight at the edge of the grave and lowering him into the grave. They scrambled out of the grave, raining dirt down on Tate as they climbed out. Matt looked around. Hugh and Geoff glanced at him and then looked down to the grave.

"Rest in Peace, my best friend. You can never be replaced. God, heal my heart of the grief it is feeling. Guide me through the future without him. All I want now is revenge. May Tate rest in peace," Matt said.

He nodded at Hugh. Hugh said some words. When he'd finished, he looked at Geoff. Geoff said some words. When Geoff had finished, he looked at Matt. Matt opened the Bible, paged through it, and found Psalm 23. He read Psalm 23 over the grave. At the end, they all said, "Amen."

Without a word, they picked up shovels. Hugh and Geoff waited for Matt to throw the first shovel of earth into the grave. Matt sighed and threw the first shovel of earth. Hugh and Geoff followed. Once they'd thrown the first shovels of earth, they worked at a fast pace.

Once they had filled the grave in, Matt said, "Okay, let's try and get some sleep now. I'll do something to mark the grave tomorrow."

They trudged up to the cabin and turned in for the night or what was left of it.

———

Chapter 34

Matt lay on the bed. Thoughts of Tate churned around in his head. He listened to the owls and the coyotes, but tonight they didn't bring peace and joy. They sounded mournful.

It seemed to Matt that he had only just fallen asleep when he heard the clatter of plates as Hugh prepared breakfast. Tate again crowded into Matt's mind, and his stomach churned. He climbed out of bed, yawned, bowed his head, and resisted flopping back onto the bed. He looked around. He didn't see Geoff but presumed Geoff was outside doing something.

"I'm glad you're up cooking breakfast, Hugh," Matt said. "If you hadn't got up, I think I would've slept the rest of the day."

"I guess that might have been a good thing," Hugh said. "It would stop you from churning thoughts of Tate."

"Yeah, there is that," Matt said. "All we can do now is focus on growing this ranch into something Tate would be proud of. Now though, the only thing I can think of is revenge. The only obvious target now is the Apache, but I think they were set up by George. I need to prove that before I do anything."

They finished breakfast. Hugh and Geoff headed out onto the ranch. As they headed out, Matt said, "I'll join you later. I've got some things to do here. If you hear some shots from here, don't worry about it. I'll be getting some practice. In fact, I'm going to get some practice in every day from now on."

Hugh and Geoff turned their horses around and headed out with a wave to Matt.

Matt collected some tins from the rubbish heap and set them up on a log about 20 yards out. He checked behind the tins. There were no rocks to send the bullets ricocheting back to him. He walked back the 20 yards and drew a line. He unhooked the loop from his Colt, turned with his right side facing toward the targets, took a deep breath, and let the air out, relaxing his muscles as he did so. He drew with minimal movement. The first can went down. He holstered his gun and did the same with the remaining five. He thought *the problem is I don't know how fast I am or whether I'm getting quicker. I'll have to think about how I measure that.* He practiced for a while longer, hitting the target every time. He then set the cans up at 70 yards and practiced for a while with his Winchester. Next, he stripped off his shirt and worked on the fighting skills he'd been taught in his youth. Again, he thought, *I don't know whether I'm good, bad, or indifferent at fighting. I think I'm going to have to get Hugh and Geoff into fighting and shooting. It'll be good for two things, I'll know whether I'm the best, and we'll all improve our skills to help us defend this ranch and ourselves.*

He headed out on one of the cow ponies to find Hugh and Geoff. Sox stood at the corral rails and watched Matt ride out. Matt found Hugh and Geoff where they said they'd be.

"So, how's it going?" Matt asked.

"All looks good at the moment. The cattle are in good condition, and we aren't missing many," Hugh said. "We need to finish off the dam before the rains start. Luckily there's not much to do. Maybe we can start on that tomorrow."

"You're right," Matt said. "We need to figure out a way of getting the water from the dam onto the hayfields in case we have a poor rainy season."

"Yeah, you're right," Hugh said.

"I want us all to practice shooting with our sidearms and rifles every morning. And when we're done with that, practice hand-to-hand fighting," Hugh said. "Are you both all right with that?"

"I'm good with that," Geoff said. "I think it's a good idea. We can build this into a great ranch, but we're going to need to defend it against George Hamilton and the Apache."

"I'm in," Hugh said.

"Good," Matt said. "At some point, I'm going to take the fight to them. Although, I'd like to live in peace with the Apache. I think that can be done, but not while George Hamilton is around."

"Yeah, I'm not so sure about living in peace with the Apache. I don't think they'll ever be peaceful," Hugh said.

"You may be right, but I'm willing to try," Matt said. "That'll be first prize. If we see that's not going to happen, then we'll have to wipe them out. But we'll be in a stronger negotiating position if we show strength."

They moved the cattle along to a different pasture. The cattle preferred certain sections of the ranch and overgrazed these. Matt guessed the grass must taste better in certain parts. Once they moved that herd of cattle along, they rode on to find the next herd.

They rode back to the cabin as the sun touched the horizon. They'd moved a few herds onto different pastures during the day, and all were in good condition. They'd planned it so that they'd be close to the cabin by the end of the day.

The next morning before heading out for the day's work, after breakfast, they started the new routine.

"I can't afford to pay a prize for every day," Matt said. "But I'll put a prize up for each activity after one month. At the end of the month, we'll have a competition on each activity, fast draw competition, rifle shooting competition, and hand-to-hand combat. For each of those activities, I'll put up a $50 prize. I'll supply all the ammunition in case you were worried."

"That's great, boss. It'll certainly provide us incentive to be the best and work at it," Hugh said. "And thanks for supplying the ammunition. I was going to ask about that. I couldn't afford the ammunition on my pay."

"Each day, we'll start off with the fast draw competition, then move to rifles, then hand-to-hand combat. Each day will be a competition but with no prize. Whoever is the winner for the day gets off any domestic chores for the next day. If each of us wins one competition, then no one gets off any chores. All happy with that?" Matt said.

"Happy." Hugh and Geoff said together.

They started off with the fast draw competition. They each had a line of cans to knock off. As soon as someone finished their line, he shouted stop, and everyone had to stop shooting. They then replace the cans and go again. They marked in the dirt a point under each name, whoever won. Matt won every round. The rifle shooting was a similar scoring system, but there was no timing. It was whoever hit the cans and how many they hit. None of them missed on the first round, so they moved the cans further out until there was a winner. Hugh won the rifle shooting.

The hand-to-hand combat was in two sections, no-rules wrestling and kickboxing. The one not fighting was the referee. Punches were counted if they got through the defense and hit anywhere on the body. Punches were not allowed to be hard enough to bruise; otherwise, the fighter was disqualified. They all learned from each other. Geoff won the hand-to-hand combat. He was 6 foot four and athletically built, compared to Matt's 6 foot and Hugh's 5 foot 10. He used his extra reach and athletic ability to good advantage.

At the end, Matt said, "that worked out well. From tomorrow on, after each activity, we'll have a debrief and can criticize each other's performance with the objective of coaching us all to be better. By the looks of it, we'll end up with the same results each day."

They jumped in the stream that ran next to the cabin, yelling and splashing to fight off the cold. The water came from somewhere further up the mountain, and they were just coming out of winter.

"Well, one good thing about this is the icy water will toughen us up, and we'll be clean, so we'll have the pick of the ladies in town." Hugh grinned. "Although, from what I see, boss, you and Julia are an item already."

"I don't see how you jump to that conclusion," Matt said. "At this point, I'm the last on her list. Once we start tackling her father on him setting us up with the Apache and stealing our cattle, I'll be done for."

"Well, since we'll be the only clean men in town, she might overlook that," Hugh said.

For the next five days, they worked on the dam to completion. They mounted their horses and turned back toward the dam, admiring their handiwork.

"I think we'll have a break from that hard work," Matt said. "We'll work the cattle tomorrow and for the next week. Then we'll get on with the backbreaking work of digging the drainage ditches for the irrigation."

Chapter 35

The next day they checked on the cattle. They were looking at a herd that was far away from the cabin. "This herd has thinned out substantially since I last saw it," Hugh said.

"You're right," Matt said. "Either the herd has split up, or someone has been stealing. Let's split up and see if we can figure out what's happened."

They agreed on who would look at which sections and headed out to determine what had happened. They circled around the herd. Matt found tracks of un-shod ponies. "Those damn Apache." He muttered. He fired off a couple of shots to attract Hugh and Geoff's attention. They waved their hats in acknowledgment and headed toward Matt. Matt carried on following the tracks. When Hugh and Geoff caught up with him, he said, "it looks like the Apache have been stealing from us. I don't want to leap to conclusions too soon. I wouldn't put it past George to try and put the blame on the Apache by using unshod horses."

"Yeah, it's a strong possibility," Hugh said. They followed the tracks for half an hour. They were heading the same way as the Apache always headed. Then the tracks of the cattle and horses disappeared. They circled around for a while. Geoff picked up the tracks again. This time they were heading toward George Hamilton's ranch. They continued to follow them and found them in a canyon on George's ranch.

"Looks like we were right," Matt said. "There's too many of them to start a fight. We'll leave the cattle here and fetch the sheriff. He'll need to do his job, but he'll need our help and some of the other townsfolk."

Hugh and Geoff agreed. "Yeah, I don't feel like taking George Hamilton and his band of men on. It'll only end one way for us."

———

Chapter 36

The three of them headed to town. They dismounted outside the sheriff's office. Matt looked down the street. The town was quiet. There were a couple people walking on the sidewalks, and four horses hitched to the hitching rails at various points in the town. The door to the sheriff's office was open. Matt knocked on the door as he walked in. The sheriff looked up from his newspaper. He had his feet on the desk and a cup of coffee on the right-hand corner of his desk. He dropped his feet to the floor and looked up at Matt. "Morning Matt, what's this? More trouble."

"Afraid so," Matt said. "This one's going to test you."

"Two of you can sit. I'm afraid I haven't got enough visitors' chairs." The sheriff said. "I can offer you all coffee, though. I have enough of that."

They accepted his offer of coffee. Matt and Hugh sat, and Geoff leaned against the wall. No one said anything while the sheriff poured the coffee. The sheriff ladled three spoons of sugar and three of coffee into each of the cups without asking who wanted what. There was no milk. He handed the coffee out and then sat. "Okay, let's hear it," he said.

"We haven't told you about Tate yet. I need to tell you about Tate to give the rest of the story some context," Matt said.

"What about Tate?" The sheriff said.

"Tate was killed in another Apache attack," Matt said.

"What? Another Apache attack. This can't continue. We'll need to call the Army in." The sheriff said.

"It's not as straightforward as it seems," Matt said. "The Apache attacked us because they found four of their horses on my ranch. That's the reason they attacked us. They took the horses back."

"Are you saying you stole horses from the Apache?" The sheriff asked.

"No, I'm not saying that. What I did say was that they found their horses or four of their horses on my ranch," Matt said. "But none of us put their horses there or had anything to do with stealing their horses. We're certain that this is a George Hamilton trick."

"What makes you say that?" The sheriff asked.

"We all know that George wants to be the only person in this area and own all the land. We believe he stole the horses from the Apache and placed them on my land so that the Apache attack me and wipe me and my hands and partner out. The plan was semi-successful. The Apache did believe it was us and attacked us. Luckily, they only killed one of us. Although, life will never be the same without my best friend and partner, Tate," Matt said.

"I'm sorry for your loss." The sheriff said. "I know you and Tate have been friends forever."

"Thanks. Do you see what I'm saying?" Matt said.

"I do, but it's going to be impossible to prove that, and therefore we won't be able to do anything about it." The sheriff said.

"The story doesn't finish there," Matt said. "After the Apache attack, we checked the ranch, and all our cattle were still there. Once we'd finished checking on the cattle, we spent a few days fixing up the dam. So, we didn't check the cattle for those few days. Once we finished with the dam, we went back to checking the cattle and found a whole bunch was missing. We had a look around and found the tracks of unshod ponies driving the cattle off. They headed off in the direction in which I had tracked the Apache before. The tracks disappear, but we found them again. The tracks then turned toward George Hamilton's ranch, and we found the cattle on Hamilton's ranch."

"But you don't know that the Apache aren't trying to set you and George against each other." The sheriff said.

"It's a possibility but unlikely. I'm sure that's what George will claim," Matt said.

"I guess I can go in and question him." The sheriff said. "But we all know what he's going to say. Then what?"

"I think it's a good enough reason to arrest him and put him on trial," Matt said.

Matt looked at the sheriff. The sheriff stared at his desk with a frown.

"I expect your theory is right." The sheriff said. "But he'll have a different story, and I don't think there'll be any way of disproving the story. I guess one of the advantages of having so many fighting men and being so powerful in the area is that no one wants to tackle you. If it was a one-man band rancher, struggling along, I'd happily go along and tackle him."

"You'll need us and a good few of the townsfolk to come along to brace George Hamilton," Matt said.

"Give me a day or so to think about it." The sheriff said. "It might be better if first I go on my own and question him. But, if he's as bad as you make out, he may well take me out when I'm there. Talking it through with you out loud, I think it's unlikely he'll take me out. So, I'm going to go out there and question him on my own, but I'll make it low-key at this point. Check back with me tomorrow as to what transpired.

Thinking about it further, I trust his daughters, and although they believe the best of their father, I don't think they would condone him shooting the sheriff, and I don't think he wants to totally alienate his daughters. I'm going to call in on Melissa and Julia before I go out and figure out with them how to approach it."

"I don't know about that, sheriff," Matt said. "I get the impression they are ruled by their father. The apple doesn't fall far from the tree."

"Well, that's the way I'm going to do it. I think my reading of the situation is right." The sheriff said.

"Okay, good luck, sheriff," Matt said as he stood up. "I'll drop by tomorrow and see how it went. I hope you're still here tomorrow. You're a good man. Do you want to go out and check the facts we've given you? Look at the cattle and the tracks."

"You should be the sheriff, Matt." The sheriff smiled at Matt. "You're right. That's what I should do if I'm operating with an open mind. The reality is I trust you and know that what you say is true. But, to do the job properly, I'm going to come out with you, and you can show me the facts. Can you wait here in the office while I go and talk to Julia and Melissa?"

"We'll do that, sheriff," Matt said.

———

Chapter 37

The sheriff stood up, lifted his Stetson off the hook, placed it on his head, and walked out onto the street heading for Julia's surgery.

At Julia's surgery, he walked into the reception area. There were two men waiting there, sitting in chairs in the reception area. Julia's surgery door was closed. The sheriff greeted the two men by name and sat down to wait for Julia to come out.

Five minutes later, Julia opened the door. Julia ushered a man out.

The sheriff stood up and looked at the two men, "sorry to push in folks. This is official business. Hello Miss Hamilton, I'd like a few minutes of your time."

One of the men waiting said, "hey, I don't care whether it is official business or not. You wait your turn."

Julia turned to the men, "I'm sorry, I need to deal with the sheriff first since it's official business."

The men frowned but said nothing further.

"Come in, sheriff. I hope this will be quick," Julia said.

"I hope so too." The sheriff said.

"Sit," Julia indicated the seat in front of the desk.

The sheriff sat. He leaned forward, holding his Stetson between his legs, twisting it. "This is a tricky matter which concerns your father. I ask that you hear me out before reacting."

Julia leaned back and frowned at him.

"Will you hear me out before reacting?" The sheriff said.

Julia's frown deepened. "Okay."

"I could go straight to your father." The sheriff said. "But I'm concerned about his reaction, and I'm looking for your advice on how to approach him. Also, if he knows you know the story, he's unlikely to shoot me or have one of his men shoot me."

Julia's face flushed. She opened her mouth and then closed it, raising her hands. "Go on, I promised not to react."

"Thank you." The sheriff said. "This is the story, and I gather you know part of it already. You know the part about the Apache horses being found on Matt's ranch. And I presume you also know about Matt's suspicion that it was your father who set that up. I gather he came and collected you for you to attend to Tate."

Julia nodded.

"The next part of the story you don't know. Matt found a whole lot of his cattle were missing. He tracked them and found that they had been stolen by a party with unshod horses. The herd was initially driven toward where the Apache have headed in the past. Then the tracks disappeared. Matt and his men found the tracks again and followed them to your father's ranch, where he found the cattle."

Julia raised her eyebrows. The flush had come back to her face.

The sheriff raised his hands. "Wait, I haven't finished yet. I realize that it's possible that the Apache want to set your father and Matt against each other, but it's my job to investigate the matter properly. I, therefore, need to go and talk to your father and establish his side of the story. But I'm worried that he won't let me get far in my investigation and will have me shot by his men. I'll be outnumbered by a long way, and I don't want to pitch up there with a whole bunch of men and start a war. I'm coming to you for advice on how I do this. Okay, I'm finished." He looked at Julia.

Julia had composed herself but was still frowning. "I was angry at first when I heard what you had to say. But I realize you must do your job and do it properly. I know my father had you elected, and you're a good choice. He may be regretting it now. He thought you would be a pushover."

Julia flashed a smile. "We finish supper at seven. I think that's the best time to approach him when we're all there. When you arrive at the door, I'll come out with him to see who it is. I'll insist on staying with you when you question him. I suggest you back that idea and say that you think it's a good idea that I'm there and Melissa. Leave my mother out of it. She'll do whatever he says. I'll talk to Melissa beforehand. But I don't think your assessment is correct. My father wouldn't stoop to stealing cattle."

"I appreciate your help in this and realize you're putting yourself out there standing up to your father." The sheriff paused. "Maybe there is another explanation. But I know he has ambitions to take over Matt's ranch, and he was angry that Matt was able to register it without him knowing. He also hates Matt. We all know that, and I certainly wouldn't put it past him to try and set Matt and the Apache against each other."

"It's a possibility," Julia said. "But I don't believe it."

"Thanks again, Julia." The sheriff stood up and smiled at her. "I'll let you get on with your doctoring. I'm glad to see you're getting some patients now. You deserve to be successful."

"Thanks, sheriff. I'll see you this evening." Julia stood and walked the sheriff to the door. She saw the sheriff out and asked the next patient in.

The sheriff walked back down the street and into his office. Matt looked at him and raised his eyebrows.

"Julia suggests I arrive at the ranch at 7 o'clock this evening when they finish supper. She insists that she and Melissa sit in on the conversation. She's a brave lady to take on her father." The sheriff said.

"She is," Matt said. "That sounds like the best plan to me. We're lucky that George has two feisty daughters. We're out of here, thanks, sheriff. We'll check in tomorrow."

With that, Matt, Geoff, and Hugh left the sheriff's office and headed back to continue with their ranch work. On the way out to the ranch, Hugh said, "I don't envy the sheriff's job. I hope he survives."

———

Chapter 38

That evening the sheriff rode out to the ranch. He saw some of the hands playing cards at the table outside the bunkhouse. He noticed one get up and lean in the door of the bunkhouse. A few seconds later, Knox appeared at the door. Knox stopped, looked at him, and then followed him to the ranch house door. The sheriff knocked on the door.

"What are you doing here?" Knox asked behind him.

The sheriff glanced at him. "None of your business. I've got business with your boss."

"Any of your business with my boss is my business," Knox said.

The sheriff ignored him. Knox placed his hand on the sheriff's shoulder and tried to turn him. "Don't you turn your back on me," Knox said through gritted teeth. The sheriff didn't move. He was at least 6 inches taller than Knox and 50 pounds heavier, all of it muscle.

Julia opened the door. "Well, hello, sheriff." She smiled at him. "What can we do for you this evening? It's late for you to be visiting."

"I've come to ask your father some questions. I'm carrying out an investigation." The sheriff said.

"Hello, Mr. Knox, I'll go and fetch my father, sheriff. In fact, rather follow me. I think he'll want to see you in his study, he's there now. Follow me," Julia said.

The sheriff turned to Knox and said, "we won't need you. This is a private matter."

"I'm coming anyway. As I said, my boss's business is my business," Knox said.

"If you come, I'll have to arrest you for obstructing justice." The sheriff said.

"Mr. Knox, don't cause unnecessary trouble. The sheriff is just here to talk to my father." Julia smiled at Knox.

Knox glared at the sheriff for a moment, turned, and went back to the bunkhouse.

"Shew, I owe you again, Julia, thanks. That was getting tricky." The sheriff said, letting out a deep breath.

Julia led the way to her father's study. "The sheriff's here to see you, Papa."

"Come in, sit down." George indicated the chair in front of his desk. "What's this about? Julia, close the door on your way out."

"I think this has something to do with the events the other evening and the Apache," Julia said. "I think I know a bit more about the Apache than anyone else here." Julia sat in the other chair in front of the desk.

"I think Julia could be helpful, so I'd like you to stay." The sheriff said.

George frowned, sighed, and sat down. "Let's see what you've got to say, sheriff."

The sheriff looked down at the desk for a moment, cleared his throat, and said, "I have a duty to investigate thoroughly any reports that indicate criminal activity. Understand I'm not accusing anyone of anything. I'm trying to get to the bottom of matters and understand what is happening to my satisfaction."

George tapped his fingers on the desk and said, "get on with it, sheriff."

"As Julia said, the events I want to talk about relate to the other evening when the Apache attacked Matt. Or at least I think they are related. I received a report this morning from Matt that several of his cattle had been stolen." The sheriff said.

"I'm not sure what that's got to do with me," George said. "That's his problem."

The sheriff continued as if George hadn't spoken. "When Matt found the cattle missing, he proceeded to examine the tracks to see what had happened. He noted a number of unshod ponies appeared to have been involved in rounding up the cattle."

George interrupted again. "So clearly, it was the Apache. I'm not going to get into a war with the Apache for the sake of Matt."

The sheriff continued. "He then tracked the herd, and they headed off toward where the Apache seemed to go every time."

George sighed.

"But then the tracks disappeared. Matt found the tracks again, and they led him back to your ranch, where he found the cattle. I rode out there and checked his story. The cattle are there on your ranch. What do you think this means?" The sheriff looked up at George.

George leaned forward and glared at the sheriff. "Are you accusing me of rustling cattle?"

"No, I'm pursuing all avenues to find out what happened." The sheriff said.

"Well, it's obvious," George said. "Either the Apache are trying to set Matt Teeson and me at war. Which is not necessary because he is my enemy anyway. Or, more likely, Teeson is creating an elaborate story to make it look like I'm a cattle rustler. So that a dumb sheriff like you arrests me, and then Teeson has got rid of his number one or maybe it is number two enemy, I'm not sure which."

"Those are possibilities." The sheriff said. "The first thing to do is to get those cattle back to Matt Teeson. So tomorrow, I'll tell him he can collect his cattle, but I don't want you shooting at him."

"Well, my men and I will be there to check that he doesn't steal any of my cattle," George said.

"That's fine, but I'll also be there. Make sure you or your men don't start a war." The sheriff stood up. "I'll be doing more investigation and will probably have to ask you more questions."

"I don't know what further questions you have. I can't imagine they'll shed any light on the matter," George said. "It can only be one of the two possibilities that I suggested to you. Good luck with figuring out which one of those it is. Good night to you, sheriff."

"Good night, George. Sorry to disturb your evening." The sheriff waved as he walked out the door. Julia followed him.

"Thanks for being there, Julia. It was a big help." The sheriff said.

"No problem. I'm going to come out to your horse with you to make sure nothing happens as you leave the property. Good luck with your investigations. I still don't believe my father had anything to do with those cattle being on the ranch. I think you should focus your attention on the two suggestions he made."

The sheriff showed no reaction to Julia's suggestion. Julia watched him ride off the ranch. She saw Knox looking from the door of the bunkhouse, also watching the sheriff ride off the ranch.

———

Chapter 39

The next day Matt rode into town to find the sheriff. He stopped at the sheriff's office. The sheriff wasn't there. Matt left his horse outside the sheriff's office and wandered down to Melissa's coffee shop. He found the sheriff having a late breakfast there.

"Morning, Matt." The sheriff said. "Join me for a cup of coffee or breakfast if you haven't had. I'll pay. Then I can fill you in on my conversation with George, and we can debate the plan of action."

"I haven't had breakfast yet, and since you've offered to pay, I don't want to pass up that opportunity," Matt said.

Matt sat. The waitress wandered over. "Can I get you anything?" She asked.

"I'll have three fried eggs, bacon, sausages, and beans. And, of course, a cup of coffee," Matt said.

"You're certainly taking advantage of my generosity." The sheriff said. "I should've limited you to two eggs, and that's it."

The waitress went off to place his order. The sheriff put down his knife and fork, finished his mouthful, and said. "I went out to George's last night, and Julia, true to her word, came in with me to talk to George. She didn't ask Melissa. It would've disrupted things if she'd gone to fetch Melissa at that point in time."

"Finish your breakfast first, sheriff. We can talk about this over coffee once you've finished breakfast," Matt said.

"Thanks, good idea. It'll give us indigestion if we talk about it over breakfast." The sheriff said.

Matt's breakfast arrived. They ate in silence. The sheriff finished first.

"I've finished my breakfast, so I can start telling you the story." The sheriff said. "When I arrived there last night, Knox followed me to the door and wanted to be part of the meeting. I told him he couldn't. He got angry about that, but Julia appeared at the door and sent him nicely on his way. Once I got past Knox, George wanted to be without Julia. But Julia insisted on staying, with the story that she should be involved since it's related to the events when Tate was killed. In short, George says there are only two possible scenarios. The Apache are trying to set him against you. Which is not necessary since you're enemies anyway. Or you're trying to make out he is a cattle thief and get him locked away and, therefore, your enemy out of the way for you to take over his ranch. That's it. I then left and didn't push it any further so that I could come up with a plan. Oh, I did agree with him you could fetch your cattle tomorrow morning. I'll come with you. He'll be there with all his merry men. But I told him not to cause any trouble. I don't think he will since Julia was there when all of this was discussed. What do you think we should do next?"

"I don't know. It's a tricky one. That's your job." Matt smiled at the sheriff.

"Yeah, you're right. But I'd be happy to have your advice." The sheriff looked at Matt.

Matt finished his breakfast and leaned back. He looked at the ceiling, brow furrowed.

"If you look at it from an outsider's perspective, the scenarios he presents are possible. It'll be difficult to disprove unless one of his hands jumps ship and comes clean. It's unlikely but not impossible," Matt said.

The two men sat in silence, thinking for a while. "Well, I don't think we'll come up with a solution today." The sheriff said. "We'll think about it and check in tomorrow when we meet to pick up your cattle. Can we meet here and then leave from here to fetch your cattle?"

"I'll see you here tomorrow at about seven," Matt said.

The waitress came over to check on them. The sheriff said, "that's all, thanks. You can bring us the bill."

The sheriff paid the bill, and they wandered back to his office. Matt said goodbye to the sheriff before getting on Sox. He knew he'd be too occupied trying to stay on Sox to be saying goodbye to the sheriff. He climbed onto Sox, and as predicted, Sox set off down the street with a couple of bucks, settling down as they left town.

The next morning, Matt, Geoff, and Hugh met the sheriff at his office. Matt led the way out to where the cattle were on George's ranch. They stopped on a hill overlooking the cattle and scanned for George and his men. There was no sign of them.

"I don't know whether that's a good sign or a bad sign that we can't see George and his men." The sheriff said. "Either they're hiding and intend to ambush us, or they've decided they're wasting their time pitching up. What do you think, Matt?"

"I think they've decided it's a waste of time pitching up. I suggest you stay up here, sheriff out the way, and be ready to hightail it out of here while we round up the cattle," Matt said.

"That sounds like a plan, particularly since it keeps me safe." The sheriff smiled at Matt.

Matt and his men rounded up the cattle and herded them back to his ranch. The sheriff followed at a distance, keeping an eye out for George and his men. Once the cattle were safely on Matt's ranch, the sheriff waved at Matt and his crew and headed back to town.

Over the next few weeks, Matt and his crew carried on with the ranch work. There were two problems. They were losing cattle daily, not big numbers, but enough to cause financial distress in the longer term. The other problem was that the rains should've started. The dam had filled up from the stream, but the grass on the ranch was becoming sparse. The two problems combined could cause ruin for Matt.

Matt rode into town and reported his losses to the sheriff.

"The sheriff said. "There's little I can do about it."

"I know," Matt said. "But maybe it'll all add up to something in the end. I can't not report it. At this rate, though, with the lack of rain and the theft, I'll go out of business."

"I've been thinking about this problem and George blaming it on the Apache. Julia seems to have a good relationship with the Apache. She can talk to the chief and get his side of the story. The problem is we can't have the Apache testifying in a court. No one will take their word against that of a white man. We'll know the story, but the jury will go with whatever story George tells. But the more we know, the more likely we'll get to the truth and get George to trial. I'm guessing he hasn't given up on getting your ranch yet. You need to be awake to that. The more information we have on the other stuff, the more careful he'll have to be." The sheriff said.

"I don't want Julia involved. It'll be dangerous for her to get in the middle of the Apache and her father," Matt said.

"I agree, it's a worry." The sheriff said.

"I'll be on my way, but I'm relying on you to keep your eye out for any criminal activities of George," Matt said.

———————

Chapter 40

George called Maria and asked her to fetch Knox to his office. When Knox arrived, George said, "sit, Knox. You want some coffee?"

"Yeah, I'll have a cup of coffee, thanks. What's up, boss?"

George waved his hand at the coffee pot. Knox stood up and poured himself a cup of coffee.

"I'm tired of Matt Teeson," George said.

"Me too. I'm happy to do something about it for you," Knox said.

"I'm pleased you said that. That's exactly what I want, and that's why I employ you," George said. "I want you to pick a fight with Teeson and get rid of him. But you'll need to make it look like he was the aggressor and we haven't had this conversation."

"That's not an easy task," Knox said. "I'll need a bonus for this."

"Hey, I'm already paying you a fortune, and so far, you've done nothing," George said.

"Yeah, well, I don't think it's enough for this job." Knox stared at George.

George shifted in his seat. Eventually, he said, "Okay, I'll pay you a $200 bonus for this job only. Don't think this will be the norm. Otherwise, your contract will be finished here."

Knox stared at George and smiled. George shifted in his seat. He interpreted Knox's smile in the way it was meant. "Anything else, boss? Is that it?"

"That's it," George said.

Knox rose from his chair and walked to the door. At the door, he turned, "don't forget the $200."

George said nothing. Knox walked out the door.

Later that afternoon, Knox knocked on George's door and walked in without waiting for an invitation. "Boss, I been thinking about this. It's going to be difficult to meet with Teeson on his own. If I ambush him, the sheriff's going to be led back to you. I think the best thing is that you invite him for a discussion at the saloon to patch things up. We'll get him to draw on me in front of witnesses at the saloon. That way, no one can accuse you of murdering him. Besides, it's not my style to shoot someone in the back. There's no one quicker than me."

"Okay, I'll send someone out to Teeson's and invite him to peace talks at the saloon tomorrow evening at 7 o'clock. I'll make a convincing story so that he'll come. But how are you going to get him to draw on you? I think he's too smart to be pushed into a fight," George said.

"You do your bit. I'll do my bit," Knox said.

"All right, I'll do my bit, and I'll leave you to do your bit," George said.

Later that afternoon, Matt, Hugh, and Geoff were moving some cattle from one pasture to another when Hugh said. "Someone riding this way, boss."

They all stopped and watched the rider approach. Matt said. "I recognize him as one of George's hands, but I don't know his name."

The rider stopped in front of them. His hands were well away from his gun. Matt noticed the loop was still on his sidearm.

"Good day to you. What can we do for you?" Matt said.

"George sent me. He thinks it's time you and he made peace. He wants to meet you at the saloon at 7 o'clock tomorrow evening to agree to a sort of peace treaty." The rider said.

"That doesn't sound like George to me," Matt said. "But no matter, I'll meet him. At least it's a public place, and he can't dry gulch me, which is his style."

"I'll tell him you'll see him at the saloon tomorrow night at seven. I won't tell him the last bit." The rider said as he turned, touched his hand to his hat, and rode back the way he'd come.

"You're taking a chance, boss," Hugh said.

"I know, but we need to bring this battle between us to a head sooner rather than later. I can't afford to carry on losing cattle at the rate I am and being distracted from running the ranch by a war with Hamilton," Matt said.

"I presume we're going to come with you," Hugh said.

"No, you're not," Matt said. "Who knows what he's up to. Maybe he wants to get us all off the ranch and, while we're away, do more damage to it."

"It's dangerous you being in the saloon there on your own with him. His men, I'm sure, will be there," Hugh said. "Maybe you should ask the sheriff to be there as well."

Matt sat on his horse, staring into the distance. "No, I think I'll take my chances on my own. Otherwise, I'll be putting the sheriff in a spot, and he might end up dead as well."

The next day Matt rode into town, arriving at the saloon at six thirty. The saloon was bustling. Matt unhooked the loop from his sidearm and walked into the smell of stale beer and cigarettes. A haze of smoke lurked around the ceiling. He looked around. He saw none of George Hamilton's men or George. He walked up to the bar, greeting people as he made his way around the tables. At the bar, he ordered a beer and struck up a conversation with the two men next to him. He turned and leaned with his back to the bar and watched the door. He looked around to see if there were any spare tables. There were none. At seven fifteen, George had still not appeared. Matt wondered whether this was a show of power or whether he was waiting for Matt to get bored and leave and then dry gulch him on the way home. As he was thinking this, he saw Knox walk in with five men from the ranch. Knox stopped at the door and looked around. He spotted Matt and strode across to where Matt was.

Knox stared Matt in the eyes with his piercing blue eyes. "Evening Teeson. George won't be joining us. He asked me to apologize, but something's come up. He asked me to represent him."

"He said he would be here. I'm not talking to you about this. This is a matter for George and me to discuss. You're just a gunman for hire," Matt said.

Knox stared at Matt. "I'm not a gunman for hire. I may use a gun when necessary. Are you going to talk to me or not?"

"Or not," Matt said.

"So, you don't want peace?" Knox said

"I do want peace between us," Matt said. "But you and I coming to that is not going to work. It must be between Hamilton and myself. Imagine if it had been the other way around and I'd sent either Hugh or Geoff, and Hamilton had been waiting here expecting me. What do you think his reaction would be?"

Knox stared at Matt.

"No answer to that, have you?" Matt said.

"Maybe I should solve the problem for George. Maybe I should draw on you now and end it," Knox said.

Matt noted that the loop was off Knox's colt, "I'm sure this was the plan all along," Matt said. "But I'm not going to be drawn into this." As he said that, he saw Knox go for his gun. Matt drew and fired, the bullet hitting Knox's gun arm as his Colt was about to clear the holster. Matt saw the look of surprise in Knox's eyes. Matt stepped forward and pressed his firearm into the soft skin under Knox's chin, pushing his head up and backward. He whipped the gun up, tearing the skin under Knox's chin with the sight. He brought the barrel of the gun down hard against Knox's temple. Knox dropped to the floor without a sound. He turned around, covering the rest of Hamilton's men, who were all foolishly bunched together. They were surprised at the speed at which things had happened. None of them had moved. "Okay, you're all going to place your sidearms on the floor and kick them

218

toward me one by one. Starting from the left, you first, he pointed to the man on the left. The man lifted his gun out of the holster, watching Matt as he did it, making sure Matt knew he wasn't going to try anything. Matt went along the line of men until they'd all placed the guns on the floor and kicked them toward him. "Now, all of you get out of here, walk slowly, I'm going to be behind you, and I'm gonna watch you get on your horses and ride out."

The men turned and headed for the saloon doors, with Matt a few paces behind them. He watched them mount up and ride down the street toward George Hamilton's ranch. When they were 50 yards away from him, he fired three shots from Knox's gun into the ground behind the horses. He had tucked Knox's firearm into the back of his pants. He wanted to make sure he had enough bullets in case some of the men had backup firearms. The horses took off at a gallop toward the ranch. Matt watched them go. He saw sheriff Gamble come running out of his office. He waved Gamble toward him and pointed to the saloon. Matt went back into the saloon. Knox was still lying out cold on the floor. As the sheriff walked up to Matt and asked him, "what's going on here?" Knox moved and groaned.

"Before you do anything, sheriff, handcuff Knox in case he tries to shoot someone else, and then I'll explain to you what happened. There are plenty of witnesses to confirm my story." Matt looked around at the saloon patrons. The heads were nodding. George Hamilton and Knox were not popular in town. They ran roughshod over the townsfolk feeling secure in their position of power.

The sheriff unclipped his handcuffs from his belt, hesitated a moment, seeing all the blood on Knox's right arm, then got over it and pulled Knox's arms behind his back and handcuffed him to yells of pain from Knox.

"Okay, now that's done." The sheriff said. "We need to get a doctor to him."

"All we need to do is stop the bleeding," Matt said. "George's other hands were here earlier. I've sent them packing back to the ranch. I'm sure they'll send Julia back here to look after Knox."

"Anyone here handy at stopping bleeding." The sheriff shouted.

A man in the far corner said, "I can do it. I was a medic in the war." He walked forward to the bar and squatted down next to Knox. He turned and looked up at the people around and said, "help me get him up onto the bar counter. It'll be easier for me to work up there."

The men helped get Knox up onto the counter amid further yells of pain from him. The men were not gentle in depositing him on the counter.

The sheriff turned to Matt and said. "Tell me what happened."

"George sent one of his hands out to my ranch yesterday to arrange a meeting here this evening to discuss a truce between us. Turns out it was a ruse to get me here with Knox and for Knox to kill me," Matt said. "That's all there is to it."

"That sounds too simple to me." The sheriff said. "Give me the full story of what happened here, and then I'll verify it with the witnesses."

"We were due to meet at seven," Matt said. "Of course, no one was here at seven, and I began to think maybe George wanted me to leave the bar, and someone would dry gulch me on the way back to my ranch. As I was about to leave, Knox arrived with a whole bunch of George's hands. He said George was now unavailable and sent him to negotiate the truce. Naturally, I wasn't interested in talking to Knox. I said, imagine what would've happened if I sent one of my hands in to talk to George. George would've been insulted. Anyway, Knox pushed a bit more, and then, while we were talking, he went for his gun. I drew and shot him in the arm as his gun cleared leather. I could've shot him in the heart, but I chose not to."

The sheriff looked around. "Anyone disputes Matt's story?"

No one said anything. They shook their heads.

"Is that a yes, or no?" The sheriff said.

There were mumbles of. "It's exactly as Matt said it happened."

"Anyone disputes that? If you do, raise your hand." The sheriff said.

Knox groaned and said, "that's nonsense."

"What's your story, Knox?" The sheriff asked.

Knox groaned but said nothing further.

"I thought so." The sheriff said. "You don't want to say anything here because it'll be lies, and everyone here will dispute you."

"I'm going to need all your names here in case you need to testify in court. You never know. Knox might die." The sheriff said. He kept the, *with luck*, in his thoughts. He decided that might be interpreted as bias if he said that. The sheriff set about taking everyone's names down.

The man who'd been working on Knox said, "I've stopped the bleeding. You can take him off to jail, sheriff. He'll be fine. But it'll be good if Julia has a look at him."

"Thanks. Appreciate your help, there." The sheriff said.

The sheriff grabbed Knox's good arm and hauled him off the counter.

Knox gritted his teeth and said, "Sheriff, you're living a dangerous life. I'm going to get you. You better keep an eye out over your shoulder."

"Threatening an officer of the law is an additional offense to that of trying to murder a man." The sheriff said. He looked around at the witnesses whose names he'd written down. "You all heard that, did you? And you'd be prepared to be witnesses to it?"

There were nods and a chorus of yeses. The sheriff pushed Knox out of the bar in front of him and walked him down the street to the jail, where he locked Knox in the jail after removing the handcuffs.

"I suggest you get some sleep. Tomorrow morning I'll read you your charges and inform you of what is going to happen to you. I guess Julia will come in tonight and fix up your wound a bit more if you're lucky." The sheriff said.

Knox eased himself onto the bed, groaning through gritted teeth.

The sheriff contemplated whether he could leave the jail. The town never appointed a deputy or even a jailkeeper. The sheriff would do his rounds and hoped that no one would break into the jail and rescue the inmates. Generally, that wasn't a concern. Most of the inmates he'd had in the past were drunks who were sleeping it off. He worried about

Knox, though. George might send some of his hands to break Knox out. He decided to do his rounds but spent most of his time walking the streets where he could see who was coming into town. An hour into his rounds, he was almost finished and about to turn back to have a cup of coffee at the jail and then go to sleep on the bed in the jail. He saw Julia coming into town with two of George's hands. He increased his pace back to the jail and arrived there shortly after Julia and the hands arrived there. They had seen him coming down the street.

"Good evening, sheriff," Julia said.

"Good evening, doctor." The sheriff nodded at the two hands. "I guess you're here to attend to Knox." He looked at the two hands and said. "You two can go and wait in the saloon, or anywhere else you choose." The two scowled at him but said nothing. They turned their horses and headed off to the saloon.

"That made me feel good," Julia said. "People have hardly ever called me Doctor up to this point."

"Matt has been singing your praises as a doctor." The sheriff said. "I figure you deserve the title. I see you're getting more and more customers."

"Yes, I am. I'm feeling good about it," Julia said. "Let's have a look at Knox. He sounds like he's not badly injured."

The sheriff ushered Julia into his office. "No, he's not, although he makes out like he is. I should search you for a firearm or weapon, but I wouldn't feel right doing that to you, so I'm going to ask you and trust you."

"I have no weapons," Julia said. "My only interest is doing my job as a doctor, and I'm not going to mess up my reputation by doing anything beyond that."

The sheriff watched Julia attend to Knox.

Knox said, "Get me out of here, Julia. This is a lot of nonsense. This was all that Matt Teeson, starting a fight. I was doing your father's bidding. Trying to negotiate peace between Teeson and your father."

"Don't listen to a word he says." The sheriff interrupted. "He's talking a lot of nonsense, and I have a whole bunch of witnesses who'll confirm that."

"I'm going to focus on my doctoring," Julia said. "I'm not interested in what the cause was."

Knox groaned from time to time as Julia tended to the wound. She placed a cloth between his teeth and said, "bite on that. I'm going to sew up the wound now. It's going to hurt like crazy."

While Julia sewed up the wound, Knox bit down on the cloth but still moaned from time to time.

Once Julia had finished attending to Knox, she mounted her horse and rode back down the street to the saloon. The sheriff walked with her and went into the saloon to call out the two hands to escort her back to the ranch.

———

Chapter 41

Julia arrived back at the ranch house. One of the hands took her horse and attended to it. She walked into the house and through to her father's study. He had demanded that she come and see him and report back once she had attended to Knox.

As she walked into the study, her father said. "So, what's the story with Knox?"

"Well, if you hired him for his gun skills, I don't think you're going to get much use out of them for a while. But otherwise, he'll be fine," Julia said.

"Has that useless sheriff arrested Teeson?" George glared at Julia.

"No, he hasn't. And he won't," Julia said.

"What d'you mean he won't? Teeson shot Knox unprovoked," George said.

"You're misinformed," Julia said. "Knox drew first, and he was apparently instigating the fight. Did you ask him to do that?"

"No, I didn't," George said. "I can't believe that Teeson managed to shoot Knox if Knox drew first. That's not possible. Knox is meant to be one of the fastest gunmen around. That's why I hired him."

"Well, he was beaten, and he did draw first. Everyone in the saloon attests to that, and the sheriff took down their names as witnesses for the trial," Julia said.

"I'll stop them testifying," George said.

"You can't do that. That's interfering with the law," Julia said.

"I can do that. I'll also get sheriff Gamble fired," George said.

"Good night, Papa. I'm tired. I'll see you in the morning," Julia said.

George frowned at Julia, shouting good night when she disappeared down the passage.

The next morning, the sheriff had breakfast at Melissa's and walked back with some breakfast for Knox. When Knox had finished his breakfast, the sheriff sat on a chair outside the cell and said to Knox, "I'm going to read the charges to you, but first, I'm going to read you your rights."

Knox started in with his normal refrain. The sheriff interrupted him. "I'm not interested in that. Do you understand your rights?"

Knox glared at the sheriff. "Yes, I do."

"You're charged with disturbing the peace and attempted murder. The judge will be here in two weeks' time. Do you want me to get a message to George Hamilton to arrange a lawyer?"

"I'm innocent. Yes, get George to arrange a lawyer. If he doesn't break me out of here before then," Knox said.

The sheriff said, "I'll arrange for George to appoint a lawyer for you. That's assuming he isn't going to leave you to our own devices."

"He'd better not," Knox said. "I was carrying out his instructions."

"Well, that's a problem. George is also going to need a lawyer because now you've implicated him in your crime. I guess he might have a conflict of interest and may only want to appoint a lawyer for himself. Or appoint a good lawyer for himself and a bad one for you." The sheriff said.

Knox stared at the sheriff. "I withdraw that comment. Ask George to appoint a lawyer for me."

"I'll do that." The sheriff said. He was wondering whether he should charge George Hamilton based on Knox's comment. He decided he probably wouldn't get anywhere since Knox had withdrawn it. The sheriff wandered back to his desk and rummaged in his drawer for some paper and a pencil. He pulled them out of the drawer and set about writing a note to

George requesting he appoints a lawyer for Knox as per Knox's request. Once he'd finished writing the note, he folded it, stood up, and walked out the door. He wandered down the street looking for little Johnny Harlow. As expected, he saw Johnny further down the street, loitering around, hoping that someone would give him something to do and pay him. The sheriff walked up to Johnny and said, "morning Johnny, do you want to earn some money?"

"For sure, sheriff. What can I do?"

The sheriff held out the note toward Johnny and said, "you can take this out to George Hamilton, wait for him to read it and see if he has any note to send back." The sheriff dug in his pockets for a coin, pulled one out, and handed it to Johnny.

"Thanks, sheriff. I like running errands for you. See you later." With that, Johnny turned and walked down the street to his scruffy, pie bald horse, tied at one of the hitching rails.

———

Chapter 42

Chief Mescal called his warriors together. Once they were all paying attention, he spoke to them. "It seems that Miss Julia was wrong about Matt Teeson. He doesn't want peace with us. The fact that he stole some of our horses proves that. We're going to teach him a lesson. There are only three people on the ranch now, but they are good fighters. So, we'll only engage in a fight with them if it's unavoidable. We're going to steal his cattle and horses. He doesn't know where our camp is, so we will cover the tracks, and he'll never be able to recover the horses and cattle. I would've liked to have killed him, but he seems to get the better of us each time we attack him."

One of his warriors said, "I think we should kill him and his two men. We can easily defeat them."

"No, we are not going to lose any more warriors. Also, if we kill them, we'll have the Army chasing after us. That's my final decision." The Chief said.

Two days later, the Apache headed out to Matt's ranch, arriving there as the sun set.

"We'll wait here and only steal the horses and cattle at two in the morning when they are all in a deep sleep," Chief Mescal said.

The Apache dismounted and took the horses to the stream and left them next to the stream to wander around and eat the green grass growing next to the stream. They climbed up the hill leading from the stream and settled themselves next to some rocks below the top of the hill. They surveyed the ranch in the fading light and discussed tactics. They picked out a herd close to the edge of the ranch that would be easy pickings. The horses would be more of a problem. They were located close to the ranch cabin. They decided they would collect the horses first, and a group of them would set off with the horses toward the camp, leaving the rest of the warriors to round up the cattle.

By two in the morning, four of the Apache were at the cabin. There was no sign of any life at the cabin, an owl hooted, but other than that, everything was quiet. The horses had been left to graze in an unfenced pasture near the cabin. The Apache had left their horses some way back from the cabin and were all on foot. They eased the horses away from the cabin. The horses wandered away from the cabin cropping the grass as they went, unperturbed by the Apache. They moved along as the Apache moved toward them. Once the Apache had got the horses moving, the horses continued moving, joining up with the Apache horses. The Apache jumped on the back of their horses and continued herding the horses at a faster pace. The rest of the Apache had started moving the herd of cattle off the ranch. The Apache had decided to hold the horses and cattle at a different camp to the one they were currently using. They moved around between the camps as the game moved during the year. Mescal figured that Matt would know the general direction of their camp, and the cattle would be moving slowly so Matt would catch up with them. For that reason, he was taking them to the other camp. He gave instructions for three Apache to drop behind and wipe out the tracks. He hoped that Matt would try and shortcut the process and go straight in the direction that the Apache had previously gone. That would lose Matt a lot of time. In addition, Matt would have no horses. By the time he'd realized that they had gone that way, Mescal would have the cattle and horses hidden.

———————

Chapter 43

The next morning Matt, Hugh, and Geoff set about their normal routines. Geoff normally checked the horses before breakfast, which he did this morning.

He ran back to the cabin shouting as he went, "the horses are gone."

"Dammit, it's those Apache. I don't think it's George this time," Matt said. "Has Sox gone?"

"Yes, I'm afraid Sox has also gone," Geoff said.

"That's the worst of it," Matt said. "I love that horse. He's irreplaceable."

They abandoned the idea of breakfast and set out on foot to try and see which way the horses had gone. Hugh found the direction of the horse tracks and the bare feet prints overstepping the tracks. Next, they found where the Apache had mounted their horses.

"It's definitely the Apache this time," Matt said. "We'll never get to catch them. We'll need to walk to town and buy some horses and only then follow them. By that time, I'm sure they would've disappeared," Matt said. "We might as well have breakfast and get our strength up for the walk to town.

They had breakfast and then set off to town, only arriving there in the evening. The livery stable was closed, so there was no buying horses that evening.

"Let's go to the saloon and have a drink or two," Matt said. "The drinks are on me this evening. I'm sorry you've all had such a long walk."

They went down to the saloon and set about drowning their sorrows. Matt told the story. He asked around the saloon if anyone had come across the tracks of the horses or had seen the horses. No one had seen anything.

They stayed in the town's only hotel overnight. With no competition, it was probably generous to call it a hotel.

The next morning, they had breakfast at Melissa's and then headed up to the livery stable. Matt purchased a horse each for them after haggling on price. None of the horses were going to win any races, but they were all that were available. They rode back to the ranch bareback. At the ranch, they saddled the horses, packed supplies for a few days, made sure they had plenty of ammunition for their firearms, and then headed out to where they had lost the tracks and continued following them. They lost them soon afterward. Matt said, "We can short-circuit this and head straight to where we lost the Apache tracks before. That'll help us catch up. I'm sure they would've gone in the same direction. Although we don't know where their camp is, we may be able to find it by tracks from where the tracks disappeared. Maybe they won't feel it necessary to cover the tracks."

"That's a good idea, boss," Hugh said.

They rode out for a day to where Matt had seen the tracks end previously. When they arrived there, they circled around but could find no tracks. They moved out in a wider circle and still found no tracks.

When they next met after the search, Matt sighed and said, "it looks like my shortcut hasn't paid off. There haven't been any people this way for a while. There's nothing for it but to go back to where we lost the tracks and see if we can pick up from there. In fact, the ranch work needs to continue, so I'm going to leave you two to carry on looking after the ranch, and I'll look for the Apache. One way or another, I'm going to find the Apache and get the cattle and horses back and avenge Tate's death. Don't expect me back for a couple weeks. I'm not going to stop until I find them and avenge Tate. I'll come back to the ranch with you now and pick up some supplies and then head out."

"There's no way you can defeat the Apache on your own," Geoff said. "We'll come with you. The ranch will have to look after itself for a while."

Matt turned his horse and headed back the way they had come. "No, you two must look after the ranch. I'll come up with a plan to deal with the Apache."

Geoff said nothing further. He could see Matt had made up his mind. He knew when Matt made up his mind, there was no changing it.

They arrived back at the cabin too late for Matt to set out again. Matt lay awake half the night plotting how he was going to deal with the Apache. The plan formed in his mind.

The next morning, he rode into town with a packhorse in tow and went to the general dealer store. He asked Bones, "do you have any dynamite you could sell me?"

"Surprisingly, I do. Sometimes people use it for blasting rocks when they're making dams. What do you want it for?" Bones asked.

"I'm building a dam," Matt said. Matt had always had difficulties telling lies. He felt better about himself that he was sort of telling the truth. Yes, he was building a dam. He didn't need to elaborate that that's not what he needed the dynamite for. Matt paid for the dynamite, and Bones helped him load it onto the packhorse.

"Do you know how to handle this stuff?" Bones asked. "I would hate you to blow yourself up. It's never good to lose a customer."

"Yeah, I've used it before. I'll be careful," Matt said.

Matt headed back to the cabin with the dynamite. He was delayed another day. It was too late in the day to set out. He spent the remaining time packing for his journey so that it would be quick tomorrow morning to be on his way. Amongst the things that he was taking were the bows and arrows that they had captured from the Apache. They formed a part of his plan together with the dynamite.

The next morning, he set out to the spot where he had originally lost the Apache.

He had had some conversations with Julia about where their camp was, but she'd not been forthcoming. He was going to have to figure it out on his own. He'd been thinking about it for a long time now, and he had an idea of where their camp might be. A year back, he'd been talking to someone who'd left the Army, and he had mentioned the camp over in an area that Matt knew. If it wasn't there, then Matt would be at a loss and have to start from square one again. The more he thought about it, the more convinced he was that that's where the camp was. He rode for two days, constantly scanning for signs of the Apache. There were no tracks or signs. At some points, he would think of turning back, and then he would realize that he had no alternative, so he would continue.

Chapter 44

He arrived at the spot where he expected the camp to be as the sun was setting. He tethered the horse and the packhorse below the crest of the hill. He crept up to the top of the hill and looked over. He let out a sigh. Below him was the Apache camp. The question now was, would it be better to attack them at night or during the day. He decided early morning would be best while everyone was carrying out morning activities, but no one had left the camp. It would also give him time to prepare for his attack. He crept back down the hill. He mounted his horse, dragged the packhorse behind him, and headed off to find a campsite that was hidden and had water and grass for the horses. He had passed one that looked suitable a little way back. He found the spot that he'd identified earlier as a campsite and tended to the horses, tethering them on some green grass near the stream. He built a fire among some rocks, blocking the view of the fire from anyone that might be looking out. He cooked a prairie chicken that he'd shot earlier in the day. After eating, he prepared for the next day. He took out the arrows that he'd captured from the Apache and attached a stick of dynamite to each one of them. He placed the arrows in his saddle bag, ready for the morning. He then checked out the two bows that he had brought with him. He'd already checked them previously but wanted to make doubly sure. Satisfied, he turned in for the night. He struggled to sleep. Eventually, the noise of a whip-poor-will and an owl lulled him to sleep. The next morning, he was up before first light. His stomach churned. He thought about eating but found he couldn't. As the sun crept over the horizon, he mounted up and headed toward the crest of the hill with the packhorse in tow. He tethered the horses and then carried the two bows and the arrows with sticks of dynamite to the crest of the hill. He went back down, fetched his Winchester, and returned, lying on his stomach surveying the camp. The light was only just reaching the camp. The camp was a hive of activity. The women were lighting fires and cooking. The children playing. Matt saw his horses in amongst the rest of the Apache remuda. He hadn't noticed that the day before because the horses had been somewhere else. Someone must have moved them closer to camp for the evening. Matt didn't see the cattle but guessed they would be somewhere around. He thought *this chief is smart. He seems to have planned everything out to mislead me and succeeded.* He watched the women and children for a bit longer. His plan had been to fire the arrows with the dynamite into the camp. He expected to take many of the Apache down with the dynamite and then take the rest out with the Winchester in the confusion. Now, looking at the women and children, he had second thoughts. Then he thought about Tate. Thinking about Tate did not take away his concerns for the women and children. They were innocent in this. He could never harm women or children. That led him back to his original goal of wanting to live in peace with the Apache. He sighed, picked up the arrows and the bows, and took them back down to the horses packing them into the saddlebags. He went back up and fetched his Winchester. He trudged back down the hill, unhappy. He'd wasted a whole bunch of time and achieved nothing. He clumped down the hill, head down, thinking of his failure. He saw a blur to his right and, behind him, felt a sharp crack on his head, and then the world went black.

———

Chapter 45

When Matt came to, he was sitting in the middle of the Apache camp, tied to a stake. There were two warriors guarding him and a bunch of children and women looking at him curiously. His head throbbed. He cursed himself. His softness had got him captured and would be the death of him. One of the warriors talked to one of the women, who turned and walked away. Ten minutes later, Matt saw the chief walking toward him.

"You've been trouble to me." The chief said. "You wounded my warriors and stole my horses. Now I see you're planning to dynamite my village. You must pay for this. You will die a long and painful death. The only question is, will you die a brave warrior, or will you cry and plead."

"I guess it won't make any difference to you, but I'd changed my mind about attacking your camp with the dynamite. I decided I could not attack women and children. You can check with your warrior who caught me. I was walking back down the hill having packed up the dynamite," Matt said.

"That's your story. According to the warrior, you were walking back down the hill to fetch the dynamite." The chief said.

"I can see why he might think that, but it's not true," Matt said.

The chief issued instructions. The two warriors untied Matt and pulled him away from the post he was tied to. As his arms came free, Matt brought his hands up and crashed the two warriors' heads together. He grabbed a knife from the one on his right's belt. As he did that, he thought, *this is not going to end well for me, but it's my only chance.* He pulled the knife from the belt and rammed it into the warrior's back. He pulled the knife out and turned toward the other warrior. The other warrior had dropped to the ground. Matt changed the trajectory of the knife but stabbed more ground than flesh and was forced to leave the knife. The chief shouted, summoning other warriors. The chief took off after Matt. Matt could hear the chief catching him. Before Matt reached the edge of the camp, the chief leaped on his back. Matt kept running for a few paces trying to keep his balance, carrying the chief on his back but fell onto his face. The chief landed with his chest on Matt's head, pressing it into the ground, stunning Matt. Two other warriors and the chief hauled him to his feet.

"You have made it worse for yourself." The chief said. "Your death now will be longer and more painful."

This time the warriors that had a hold of Matt gripped him tightly and were clearly not going to be caught by surprise.

More warriors surrounded them. The warriors stripped Matt naked and tied him spread-eagled in the center of the village. The warriors had pulled the ropes on his legs and arms tight, allowing him no possibility of movement. It was now a question of how long and painful his death would be. The Apache had lost interest in him for the moment. Occasionally someone would pass by and stare at him, some spat at him. Some spoke to him in Apache, Matt presumed cursing him.

The chief summoned two warriors. "Fetch Julia to attend to our wounded brother."

The two warriors nodded and headed off to their wikiups'. They emerged a few minutes later with their weapons. The chief watched them go and then held discussions with some of his other warriors on what to do with Matt.

———

Chapter 46

The warriors rode hard, but it still took them more than a day to get to George's ranch. They were near the ranch toward evening. They watched and waited until the lights had been turned off and the ranch had been quiet for two hours. They walked to the ranch house, there was no cloud, but there was also no moon. They crept around the house, looking in all the windows. All the windows of rooms with people sleeping in them were wide open, letting the fresh night air in. Two of the warriors were of the three that previously abducted Julia. One of them signaled to the other that he had found Julia. He pointed into the room. He signaled for the one to wait outside. He climbed in the window and stood briefly, noting from Julia's breathing that she was sound asleep. He clamped a hand over her mouth and lifted her out of bed, and carried her to the window. His fellow warrior grabbed her legs and helped get her out of the house. Julia kicked and wriggled. She tried to scream, but when she found little sound escaped through the hand with a cloth clamped over her mouth, she tried to bite into the hand, with no success. The wriggling was of no help either. The Apache were far more powerful than she was. Outside the window, the one Apache tied a gag over her mouth, slipped a blindfold over her eyes, and then tied her hands behind her back. The Apache that had been holding her picked her up in a fireman's lift. She kicked her legs and then felt them grabbed, and a noose of rope slipped over them, pulled tight, and knotted. She was unable to move and decided it was pointless to wriggle further. She relaxed and let her breath out. As she thought about it, she calmed down. She realized it was likely the Apache again wanted her help. She knew that they couldn't just ride in and ask her for help as they were still considered enemies by everyone, and no peace agreement had yet been made. The Apache placed her across one of their horses. She felt the Apache jump up behind her and hold her in place. They had placed her across the horse with her legs on one side and face on the other. She hoped that, at some point, they would make her more comfortable. The horse moved off at a walk, its backbone digging into her stomach. After an hour of riding, when she felt like she was unable to take the discomfort any longer, she felt the horse stop. The Apache behind her jumped off the horse. She was lifted gently off the horse and placed on the ground. She recognized the two Apache as being the ones who had abducted her before. One of them was the one that spoke English.

He said, "sorry we had to kidnap you like that. But we couldn't just come and ask you. Your people would have killed us."

"So, why are you kidnapping me this time?" Julia asked.

"Your friend Matt came to try and kill us all." The Apache said. "Luckily, we caught him, but after we caught him, he tried to escape and wounded two of our warriors. The chief asked us to fetch you to attend to their wounds. They are serious. Can we trust you to ride with us without us tying you up now?"

"Yes, you can trust me," Julia said. "I told your chief he didn't need to abduct me in the future. I'm happy to come and help him. But I understand since we aren't at peace, it was impossible for you to walk in and then ask for me."

"We didn't bring a spare horse, so you'll have to ride in front of me." The Apache said. "You can jump up now."

Julia hitched up her nightdress and vaulted onto the horse. She pulled her nightdress down over her legs as far as possible to preserve her modesty. The Apache vaulted onto the horse behind her. They rode in silence until they arrived at the camp the next morning. As they rode into the camp, Julia saw a man staked out in the center of the village.

"Who's that?" She asked. "I need to attend to that person as well. You should let him go."

"That won't be necessary. That's your friend Matt. Since he wanted to kill us, he will now suffer and eventually die. He won't need your help unless it is to keep him alive a little longer to experience more pain." The Apache said.

Julia said nothing realizing that the two escorts had no power to make any decisions. It was the chief's decision to make. She hoped she would be able to persuade him to release Matt. They pulled up in front of the Chief's wikiup. He was sitting out in front.

"Thank you again for coming." The chief said.

"As normal, I had no choice," Julia said.

The Chief smiled. "Well, it looks like this is the way you will always visit us since your friend was trying to kill us and clearly has no intention of living in peace with us. I need you to attend to two warriors that he wounded."

"After I've attended to them, can I talk to Matt Teeson and find out what he was up to and why?" Julia asked.

"Yes, you may." The chief said. "But nothing he says or you say will make any difference."

Julia sighed. "Ask your man to show me your wounded warriors so I can attend to them."

The chief issued an instruction in Apache. One of the warriors said, "follow me."

Julia followed him to the same wikiup where the other wounded warriors had been previously. This appeared now to be the hospital. Julia knelt next to each warrior to check them, identifying which needed attention first. She started work on the warrior in the worst condition. Half an hour later, she was done with him and turned to the other one. Liluye watched Julia attend to the warriors. Julia turned to her and said, "they should be fine in a week. I've done all I can to help them now. You need to change these dressings daily and put this on. She indicated an ointment that she had applied to their wounds."

The medicine woman nodded her understanding.

Julia turned to the warrior who was waiting outside the wikiup and said, "please take me to talk to Matt Teeson now."

The warrior said, "I can't do that. Only the chief can give you permission."

"He said once I'd attended to the wounded warriors, I could speak to Matt," Julia said.

"I'll take you to the chief, and he can confirm that." The warrior said.

Julia followed the warrior back to the chief. The warrior spoke in Apache to the chief. The chief said something back in Apache to the warrior and smiled at Julia. "You may go and talk to Matt now."

The warrior escorted Julia across to where Matt was staked out. His eyes were shut. He looked to be in pain.

"Hello, Matt," Julia said. "What have you got yourself into now?"

Matt opened his eyes and stared at Julia. He said nothing.

"The chief said you tried to kill all the people in the village," Julia said. "But luckily, they managed to catch you before you did."

"Water." Matt croaked.

Julia turned to the warrior with her. "Please, can you fetch him some water?"

The warrior hesitated, then decided that would be all right. He walked away and came back a couple minutes later with some water in a cup. He passed it to Julia. Julia knelt beside Matt and trickled the water into his mouth so that he wouldn't choke. Some of it dribbled down the side of his mouth.

"Now, are you able to tell me what's going on?" Julia asked.

"I did come here with the intention of wiping out the village. There is only one of me, so I had a plan to use dynamite to wipe out the village. But when I saw the women and children, I couldn't carry on with my plan. I picked up the arrows with the dynamite and the bows that I had moved to the top of the hill overlooking the village and took them back down to the horses, packing them into the saddlebags. I then went back up the hill and fetched my Winchester. On my way back down to the horses with my rifle, the Apache warriors captured me," Matt said. Talking was a major effort for him. He shut his eyes again.

"That was dumb," Julia said. "Why on earth did you want to wipe them out, having said you want to live in peace with them? I told the chief that you want to live in peace with them. Now in the future, he won't believe anything I say."

Matt said nothing. Julia waited. "Water," Matt said.

Julia poured some more water into his mouth.

"The Apache stole my cattle and some horses, and more particularly Sox, who is irreplaceable. I needed to get my cattle and horses back and stop them from stealing in the future," Matt said.

Julia could see some logic in what he was saying.

"I can't believe you're so stupid," Julia said. "You couldn't have expected this to turn out any other way, except maybe you being killed outright and not having to suffer the torture."

"So, you're on their side," Matt said.

"No, I'm not on any side. I think they're wrong too and should sit down and talk with you and come to some agreement with you," Julia said. "In fact, I'm going to go talk to the chief now about that and suggest that I sit in as an intermediary," Julia said.

"Good luck with that," Matt said. "I think the chief has made up his mind."

Julia rested her hand on Matt's arm and said, "I'll see what I can do. But the big question is, would you be prepared to talk peace with the chief."

"I don't have much choice," Matt said. "If I don't talk to him, I'm dead anyway. At least I have a chance if I can talk to him."

"Will you stick to any agreement you come to with him?" Julia said.

Matt frowned at her. "Of course, I will. I'm a man of my word. You should know that by now."

"No. I don't know you that well," Julia said. "What I've seen is that you've already broken your word. You said you want to live in peace with the Apache, and here you are attacking them."

"That's hardly fair judgment on me," Matt said. "They attacked me and stole my animals. What do you expect me to do?"

"I expect you to stick to your word and try and talk to the chief and make an agreement, not try to wipe them out," Julia said.

Matt snorted, closed his eyes, and gritted his teeth. He opened his eyes again. "And how was I going to do that? I couldn't just ride up here and ask to talk to him. The result would be the same as now."

Julia didn't have an answer for that. "I'm going to go and talk to the chief." Julia strode off.

She stopped in front of the chief. "I would like you to talk to Matt and see if you can come to a peace agreement with him."

"No, I can't do that." The chief said. "We come to an agreement here, and then he'll break it. He said before he wanted to live in peace with us, but what did he do? He came and attacked my village. With the intention of killing us all."

"It's not as if he could have ridden here to talk peace with you," Julia said.

"There is no changing my mind." The chief said, "I'll have my warriors take you back now."

"You're a bad man," Julia said. "You're going to cause your tribe to be wiped out."

"Are you saying you're going to bring men here to wipe us out?" The chief said. "Maybe I should keep you here, make you the wife of one of my warriors."

"No, I'm not going to bring anyone here. And that also shows what kind of man you are. I have helped you, and now you're threatening me. What happens when your men are wounded in the future, and you want me to come and help you? I won't be around to help you anymore," Julia said.

"You will be. You'll be here all the time." The chief said. "I'll get my warriors to take you back." He smiled at her.

Julia opened her mouth to continue the argument but closed it again. The chief shouted across to his warriors to escort her back to her father's ranch. She decided it would be better to keep quiet and live another day.

Chapter 47

The warriors blindfolded her for the return journey. Back at the ranch, she found no one around other than her mother and a couple of hands who had been left to keep guard.

"Where's everyone, Mama?" Julia asked.

"Oh, I'm so pleased to see you back. No one knew where you were. They went out looking for you." Amy said.

Her mother shouted to one of the hands. He came across. "Go and find George and the rest of the crew and tell them Julia is back." The hand acknowledged and walked off to fetch his horse.

A few minutes later, he cantered away from the ranch.

Amy said to Julia, "you're alright?"

"Yes, I'm fine, Mama," Julia replied.

Julia's mother called to Maria to bring them some coffee and then turned to Julia and said, "come tell me what happened."

Julia sat with her mother and told her the story. "I don't know what we're going to do," Julia said. "We can't go on like this, fighting with the Apache."

"I know what your father will say," Amy said. "He'll say the simplest way is to wipe out both Matt and the Apache, and then there'll be no more trouble."

"You're probably right," Julia said. "You need to help me persuade him to do the right thing and bring peace between himself, Matt, and the Apache."

"I'll do what I can," Amy said. "But you know him. He never pays attention to women."

Julia organized for Maria to pull her a bath. She bathed and changed into her nightclothes, and went to sleep.

Julia was woken by a hammering on her door. "Julia, I need to talk to you now," George shouted through the door.

"Okay, I'm coming. I'll see you in your study in half an hour," Julia said.

"You'd better be quicker than half an hour," George said as he walked away from the door.

Julia was in his study in 20 minutes.

"I've heard the story from your mother," George said. "I'm going to go and wipe that Chief Mescal and his tribe out, and I'll deal with Matt at the same time if he is not already dead."

"You can't do that," Julia said. "I'd be happy if you'd rescue Matt and then arrange peace talks with the Apache."

"That's a ridiculous idea," George said. "To rescue Matt, I'd have to wipe out the tribe anyway."

"I don't think you would have to," Julia said. "You clearly had better weapons than the Apache, and you'd catch them by surprise, so why don't you go there and get the drop on them. But instead of wiping them out, talk peace with them and arrange to have Matt released."

————————

Chapter 48

Sheriff Gamble had a dilemma. It seemed the Judge would not be visiting the town for some time. He didn't think Knox's case was worthy of a special visit. It was costing the town to keep Knox in jail. The sheriff decided he had no choice other than to release Knox. He considered whether he should consult with Matt first. He thought. *I'm the sheriff. It's my decision. I don't need to consult with anyone. There's no alternative, anyway.*

The sheriff sighed and wandered to Knox's cell door. "I'm going to release you." He said as he inserted the key in the door.

"Hah," Knox said. "I told you, you had no case."

The sheriff said. "Be grateful I'm letting you go. It's costing the town to keep you here, and the judge has indicated he won't come for one case. I'll reserve the right to arrest you again if you cause further trouble, however small."

Knox snorted and said, "and go through the same thing all over again. You think the judge will do anything different the second time?"

Knox walked out of the jail. "Hand me my guns." He said.

"You can send someone from the ranch to collect them. I'm not stupid enough to trust you with them now." The sheriff said.

"You're right not to," Knox said. "You're going to pay for what you've done."

"Are you threatening a peace officer again?" Sheriff Gamble stared at Knox.

Knox held his gaze, eventually looking away and leaving the jail without another word. He walked down the street to Melissa's. The sheriff watched him go into Melissa's and come out a few minutes later. Knox summoned Johnny Harlow. The sheriff saw Knox hand Johnny some money. A few minutes later, Johnny headed out of town on his pony toward George Hamilton's ranch.

———————

Chapter 49

Julia's father stared at her for a moment. "I'll do it your way. I'll go and try to rescue Matt, but if it fails, which I'm sure it will, I'll end up wiping out the Apache tribe. But I'll try and do it your way first." Julia's father said.

"Thank you, I appreciate you trying," Julia said. "But you must genuinely try." She stared at him, trying to gauge his true intent.

George said nothing. He was deep in thought. "Okay, you can leave now," George said. "I need to plan." Julia stood up and walked out.

George went out to the bunkhouse and asked one of the hands to fetch Jim and Knox and send them to his office.

Half an hour later, Jim and Knox were in his office.

George launched straight into it without any greeting. "You both know the Apache kidnapped Julia again to help with a couple of their warriors who Matt Teeson wounded. I'm tired of the Apache and Matt Teeson. Julia has asked me to try and rescue Matt Teeson. I said I would."

Knox raised his eyebrows.

"No, I'm not actually going to do that," George said. "I'm going to make out like we tried to rescue Teeson, but I'm going to wipe out the Apache, and if Teeson is still alive, I'll kill him as well. That way, I'll keep my family happy. I'll say I tried to rescue Teeson, but the Apache attacked me, and I had no alternative other than to defend myself. So that's the story you're going to tell when we come back, and make sure all the hands tell the same story. Get everyone ready and fully armed with lots of ammunition, and we'll be on our way today. The Apache think we don't know where their camp is, so we'll be able to catch them by surprise," George said.

Jim and Knox left the office. As they walked toward the bunkhouse, Knox said. "It's about time we did this. The Apache and Teeson are trouble. They get in the way of our plans every time. It'll be great to be rid of them. I'll enjoy it. I suspect Teeson is already dead anyway and a painful death." Knox smiled.

Three-quarters of an hour later, everyone was ready to leave. Julia watched them leave with doubts in her mind. She wondered whether her father had any intention of trying to make peace with the Apache and rescue Matt.

She waited a while and went out and saddled a horse. She followed the group. She would see for herself what transpired. She thought her father would probably do what he said, but she had doubts. She decided it would be a good idea to see what actually happened.

———————

Chapter 50

Chief Mescal summoned his warriors. "George Hamilton knows where our camp is now. We need to be ready for him to attack. Julia Hamilton will not send him here, but I know the man. He'll feel he has to wipe us out because we kidnapped his daughter. I want you to take the dynamite that Matt Teeson brought here and surround the camp with it and then make fuses that lead from the camp so that we can kill some of his men with the dynamite. The rest we'll kill in the confusion caused by the dynamite.

The warriors left and set about their task. Chief Mescal had not tortured Matt anymore. He would deal with him after he had fought off the attack by George Hamilton. Depending on how things turned out, he decided he might try and go with Julia's plan.

Two hours later, one of his warriors reported back to him they were ready. Chief Mescal said to the warrior, "give Matt Teeson some water. I might decide to spare him." The warrior acknowledged the chief and took some water to Matt. Matt was surprised to receive the water but grateful.

George Hamilton's men camped the night en route to the Apache camp. They reached the Apache camp at midday the next day.

George peered over the hill at the camp. He saw women and children, saw Matt Teeson staked out in the middle of the camp, and one or two warriors wandering about. "I wonder where the rest of the warriors are." He mused.

Knox said. "Maybe it's siesta time."

George turned and scanned around. "I can't see any warriors anywhere else, and they don't know we know where their camp is. I can't imagine they're waiting to ambush us."

George issued instructions for the men to set up around the camp to attack the camp from all sides. He gave instructions that no one was to attack until he fired the first shot. Then they would all ride in on their horses and kill the Apache in the camp. George waited for the men to surround the camp. He fired a shot in the air. The Apache, on hearing the shot, lit the fuses to the dynamite.

————————

Chapter 51

Matt felt the sun burning his skin. He couldn't take much more of this. He closed his eyes and tried to relax and ease the pain. He was surprised to hear shots ring out. He wondered whether someone had come to rescue him. He doubted it. It was more likely George Hamilton come to attack the Apache and at the same time get rid of him. He didn't believe Geoff and Hugh would mount an attack. It would be suicide. He wriggled and pulled at the ropes binding him. He needed to escape. Whatever happened, someone would kill him, whether it be the Apache or George Hamilton. This would be his only chance.

Shots came from all sides now. The Apache were shooting at whoever it was and defending themselves. There was a deafening explosion, and clumps of earth rained down on Matt. A black cloud of smoke lingered in the air. Matt surmised the Apache had made use of his dynamite.

The next moment Nitis was beside him. "You saved me once, Matt Teeson. I'm going to save you now."

"I'm happy that you're going to save me. But I'm not sure it's a good idea for you to do that for yourself. You'll be an outcast with your tribe," Matt said.

"It doesn't matter. I pay my debts. If we carry on warring with you whites, we'll all be wiped out. I want to stick with you and try and build peace between us. Before I release you, do you give me your word that you'll work with me toward this?" Nitis said.

"For sure, you have my word," Matt said. "That's been my goal all along, so we'll be working together toward the same goal. Unfortunately, I keep having to defend myself against your tribe."

Nitis sliced the ropes off Matt's arms and legs. "We don't have time to get you dressed. I've got clothes with me, and I've got water and food. We need to run now while there is chaos," Nitis said.

There was a shot from their right. "Nitis, what are you doing?" The warrior shouted.

"I'm getting Matt to safety. Chief Mescal will not be happy if he is rescued or killed in this skirmish," Nitis said.

The warrior hesitated, frowning at Nitis while he processed what Nitis was saying.

"Come." Nitis pulled Matt along. Matt stumbled and fell on his face. His legs didn't want to move, having been tied for so long. Nitis pulled him up and draped Matt's arm over his shoulder. "Come on." He said again.

"I'm trying," Matt said. "My legs don't want to work."

"Well, make them work," Nitis said.

They struggled along. No shots came their way. Matt guessed that George Hamilton, or whoever it was, was occupied defending himself after the surprise of the dynamite, and the Apache warriors would be unsure what was happening. They would guess that Nitis was going to keep Matt as a captive and ensure he wasn't killed in the crossfire.

Nitis paused behind some rocks to assess where best to go next. He saw a gap where there were no Apache and headed for it. Suddenly shots came from the attackers toward them. It confirmed to Matt it was most likely George Hamilton, and he and Nitis needed to get away. It would be difficult without horses, but there did not seem to be any Apache horses nearby.

They continued hobbling along. The shots died out as they clambered behind the cover of some rocks. The shots were coming from behind them but not coming toward them. Nitis stopped and pointed. Matt looked at where he was pointing. George Hamilton's horses were all tied and guarded by one man.

Nitis whispered in Matt's ear. "You stay here. At the moment, you're useless. I'm going to kill that man, and we'll take four horses and chase the others off.

Matt nodded as he watched Nitis disappear. He watched the man guarding the horses. The man wasn't paying attention around him. He was focused on where the battle was taking place. As he watched, Matt saw Nitis behind the man, grab his hair pull his head back, and slice his throat. The man dropped to the ground without a sound, blood spurted from his neck. Matt jumped up and hobbled toward Nitis, who was gathering four horses together. By the time Matt got to Nitis, Nitis was on one of the horses with the reins of two horses attached to his saddle. He was holding another horse's reins. Matt climbed into the saddle, grimacing in pain with the new movement required of his limbs. As he settled into the saddle, Nitis left him and rode around the other horses cutting their tethers and whipping them on their behinds. Chasing them off, away from the battle. The horses were only too pleased to head away from the battle. Matt hoped they would head back to the ranch and leave George Hamilton and his men to walk.

Matt and Nitis rode behind the horses, encouraging the horses to go further and faster. Eventually, they heard no more shots. Whether that was because they were too far away or the battle had been won by one or other of the parties, they weren't sure.

Nitis said. "We're far enough away from them now. We should cut away from these horses and wipe out our tracks and then decide what we do once we're safely away from everybody."

"I agree. Chief Mescal is going to want revenge for this attack. He may take it out on any white person. George Hamilton is certainly not going to let me live."

They headed away from the horses. Nitis followed behind Matt, wiping out the tracks.

———

Chapter 52

Chief Mescal watched as the dynamite took out several of George Hamilton's men. He smiled. The plan was working. He continued to shout instructions to his warriors, who now picked off George Hamilton's men in the chaos caused by the dynamite. The battle raged, the forces were now evenly matched.

Chief Mescal raised his hand and signaled his warriors to cease fire. He waved at them to stay undercover. They watched and waited for half an hour and saw no movement.

Chief Mescal called across to one of his warriors, who had a great ability to sneak around without being seen. "Check around where the attackers are. See if they are still there or if they have retreated. Then come back and report to me. None of us will move until we know where they are."

The warrior nodded and was gone within a couple of seconds, out of sight. An hour later, he was back. "George Hamilton's men have retreated, but the horses have been chased off. They are setting up a defense line where the horses were.

———

Chapter 53

As Julia arrived close to the camp, her father popped out from behind a rock. "What are you doing here?" He asked.

"I wanted to check what was happening with Matt," Julia said.

"I said I would rescue him." George Hamilton said.

"Well, did you?" Julia asked.

"No, I didn't. The Apache used dynamite on us and killed several of my hands. We had to retreat. And then I found we had no horses. So, I'm pleased that you've come. Now we can use your horse to either fetch some new horses or recover our horses wherever they might be. It'll be quicker if you ride back on your own and ask Tim Curtis on the ranch to bring six horses back here. We need six horses now. There are only six of us left," George said.

Well, what happened to Matt?" Julia said.

"We saw one of the Apache pulling him away. I was surprised they didn't kill him, but maybe they wanted to torture him more before they killed him," George said.

"Can't you rescue him now?" Julia asked.

"No, we can't. He's long gone and hidden somewhere," George said. "Maybe we can look for him once we have the horses back."

"We tried to shoot the Apache who was taking him away, with no success." George lied.

————

Chapter 54

"Okay, I'll go get you the horses." Julia turned to ride off.

"Wait," George said. "We've got some wounded who you need to attend to."

"I thought I went to medical school just to find a husband?" Julia said.

George scowled at her, at a loss for words.

"Don't worry, I'm not going to endanger people's lives to prove a point to you that you need me," Julia said. She glanced around and saw the wounded in an enclosure of rocks. She went to her horse and pulled the small medical bag she'd brought with her. She walked across and knelt beside each of the men, checking who was the most urgent and in need of attention. Once she had prioritized the wounded, she set about working on them.

After two hours, she said. "I've done what I can, and I've shown one of the other hands what to do while I'm away. I'll fetch your horses now."

George nodded.

Julia camped out that night to the sounds of owls, nightjars, and coyotes. She kept the fire going all night behind some rocks to keep her warm and to keep away any predators. She enjoyed being out on her own at night. The next morning, she cooked breakfast from the supplies that she'd brought with her and then headed out toward the ranch. She arrived at the ranch at two in the afternoon.

Amy ran out to greet her. "Where've you been?"

"I decided to follow Pa and see what happened," Julia said.

"That's dangerous. You should've told me where you were going. I've been worried sick." Amy said.

"If I'd told you, you would've stopped me. It's lucky I did go because pa and his men now have no horses. I've got to take horses back to him," Julia said.

Amy said nothing. She wrapped her arms around Julia and hugged her. "I'm pleased you're safe."

"So am I." Julia smiled at her. "I'm going to have a bath, get something to eat, gather some supplies, and then head out with the horses back to Papa."

"I don't think there's much point in you going out tonight," Amy said. "You won't get far before it's dark."

"You have a point," Julia said. "I'll leave first thing tomorrow morning."

"Why do you have to go anyway?" Amy asked.

"I think it'll be too much for one hand to take six horses. Also, he doesn't know the way to the Apache camp," Julia said.

Amy looked doubtful. "Okay."

The next morning Julia and Tim Curtis were on their way with the horses. Amy gave her a hug with a worried look before she left.

The next day they arrived at George's camp with the horses.

"Am I glad to see you," George said. "We've been worried that the Apache would attack us while you're away. They must have realized we had more ammunition than them, and they would lose more men without getting any more of my men."

Within 15 minutes of Julia arriving with the horses, they were riding back toward the ranch. George had designated one of the hands to take a different route and stay off to the side and watch the back trail. If he saw the Apache coming after them, he was to catch up to them and warn them.

The hand caught up to them that evening when they set up camp for the night. "I saw no sign of the Apache following you. I think we're safe." He said.

"Even so, you must do the same tomorrow to make sure that we're not caught by surprise," George said.

"Sure thing, boss." The hand said.

The next day they arrived back at the ranch, not having seen any Apache on their tail.

"Jim, you need to employ us some more hands. Make sure they're good with guns," George said.

Chapter 55

Julia spent more time attending to the wounded. All looked like they would survive.

"Julia, I need you to come and talk to me in my study," George said.

Julia sighed and followed George into the study.

George sat back in his chair behind his desk and pulled out a cigar.

"Please don't do that while I'm here," Julia said.

George placed the cigar on his desk and threw the matches down next to it. "Julia, I don't want you going out anywhere without my say-so in future. You can't be trusted to do the right thing. You seem to have taken a shine to this, Matt Teeson. He's bad news, and I don't want you hurt by him."

"Firstly, I don't think Matt would do me any harm. Secondly, I have my doctor's business to run, so I need to go out. Thirdly, every time I've gone out so far, has helped people and built goodwill. No one has hurt me. So that says to me I've been doing the right thing," Julia said.

George scowled. "Okay, I'll let you run your practice, but you're not to go traipsing out to Matt Teeson or the Apache. Neither of them are safe."

"All my visits to them have been for doctor services. You can be sure they're not going to do any harm to me. There are no other doctors, which means they're more likely to look after me than harm me," Julia said.

"My, you're stubborn. I don't know how I brought up two daughters like you and Melissa," George said.

"I think our stubbornness comes from you. But I like to think we use our stubbornness for good." Julia said

"What's that meant to mean?" George said.

"It means you would do well to follow our example and use your good points for good. You need to start making peace with Matt and the Apache," Julia said.

"That's never going to happen. The Apache are thieves, and Matt Teeson is no better," George said.

"I'm guessing this meeting is ended. We'll never see eye to eye on certain things, in fact, most things," Julia said. She stood up. "I hope you'll think about what I said."

"Be careful, don't say I didn't warn you about trusting Teeson or the Apache," George said.

Julia raised her eyebrows as she walked to the door, opened it, and walked out, closing the door behind her.

George picked up his cigar and lit it. He took a deep suck of the cigar and blew clouds of smoke toward the ceiling. He sat for 15 minutes staring at the ceiling, wondering what to do about his daughters. He didn't like how they viewed Matt Teeson. There was only one solution to deal with that. He thought further and wondered how he was going to get rid of Teeson without them knowing he had anything to do with it. His best chance had been when Teeson was with the Apache. He'd blown that."

Julia went to bed that night thinking. *Things are heading in the right direction. I don't know about my father, though. I hope he gets on board at some point in the future. I'm starting to feel like a real doctor and doing some good.*

———

Chapter 56

Nitis and Matt rode on. Nitis rode next to Matt, grabbing him from time to time to stop him from falling out of the saddle. Nitis wished he could take Matt to Julia to attend to him. The torture inflicted on him had taken his strength.

"I need to get you away from the danger of Mescal and George Hamilton, and then we'll rest up and get you strong," Nitis said.

Matt grunted.

Nitis set up a camp at the top of a hill with rocks surrounding it. He dug a pit to build a fire in so that it couldn't be seen at night.

Nitis and Matt were now living off the land. "I need to go back to my ranch and check on my hands, that they're still there and things are running smoothly," Matt said.

"If you go back, George will kill you," Nitis said. "But you're in no state to go back now anyway."

"George won't kill me. The sheriff has shown he's not taking any sides, or George fears it's more likely to be my side. If someone shoots me, he knows it'll be George behind it. Also,

I can't leave my hands on their own. I worry that George will ambush them," Matt said.

"You're right," Nitis said. "We'll head back to your ranch once you're strong, but it'll take us three days to get there. What am I going to do?"

"Would you be prepared to work for me on the ranch? I know there'll be a lot of prejudice against you from the townsfolk, which might be hard for you to endure," Matt said.

"I can handle it." Nitis smiled at Matt. "I don't think your hands will like it, though."

"They're good people, they may have difficulty accepting you at first, but with your charm, you'll win them over," Matt said.

"You're right. I'm sure my charm will win them over. They might kill me before my charm has time to work." Nitis grinned.

It took Matt a week to recover from his ordeal. Nitis helped him gain strength, tending to his wounds and feeding him. Every day Nitis went out and came back with some form of small game for food. Every day Matt would say he's ready to move on, and every day Nitis would say you're not ready yet. Your strength is not there. You'll set yourself back. On the seventh day of having the same debate, Nitis said, "you're strong enough now. We'll head out tomorrow."

———

Chapter 57

Finding hands for the ranch wasn't difficult for Jim. Work was scarce, and a lot of people had moved to the area hoping for a better life but finding things more difficult than they'd been led to believe when they set out West.

Jim reported back to George. "I've managed to replace the hands we lost and added a few more. They're not the greatest, but they're the best of what is around. I wouldn't call them gunmen, but they can all shoot and reasonably straight."

"Good, all we need is numbers, a bit of cannon fodder," George said. "I'm going to move on to Matt Teeson's ranch and take it over. We'll have to put some hands there. I'm going to put Knox in charge of them and give him instructions to get rid of Matt Teeson's hands at some point. I'm reluctant to have him shoot them. But I hope to make them nervous enough to run off. If they don't run off, he can keep an eye on them. I'll pay them more than what Matt Teeson was paying them. That'll buy their loyalty."

"My reading of them is they're loyal to Teeson, but Knox will intimidate them enough to get them to run off," Jim said.

"Given that I'm going to take over Teeson's ranch, you should employ another two hands. We'll have too many hands to start with, but if Teeson's hands run off, that'll put it right," George said. "Bring Knox in here so that I can brief him."

"Will do," Jim said as he turned and walked out the door. Fifteen minutes later, he was back with Knox. George waved them to take a seat. They sat. He offered them a cigar each.

"Won't say no to that, thanks, boss," Knox said as he reached for a cigar.

Jim also took one.

"Knox, I want to take over Matt Teeson's ranch, and I want you to run it," George said.

"It'll be a pleasure, boss. What should I do with those two hands that he has there now? Shall I shoot them and bury them? No one will know or be interested," Knox said.

"No, you can't do that," George said. "That sheriff seems eager to do his job properly. He'll definitely smell a rat if the two hands are killed, and you've just moved onto the ranch."

"That's fine," Knox said. "It'll give me an excuse to get rid of the sheriff."

George looked thoughtful for a moment. "No. I don't think we'll go to that just yet. I want you to make them nervous and think that they're in line for being shot so that they run off."

"I can do that." Knox grinned. "How many hands are you going to send with me?"

"I'll send four hands with you, which should be more than enough," George said.

"When d'you want this to happen?" Knox asked.

"Today," George said. "I don't know what's happened to Matt Teeson. But I need to be in possession of the ranch before or if he comes back. Meantime while you're holding the ranch, I'm going to go to the government and get the ranch registered in my name."

"Consider it done, boss," Knox said as he blew a cloud of smoke at the ceiling. He stood up and said, "I'll be on my way. I'll come back in a couple of days and report to you how things are going."

"Good," George said.

Jim and Knox left the office, blowing clouds of smoke as they walked down the passage. Julia scowled at them as she walked past on her way to her room. She waved a hand at the smoke, trying to keep it out of her face. Knox laughed.

Jim and Knox assembled the hands together. They outlined the plan and identified the hands that would be remaining on Matt's ranch. They decided they would go across to the ranch with ten hands to take possession of it. Once that was done, the other six hands would return. The four that would remain on Matt's ranch were told to pack up their meager belongings so that they could settle on Matt's ranch.

The cavalcade rode out in a flurry of dust. Julia watched them go and frowned. She walked to her father's study and knocked on the door. At the command, "come in." Julia entered and shut the door behind her.

"I've just seen Knox and Jim ride out with ten hands," Julia said. "Where are they off to, and what are they going to do?"

"It's none of your business. It's ranch business," George said.

"They look like they're set up for war," Julia said.

"As I said, it's none of your business," George said.

Julia turned and walked away from her father, frowning. She went out onto the porch and watched the hands ride off in a cloud of dust. It was difficult to tell where they were heading, given that pretty much any way they were going, they would go down the ranch road first.

Geoff and Hugh were riding out on the ranch, checking the cattle.

"I don't know what's happened to Matt. We need to be paid at some point in time; otherwise, we'll run out of food. I guess we can hunt for food, but we'll run out of ammunition as well," Geoff said.

"Maybe one of us should go and have a look for him," Hugh said.

"I'm not sure where we would start," Geoff said. "My first port of call would be George Hamilton. But it's likely that Knox would shoot us on some pretext or other."

"Yeah, you're right. I'll take a ride into town and talk to Julia Hamilton," Hugh said.

"That's a good idea," Geoff said. "Maybe you can go in tomorrow."

"Yeah, I'll do that," Hugh said. "Oh, oh. I see a cloud of dust heading up toward the cabin. I wonder who that can be."

"Let's go and see," Geoff said.

They slipped the loops off their sidearms. "I don't like this," Hugh said. "We should set up above the cabin behind those rocks and talk to them from there with our rifles on them."

"That makes sense," Geoff said.

They circled around behind the cabin and hid their horses in amongst a copse of pinyon-juniper and walked down with the rifles and a supply of ammunition to the rocks. They crouched down behind the rocks with a view of the cabin to one side. They kept their rifles hidden so the sun's reflection would not reveal their position until they were ready. The cavalcade pulled up at the cabin.

Geoff shouted. "We've got you covered. What do you want?"

The group of men looked up toward where the voice was coming from and around to see if they could see anyone.

Knox spoke. "We need to talk to you."

"You can talk to us from there," Geoff said. "There's no way we're going to come down and talk to ten men."

"Okay, I understand. Maybe you don't trust us. We'll talk from here," Knox said.

"You're damn right, we don't trust you," Geoff said.

"Your boss is dead. Killed by the Apache. George Hamilton now owns this ranch. You have a choice. You can either work for him and get paid, or you can leave. If you don't choose either of those, we'll have to run you off, and you may end up dead."

Geoff and Hugh looked at each other. "What do you think we do?" Hugh said.

"I'm guessing it's possible that the Apache have killed Matt. But I don't understand how George Hamilton can suddenly own the ranch. I don't know how the law works. I don't know whether Matt had any relatives. I guess if he didn't, it's quite possible that George Hamilton could take possession of the ranch," Geoff said.

"Well, what's it going to be?" Knox said.

"Give us a moment. We're having a discussion," Geoff said.

"Well, don't take too long," Knox said. "We're going to dismount here and get ourselves some coffee, and then you need to have decided."

"Okay," Geoff said.

Geoff and Hugh conferred some more. Hugh said. "My worry is that if we say we'll join them, they'll kill us anyway."

"We'll have to ask them what assurances they can give us that we won't be killed," Geoff said.

"Let's ask them and make a decision from there," Hugh said.

"Knox," Geoff shouted.

"Yeah," Knox said. "Go ahead."

"We want to work for you because we need to be paid, but what assurances can you give us that we won't be killed. You have enough men there to run the ranch. In fact, more than enough," Geoff said.

"George Hamilton is a fair man. We'll move the extra men back to his other ranch. As you know, he wants to grow his ranching empire, so there's more than enough work for all the men," Knox said.

"I'll tell you what we'll do," Geoff said. "We'll ride into town and tell the sheriff what's going on and then come back. That way, someone will know what's happened if we get killed."

"No, that's not going to work," Knox said. "The sheriff will make unnecessary trouble and make George jump through all sorts of hoops. If you don't trust us, I suggest you move on."

"We need the wages," Geoff said. "We want to confer a bit longer on how we do this and be safe."

"Well, don't take too long," Knox said.

"We'll give you a shout shortly," Geoff said.

"What're you thinking?" Hugh said.

"I think we get the hell out of here," Geoff said.

"You're right," Hugh said. "We should go and see the sheriff and Julia and try and find some more information on Matt and take it from there. If Matt has been killed, then we'll have to find other jobs. If not, we need to find out where he is and tell him what's happening. You've bought us some time while he thinks we're conferring, but it's not much time."

Geoff and Hugh snuck back to their horses, mounted up, and headed for the town in a roundabout way.

After twenty minutes, Knox shouted up the hill. "Hey, fellas, you've had enough time. What's your answer?"

Knox waited. All he could hear was a saw-whet owl. "Okay, we're coming up. Come out with your hands up and then drop your weapons," Knox said.

Knox and three men headed up the hill. Every step they took, they expected a shot. Nothing came. They reached the spot where Geoff and Hugh had been. Knox looked around and saw the footprints and nothing else. He followed the footprints to the horses. He turned to the men and said. "Looks like they've done a runner. We need to find them and kill them. Otherwise, they'll alert Teeson and join up with him. Let's get back and fetch our horses."

They headed back down the hill, collected the horses, and rode back up to where Hugh and Geoff had tethered their horses. They followed the tracks until they came to a stream. At the stream, the tracks disappeared. Knox said. "It looks to me like they were heading to town, although not by a direct route. I think we can short-circuit this and ride straight into town and pick them up there."

Geoff and Hugh rode into town. They stopped at the sheriff's office. They dismounted outside the sheriff's office and slapped the dust off. Geoff knocked on the sheriff's door.

"Come in." The sheriff looked up at them. "What can I do for you two? Take a seat and grab some coffee."

"Thanks, sheriff," Geoff said. "Do you have any idea what has happened to Matt Teeson?"

"No, I don't. I hear rumors that the Apache captured him. I also heard George Hamilton went to attack the Apache. I haven't got an update on that. I wanted to talk to Julia about that." The sheriff said.

"That doesn't sound good," Geoff said. "I'll go and check with Julia. But we can't hang around for long. We've just come from Matt's ranch. Knox and Hamilton's men have effectively taken possession of the ranch. They wanted us to work for them. We didn't answer and snuck away. I'm sure they're looking for us now, and when they find us, they'll kill us.

"I'll have a word with Knox and tell him if you're killed, he'll be arrested and go on trial. Which will mean a hanging for him." The sheriff said. "I'm not sure what I can do about them squatting on Matt's ranch until I know what's happened to Matt."

"Thanks for that, sheriff. I'm not going to wait around and see what happens," Geoff said. Geoff and Hugh finished their coffee. "We'll be on our way. Stopping in on Julia on our way out. Once we know what's happened, we'll ask Julia to come and update you," Geoff said.

"Don't worry about sending her to me." The sheriff said. "I'll pop in and see her and get an update from her."

Geoff and Hugh mounted up and rode up the street to Julia's surgery. There were three horses tied up outside the surgery. They dismounted and walked in and found two men sitting in reception. Julia's office door was closed. Geoff sighed. Hugh and Geoff took a seat in the chairs in reception.

The door of the surgery was opened by the other patient who came out, followed by Julia.

Geoff stood. "Sorry to interrupt Julia, but we have some men looking to kill us. We'd like to ask you a couple questions and then be on our way. Geoff looked at the other two patients. "Sorry about this, but if we don't get on our way quickly, we'll become emergencies, and then you'll have a much longer wait for Julia.

The two patients scowled at Geoff. "Okay, I guess we'll have to wait. I hope you're not lying." The one said.

"Thanks, I appreciate that. I'm certainly not lying," Geoff said. "Is that alright with you, Julia?"

"I'm not happy. I don't like keeping my few patients waiting. But I think I know what this is about, so I'll have to make an exception," Julia said.

Julia ushered them into her office, closed the door behind her, and said, "take a seat." She pointed toward the seats in front of her desk. She sat down behind the desk. "What's this about?"

Geoff leaned forward. "We hope you can tell us what's happened to Matt. He went off to find the Apache and never came back. Then Knox and a bunch of men from your father's ranch came and said they were taking over the ranch because Matt has disappeared and won't be coming back."

"Well, it's news to me that Knox is taking over the ranch. I also wasn't aware that Matt wasn't coming back," Julia said. "My father said they had gone to rescue Matt from the Apache and had attacked the Apache. The Apache had captured Matt and were busy torturing him. They had also taken over Matt's dynamite, and when my father attacked the Apache camp, they blew a whole lot of his men up and then, in the chaos, mounted an attack on my father and his men. The Apache managed to beat off my father and his men. My father says he saw an Apache dragging Matt away. He was surprised that the Apache had not killed Matt. He presumes they were keeping him alive for some reason. So, this story that Matt is not coming back is not necessarily true."

"It sounds like you have the most up-to-date news on Matt. It seems that he is still captured by the Apache, which means at some point, quite likely, they'll kill him. If that's the case, Matt has no relatives to take over the ranch, so I guess it's going to be difficult to chase your father and Knox off," Geoff said.

"Yeah, I guess you're right," Julia said. "I think I'm going to head back to the Apache. They're friendly to me because I've attended to their wounded, and then I'll see what's happened to Matt and plead his case."

"Before you do that, let Hugh and I have a look around and see what we can find, and we'll come back and report. But don't tell Knox or your father that we've been here or what we're going to do. We're going to disappear for a while after that," Geoff said.

"I'll do nothing at the moment," Julia said. "Good luck. I hope you find Matt and that he's safe. I'm not sure whether it would be better if I found Matt and negotiated for him. The Apache are not going to listen to you."

"Hopefully, we'll find Matt soon. Depending on what the situation is, we'll let you know. You may still be able to negotiate with the Apache," Geoff said.

"Can you describe to us where the Apache camp is," Geoff said.

Julia grimaced.

"Don't worry, we're not going to attack them. There's no way two of us can take on the Apache," Geoff said.

"You read my mind," Julia said. She then described to them where the Apache camp was.

"We'll be on our way now. Thanks for your time, Julia," Geoff said.

Julia followed Geoff and Hugh out. "Good luck," Julia said. She turned to one of the other patients "sorry about that. You can come in now."

Geoff and Hugh mounted up and rode out of town by one of the side streets. Hugh dismounted, and Geoff led his horse while Hugh wiped out the tracks. Once they were far enough from town, Hugh mounted up again, and they took off at a canter. They rode up into the hills through some pinyon-juniper which hid them to a degree from anyone looking from town. Once they were far enough away, they pulled up and turned to look toward town.

"I don't see anyone at the moment," Hugh said.

"Me neither," Geoff said. "We'll sit here and watch for a while."

They sat on their horses and watched the town.

"That looks like Knox and his merry men riding in now." Hugh pointed.

"You're right. They'll spend a bit of time in town. Let's get going and put more distance between us. We need to find Matt. I don't know how we're going to do that?" Geoff said. "I guess the starting point is to find the Apache camp without the Apache spotting us."

Geoff and Hugh headed toward the Apache camp following Julia's directions. A day later, they arrived at the Apache camp. They tied their horses some way from the camp and then crept to the crest of the hill to look down on the camp. They found some shade under a small tree at the crest of the hill and lay down to watch the camp. After an hour, Hugh turned to Geoff and said. "It doesn't look to me that Matt is there."

"You're right. That's a problem. We don't know where to go from here," Geoff said. "Let's watch for another hour, and then we'll have to try and find Matt somewhere else. Maybe we'll have to ask Julia to go into the Apache camp and ask them what has happened to Matt. Otherwise, we may be on a wild goose chase. Maybe they've killed Matt."

They settled down for another hour to watch. At the end of the hour, they were none the wiser.

"Let's circle around the camp at a distance and see if we pick up any tracks," Hugh said.

"It's about the best thing we can do," Geoff said.

They snuck back to the horses, mounted up and rode for an hour away from the camp, and then started circling. Evening came with them still having no idea what happened to Matt. They found a spot next to a spring to camp for the night. They fed and watered the horses and then fed themselves. They were up with the sun the next morning. Geoff headed out to find some food for them. He was in two minds about whether he should be shooting game for their food or not. He decided they were far enough from the Apache camp for it not to be a problem. He came upon a black-tailed jackrabbit standing stock still, carrying out its normal defense mechanism of not moving. Geoff backed off a way and lay down in the grass. He aimed at the jackrabbit's head with his rifle, squeezed the trigger. The rifle kicked, the sound echoing around. The jackrabbit dropped where it was. Geoff picked up the jackrabbit and walked back to camp.

Hugh grinned at him as he walked into camp with the jackrabbit. "Good job Geoff. That'll make a good meal. Since you did the hunting, I'll do the skinning and cooking."

Geoff dropped the jackrabbit next to the fire. "I'm worried about the noise that it made, shooting it. While you cook, I'll keep watch."

Geoff walked to the top of the mountain near their campsite and lay down where he could see anyone approaching. By the time Hugh called him for breakfast, he'd seen nothing other than some bighorn sheep.

They ate in silence. They finished eating, rinsed the plates, and packed everything into the saddlebags. As they mounted up, a voice called out to them. "Don't move. I have a rifle trained on you. Drop your weapons and then raise your hands.

"Damn, I shouldn't have shot that jackrabbit," Geoff said as he dropped his rifle and sidearm to the ground. Hugh also dropped his weapons to the ground.

The voice came again. "Don't move. Stay facing that way."

"I recognize that voice," Hugh said. "That's Matt."

"Hey Matt, it's Hugh and Geoff. Can we put our hands down?" Hugh said.

Matt recognized Hugh's voice, and now that Hugh had said who they were, he recognized them, even at a distance.

"Okay, I recognize you now," Matt said. "You can put your hands down and jump off your horses, pick your weapons up again. Sorry about that. Don't get a fright. I've got an Apache with me. But he's a friend, not a foe."

Matt and Nitis rode up to Geoff and Hugh. Matt shook their hands. Nitis looked warily at them and touched his hand to his head in greeting.

"Where are you two off to?" Matt asked. "You're meant to be looking after the ranch."

"Well, there's the problem," Geoff said. "On instructions from George Hamilton, Knox has moved onto the ranch with some hands. Effectively George is taking over your ranch."

"He can't do that," Matt said.

"Knox said you were dead. So, from our point of view, it's difficult to argue. We aren't relatives. As far as we know, you have no relatives. That means no one could do much since we were told you were dead," Geoff said.

"Now that you put it like that, I can see the problem," Matt said.

"We made out like we'd work for George Hamilton. We were up the hill behind the cabin, and Knox was down at the cabin. We were having negotiations from those points. Knox gave us some time to make up our minds, and during that time, we sneaked away," Geoff said. "We then checked with the sheriff, who knew nothing of your whereabouts, and then Julia. Julia said the last that was known of you, you were being dragged off by an Apache from the camp when George attacked the Apache camp. I'm guessing you were being dragged off by Nitis here."

"Yes, it was Nitis who dragged me off. He saved my life," Matt said. "Chief Mescal had me staked out in the camp and had been torturing me and would have killed me at some point in time. The attack on the camp came just in time, and Nitis rescued me and smuggled me away from the camp. Now he'll be an outcast with his tribe. But it means I have a new hand, which I needed anyway. You're all going to have to get along."

"Seems we're all up to speed now. What are we going to do now?" Geoff said.

Chapter 58

"I guess, with the four of us, we could take on Knox and whoever may be left on the ranch with him. We'll have the element of surprise," Matt said. "The problem is I'm not a fan of ambushing people and shooting them in the back. If we give them any sort of warning, that would even things up which would put all of us in danger. We'll have to think of a plan."

"At the moment, I'm guessing George thinks his plan is coming together. Do you think Julia was in on the plan?" Matt said.

"No," Geoff said. "Julia is on your side. I get the impression that she doesn't think much of her father's plans to take up your ranch."

"I don't think at this point I can trust Julia," Matt said. "I'm sure family comes first."

"You may be right," Geoff said.

"Let's go and see what's happening at my ranch. Nitis is good at sneaking around. If we need anyone to get close, I'm sure you can do it." Matt glanced at Nitis.

"You're right," Nitis said. "I can sneak anywhere without anyone seeing or hearing. But you white men, it'll be like a herd of stampeding buffalo." He grinned.

Matt turned to Hugh and Geoff and said, "I'm pleased to have caught up with you. I've had trouble with this nonsense for days now."

Geoff and Hugh showed no expression and said nothing. It was going to take them a while to get used to being friends with an Apache. They headed off toward Matt's ranch, Matt in the lead.

Evening fell before they reached the ranch, so they set up camp.

"I don't think we should be shooting anything for food," Geoff said. "Some of George Hamilton's men might hear the shot."

"Don't worry, Nitis will get us some food without making any noise," Matt said.

"Sure thing," Nitis said.

Nitis left with his bow and arrows. Half an hour later, he was back with three prairie chickens. He held them up and grinned.

"You guys are going to have to up your game." Matt looked at Hugh and Geoff. "Looks to me like Nitis is the most useful of my employees." Matt grinned.

Geoff and Hugh scowled.

Nitis prepared the supper. By the time they had eaten supper, Geoff and Hugh were beginning to think Matt was right. It was not a bad thing. They would benefit from Nitis' skills.

"Good job with the hunting and cooking, Nitis," Hugh said.

Nitis grunted and raised his hand, and grinned in acknowledgment. "Watch and learn," Nitis said.

Matt sighed.

The next morning Nitis again found some game for them to cook for breakfast. After breakfast, they headed toward Matt's ranch.

At midday, they approached the ranch. Matt called a halt.

"It'll be best if we sneak around the perimeter of the ranch and up into the mountains behind the ranch so that we can see what's going on, then make a plan from there," Matt said.

The others nodded in agreement. They altered course and headed for the hills where the ranch was. Once they found a concealed spot with a view of the whole ranch, they dismounted and watched.

After fifteen minutes of watching, Matt said. "It looks like nothing's changed since you were there. I see Knox and three hands working the ranch. Although watching Knox, he seems to be bossing the rest and doing nothing, which is what I would expect. Anyone got any ideas?"

"It would be easy to pick them all off from cover," Hugh said. "But I know that's not your style."

————

Chapter 59

Over supper that evening, Julia questioned her father. "What's going on with Matt's ranch? Have you heard from Knox?"

"No, I haven't heard from Knox yet. I don't imagine much has changed. I'm sure he's just making the ranch better. That Matt Teeson had no idea about ranching," George said.

"I'm sure Matt Teeson was a good rancher. He didn't have your money," Julia said.

"Well, he shouldn't be ranching if he hasn't got money to improve the ranch. That's the problem with all the small guys. They eke out a living for a while and then go bankrupt," George said.

"I think you'll get a surprise," Julia said. "I bet Matt is alive and will return to his ranch. Then what're you going to do?"

"You seem to have a lot to say about this, Matt Teeson. I hope you're not holding a torch for him. If you are, you're going to be sad. If he's not dead now, he will be sometime soon," George said.

"So, it's your intention to kill him, is it?" Julia said.

"No, it's not, but I'm sure a hothead like him will get himself killed soon enough," George said.

"He's not a hothead at all," Julia said. "It's just that you and Knox, or more you, are after him. Knox just does your bidding."

"That's nonsense, and this conversation is now over," George said. As he said that, Melissa walked in to join them at supper. She raised her eyebrows at Julia as she sat down.

Julia gave a slight shake of her head to Melissa.

Shortly afterward, Knox walked in.

"How's it going on the new ranch?" George asked.

"It's going well. It's a good ranch. You made a good acquisition," Knox said.

Melissa raised her eyebrows again but said nothing. The rest of supper was spent discussing the two ranches between Jim, Knox, and George. Julia and Melissa said nothing.

After supper, George, Jim, and Knox went to George's study and carried on the discussion over cigars and brandy. Melissa, Julia, and Amy went to the lounge.

"I don't know what to make of Papa," Julia said. "He's my father, so I like to think the best of him, but what I've seen of him recently doesn't make me happy. He's not the same man. Power is going to his head. He thinks he can take over any ranch now without going through the normal process of buying someone out and accepting their word if they say they don't want to sell."

"Leave it to your father," Amy said. "He knows what he's doing. He's successful because he's smart."

"You have to say that. You're his wife," Julia said. Amy didn't respond. "I think Papa will get a surprise. Matt will come back and take back his ranch. Someone is going to get killed. Or more than one person. Maybe Papa, maybe Knox, maybe Matt.

"What's happened to Matt?" Melissa asked.

Julia brought Melissa up to speed.

"Oh, at last, all these snippets of conversation I've been picking up make sense now," Melissa said.

"I have a bad feeling. This is not going to end well," Julia said. "Good night. I'll see you at your restaurant for breakfast tomorrow morning, Melissa. I'm making enough money now to pay you for breakfast, and I have to get to the surgery on time. I'm picking up a lot of patients."

———

Chapter 60

Matt, Nitis, Geoff, and Hugh continued their vigil over the ranch.

Over supper that evening, Matt said, "I'm going to go into the lion's den to talk to George, and see if we can't sort this out."

"You're crazy," Hugh said. "We can't have that. If you die, then George Hamilton gets the ranch, and I'm sure we'll have to move away from the area, or he'll kill us as well."

"I'll have to think about the plan to ensure that I don't get killed. I need to get George Hamilton on his own. The problem is he never seems to be alone," Matt said.

"Nitis, you'll need to come with me and teach me how to sneak around. You can also cover me without anyone knowing," Matt said.

"I don't like this idea," Nitis said. "That's asking for trouble. But if that's your plan, I'll come with you and cover you."

"Appreciate that," Matt said.

"I echo everyone else's comments," Geoff said. "This is not a clever idea. I'm going to turn in now. Good night."

Everyone followed Geoff's example and turned in. Nitis took longer. He checked on the horses first before turning in.

The next day they continued with their vigil on the ranch. During the afternoon, Matt said. "I've heard that George likes to go to his study after supper, like clockwork, usually about 8 o'clock. The trouble is he usually has some of his men join him there, which could cause a problem. Anyway, I'll play it by ear. Nitis and I will sneak down and see what's happening. If it looks too dangerous, we'll come back. Otherwise, I'll talk with him."

"I'm not going to say anything further. You know my views," Geoff said.

Nitis and Matt rode out later that evening, planning to arrive at George Hamilton's ranch by 8 o'clock. It was a half-moon which made riding easy. They arrived close to the ranch and tied the horses off in the bushes. Nitis and Matt crept to the ranch house. Matt led the way to George's study window. They crouched below the window and listened. It sounded like it was, as predicted, George, Knox, and Jim. The window was wide open. Matt signaled Nitis to follow him away from the study. Once they were far enough away, Matt whispered to Nitis, "I'm going to point my firearm in the window and tell them to drop their weapons. You stay out of sight, but keep your weapon drawn and be ready to help me. You won't be able to see in, but hopefully, you'll know what's going on by the conversation. First, though, we need to get one of his horses."

Nitis nodded his understanding. They crept to the stables and saddled one of the horses. Nitis took the horse back to where their horses were tethered. They then snuck back to the house. Once they were both in position, Matt stood up and pointed his weapon at George. "Everyone, place your weapons gently on the floor. Any false move and George dies," Matt said.

George's mouth dropped open in surprise. Knox reached for his weapon. "Knox, stop, or George is dead."

Knox stopped.

"Huh, the prodigal son returns," George said. "What can we do for you?"

"First thing you can do is place your weapons on the floor, there where I can see them." Matt pointed to a spot on the floor.

Knox, Jim, and George placed the weapons where Matt had told them to. "Knox, I know you have a backup weapon place that there as well."

Knox reached into his boot and drew out another weapon placing it amongst the rest.

"Now we're going to have a talk," Matt said. "First thing, you can move your hands off my ranch. The sheriff is aware of what's going on and will back me on this." Matt lied. In doing so, he decided that it would be a good idea to let the sheriff know. He would do that when he'd finished here."

"George, you're going to come with me as a hostage. You'll be released as soon as your hands are off my land," Matt said.

"That's not necessary," George said. "I give my word."

"I'm afraid history has proved your word is worth nothing," Matt said. "So, this is the way it's going to be."

"Anyone follows me, and George dies. I have one of my hands with me, and you won't know where he is, but if he gives me the signal, then George dies," Matt said. "Okay, George, move across here and climb out the window. Wait. First, you can pick up each of the weapons by the barrel and hand them to me."

George moved forward and picked up each of the weapons by the barrel, and handed them to Matt. Matt handed them to Nitis. "Okay, now you can climb out the window," Matt said.

George climbed out the window. Matt waved his gun at him. "Turn around, head on the wall, hands behind your back." George complied. Nitis tied his hands behind him with pigging strings. Matt continued to keep an eye on Jim and Knox, who didn't move. "Knox, make sure those men are off my land tomorrow, and then you'll have George back, and he can pay you."

Nitis disappeared into the shadows. Matt led George to the horses. Matt helped George Mount his horse. It was a struggle with his hands tied behind his back. Nitis untied George's hands and re-tied them to the pommel. Once that was done, Nitis mounted his horse and disappeared. Matt led George's horse, and they headed back to Matt's ranch. They arrived at Geoff and Hugh in the early hours of the morning. Geoff was keeping watch while Hugh slept. Matt guessed they'd been taking it in turns. George had said nothing on the ride to the ranch. Matt figured this was probably a bad thing. He must be scheming. Nitis appeared shortly afterward. They tied George to a tree. "Hey, you can't do this," George said. "You can trust me. I'm not going to run away."

"We've had this discussion about trusting you before," Matt said.

Once George was secured to a tree, Matt summoned the others away from George so that he could talk to them without George hearing. They kept an eye on George.

"I'm going to ride into town after I've had some sleep and talk to the sheriff. He needs to know what's going on here," Matt said. "Can you guys set up a roster for keeping watch until morning? I'm exhausted. You might have to give Nitis a break on the watch as well."

"That's fine," Geoff said. "Hugh and I will take turns."

Matt woke at first light. He had a wash in the stream, it was cold, but he managed to keep the screams to himself. He then said to Geoff, "I'm on my way to see the sheriff now. I'll get some breakfast at Melissa's after I've seen the sheriff. You're in charge. Make sure George doesn't escape. I suggest you post Nitis somewhere away from the camp where he can keep an eye for anyone approaching."

"Will do, boss," Geoff said.

Matt rode off to town, taking a roundabout route. He didn't want to bump into any of George Hamilton's men on the way. He tethered his horse a little way out of town among some trees and then snuck into town by one of the side streets. He came up the side of the sheriff's office, glanced up and down the street, saw no one was looking at the office, and barged into the sheriff's office. He came face-to-face with the sheriff. The sheriff was sitting at his desk, his firearm drawn and pointed at Matt.

"You nearly died there, boy." The sheriff said.

"Sorry, sheriff," Matt said. "I didn't want anyone to see me, so I couldn't stand outside your door knocking."

"Well, it's good to see you, Matt. No one was sure whether you were dead or not." The sheriff said.

"I nearly was. That chief Mescal was torturing me. He was going to eventually kill me. I've got George Hamilton to thank for being alive," Matt said.

"I heard he attacked the Apache camp, and you were dragged off by one of the Apache." The sheriff said.

"Yes, that's right. The Apache who dragged me away was an Apache called Nitis. He rescued me because when the Apache attacked me and my ranch, I spared his life. He has a sense of honor and wanted to repay me," Matt said.

"That's good." The sheriff said.

"I need to update you on something," Matt said.

"Go ahead." The sheriff said.

"George Hamilton put his hands onto my ranch, well, Knox and three others. He figured that I wasn't coming back and that he could take over the ranch since I have no relatives. Which was probably not a bad idea if I'd been dead. I've captured George Hamilton and am holding him at a secret location until his hands have moved off my ranch. But I thought I'd better let you know what's happening so that if I disappear, suspect number one will be George Hamilton," Matt said.

"Are you going to let him go?" The sheriff asked.

"I'll let him go as soon as his hands are off my ranch and back at George's ranch," Matt said. "None of this is of my doing. I don't want any trouble. I want to get on and run my ranch."

The sheriff sighed. "I know. Okay, I'm now aware of what's going on, and I'll keep an eye on it. Good luck."

Matt left the sheriff's office. He changed his mind about having breakfast at Melissa's. He guessed that he was probably not popular with Melissa. He decided to head out of town hungry and get something to eat when he got back to the camp.

When Matt got back to his camp, all seemed to be in order. George was still tied up.

"So, what's happening with George's hands? Have they left the ranch yet?" Matt asked.

"They have," George said. "Your men should've released me by now. Your ranch is free for you to return to."

No one said anything. They looked at Matt. Geoff knew that Matt would not have been happy if he'd just let George go.

"So, Geoff, have they gone?" Matt asked.

"They appear to have gone," Geoff said. "Nitis has followed them. We'll see what he says when he gets back."

"Okay, we'll wait for Nitis," Matt said.

George scowled at Matt.

Five hours later, Nitis rode into camp.

"So Nitis, what's happening?" Matt asked.

"They're heading back to George's ranch," Nitis said.

"Okay, George. It seems like you're free to go. But before we do that, we need to talk," Matt said.

"It seems like you'll stop at nothing to get my ranch. You have a lot more men than me. So, are you still going to try and take over my ranch?" Matt asked.

"No, of course not," George said. "You have my word."

"We've had this conversation about your word before. It isn't worth much," Matt said. "In this case, I'm going to take your word. But be warned, if you break your word, I'm not going to treat you the same way I've treated you so far. I've treated you with kid gloves. Going forward, any trouble from you and those gloves off.

"Okay, you can release George and send him on his way," Matt said.

Geoff released George. George stood there rubbing his wrists for a while. "Are you going to give me a gun?"

"Not a chance," Matt said.

George scowled at him. Nitis brought his horse to him. George mounted up. As he rode off, he said, "you'll be hearing from me and my men, don't think you'll get away with this unpunished."

"You never learn, do you?" Matt said. "We need to live in peace with each other and get on with our own ranches. If you try anything, someone's going to be killed, and it might be you."

George kicked his horse into a canter with no further comment.

"Well, we haven't heard the last of this," Hugh said.

"No, you're right," Matt said.

———

Chapter 61

Back at the Hamilton ranch for supper that evening, George, Amy, Julia, Melissa, Jim, and Knox were all eating. The only sound was the clinking of cutlery on the plates.

Julia broke the silence. "We're glad you're back, Papa, but we hope you're now going to leave Matt Teeson alone, and you get on with your ranching and let him get on with his. You're lucky no one was killed through this."

George glared at Julia. "He can't get away with this. I'll see he pays."

Julia said nothing further. She could see if she persisted, her father would fly into a rage. She decided to warn Matt of her father's thoughts.

George sighed. He was surprised Julia said nothing further. He knew there was something going on in that brain. George carried on eating in silence, thinking. *I need to break up the alliance between Julia and Matt. I want her to think he's a pariah. I'm not sure how I'm going to do that, but I'll come up with a plan.*

Julia went into town as normal. She had breakfast at Melissa's and then went to her surgery. George had sent one of the hands to town to keep an eye on her and watch her all day to make sure she stayed at her surgery. He told the hand not to do anything if she went anywhere, just to follow her and see what she did and report back to him. Julia was finished with the patients by noon. She put the closed sign up on the door, walked across to Melissa's, had lunch, and then rode out of town toward Matt's ranch. The hand followed her.

Julia rode into Matt's yard. He was in the corral training a horse. When he saw her, he left what he was doing and came over. "Well, this is a pleasant surprise, Julia. Good to see you. There are some Hamiltons I'm happy to see. Others, not so much."

"Well, it's those other Hamiltons I want to speak about," Julia said.

"Now, I'm disappointed. I thought you just wanted to come and talk with me," Matt said.

Julia smiled. "Well, I guess that's part of it."

"Can I offer you a cup of coffee?" Matt asked.

"Yeah, I wouldn't say no to a cup of coffee," Julia said.

Matt led her across to the porch. "Take a seat. I'll bring your coffee out to you. It's fresh."

Julia sat on a chair on the porch and waited for Matt to reappear with the coffee. Matt handed her the coffee. "Okay, let's get the serious business out the way," Matt said.

"I came to warn you about my father," Julia said. "He's not happy about you reappearing and chasing him off the ranch. And, more particularly, humiliating him by bracing him in his own home. He won't forgive you for that. I'm warning you to ride carefully and keep a lookout."

"Thanks for that," Matt said. "I appreciate you doing that. I know how hard it must be for you. After all, he is family."

"I suspect he's got someone watching me. So yes, it is hard, and supper tonight is going to be an unpleasant affair, I'm sure," Julia said.

"Sure, it would upset him, but I didn't know what else to do. I couldn't leave his men on my land, and that's the best way I could think of to get them off without any bloodshed," Matt said. "How's the doctoring going? Are you getting more patients?"

"It's going well. I'm getting a few patients every day. Not enough to keep me busy all day, but it's at least giving me an income, and if my father cuts off the rental on the premises, I'll be able to afford it out of my income. I've got you to thank for that. You brought me my first patient. I hope you sang my praises after that, as you promised you would."

"I did, and my hands did as well. You have a lot of admirers," Matt said.

They carried on talking for a while about the ranch and how it was going. Julia stood up. "I must be going. I want to get back to the ranch before dark. It's been good talking, Matt."

Matt watched Julia ride down the hill. Thinking *that's a beautiful girl, and she went out of her way to warn me against her family. Interesting, but I have a fear our families will always be at war.*

He stood up and went back to the corral to continue with his work with the horse. The horse appeared to have regressed its training. Matt realized it was because Julia was now a distraction, and he wasn't focused on what he was doing. He gave up the attempted training of the horse and selected one of the cow ponies to ride out and see how the work on the rest of the ranch was going.

All the way back to her father's ranch, Julia had this uncomfortable feeling that someone was following her. She turned around from time to time to see if she could spot anyone. But each time, she saw no one.

At supper, Julia noticed her father glancing at her from time to time. She said, "is something bothering you, Papa?"

"Well, now that you raise it, yes, something is bothering me. You went to visit Matt Teeson today. What was that about?" George said.

"Oh, so you're having me followed, are you?" Julia said.

George hesitated but recovered quickly. "I'm not having you followed. I've got someone protecting you."

"I don't need anyone to protect me. I make friends, not enemies," Julia said.

"We can't be too careful," George said. "I have enemies. They might find it easier to get to me through you."

"Your enemies are not as ruthless as you. They wouldn't do anything to me to get you," Julia said.

"What did you say to Teeson anyway?" George asked.

"I warned him to be careful of you. I feel it's only right. My job as a doctor is to save people. It's better to ensure they don't get shot rather than let them get shot and then have to attend to them. If they get shot, they may not even live for me to attend to them," Julia said.

George snorted. He said nothing further. Supper continued in silence.

Knox broke the silence. "Julia, I don't think you should get too attached to Matt Teeson. He's his own death warrant."

"He's not his own death warrant. He tries to mind his own business, but you and Papa keep interfering. And what you're trying to do is no better than straight-out theft," Julia said.

George went red in the face. "How dare you accuse me of theft. Our suppers seem to deteriorate every night into an argument. I think we need to eat separately in the future."

"You're right. Yes, it would be better if we ate supper separately. You need to stop having me followed. I'm a grown woman. I need to live an independent life," Julia said.

"Well, if you want to be independent, maybe you should move out. Then where would you be," George said.

"You're so busy fighting your wars you don't know what's going on in my life," Julia said. "My practice is doing well." She stopped short there. It would be a struggle for her to move out and pay for the practice rent. She hoped her father would settle for her living independently at home.

George said nothing. He glared at her and then, as per normal, turned to Jim and talked ranch matters. Julia finished supper and was about to leave the table.

"I repeat my warning, don't get too attached to Matt Teeson. He'll be dead by the end of the week," George said.

Julia stopped mid-stride, half turned toward her father, hesitated, and then carried on walking out of the room, saying nothing further.

She lay in bed that night, thoughts churning. Wondering what to do. She'd already warned Matt. But she felt maybe her warning hadn't gotten through, and with her father's latest threat, she decided she needed to emphasize things and get Matt to take the threat seriously and do something about it. Not that she knew what he could do about it.

The next morning, she was up early and off for breakfast at Melissa's. Melissa rode with her into town.

"I can see you're getting quite attached to Matt Teeson. I don't think it's going to end well, though, with Papa's attitude. And there's nothing we can do about it," Melissa said.

"I think you're right, but I must try and do something. I'm going to see Matt again and get him to take precautions," Julia said.

"That might only make things worse for him," Melissa said.

"That is a worry, but I can't sit back and do nothing," Julia said.

"I know. Look what happened to Patrick. I didn't know what was going on. I had no opportunity to warn him. So, you're right to try and do something," Melissa said.

"I'll try and get him to come in to see me some time. It worries me that someone is following me. I think it would be safer for him to come and see me," Julia said.

They arrived at Melissa's. The waitress had already opened up and had the coffee going. Melissa turned to Julia and said. "Your breakfast will be along shortly. You can drink your coffee in the meantime."

Chapter 62

Julia contemplated how she'd get a message to Matt while she ate breakfast. She thought maybe little Johnny Harlow could take a message out to Matt. She left money on the table to pay for breakfast and wandered past the kitchen, and said goodbye to Melissa. She headed out along the street toward her office. As she was walking, she saw Johnny Harlow loitering outside one of the shops. He was sitting on the sidewalk whittling a piece of wood. She changed direction and headed toward Johnny. "Good morning, Johnny. Can you run an errand for me?" She asked.

"Sure, Miss Hamilton," Johnny said. "What is it?"

"I need you to take a note out to Matt Teeson on his ranch. You know where that is?" Melissa asked.

"Yeah, I know it," Johnny replied.

"Can you pop past my office in ten minutes, and I'll have the note ready for you and your money," Julia said.

"See you in ten minutes, Miss Hamilton," Johnny said.

Further down the street, George Hamilton watched Julia. He'd come into town for some supplies. He was curious as to why Julia was talking to little Johnny Harlow. He watched Julia go into her office and Johnny loiter for a bit longer. He surmised that maybe Julia was sending a note to Matt. He frowned as he pondered how he might make use of that. The frown disappeared as he hit on an idea. It depended on him being right in his assumption. He continued to watch and saw Johnny go into Julia's office. George popped into a store where one of his hands was buying supplies.

"I want you to follow little Johnny Harlow. I think he's taking a message to Matt Teeson. I want you to catch up with him and tell him Julia's changed her mind and has a different note for him to deliver. You can then hand him a note. I'll write that note now to replace the one that Julia has given him.

George asked for some paper and a pencil from the shopkeeper, who dug under the counter and handed him a pencil and paper. George scribbled a note. He asked the shopkeeper if he had an envelope.

"Sure, I've got an envelope, but you'll have to pay for it." The shopkeeper said.

"No problem, add it to my bill," George said.

The shopkeeper handed the envelope to George. George slipped the new note inside the envelope and wrote Matt Teeson on the outside. He'd been watching Julia's office through the window. George and his hand walked out of the shop. George pointed down the street, "there goes Johnny now. Give him a couple minutes to get around the corner there and then chase after him," George said.

The hand took the message, climbed onto his horse, and walked down the street. Once Johnny was around the corner and out of sight, he spurred his horse into a canter. Johnny was moving fast. It took the hand a while to catch Johnny. Johnny heard the clatter of hooves behind him and looked to see who was coming. He was in two minds about whether to try and outrun his pursuer or not. He decided to stop and wait for him. He thought if he didn't stop, it was likely the pursuer would catch up with him anyway. He turned his horse and watched the rider approach. He recognized him as one of George Hamilton's hands.

"Hi Johnny, I'm pleased you slowed down. You were going fast. Miss Julia changed her mind and wrote a different note." The hand said. "Give me that note and take this note to Matt."

Johnny thought about it for a second or two. He was wary of adults and never wanted to cause trouble. That usually ended up with a whack around the ear. Besides, it was one of George Hamilton's hands who Julia would know. He figured it must be all right. He took the note and said, "Okay, I'll take this note to Mr. Teeson.

Johnny took the note, turned his horse around, and headed off in the direction of Matt Teeson's ranch. George Hamilton's hand watched Johnny head off with the note and smiled. *Looks like Johnny is buying it*. He thought. He turned and headed back to town. George was waiting for him. "Well, is Johnny going to deliver the new note?" George asked.

"It looks like it. He looked puzzled for a second but then accepted it and headed off with the new note. I've got the old note. Here it is. He handed the note to George.

George opened the note, read it, and smiled. The smile disappeared. He frowned as the execution of his plan came to mind. All sorts of things could go wrong, and he was going to have to sacrifice his gun for hire. He had second thoughts. *Oh well, I still have time to think about it and decide*. He thought.

George headed to the undertaker shop. As he walked in the door, Bones greeted him. "Good morning Mr. Hamilton. What can I do for you? I hope you've come to buy something." Bones said.

"Well, I haven't come to buy anything," George said, but you'll like this even better. I've come to give you money."

"I always like money. But I also know there's no free lunch." Bones said.

"You're a wise man."

Matt was out on the ranch with Hugh moving cattle. He spotted a horseman in a cloud of dust coming up the trail to the ranch house. "Looks like we have a visitor," Matt said.

"You want me to come with you?" Hugh said. "In case it's trouble."

"No, don't worry. It's only one person. I'm sure I can handle it," Matt said.

Matt turned and headed toward the ranch house. Johnny had pulled up at the ranch house and jumped off his horse. He was knocking at the door. There was no answer. He peeked in the window but couldn't see anyone.

"Hello, Johnny," Matt said. "What brings you here?"

Johnny jumped and turned around. "You gave me a fright Mr. Teeson," Johnny said.

"Sorry, Johnny, what have you got for me?" Matt said.

"Miss Julia asked me to deliver this note to you." Johnny held the note out to Matt.

"Thanks, Johnny. Hang on in case I need to send a reply," Matt said.

He read the note.

Dear Matt,

My father has plans. I need to talk to you. Meet me outside the saloon in the alley at 6 o'clock tomorrow morning. Don't send a reply. He has people watching me all the time. I don't want the reply intercepted. If you're not there by 7 o'clock, I'll leave. No harm done.

Julia.

"No reply needed, Johnny, you can go. Thanks," Matt said.

Johnny touched his hand to his hat, turned, and rode off down the trail.

Matt read the note again and frowned. The writing wasn't quite like he would imagine Julia's was. It looked more masculine. He thought maybe because she was a doctor, her writing was more masculine because she was doing a man's job. With that thought, he pushed the note into his pocket.

He rode back out to Hugh.

"What was that about?" Hugh asked.

"Nothing much. Johnny delivered a note from Julia to me," Matt said.

Hugh looked at Matt and raised his eyebrows with a smirk. Matt ignored him and carried on with the work they were doing.

George sat in Melissa's restaurant, drinking a cup of coffee. He watched the street for Johnny's return. He saw Johnny returning to town after his 3rd cup of coffee. He jumped up from the table and headed out to the street, leaving no money behind for his coffee. It was his right. He had set Melissa up, and she was still staying under his roof.

He intercepted Johnny as Johnny climbed off his horse.

"Hello Johnny, did you deliver the message to Mr. Teeson," George said.

"Yes, sir, I did," Johnny said.

"Well, you better not say anything to anyone about that. Because I know you didn't deliver the correct message. Julia gave you a message to deliver, and someone intercepted you and gave you a different message," George said. "I think that message that you delivered might be trouble. You should've insisted on delivering the message that Julia gave you."

"But the message I delivered was given to me by one of your workers, Mr. Hamilton. So, I thought it would be fine." Johnny said with a frown.

"Well, you shouldn't be thinking. You should just do what you're told. Luckily for you, I'm going to help you out," George said. "I'm going to give you $10 to keep your mouth shut about delivering the message. If Julia or anyone asks you, you apologize to Julia and say you're sorry you lost the message. Here's your money back. I suggest you don't think of saying anything else, or you might just disappear."

"Yes, sir," Johnny said, tears filling his eyes.

"Good, I'm pleased you understand," George said. George turned and marched back down the street to his horse. He mounted and headed out of town toward his ranch. Johnny watched him, his heart thumping. This didn't feel right. He was now stuck. He'd taken the money from George. Plus, George was more to be feared than Julia.

Back at the Hamilton ranch, as George was riding into the yard, he came across Jim. "Jim, send Knox into my study when you find him," George said.

"Sure, boss, anything I can help with?" Jim asked.

"No, I've got a small job for Knox," George said.

Jim headed out to find Knox. George headed for his study. In his study, he pulled out a cigar, lit it, and blew smoke at the ceiling, thinking about his plan. There was a knock on the door. Knox stepped in without waiting for George to invite him in.

"I believe you've got a job for me?" Knox said.

"Yes, I do. But you need to keep it to yourself. Don't talk to anyone about it," George said.

"That sounds like the sort of job I like," Knox said.

"Take a seat." George waved toward one of the chairs in front of his desk. "As you know, I've been wanting to get revenge on Matt Teeson for a while. I'm now tired of him. I want him out the way. I have arranged for him to be in the alley behind the saloon tomorrow morning at 6 o'clock. I want you to go there and kill him. Do you think you're able to kill him in a gunfight?"

"For sure, boss. There's no one that can beat me. He caught me by surprise the last time. It won't happen again. He's as good as dead," Knox said.

"When you've done the job, come back and tell me. I'll be a happy man. I'll tell you how happy. I'll give you $500 once you've done the job," George said.

"At last, a proper job," Knox said. Knox stood and left the study. George sat a while longer, finishing his cigar, watching the smoke crowding the ceiling. He smiled. It was easy to promise money to a man who would be dead.

George stood up and walked out into the yard. He glanced around. He was looking for Adam Carter. He saw Adam training a horse in the corral. He went and stood at the corral rails and watched Adam trying to stay on the bucking horse. He wasn't on long before the horse deposited him in the dust. "Take a break from him. Get one of the other hands to try. I need to talk to you. Come to my study as soon as you're ready."

George wandered back to his study and sat down. He contemplated having another cigar but then decided he needed a brandy. He poured a brandy and took a sip. Ten minutes later, there was a knock on the door. "Come in," George said and waved Adam to a seat. "You don't like Knox, do you?" George said.

Adam frowned. He said nothing. He tried to figure out what the right answer to the question was.

"Don't worry, I don't hold it against you not liking Knox. He's not a likable person. The only thing he lives for is killing people and proving he's the fastest gunman. Let me ask the question again. You don't like Knox, do you?"

"No, I don't. But I'm wary about sharing it. He's likely to kill me." Adam said.

"How would you like to get rid of him?" George asked.

Adam hesitated again. "My life would be much happier if he wasn't here."

"Well, you can earn yourself $500 and be rid of Knox," George said.

Adam's eyebrows shot up, "that sounds attractive."

"What I'm going to say to you now must not go beyond this room. Do you understand what I'm saying?" George asked. "I need your word on this before I continue."

"You know I'm totally loyal to you, boss," Adam said.

"I'm sure you are, and I'm sure the $500 helps your loyalty," George said

"For sure it does. That's more money than I've ever seen. Or will ever see." Adam said. "What do you want me to do? For that kind of money and to prove my own loyalty, I'm willing to do pretty much anything."

"Well, that kind of money doesn't come for nothing. You're going to earn it," George said.

"Here's what I want you to do," George said. "Tomorrow morning, Knox is going to town, and he's going to meet Matt Teeson in the alley behind the saloon. Knox is going to provoke a gunfight with Matt Teeson and kill him. The problem is I worry about having Knox working for me. He's a dangerous man. He can turn at any time. I also want Matt Teeson out of the way, but in getting him out the way, I want it to look like Matt Teeson is a criminal. Well, he is a criminal, but I want everyone to know it. What I want you to do, is be at the alley before either of them arrives. I want you on the roof of the saloon behind where Knox will be. If my plan works, he'll be last to arrive in the alley, so you should be on the saloon roof on the main road side. I want it to look like Teeson has shot Knox in the back. So, you need to train your rifle on Knox, and as he starts to draw, shoot him in the back."

Matt was up before 1st light the next morning. He figured he could get breakfast at Melissa's once he'd seen Julia. He decided not to wait for Hugh to finish cooking breakfast. He couldn't afford to wait. Otherwise, he'd miss the meeting with Julia, which he definitely didn't want to do. He arrived in the alleyway next to the saloon shortly before six. Looking at the alley, he thought this was not a great place for Julia to be. She hadn't arrived yet. He wandered down the alley to check if she was there. He turned around to see if she'd come in behind him. A look of shock crossed his face. He was surprised to see Knox standing in the alleyway. *Julia's set me up*. He thought.

"Didn't expect to see me here, did you?" Knox said. "Looks like the beloved Julia has set you up. It doesn't matter anyway because you're not going to walk out of here alive."

Matt cursed himself. He always tried to train himself to remove the loop from his sidearm every time he dismounted. He hadn't been able to get into that habit. He noticed Knox had removed the loop from his sidearm.

"So, this is how it was with Patrick O'Hagan. You weren't fast enough. You needed an advantage. I think the loop was still on his gun when you drew. From what I hear, you went up afterward and removed it. You're a coward Knox," Matt said.

Matt could see the wheels turning in Knox's head. Knox decided Matt was trustworthy, unlike Knox himself. Knox raised his hands above his head. "Okay, remove the thong from your firearm."

Matt watched Knox. Matt slowly moved his hand to his thong and slipped it off. He then moved his hand slightly away from his gun.

"See, you don't know what you're talking about. I'm not a coward. That's not what happened to Patrick O'Hagan," Knox said. "I'm going to count to three. On the count of three, we draw."

"I see you still want the advantage. You doing the counting," Matt said.

"Well, that's how it's going to be. One, two, three." Knox was drawing before he got to three. A surprised look appeared on his face as Matt's bullet passed through his chest. Knox managed to get a shot off. Matt felt a searing pain in his left arm. He looked down and saw a fountain of blood spurting from his arm. He dropped his firearm and clamped his hand over the wound to stem the flow of blood. Even though Matt had waited for the count of three, his practice had paid off. At the same time, a look of surprise crossed Matt's face when he heard a rifle shot. He fully expected to feel another bullet pass through him. Knox fell face down in the alley. Matt walked up to Knox. The world was becoming fuzzy. Matt was surprised to see Knox had a hole where a bullet had entered his back.

Everything went black, and Matt collapsed to the earth next to Knox.

Nitis had had a bad feeling about Matt heading into town. He followed him. He didn't tell Matt he would come to town with him. He knew Matt would say, *all's good, don't worry, you've got work to do on the ranch.*

Nitis witnessed the shooting, the three shots. He knew where the two shots had come from, but the third shot sounded like a rifle shot. He tried to figure out where the third shot came from. He saw Knox drop to the ground. Nitis crept toward the alley. He saw Matt walk up to Knox and stare down at him and then collapse. Nitis broke into a run. He looked at Knox and saw the bullet hole in Knox's back. He turned and looked around to see if he could see where that shot had come from. He saw nothing. He slapped Matt's face and said, "Matt, we need to get you out of here."

Matt didn't move. Nitis glanced at the wound on Matt's arm. Blood flowed from the wound. He surmised it wasn't fatal. His priority was to get Matt out of there. He lifted Matt on his shoulder and ran out the end of the alley, away from town and toward his horse. By the time he got to his horse, he was exhausted. He heaved Matt into the saddle and held him there, mounting behind him. He clutched onto Matt, struggling to hold him in the saddle as they galloped off.

The next thing Matt knew, he was lying on a bedroll somewhere out in the wilds. Nitis was cooking something over a fire. He groaned and said, "where am I? What's happened?"

————

Chapter 63

Nitis glanced up from his cooking. "I'm pleased to see you're awake. It's about time you woke up and started carrying your own weight."

Matt tried to sit up but dropped back down. A dizzy spell overtook him. Nitis walked over to him with a canteen of water and helped him to sit up, placing the saddle closer against his back to help him sit. "Here, drink this," Nitis said.

"Tell me what happened?" Matt said.

"It seems you were lured into that alley next to the saloon with the sole purpose of Knox killing you. You were quicker than Knox. Your shot would have killed him, but it looks to me like someone else shot at Knox from the back. I figured I couldn't wait and let things take their course because it's not clear what happened."

"It's coming back to me now," Matt said. "Little Johnny Harlow gave me a note which asked me to meet Julia in the alley behind the saloon. He said Julia had given him the note to bring to me. I was a little suspicious as the writing looked more like a man's writing. But I guess my eagerness to see Julia overcame my concerns. How come you were there?"

"I asked Hugh if he knew where you were off to you. Hugh told me you got a note from Julia. And maybe that was where you were heading. That made me suspicious, so I thought I would get your back, as I always must," Nitis said.

"Well, thanks for that. What should we do now? Should we head back to town and explain to the sheriff what happened? He always seems to trust and believe me," Matt said.

———

Chapter 64

George had also gone into town early that morning. He went straight to the sheriff's office. The sheriff, as always, was early. He looked up at George. "You're early. What can I do for you?" The sheriff said as he stood. He didn't proffer his hand. He felt better being on the same level as George.

"I'm worried. Knox went into town. One of the hands said he was going into town to meet Matt Teeson," George said. "I think Teeson plans to ambush him and get him out the way. That would be a big step toward Teeson meeting his ambitions and eventually being able to take over my ranch. He knows that Knox is probably the only one who can take him on," George said.

Three shots rang out close together. "I think I'm too late to warn you."

The sheriff grabbed his hat off the hook behind the door, adjusted his gun belt, and said, "let's go."

The sheriff and George strode down the street toward where they'd heard the shots come from. "It sounds like the shots came from the saloon." The sheriff said.

"Yeah, I think you're right," George said.

They arrived at the saloon. The saloon was closed. They stared in the windows of the saloon. It was dark inside. They walked around. All the doors and windows were shut. As they came round the side going up the alley, George said, "someone's there lying on the ground."

George and the sheriff stared at Knox on the ground. He was lying on his front.

"Looks like someone bushwacked him," George said.

The sheriff crouched next to Knox and felt for a pulse. "No pulse. He's gone.

They then looked around to see if they could see anyone. "Well, whoever shot Knox seems to have disappeared." The sheriff said

"You can be sure it was Matt Teeson. We need to find him. I'm sure that won't be difficult," George said.

They wandered up the alley but didn't pick up anything else. "You stay here and keep an eye that no one else comes here. I'm going to go and fetch the undertaker." The sheriff said.

The sheriff came back half an hour later with the undertaker. "Bones, I'll come through later to see you and see what your conclusions were on the cause of death, although it looks obvious."

"Come through in about three hours. I'll be ready for you then." Bones said.

George and the sheriff searched the alley further. "I see there are moccasin tracks here," George said. "Maybe I'm wrong. Maybe it wasn't Teeson who shot Knox. I hear Teeson teamed up with one of the Apache. Maybe he got the Apache to do his dirty work for him."

"It's hard to tell what happened in this alley. It's a common thoroughfare, and there are lots of tracks here. I don't think we can jump to conclusions." The sheriff said. "Given what you say, it's likely that it was Teeson who shot Knox. We'll see what Bones says about the shots."

Three hours later, the sheriff headed to Bones' shop. George made to follow him. "I'm going to see Bones on my own. You can go and have a cup of coffee. I'll tell you what Bones' conclusion is." The sheriff said.

"I want to see what happened as well," George said. "He was my employee. I should be there as well."

The sheriff shrugged. "Okay, I suppose there's no harm in it."

George and the sheriff walked down the street to Bones' shop, knocked, and were invited in.

"Hello sheriff, hello George." Bones said. "Are you ready to hear my conclusions? Can I offer you some coffee first?"

"No thanks, I've had plenty of coffee this morning." The sheriff said. "You can go ahead and let us know your conclusions."

"I'm going to state the obvious, he died of gunshot wounds." Bones said. "Both shots were from the back."

"Thanks, Bones." The Sheriff said.

"I'm going to form a posse. We need to capture Teeson as soon as possible before he kills someone else," George said. "Then he needs to hang. We don't need a trial. It's obvious what happened. To save everyone a whole lot of trouble, we'll hang him ourselves," George said.

"I'll form the posse and bring him in." The sheriff said. "I'm not having vigilante justice."

"Well, I'm also going to form my own posse," George said. "Knox was my employee."

"Well, if you do catch him, you better bring him in. Do not administer your own justice." The sheriff said.

George ignored him and walked away.

———

Chapter 65

George rode back to the ranch and called his men together. He explained to them what had happened. Matt Teeson had bushwhacked Knox. He called for eight volunteers to form a posse with him to go and catch Matt Teeson. All the hands volunteered. It didn't necessarily mean that they were all out for justice for Knox, but no one wanted to be the odd one out. George then selected the eight hands that he wanted. He selected them based on who he thought would be comfortable with vigilante justice.

Over supper that evening, Julia quizzed George on what had happened. "I hear Knox was shot today," Julia said. "The sheriff tells me that Matt Teeson shot him in the back. I don't believe that. He also tells me that you are forming a posse to catch Matt Teeson."

"Your information is all correct," George said. "I'm heading out with a posse tomorrow morning. We'll find him. That sheriff talks too much. This is men's business."

"What are you going to do when you find him?" Julia asked.

"I'll decide what to do then. But I don't want him being released because someone says there's not enough evidence," George said.

"I hope you're not thinking of carrying out the hanging yourself. I'll never talk to you again," Julia said.

"Well, you can't look at this independently. You're too close to Teeson. We can't have people like him running around shooting people in the back," George said.

"That's not the case," Julia said. "I don't condone Matt Teeson shooting anyone in the back or anyone else shooting anyone in the back. But we can't have people taking the law into their own hands. It's up to the sheriff to arrange for a proper trial and put Matt Teeson in jail. He must then have a proper trial and let the law take its course. In fact, I have no time for Matt Teeson. I didn't like Knox, but shooting someone in the back is worse than anything Knox has done."

"That'll take too long. That's not how it works out here," George said. He then turned to Jim and started talking ranch matters. Julia gathered the conversation was now over.

Julia carried on eating supper, deep in thought. She still couldn't quite reconcile what Matt had done to the person she knew. But then she had to concede she didn't know Matt well. She wondered what had happened to the message that Johnny had delivered. She would've thought that Matt would at least try and see her before he did anything stupid. She decided she needed to talk to Johnny and see if he did deliver the message. He'd been reliable in the past.

The next morning Julia watched George mount up and lead his eight men out. Shortly after that, she headed to town with her normal routine to have breakfast at Melissa's and then head to the surgery. Once the patients dried up by about midday, she set out to find Johnny. She turned the notice on the door to, *closed,* and walked down the street. Johnny, as normal, was outside one of the shops sitting on the sidewalk whittling some wood.

She stopped next to Johnny. He carried on looking down, whittling his wood. It didn't seem quite like the Johnny she knew. Normally he would look up, stand up, and greet her politely.

"Hello, Johnny. You're focused on what you're doing there. What are you making?" Julia said.

"I'm making a gun so that I can practice with it until I'm big enough to get a real gun," Johnny said.

"Johnny, did you deliver the message that I asked you to deliver the other day?" Julia asked.

Johnny burst into tears.

"What's wrong, Johnny?" Julia asked.

"I didn't deliver the note. I lost it on the way. It fell out of my pocket. I went back to find it, but I couldn't find it." Johnny stood up, dug in his pocket, and pulled out the money that Julia had given him. "Here's the money you gave me. I'm sorry, Miss Hamilton. I was too scared to tell you I hadn't delivered it. I should've told you."

"Johnny, I hope you've learned your lesson. In future, when something like that happens, you need to tell the person. Otherwise, the person you're running the errand for makes all sorts of wrong assumptions that can lead to all sorts of troubles. You can keep the money, but I'm not sure I'll ever give you an errand to do again. I can't trust you." Julia said, frowning at Johnny.

Johnny looked at her and said nothing. He continued to sniffle. Julia turned and left Johnny without another word. She thought *I guess it's also quite scary to a small boy. I shouldn't be too harsh.*

She walked down the street to Melissa's. Melissa saw her and said. "I'll be along to join you for lunch with your normal."

Fifteen minutes later, Melissa joined Julia with a light meal for both. Julia brought her up to speed on the events and told her about Johnny.

"That seems strange," Melissa said. "I like little Johnny Harlow. It doesn't seem like him, but I guess maybe he's scared of adults."

Chapter 66

"We need to find out what's going on," Nitis said. "Maybe, there's no problem, and we can continue life as normal. Or, in fact, better than before, now Knox is gone."

"Yeah, you're right. You should sneak back to my ranch and get Hugh or Geoff to find out what's going on. Then we can decide what to do," Matt said.

"Tomorrow morning, I'll head out and get hold of Hugh or Geoff," Nitis said.

The next morning Nitis set out back to Matt's ranch. When he got there, he saw Geoff and Hugh riding out herding some cattle. He pulled up next to them and said, "what can you tell me about what's going on?"

"What d'you mean, what's going on?" Geoff asked. "We haven't heard anything, although we haven't seen Matt since he left early yesterday morning. What can you tell us?"

"Oh, I was hoping to find out from you what's going on. It seems like I know more than you," Nitis said. "Knox and Matt had a gunfight early yesterday morning. Matt won. But there's a twist to it. Someone, I don't know who shot Knox from hiding. Matt was wounded. I figured it best to get Matt out of there, as I didn't know what was going on. I've got

Matt in hiding, but I wanted to find out from you what was going on to see whether we can come back in."

"How badly is Matt hurt?" Hugh asked.

"It's not bad. I've cleaned the wound and bandaged it. It's his left arm. He'll be fine if we can keep him safe from whoever's trying to kill him, which I guess is George Hamilton. It's a real puzzle, though, who shot Knox, and whether that person is on our side," Nitis said. "Do you think one of you will be able to go into town and find out what's going on?"

"It sounds dangerous for any of us to go into town," Geoff said. "But we need to find out."

"It seems to me that Julia might've set him up." Hugh said, "little Johnny Harlow came here with a note which he gave to Matt. Matt wouldn't tell me what the note said. He just said it was from Julia. He seemed to be reluctant to tell me what was in the note. I was about to tease him, but with the look on his face, I refrained. Given that it was maybe Julia that set him up, I don't know who our friends are and who to check with.

"I'll check with the sheriff. He seems to be neutral and do what's right," Geoff said.

"In the meantime, I'm going to go back to Matt. We'll stay hiding out," Nitis said. He described where he had Matt. "Once you know what's going on, you can find us there. On second thoughts, I'm going to move from there in case sheriff Gamble forces you to tell him where we're at. But you can still go there. I'll find you."

Nitis turned to ride away. "Good luck. Let me know as soon as you know what's going on."

"Will do," Geoff said to Nitis' back.

"What do you think?" Hugh said. "Do you think we'll be all right going to see sheriff Gamble?"

I think it'll be fine if it's only sheriff Gamble," Geoff said. "Who's going to see the sheriff?"

"Let's draw straws," Hugh said. "Whoever draws the short straw goes to see sheriff Gamble. But the one who doesn't draw the short straw will need to be somewhere around to try and sort things out if things go pear-shaped."

Geoff climbed off his horse and pulled a straw stem from the ground. He broke it into two parts of unequal length. Sorted them behind his back and then said to Hugh, "pull a straw."

"Aagh," Geoff said. "It looks like it's me."

Hugh grinned. "Yup, it's you. When are we going to do this?"

"I think we should go to town this evening. Normally sheriff Gamble does an early round, and then he's in his office from seven till nine, then he goes out again. Maybe we can catch him between seven and nine in his office." Geoff said

"That sounds like a plan," Hugh said.

They rode into town and arrived in town at about six in the evening. They tied their horses to the rail at the quiet end of town, away from the saloon, and then walked down to the sheriff's office. The light was dim enough that it would make it hard for anyone to recognize them. They tried the sheriff's door. It was locked. They moved across the street to the alley on the other side, which was dark. True to form, sheriff Gamble arrived at his office at seven, opened up, and went inside, shutting the door behind him. They saw the light come on as sheriff Gamble lit a lantern in his office.

"You stay here," Geoff said. "I'll go and talk to the sheriff. We can't plan because we don't know what's going to happen. You'll have to play things by ear."

"Good luck. I hope all goes well." Hugh said

Geoff waited till the street was quiet and then headed across to the sheriff's office. He knocked and walked in before there was an answer. "Evening, sheriff."

The sheriff jumped to his feet, his hand moving to his gun, he stopped. "Evening Geoff. I wasn't expecting you," The sheriff said. "Sit. To what do I owe this visit?"

"I heard that Matt shot Knox, but I'm not clear on the circumstances. I want to hear from you what happened. The last I saw of Matt was him heading into town early yesterday.

He didn't say why he was going into town," Geoff said. "What's your take on the story?"

"Seems like Matt shot Knox in the back in the alley behind the saloon." The sheriff said.

"That sounds like nonsense," Geoff said. "Matt would never shoot anyone in the back. I can tell you for certain he was faster than Knox. We've all been practicing for some time now and drawing against each other, and Matt is by far the fastest."

Well, that's the way it looks. Bones confirms that Knox was shot in the back. We're going to have to bring Matt in, and he'll have to go to trial. It'll all depend on the trial," The sheriff said.

"Well, I don't think this is right. Something doesn't make sense to me. I'll be in touch, sheriff," Geoff said.

"You better not be harboring a criminal," The sheriff said. "If I find you have Matt and didn't turn him in, you'll also be in jail. You'll be an accessory to murder."

"I haven't seen him since yesterday morning. Thank you for your time, sheriff," Geoff said as he stood up to leave.

As he walked out the door, the sheriff said, "don't forget, if he turns up on your doorstep, you need to bring him in."

Geoff waved as he went out the door, not turning around to look at the sheriff. He walked along the sidewalk and then looked back at the sheriff's office. The sheriff had shut the door. Geoff then went down one of the other streets on the other side and came up the alley where Hugh was waiting. He called out to Hugh. "Hugh, we can go now," Hugh whipped around.

"You shouldn't be sneaking up on me like that," Hugh laughed.

"Sorry, we're not popular with the sheriff. Let's get out of here, and when we're away from the town, I'll tell you what's going on," Geoff said. They rode out of town from the back of the alley.

Once they were clear of town, Geoff updated Hugh.

Once he'd finished updating Hugh, Geoff said, "it's lucky the sheriff didn't ask me if I knew where we might find Matt. Maybe that was on purpose. He said if we were harboring Matt, we had to turn him in, or we would be accessories to murder."

"I don't like the sound of that," Hugh said. "We'll have to let Nitis know what's going on, and Nitis will have to keep Matt. It's a good thing he didn't let us know exactly where he would have Matt. How are we going to unwind this?"

They rode on in silence for a while. "This seems like an insurmountable problem. I'm sure George Hamilton is going to come back to the ranch and take it over again. I think we need to find Nitis as soon as possible, and then we can keep an eye on what's happening from a distance. They'll be chasing after Matt. They might catch him at some point. If they do, at least we'll be free and may be able to help him. We'll pick things up this evening from the ranch and then go to where Nitis told us to meet. We'll cover our tracks."

They picked up what they needed from the ranch to live out for a while and then headed toward where Nitis told them to meet. They covered their tracks as they went. They camped overnight once they were away from the ranch.

The next morning, they continued to where Nitis told them to meet. When they got there, they set up camp and waited. Hugh lit a fire and brewed a pot of coffee. Once the coffee was ready, they leaned against a rock which gave them a clear view of the approaches to the site. At two o'clock that afternoon, Nitis said, "you two would be dead in no time." Nitis appeared out of nowhere. Geoff and Hugh jumped, turning around to look at him.

"You're right, although I don't think there's anyone sneakier than you are, so luckily, you're friendly, I think," Geoff said.

"Yes, you're lucky I'm friendly." Nitis grinned at them. "So, what's the story?"

Geoff said, "it's not good. I managed to see the sheriff. The short story is he claims that Matt shot Knox in the back, and he now needs to bring Matt in for trial. He said if we're holding Matt and not bringing him in, he'll have to arrest us and put us in jail for harboring a criminal and as an accessory to murder. Which, of course, is a lot of nonsense."

"That's what I feared," Nitis said.

"We need to carry on as we are. You need to keep Matt, and we should go our own way and stay out of the way, but meet here at prearranged times so we can update each other. It's safer if we stay apart. At least someone on the outside can help you," Geoff said.

"That sounds like a good idea," Nitis said. "I'll update Matt. We'll meet here in two days' time, same time."

Nitis slipped away. "That's one sneaky Indian," Hugh said. "I'm pleased he's on our side. But this can't go on forever."

———

Chapter 67

George and his men were having no success in tracking Matt down. They set up camp for the night.

"How long are you going to keep this up, boss?" One of the hands asked. "We can't go on searching forever."

"At some point, we'll have to go back to the ranch. But that may be a while. I'd like to find him soon and hang him. We're not going to wait for the sheriff or any court. If we catch him, we'll hang him," George said.

Some of the men agreed and shouted their agreement. A couple of the others followed along, but their agreement was less determined.

The next morning, they set out again. Two of the men were good trackers. The rest were worse than average. The worse than average ones looked at the ground and talked as they went. It annoyed George, but he realized nothing he said was going to change them. At least they'd be useful when it came to capturing Matt and hanging him.

One of the men, one of the not so good trackers, who was busy talking, stopped talking. He pointed at the ground. "This looks like an un-shod pony has passed this way."

The rest of the men stopped. George came up and had a look. "Well done, you surprise me. I didn't think you were much of a tracker, but it looks like you found something. Let's follow these tracks. We need to split up. We don't want to be ambushed in a clump."

George set two men to follow the tracks, and the rest spread out on the flanks and followed at a distance. After a while, one of the two men following the tracks called a halt. He waved George across.

When George came up to him, he said, "We're close. These tracks are fresh."

"We'll have to spread out more. You'll have to be careful they don't ambush you," George said.

George spread the men out further. They continued following the two men tracking. The two men stopped and waved to everyone else to stop. They then rode across to George.

"We've found them. They're camping by a stream over this hill. It looks like it's an Apache and Matt. Matt appears to be wounded." The one tracker said.

"Well done, boys," George said. He signaled to the other men to come to him. Once everyone was around him, he said. "We'll pull back here and draw up a plan of attack."

They pulled back away from the campsite and crowded around George on their horses.

George said, "we could shoot them where they are. That would be the simplest thing to do. But that's too easy and good for Matt Teeson. I want everyone in the area to realize they don't mess with me."

After that, George outlined a plan of action and confirmed that everyone understood. He then said, "let's get to our positions."

The men rode closer, tethered their horses, and proceeded on foot. Once the camp was surrounded, George called out, "Matt Teeson and friend, I have you surrounded. Put down your weapons, or you die where you are. It'll be easier for me to shoot you where you are, but justice needs to be served."

Matt and Nitis looked up. They saw where George was. George said, "look around if you don't believe me."

Matt and Nitis looked around and realized they were surrounded and had no chance. Nitis said, "I don't know how they found us. They caught me napping."

Matt and Nitis placed their sidearms on the ground and stood up, hands raised.

"Good decision, boys," George said. "Stay facing me. Don't move an inch."

George signaled two men from behind to come down. The men slithered down the rough, loose rocks to the campsite. One of the men said, "you first, Indian, bring your hands down slowly behind your back, don't try anything, or you'll both die."

Nitis did as he was told. The men tied his hands behind his back with piggin strings. He then repeated that with Matt. "Right, now lie face down on the ground, both of you."

Nitis and Matt complied. Matt's heart beat fast. He couldn't imagine that George would take him in for trial. This looked like the end. He heard the other men sliding down the loose rocks.

"This is the end for you, Matt Teeson," George said. ""You'll hang now for the murder of Knox. He was a good man."

"I wonder if you even believe your own lies," Matt said. "You know very well what happened to Knox. I think you were worried he might turn on you, so you had him shot and blamed it on me."

"Good story," George said. "But it doesn't wash. Enjoy your last few breaths. Isn't it a tradition to offer a man who's about to die his last cigarette? Oh, I know, you don't smoke."

"Well, now's a good time to start," Matt said. "Let's see what I've been missing. Do you have a cigar for me? I might as well go big in my last minutes on earth. I know you smoke cigars."

"Never let it be said that I'm not a generous man," George said. "I do have a cigar, an awfully expensive one because I'm so generous I'll let you have it. In fact, I'll even let your Indian friend have one. That's another thing you've committed, joining up with the Apache." George moved his face down near Nitis. "Can I offer you a cigar as well?"

"I might as well have one," Nitis said.

"Get yourselves up. You can lean against those rocks over there." George pointed. "Have your last cigars there. I want you to enjoy them. I don't want them wasted."

Matt and Nitis struggled to their feet, their hands tied behind their back, and moved over to the rock and leaned against the rock. George stared at them, frowning. "Hmmm, this is a problem. It's going to be difficult for you to smoke cigars with your hands tied behind your back. I guess I'll tie your feet first and then release your hands." George signaled for one of the men to untie their hands but first tie their feet. The man stepped forward. He first attended to Matt and then to Nitis. George then handed the cigars to the man and said. "You can give them the cigars and matches. I guess you hoped I'd come up and put the cigars in your mouth and light them for you, give you a chance to grab me. I'm not stupid," George said.

Matt and Nitis lit the cigars. They immediately coughed and sputtered, puffing out clouds of smoke.

"Girls." George laughed.

Matt and Nitis persisted, having to relight the cigars from time to time. "Don't worry, boys, we've got all day. This is prolonging your agony, which makes me happy," George said.

The cigars still had a bit to go. George said, "I've been patient enough. I think you've had a long enough smoke. Let's get on with it, boys."

Two of the men took their lassos off their saddles. They fashioned hangman's nooses. They then walked up to Matt and Nitis and placed the ropes around their necks.

"You can stand up now," George said. Matt and Nitis stood. "Hands behind your back again." Nitis and Matt placed their hands behind their backs. The men re-tied their hands. They then untied their feet.

The men led Matt and Nitis across to their horses. "Climb aboard now, boys," George said. Both Matt and Nitis racked their brains. This looked like the last moment. Matt dived to the ground, given he couldn't think of anything else. "That's not going to save you," George said. "Here, throw me that rope." George said to the man holding the rope around Matt's neck." George turned the end of the rope around the pommel of his saddle and kicked the horse into a canter. Matt bounced along behind. George stopped after about 10 yards. "I don't want to kill you by dragging you behind my horse. I want to see you hang." Matt was bleeding from his face, he managed to avoid being hit by any rocks, but the times when he wasn't able to keep his face off the ground, his face had a good scrubbing. "That'll teach you a lesson. Unfortunately, it's not going to be of much use to you in the future." George turned his horse and dragged Matt back to the circle of men. "Stand up now and climb on your horse." Nitis was already on his horse, the rope around his neck and held by the other man. Matt climbed onto his horse. He figured this was it.

"No one move."

George looked around. He glared at the sheriff and the posse behind the sheriff. The sheriff was off his horse behind a rock, his rifle resting on the rock aimed at George.

"You can kiss your job of sheriff goodbye," George said. "I brought you in, and I can take you out."

"That's not how it works." The sheriff said. "I'm appointed by the people. And I'm going to do the job I was appointed for."

"I know you have always been friends with Matt Teeson," George said. "So, whatever he does, you're going to support him."

"That's not correct." The sheriff replied. "I am making sure the law is applied. You cannot exercise vigilante justice. I'm going to take Matt Teeson into town and put him in jail, and he'll have a fair trial. His fate will be up to a judge, not up to you, as for the Apache. He can go. He's not wanted for any crime."

"The Apache is just as guilty," George said. "He's been harboring a criminal."

"We don't know that Matt Teeson is a criminal until he's had his trial." The sheriff replied. "So, the Apache goes free. I should arrest you for criminal activities. But I'll stop short at that, at this point, if you cooperate. I want you to leave those two men where they are and ride away. But before you do that, I want you to deposit your firearms. You can collect them tomorrow from my office."

"You're going to pay for this," George said through gritted teeth, his face flushed.

"Are you going to cooperate?" The sheriff asked.

George instructed his men to place their weapons in a pile in the center of the clearing.

As he was doing that, the sheriff said. "One of my men will check you all to make sure there are no hidden weapons, and then you can go."

Once all the weapons were placed in a pile in the center, the sheriff instructed the men to come forward one by one with the horses for two of his men to check and make sure there were no remaining weapons. Once that was done, the sheriff said, "I'll see you tomorrow when you collect your weapons."

George rode off with his men, not bothering to reply.

"Right, Matt, I'm going to take you in." The sheriff said. He turned to Nitis and said, "you can go, but before you go, you need to put your weapons here." He pointed to the spot in front of him.

"But I can't survive without weapons. I need to hunt," Nitis said.

"You can collect them from me this evening. I'm sure you can survive that long without food." The sheriff said.

"Okay, I'll see you this evening," Nitis said.

The sheriff had one of his men get Matt onto his horse and tie his legs underneath and his hands to the pommel. He was taking no chances. He then delegated one of the men to lead Matt's horse. They set out toward town, Matt in the middle of the column of men.

————

Chapter 68

They arrived in town in the late afternoon. Sheriff Gamble placed Matt in jail.

As he clanked the door of the jail shut, Matt said, "you seriously don't believe I did this, sheriff."

"It's not my job to judge." The sheriff said. "That's up to the judge when he arrives. That'll be in three days' time. "

"You've known me a while now, sheriff. Surely you know by now that even if I didn't think I could beat Knox, there'd be no way I'd shoot him in the back. Geoff, Hugh, and I have been practicing every day for some time because we knew this battle with George was coming. I'm far quicker than Geoff or Hugh, and I bet that I'm probably quicker than most people," Matt said.

"As I say, it's not me for me to decide, save you arguments for the trial. You heard George. He says I favor you already, so I couldn't show you any more favor by releasing you without a trial." The sheriff said.

"That's the problem with the law. It depends on a jury and who might be able to show enough evidence either way as to what happened, so I'll be hung regardless," Matt said.

"The evidence against you is strong." The sheriff said.

"What evidence?" Matt said.

"Your best bet is to get yourself a good lawyer." The sheriff said.

"Well, there's the problem. There's not one lawyer in town. So, does that mean you're going to delay the trial until I can find a lawyer who will represent me? It's going to be difficult because I don't have much money to pay for a lawyer. I guess I may have to offer that lawyer capital with some of my land. It would be better than me being hung for no reason. Do you have any suggestions of who I can get as a lawyer?" Matt said.

"I can't recommend you a lawyer. It would be a conflict of interest." The sheriff said. "I'll bring you some supper later. Let me know who you want me to contact to represent you."

Matt lay on the bed. It was rough hessian material stuffed with hay. Matt suspected he would soon be itching. It was probably full of bedbugs. His hands behind his head, he thought about his predicament. Who could he get to represent him? His thinking wasn't helped by the bugs crawling over him, making him itch. Eventually, he gave up thinking about who could represent him and tried to get to sleep. It took him a long time to get to sleep.

———

Chapter 69

Matt woke before it was light. He could hear an owl hooting. Even in town, the wildlife could be heard. The town did not stretch far. He went back to the problem of who could represent him. Melissa popped into his mind. He remembered someone saying she wanted to be a lawyer. Matt thought about it further. It was unlikely she would represent him, particularly as her father was more likely the culprit. But then again, she might want to get to the bottom of who shot Patrick, and she probably suspected it was something to do with her father. The other problem was Melissa knew nothing about the law as far as he knew. Would the judge even allow her to represent him? From what he knew of these things, because of the shortage of lawyers, almost anyone could represent anyone. As long as the so-called client confirmed that he was aware that the person was not an admitted lawyer. The other thing that might help is Melissa was well-respected in the community. That would give him support from the jury. Having made a firm decision, he fell asleep. He was woken by sheriff Gamble clattering the bars.

"Here's some coffee. I'll get you some breakfast once Melissa's is open." The sheriff said.

Chapter 70

George woke up excited. His plan was coming together. He would soon have possession of Matt's land. He could barely contain himself to get going. He sat with Jim at breakfast. "Well, Jim, things are coming together. We'll soon be able to join Matt Teeson's ranch to mine. I want you to send four men over there to start working the ranch and keep it in good order. I'm going to go and arrange for it to be registered in my name."

Jim looked at him. "Yes, boss." He carried on eating in silence. He was beginning to feel uncomfortable carrying out his boss's biddings unquestioned. The pay was good, but effectively he was selling his soul.

After breakfast, Jim selected four men to head across to start working Matt's ranch.

"But won't Matt's hands shoot us if we try and take over?" One of the hands said.

"No, Matt Teeson is in jail, and Geoff, Hugh, and the Apache are hiding out somewhere. I don't think it's on the ranch." Jim said.

George saddled his horse and headed out for the land registry of the territory. It would take him a day to get there. He booked himself into a hotel for the night when he arrived.

The next morning, he was in the office of the land registry first thing. He stated what his business was. A clerk called him through.

"I want my title to a ranch registered." He quoted the plot numbers.

The clerk wrote the plot numbers down and opened a ledger. He paged through it and then ran his fingers down the page. "Ah, here we are." He frowned. "It seems these plots are already registered to a Matt Teeson. What did you say your name was?"

"My name is George Hamilton. Yes, the land is registered to a Matt Teeson. But he's in jail and shortly to be hanged. He has no relatives, so to make sure the land is worked, it needs to be passed on to someone else, and that person should be me."

"I'm afraid we can't do that, sir. We need to see a death certificate, and then there needs to be a search for relatives." The clerk looked up at him.

"I'm sure I could make it attractive for you to register the transfer," George said.

"Are you trying to bribe me, sir?" The clerk asked.

"No, I didn't say anything about bribing you." George smiled at him.

"Well, how are you thinking of making it attractive for me to register the property in your name. In any event, why wouldn't you wait until the man has been hung?" The clerk said.

"The early bird catches the worm," George said. "I'm sure you want to do your job properly and make sure the land is well looked after and developed."

"Well, there is that. There is a fee for doing transfers. That fee is negotiable." The clerk said.

"Well, how negotiable is it. I could afford $500," George said.

"I think that would do it." The clerk said. "But it is cash."

"No problem," George said. He fished in his pocket and pulled out $500, placing it on the counter. He kept his hand on top of the $500. I'll hand this over once you've registered the land in my name."

The clerk looked at him. "Err, that's not how it works. Cash first, and then I do the transfer."

George stared at the clerk, frowning. He pushed the $500 across the counter to the clerk. The clerk whipped the $500 off the counter and stuffed it into his pocket.

"I'll attend to the transfer now, sir." The clerk said.

"Thank you, it's a pleasure doing business with you." George smiled.

He watched the clerk write the transfer up in the ledger. He was finding difficulty keeping the smile off his face. *My plan has come together at last*. He thought.

He turned away from the counter and paced. The clerk was now writing out the title deeds. George was struggling to hold his impatience to get hold of the certificates. The clerk was not the quickest writer, but he was meticulous. George guessed he would also be a happy clerk, and this was the most money he'd ever seen.

"Here are your certificates of title, sir." The clerk held the certificates out to him. "It's been a pleasure doing business with you, sir."

George took hold of the certificates. "Thank you, I'll be on my way now."

George strode out of the office and back to his hotel room. He packed his few items into his saddle bag and checked out of the hotel. He was tempted to stop for a celebratory drink at the saloon. He resisted the temptation. He was more interested in getting the title deeds into his safe at the ranch. He wouldn't be content until they were safely in there. He rode out of town, whistling. He wouldn't make it to his ranch tonight. He'd have to camp overnight. He stopped shortly before the sun went down, giving himself enough time to set up camp in the light. He ate the cold food he had bought from the hotel. He lit a fire to keep himself warm and heat himself up a cup of coffee. While he was drinking coffee, two men rode up and asked if they might join him. As they rode up, George slipped the loop off his firearm. George looked them over. They looked like they were harmless. But he wasn't sure.

"I don't want to sound inhospitable," George said. "But I prefer to keep my own company." While he was talking, he noted that the loops were still on their firearms.

"We don't want to cause you any harm." The one said. "We just wanted some company and felt we would be safer together."

"Well, I feel safer keeping my own company," George said.

"That's not very neighborly of you. We'll be on our way." The one man said.

The two men turned and headed the horses away from George's camp. George watched them go. He had a feeling they'd be back.

Once they were out of sight, he placed the bedroll near the fire and stuffed it with leaves. He placed his hat on his saddle at one end. He finished his cup of coffee around the fire and then moved away from the fire, wrapping up in his thick jacket. He sat against a tree and closed his eyes. It wasn't comfortable, but it was better than being surprised by the two men.

At about two in the morning, he was awoken by shots. He opened his eyes and watched as the men ran across to his bedroll to check on their handiwork. He drew his sidearm and took aim at the one that was slightly in front. He squeezed the trigger. The man yelled, threw up his hands, and fell to the ground. The other one stopped as George turned his firearm onto him and squeezed the trigger. He grunted and fell to the ground. George stood up and walked across to them. He checked for a pulse on each but found none. *Good riddance. That'll teach them.* Then he thought, *I guess it won't teach them. They're dead. At least that's two fewer troublemakers in the world.* George dragged them away from the camp. Once they were clear of the camp, he settled into his bedroll and went to sleep. The next morning, he was up early, had a cup of coffee, saddled his horse, and was on his way. He chewed beef jerky while he rode. Once he had the deeds in the safe, he would head to Melissa's and get himself a good breakfast. In fact, he thought, it'll be closer to lunch. He rode toward his ranch, thinking of how he'd now rule the area with the combined ranches. He would be by far the biggest and most important ranch in the territory. He figured the first thing he would do would be to get rid of sheriff John Gamble and appoint someone who was more willing to do his bidding. He arrived at his ranch later that morning. He removed the title deeds from his saddlebags and headed for the safe. He greeted Maria and Amy as he walked in but continued striding toward the safe. He opened the safe and placed the title deeds in the safe, and then relocked it. He breathed a sigh of relief. That was done. No one could take Matt Teeson's ranch away from him. It would complicate things if Matt Teeson wasn't hung, but he didn't think that was likely. He went outside, mounted his horse, and headed into town to get a meal at Melissa's.

George dismounted in front of Melissa's and hooked the horse's reins over the hitching rail. He strode into the restaurant. The restaurant was half full. He found himself a seat near the window facing the door. The waitress rushed across to him. "Hello, Mr. Hamilton. What can I do for you?"

George said, "you can bring me four eggs, bacon, sausage, beans, and flapjacks. Oh, and a pot of coffee."

The waitress paced off to place his order. As she entered the kitchen, she said to Melissa. "Your father's here."

Melissa grimaced and headed out of the kitchen. She walked across to George's table. "Hello, Papa. Where've you been?"

George smiled at Melissa, stood up, and gave her a hug. Melissa was surprised and thought. *That's unusual. I wonder what's up with him.*

"I've got great news. I've secured Matt Teeson's ranch," George said.

"What do you mean you've secured Matt Teeson's ranch?" Melissa asked. "You can't just secure his ranch because he's in jail. You need to wait until after the trial before you do anything, and then I don't think you'd be able to do anything anyway."

"Details, details. I've been to the land registry office, and I've had Matt Teeson's ranch registered in my name," George said.

"I don't understand how you could've done that. Surely that's not legal?" Melissa said.

"Of course, it's legal. Matt Teeson's in jail. He can't do anything about looking after the ranch. The government wants ranches to be looked after and grow. They don't want ranches lying fallow. Anyway, he'll be dead in a few days," George said.

"I wouldn't be so sure," Melissa said. "I don't believe Matt Teeson is a murderer."

"Well, I think he'll be proven guilty anyway. He has no one to represent him. There are no lawyers in this town. So even if he was innocent, he'll still hang," George said.

"And that doesn't bother you? That an innocent man hangs through lack of representation," Melissa said.

"Not at all. Especially if it's Matt Teeson. He's been a thorn in my side for a long time. It's time someone sorted him out," George said.

Melissa frowned, sighed, and walked away. *This doesn't seem right that Matt Teeson can't get representation or he gets hung just because he has no representation.* She thought.

———————

Chapter 71

George left his breakfast table without paying for the meal or leaving a tip. After his breakfast, George headed across to the saloon. When he got there, he announced, "drinks on the house for everybody." The saloon was half full. A few of the cowhands had somehow managed to sneak off for a lunchtime drink. His offer was greeted with cheers.

One man asked him. "So, what are we celebrating?"

"We're celebrating me acquiring Matt Teeson's ranch. Since he's going to be hung, he won't be needing it. In fact, I think it's pointless waiting for the trial. We should go and deal with the hanging now," George said.

"We need to have a few more drinks before we're ready to do that." One man shouted.

"You're right. You can have a few more rounds on me. Then we'll head over to the jail and break Matt Teeson out and save the territory a trial. It's pointless having a trial. We know what the result will be. Why go through that farce?" George shouted.

A round of cheers greeted his statement.

George bought more rounds of drinks. The noise in the saloon increased. George figured spending the money on the drinks was worth it. After an hour, the men started chanting, "let's go and hang Matt Teeson. Hang Matt Teeson."

The men surged to the door of the saloon. George Hamilton pushed his way through the crowd and led them to the jail. The sheriff heard the crowd coming down the street. He stood at the door of the jail with his rifle. Once the crowd was within hearing distance, he said, "that's far enough." The crowd continued advancing on the jail. Sheriff Gamble lowered his rifle and aimed fractionally above the heads of the crowd, and pulled the trigger. He was surprised at how close his shot was. It was closer than he meant it to be. It whipped the hat off one of the men near the front. The man dropped to the ground in fright. That caused the crowd to stop.

"Sheriff, you're wasting your time. You're not going to be sheriff for long. And you can't hold this crowd off. There are too many. If you kill one person here, you'll be hung as well. It'll be good for Matt Teeson to have company. You and he are as bad as each other." George shouted.

"If I must shoot someone, I will. The first person I shoot will be you." With that, the sheriff aimed at George Hamilton's chest. George Hamilton stood dead still. The crowd jostled him forward. That made him nervous. He turned around. "Hey, stand still." He said.

Julia, in her office, was alerted by the noise. As soon as she finished with the patient she was busy with, she went outside to see what was going on. She saw the crowd in front of the sheriff's office. It was vague at this distance, but it looked like her father was at the head of the mob. She walked down the street. As she got closer, she knew for sure it was her father. She walked up to her father. "What's going on here, Papa?"

"This is none of your business," George said. "Go back to your office and do whatever it is you do there. This is man's business."

"No, I'm not going anywhere until I know what's going on," Julia said.

Matt was at the cell bars. He could hear what was going on. It seemed to him he was getting support from different quarters.

"You do as you're told," George said. He was going red in the face from anger and embarrassment at being disobeyed by his daughter in front of the crowd.

"I suggest you be on your way." The sheriff said. "Otherwise, innocent people are going to get hurt, and it'll be on your head."

George glared at his daughter. He saw no give in her return stare. Rather than look even more foolish in front of the crowd, he turned to the crowd and said. "Let's go and have another drink. Matt Teeson's going to be hung anyway, whether it be by us or after the trial by the sheriff. Maybe the sheriff wants to save that task for himself." George laughed.

The crowd turned and headed back to the saloon with a few comments of, "yeah, let's have another drink."

The sheriff watched the crowd head back to the saloon. He walked up to Julia. "Thanks, Julia. That was a help. I'm not sure what would've happened if you hadn't appeared." The sheriff said.

"It looks like you had it under control." Julia smiled at him. "I'm pleased we have an honest and decent sheriff who isn't intimidated. And particularly, is not intimidated by my father. I hope Matt gets a fair trial. He doesn't seem like a murderer to me."

"It's a pity there are no lawyers to represent him." The sheriff said. "He's at a big disadvantage trying to defend himself, even though he's smart. It would be more credible if he had someone else defend him, even if that person is not a lawyer."

———

Chapter 72

Nitis had watched the spectacle of the crowd approaching the jail from the gully on the edge of town. *I need to break Matt out of there. It's only a matter of time before that crowd lynches him. Particularly if they've gone back for more drinks. I hope that the sheriff can hold them off.* He thought.

Nitis wondered what he should do next. He decided he needed to speak to Matt and arrange for him to break out of jail. He watched from the gully until the sheriff left the jail on his rounds. It was dusk, and there seemed to be no one around the jail. Nitis made his way from the gully to the windows of the jail. He thought it unprofessional of the town to not have cleared away the bush and rocks near the jail. It made it easier to sneak up to the jail windows. He guessed once they had a breakout, they would sort it out for the future.

He tapped on the bars of the jail with his knife. "Hey, Matt." He whispered.

Matt got up from his cot. "Hey Nitis, good to see you."

"I need to break you out of here," Nitis said. "I'll do it at 2 AM this morning when the town is quiet. I'll create a diversion somewhere else in town, and when the sheriff heads to the diversion, I'll come and break you out."

"You don't need to break me out," Matt said. "I've been thinking about it. If you break me out, I'll be running forever."

"But if I don't break you out, you're going to hang, and then you're going to go nowhere," Nitis said.

"I've made up my mind," Matt said. "I need someone to represent me, though."

"Who are you going to get to represent you?" Nitis asked. "There are no lawyers in town or close by."

"I've heard it said that Melissa wants to be a lawyer," Matt said. "I'm going to give her her first practical experience of being a lawyer."

"She can't do that," Nitis said. "She has no experience. You'll be like a lamb to the slaughter. I know nothing about your white man's law, but I've heard it's complicated and nothing like our law which everyone knows and understands."

"She'll have an advantage. She's George Hamilton's daughter. If she's defending me, then everyone's going to have a careful look at the case," Matt said.

Nitis frowned. "You've got a good point there. It might even work. But how are you going to get Melissa to represent you?"

"That's where you come in. I want you to approach Melissa. The problem is you'll have to catch her on her own somewhere. Maybe when she's heading back to the ranch, and persuade her," Matt said. "Do you think you'll be able to do that?"

"I'll give it a try," Nitis said. "Nothing to lose. If she agrees, I think it will give you an advantage in that she's George Hamilton's daughter and going against him. It'll take a lot of courage on her part."

"Thanks, Nitis. You better be on your way. If you manage to persuade Melissa, she can just come in the front door and talk to the sheriff. He'll be obliged to let her talk to me in private," Matt said.

"Good luck Matt," Nitis said.

"And good luck to you persuading Melissa," Matt said.

————

Chapter 73

The next morning Nitis waited on the road from George Hamilton's ranch into town. He hid close to the road in a gully. He saw Melissa coming down the road in a buggy. The horse was trotting. It would be hard to catch it and stop it, but Nitis was confident he could do that. As the horse came up next to Nitis, he jumped out and grabbed the bridle, running alongside the horse. He pulled it to a halt. He said to Melissa. "Don't worry, Melissa, I'm a friend of Matt Teeson's. I'm not going to harm you. He needs your help."

Melissa had whipped out a gun from somewhere. It was trained on Nitis without a waver.

"I know you're not going to hurt me because I've got this gun trained on you, and I'm a good shot," Melissa said. "But we can talk. If you don't mind, I'll keep the gun pointed at you."

"Nope, I don't mind." Nitis raised one hand, the other still holding onto the horse's bridle.

"What help is it that Matt wants from me?" Melissa said.

"I spoke to Matt yesterday through the jail window after the sheriff left. Matt wants you to represent him in court," Nitis said. "He's heard that you want to be a lawyer. He says this is your opportunity. He'd like you to represent him. What do you say?"

"I say, that's a ridiculous idea," Melissa said. "I have no idea how to be a lawyer. He's right. I do want to be a lawyer. I was talking to my sister, Julia, about the fact that there are no lawyers in town and no one to represent Matt. Which seems unfair."

"Exactly," Nitis said. "Matt understands you know nothing about the law, but he thinks you, like your sister, are smart, and you would do a good job. He also says it doesn't hurt that you are George Hamilton's daughter. He says that'll be an added advantage. Plus, everyone respects you and knows you."

"Well, flattery will get him everywhere," Melissa said. "I think me representing him will give him a much better chance than no one representing him."

"So, your answer is yes," Nitis said.

"My answer is yes," Melissa said as she placed her firearm back in its holster. "I don't think I need to keep pointing this at you, do you?"

"No, I don't think you do." Nitis smiled.

"I'm not comfortable about doing this. My father will excommunicate me from the family. But so be it. This confirms to me what I should be doing with my life. I'm sure I'll meet tougher obstacles in the future," Melissa said. "So, what's my next move?"

"Matt said that if you agree, you should go to the sheriff and say you're going to represent Matt in the trial," Nitis said. "He said it's quite all right for you or his representative to visit him in jail and have a private conversation. The sheriff might object at first because you're not a qualified lawyer, but Matt is sure that he'll eventually agree. So, when you have a chance, go and check in with the sheriff."

"I'll do that," Melissa said.

Nitis released the reins of the buggy. "Good luck, Melissa. Thanks for doing this. I'm sure you'll be successful, from what Matt tells me about you," Nitis said.

"There you go again, or Matt goes with his flattery. It definitely helps." Melissa smiled as she flapped the reins and got the buggy in motion.

Nitis watched the buggy head off down the road with trickles of dust flying up from the horses' hooves and the wheels. As it went round the corner, Nitis walked to his horse, vaulted on, and rode off to find Geoff and Hugh. When Nitis met up with Geoff and Hugh, he updated them on events.

"Do you think we can risk going to the trial?" Hugh said.

"I think you can," Nitis said. "I would like to. To support Matt and to see Melissa in action. But the townsfolk would not be happy with an Apache being there. They would for sure kill me. I think you should both go, but be careful. Then you can update me on what's happening."

Melissa got the restaurant going for the day and then headed to the sheriff's office. The door was open when she got there. She poked her head around the door, knocking at the same time. "Good morning, sheriff." She said.

"Morning, Melissa. What can I do for you?" The sheriff asked. "Come in. Do you want a cup of coffee? I suppose not. You probably have much better coffee at your diner."

"No, I haven't had a cup of coffee this morning, so I'd welcome a coffee."

———

Chapter 74

Melissa sat while the sheriff organized a cup of coffee. The sheriff placed the cup of coffee in front of her.

"Thanks, sheriff. Now to the matter at hand. I've had a message that Matt has no one to represent him in court and that he would like me to represent him," Melissa said.

"But you're not a lawyer. How can you represent him?" The sheriff asked.

"I realize it seems ridiculous. But if I don't represent him, no one will. It's a question of whether my representing him is better than no one. I figure that it is," Melissa said. "It's true. I know nothing about the law, but I'm sure the judge will cut me some slack and guide me. He'll know that there are no lawyers around here to represent Matt. My ambition is to be a lawyer and provide defense where there is none. That's what our law is about. Everyone is entitled to a defense. The advantage I bring to the party is that everyone knows me and trusts me, and they'll see I'm going up against my father's wishes."

"You make some good points there." The sheriff said. "But is Matt happy to have you as his lawyer?"

"I understand that he is," Melissa said. "Someone got a message to me which came from Matt. I can't disclose who gave me the message. But I think it's a reliable source. Will you talk to Matt and confirm? And if he confirms, then allow me some privacy with my client." Melissa smiled. "I like that, my client bit."

"It does sound good." The sheriff said. "I'll talk to Matt while you finish your coffee." The sheriff rose and walked the few places to the jail cell. He guessed Matt would've been able to hear from the cell what was discussed.

"Hello, Matt." The sheriff said.

"Hi, sheriff. I heard what was going on out there. It's not a big building this, so whatever I do and whatever you do is no secret." Matt smiled. "Yes, my answer is I would like Melissa to represent me. And I did send for her."

"Okay, I'll let Melissa come and talk to you. It'll have to be through the bars. I can't favor you." The sheriff said. "But I'll go and park myself a little way from the jail, close enough to hear if Melissa shouts for help. But far enough so that I won't hear your private conversation."

"Thanks, sheriff," Matt said.

The sheriff walked a few steps back to Melissa. "I guess you heard that."

"Yes, I did, thanks," Melissa said.

"You can go down the passage and talk to Matt. I'll bring you a chair to sit on, and then I'll head outside. I'll be within shouting distance but not within hearing distance of your normal conversation." The sheriff said.

"Thanks, sheriff," Melissa said as she walked down the passage to Matt. The sheriff followed her with the chair and placed it at a safe distance from Matt.

"Melissa, don't move your chair closer. We don't want you where the prisoner can grab you and hold you, hostage." The sheriff said. "Not that I think you would do that, Matt. But I should treat you like any other prisoner."

"Don't worry, sheriff. I know you've got to treat me like any other prisoner, and I'm relaxed with that," Matt said.

"Thanks for coming, Melissa," Matt said. "I wasn't sure whether you would come."

"Well, I was in two minds. But Nitis did a good selling job. I don't know whether it was his flattery or whether he was passing on your flattery. But it worked," Melissa said.

The sheriff had walked out the door. Melissa and Matt waited until they felt he was out of earshot.

"So, important things first," Matt said. "This must be like a normal lawyer-client relationship. We need to agree on fees first. You should charge the normal rate that a lawyer would charge me."

"It should be lower than that," Melissa said. "Because you're not getting a qualified lawyer."

Melissa suggested a rate per hour. Matt said. "That sounds reasonable, but I think we should double it because you're going up against your father. That takes a lot of courage, and I'm sure is not good for your family relationship. The other thing is if you fail, and I hang, you won't get paid. Or I guess you might get paid, but I'm not sure how."

"That seems more than fair to me," Melissa said. "This is going to be a lot of teamwork since I guess neither of us really knows what we're doing. How do you think we go about this?"

"Well, there's a couple of things that need to be investigated that I think will prove my innocence," Matt said. "The first thing is we need to investigate the wounds on Knox's body. I think Bones was paid off. I suspect it was by your father. Don't get mad."

"Don't worry, I have suspicions of my own," Melissa said. "Don't forget, Knox shot Patrick O'Hagan, who I was very fond of."

"I think you should get Knox's body exhumed. I don't know what the law procedures for doing that are, but it needs to be done. And then get Julia to examine the body. She can then testify in court," Matt said. "What you'll find is that there is an entry wound from a bullet which came from the front, which would've been my bullet, and there'll be one from the back which was from someone else who at the moment is unknown. I know what went down. I can tell you the truth without concern. Since you're my lawyer, everything I tell you is privileged. But I'm not worried about that because everything I tell you *is the truth* and will prove my innocence. Having said that, I guess we should have a formal document that confirms that you are representing me as my lawyer. I suggest you draw that up. I presume it can be a commonsense document that says that you are representing me in this case, and we both sign it."

Matt then told Melissa exactly what had happened that morning. He also told her about the message that Johnny Harlow brought him.

"So that leads us to the next thing that you need to investigate. You need to check with Johnny Harlow the whole train of that message," Matt said. "I think you'll find that Johnny was intercepted somewhere and the original note exchanged. I, unfortunately, didn't keep the note that Johnny gave me. But it said......... I need to go to town. The note was from Julia. She'll know what the note or the original note said and be able to testify to that. Once you get the truth from Julia, I think you'll be able to extract exactly what happened from Johnny Harlow. He's probably scared now. But he's only a boy, so you'll have to go gentle on him and get the truth."

"Well, if all that pans out, I think we've got this trial won," Melissa said. "Then I'll be able to ride on the back of this trial for obtaining future customers once I've had the proper training. Is there anything else that I should be investigating?"

"No, I think when you get to the bottom of those two things, as you say, you'll have the trial sewn up, and I'm guessing you'll pick up more information as you go, which will support my case," Matt said. "Do you know what's happening with my ranch? If I survive this, I'm hoping that Hugh and Geoff will have been looking after my ranch."

"I'm afraid my father has put some of his hands on the ranch to look after it. Which is a good thing in some ways, in that, when you come out, it will have been properly looked after," Melissa said.

"Well, I guess that is a good thing. I wonder where Geoff and Hugh are. At least the ranch is registered in my name. I'll be able to kick your father off when I get out," Matt said.

"Well, there's the next problem," Melissa said. "My father went away for a couple of days and came back happy with himself. It seems he's managed to get your ranch registered in his name. I'm not sure how he managed that, but apparently, that is the case."

Matt scowled. "How's he managed that? He must've paid someone off again. He seems to think he's above the law."

"At the moment, that's the least of our worries," Melissa said. "If you hang, the ranch won't be a worry of yours. If we win the case, I'm sure somewhere along the line, we'll prove that my father's title to the ranch has been illegally obtained, and we'll be able to get it overturned. Maybe that'll be my next case, prosecuting whatever clerk registered the ranch in my father's name. I wonder if you can be a prosecutor and the defense attorney but for different clients? I think I'm getting ahead of myself."

Matt smiled. "Maybe. But it's good to dream. And I agree with you. We need to worry about the case first and the ranch second."

"Bye, Matt, I'd better get on. We haven't got much time," Melissa said.

———

Chapter 75

After leaving the jail, Melissa headed to Julia's surgery. As was normal these days, there were three people waiting outside. The door was closed with another patient in with Julia. Melissa sat and waited.

"I hope you're not going to push in." One of the patients said.

"Why has that happened before?" Melissa asked.

"Yes, I was in here the other day, and the sheriff pushed in." The patient said.

"Don't worry, I won't push in. I'll ask Julia to come and visit me at the diner when she's done with her patients." Melissa smiled at the man.

The man grimaced and said nothing further. Melissa guessed he would reserve judgment until he saw what happened. Julia came out behind her patient. "Hello Melissa, are you sick?"

"She was here after me." The patient who complained before said.

"No, I'm not sick. But I need to talk to you in private at some point. Maybe you can come past the diner when you're done with your patients here," Melissa said.

"Okay, I'll do that. I'll probably be finished around lunchtime. And then I'll come to the diner," Julia said.

Once the patients had been dealt with, Julia closed the door of the surgery offices after turning the sign around on the door to say *closed* and wandered up to the diner. She walked into the diner. Melissa's waitress saw her come in and walked over to her. "Can I get you anything, Julia?"

"No thanks, not at the moment. If you could tell Melissa I'm here," Julia said.

Julia sat down at a table next to the window, looking out onto the street, which happened to be furthest from any of the other customers. She figured if they kept their voices down, whatever it was Melissa wanted to talk about would not be heard by other patrons.

Five minutes later, Melissa came and joined her. "Nice to see you're so busy, Julia."

"Yes, I'm getting more and more patients each day. At least I'm proving father wrong and Matt Teeson. Although, I guess it doesn't matter what I prove to Matt Teeson anymore. Looks like he's not going to survive long." Julia frowned and blinked back a couple of tears.

"Well, Matt Teeson is what I've come to talk to you about," Melissa said. "This is going to sound crazy to you, and you might be angry to start with anyway."

"I can't imagine you doing anything that would make me angry." Julia smiled at Melissa.

"Well, I think this is going to be a first, then," Melissa said. "And you'll think I've taken leave of my senses."

Julia raised her eyebrows and stared at Melissa.

"Here goes," Melissa said. "As you know, there are no lawyers in this town, and Matt has no one to represent him in court. He asked me to represent him."

"That's ridiculous. How stupid can he be?" Julia said.

"After giving it a lot of thought, I don't think it's so stupid," Melissa said. "I've agreed to represent him."

Julia frowned and snorted.

"Firstly, he needs someone on the outside to help him," Melissa said. "Secondly, everyone knows me, and if they see me defending him, and particularly the jury, they'll think maybe he is innocent. And they'll wonder even more given that I'm risking going against Papa."

"You've definitely taken leave of your senses," Julia said. "You don't even know that he is innocent. You know nothing about the law, and Papa is going to be furious with you."

"Since when have you worried about Papa being furious? You're always knocking heads with him. I'm sure Matt is innocent. He's given me a few pointers, and once we've established those, you also will know he's innocent. I need your help. Not knowing the law is a problem, but apparently, there's nothing to stop me from representing Matt if he is aware and has signed that he is aware that I'm not a qualified lawyer. Will you help me?" Melissa asked.

Julia frowned at Melissa. "Why did he ask you anyway?"

"You mean instead of you?" Melissa said. "He knows you're already busy as a doctor. He also knows you're never going to want to change from being a doctor to a lawyer. He knew from somewhere that I wanted to be a lawyer." Melissa smiled. "I think that's your biggest concern."

"What's my biggest concern?" Julia glared at Melissa.

"I think you're fond of Matt, and now you're disappointed that he didn't ask you for help," Melissa said.

"Hah, that's a lot of nonsense. He's been a problem to me from the beginning. He had this view that I couldn't be a doctor because I'm a woman. So, I've never been fond of him," Julia said.

Melissa smiled, "you're bad at covering up your feelings for him."

"I've got no feelings for him," Julia said.

"Well, let's change the topic and get back to what's important," Melissa said. "Are you prepared to help Matt?"

"Well, since it's helping you, the answer is yes," Julia said. "I also want to get to the bottom of whether he's innocent or not. You may be right. I possibly have some feelings for him." Julia smiled briefly.

"Shew, thank goodness that part of the discussion is over," Melissa said. "Now, we need to get to the details of what we're going to do. Firstly, we need to talk to the sheriff about how we get permission to exhume Knox's body. It's not going to be a pleasant task, exhuming the body. But I need you to look at the body and identify where the bullet wounds were and came from. According to Matt, he was quicker than Knox, and there'll be one bullet wound from the front, which will be Matt's. Then there will be one from the back, shot by an unknown person with a rifle. Matt thinks the bullets are still in the body. It's possible Bones may have taken them out. If the bullets are there, it will give us even stronger evidence if we can identify one as from Matt's pistol and one from a rifle."

"We'll have to do that without Bones knowing," Julia said. "Otherwise, he's going to block us."

———————

Chapter 76

"When shall we go and talk to the sheriff?" Melissa said. "I'm thinking there's no time like the present."

"Let's get this over and done with," Julia said.

Melissa left a tip on the table for the waitress, as she always did, even though she wasn't paying for the meal since it was out of one pocket and into the other. They walked down the street to the sheriff's office. The sheriff wasn't in.

"I need to go and check whether I have any more patients," Julia said. "Will you wait here for the sheriff and talk to him? Whatever happens, I'll wait at my office and either deal with patients or wait for new patients. Once you've talked to the sheriff, you can come and fetch me."

"That's fine," Melissa said as she leaned against the wall to wait for the sheriff. "I'm going to suggest to the sheriff he puts a bench out here. He's often doing his rounds when people need him. At least then we could sit and wait for him."

Julia walked down the street to her surgery. There were two patients waiting outside. One of them said to her, "we were about to leave. We didn't know whether you were coming back."

"Sorry about that," Julia said. "You make a good point. I'm going to stick something on the door so that I can slip the time I'll be back in. Then people know whether to wait or not."

Julia opened up and let the patients in.

Melissa stood outside the sheriff's office for half an hour. She was thinking of leaving when she saw the sheriff walking down the other side of the street. She waved to him. He waved back and cut across the street toward her.

"Hello Melissa, back again. I guess it's the same matter." The sheriff said as he unlocked the door. "Come in." He offered her coffee, but she turned him down, given she'd already had a cup of coffee at her diner.

Once they were both seated, the sheriff said, "what can I do for you?"

"I've got over one hurdle, which was talking to Julia and getting her on side. She was skeptical at first. In fact, she's probably still skeptical. But she's agreed to help. We need to exhume Knox's body so that Julia can check the wounds. We're not sure that Bones did his job properly, or maybe he was paid off to push a certain line," Melissa said.

"You're busy incurring everyone's wrath." The sheriff said. "Bones is going to be mad at this. But that's the job of a good lawyer. You'll have to get used to it. And I believe you've got the right stuff to be a good lawyer. I'll have to write a notice giving you permission to exhume the body. I don't know what the law is, but I think that should be fine. You can't wait until the judge gets here. You need to build your case now."

"Thanks, sheriff," Melissa said. "Oh, and while I think about it, you need to put a bench outside your office. It's tiring standing out there waiting for you." Melissa smiled.

"For you, Melissa, anything, I'll get a bench put out there. It's a good idea." The sheriff said. "I'll write out the note to say you can exhume the body. I'll then arrange for two men to do the digging and help you exhume the body. The sheriff's office will pay for that. I think I'd better be there when you do it. I'm guessing people won't take too kindly to bodies being exhumed."

"Thanks, sheriff," Melissa said. "When should we do that?"

"Tomorrow morning at 9 o'clock. I'll arrange for the two men today and ask them to be there at 9 o'clock tomorrow. I'll meet you and Julia here at the office at 8:45. Does that sound alright?" The sheriff said.

"That's fine," Melissa said. "I'll go and tell Julia now so that she can put a notice on her door to let patients know, or maybe she'll attend to what patients are there before she comes here. At least she'll have warning."

"Do you think Julia will do the inspection at the graveyard? Or will she want the body taken somewhere?" The sheriff asked.

"I'll ask her," Melissa said. "I'm sure she won't want us to take the smelly body to her surgery. It's been difficult enough to get patients, and that lingering smell will chase them away for a long time."

Melissa wandered down to Julia's surgery. There was no one in reception, but Julia's door was closed. Melissa sat in reception and waited. Ten minutes later, Julia came out, following a patient. She said to Melissa, "I'll be with you shortly."

Julia took the payment from the customer, made a note in the ledger, and gave the customer a receipt. Once he'd gone, she said to Melissa, "how did it go with the sheriff?"

"Good," Melissa said. "He'll give me a signed note saying we can exhume the body and will arrange for two men to dig up the body at nine tomorrow morning. He says we should meet him at his office at a quarter to nine, and he'll come down to the graveyard with us. That'll maybe give you a chance to see your first few patients and put a note on the door as to when you'll be back for any patients that come after that. He did ask where you'd want to look at the body. I said I was sure you didn't want the body to come back to the surgery, but I'd ask you what you want to do."

"Could you ask the sheriff to arrange a flatbed wagon? Then I can do the inspection of the body on the wagon at the grave site, and once done, the two men can rebury the body," Julia said.

"I'll do that," Melissa said. "We'll meet at the sheriff's office tomorrow morning at 8:45."

Melissa turned and headed back to the sheriff's office. The sheriff was missing again. Melissa sighed and leaned against the wall to wait for the sheriff. Twenty minutes later, he came wandering back down the street.

"I'd better hurry up and get that bench put in place." The sheriff said. "I was arranging for the two men to exhume the body."

"No problem, sheriff, you're helping tremendously. I've talked to Julia, and she's happy with that plan. She asks whether you would arrange a flatbed wagon to put the body on next to the grave. She'll inspect the body on the wagon, and then once she's done, it can be reburied," Melissa said.

"I can do that." The sheriff sighed." I'll have to go back to the saloon to find someone who can rent a flatbed wagon to us for a period. I'm sure it won't be a problem."

"Thanks, sheriff," Melissa said. The sheriff turned and wandered back down the street. Melissa went back to her diner.

At supper that evening, George Hamilton said. "You're quiet this evening, girls. Normally you're moaning at me for some perceived sin that I've committed. What's going on?"

There was silence for a moment. Melissa then said. "We're worried about Matt Teeson. We know there's no point in talking to you about that because you've written him off as guilty and want him hung. So, it's better that we keep quiet."

"You're right. It is better that you keep quiet. He's guilty, and he'll hang. This town will be better without him. His ranch will prosper under me," George said. He turned to Jim and continued to talk about other ranch matters with Jim.

The next morning Melissa and Julia met the sheriff at his office at 8:45. "Morning, ladies." The sheriff greeted them. They walked together to the graveyard. They arrived there shortly after nine. The two men who the sheriff had hired to exhume the body were sitting with their backs leaning against a tree. As the three arrived, they stood up. The sheriff directed operations. The men started digging. While they were digging, a man drove up with the flatbed wagon. The sheriff directed him where to place the wagon. It took them half an hour to dig down to the coffin. The two men had their shirts off and were sweating, even though, at this time of day, it wasn't hot. Once they got to the coffin, one of them said to the sheriff. "It's going to be too heavy for us to lift this coffin."

The sheriff looked at Julia and said to the two men. "Take the lid off the coffin and pick the body up and place it on the wagon. You should be able to do that."

"We can't be picking up a dead body." The one man said.

"I told you yesterday what you'd be doing. You knew you'd have to pick up a body out of the coffin. If you want to be paid, you can't change your mind now." The sheriff said.

Amidst much grumbling, the two men removed the lid off the coffin and placed it outside the grave. "This doesn't smell too good." The one man said. Both men pulled their bandannas up around their noses. They mumbled and grumbled more while they lifted the body and placed it on the edge of the grave. They climbed out and then lifted the body onto the flatbed wagon. "We should get a bonus for this." One of them said.

"Yeah, I agree, it's not a pleasant task. I'll add a bit more to what I promised to pay you." The sheriff said.

The men's frowns disappeared. Julia tied a bandanna around her face and over her nose. She placed her doctor's bag on the wagon next to the body and set to work. Melissa and the sheriff stood ten paces off, neither of them wanting to be close to the body. They also made sure they were upwind of the body. Melissa thought, *no wonder I didn't want to become a doctor*. Julia worked for a while on the body. She pulled a bullet out from the one wound and placed it next to her on the wagon. She then asked the men to come and turn the body over. She again worked on the body and dug another bullet out, placing it next to the other one. She had a notebook next to her and described in the notebook which bullet had come from where and what she'd observed in the wound. She then turned and called Melissa and the sheriff over. They reluctantly came over.

"I think it's good to have witnesses," Julia said. She then described the wounds and pointed them out to the sheriff and Melissa and then indicated the bullets. She told the sheriff and Melissa that one was from the back and one was from the front. She pulled the rifle bullet out from the front. The rifle shot had come from the rear of Knox and had poked its way out of the front of Knox's body. Matt's bullet, or what she presumed was Matt's bullet which came from the front, had not quite penetrated out of the back of Knox's body. She'd had to dig for it with a scalpel, but not far.

"Well, that seems to back up Matt's story," Melissa said.

"It does." The sheriff said.

"I think we'll be able to get a lot more evidence than this once we've talked to Bones and persuaded him to testify and once we've talked to Johnny Harlow," Melissa said.

"Are you done?" The sheriff asked Julia.

"Yes, I'm done. The body can be reburied," Julia said.

The sheriff directed the two men to rebury the body. They did so amongst more moans and groans. The sheriff said to Julia and Melissa. "You can be on your way. You don't need to wait here. I'll see that these men finish the job and pay them off. You can get on with whatever else you have to do."

Melissa and Julia thanked the sheriff and walked away from the gravesite. Julia stopped and turned back to thank the two men who'd exhumed Knox's body. Melissa and Julia then carried on.

"What's your next step?" Julia asked.

"I'd like to strike while the iron's hot. Will you come with me to talk to Bones now?" Melissa said.

"I can do that. But what are you going to say to him? He's not going to be cooperative," Julia said.

"We need to spell out what we've done and found and suggest to him that he needs to put things right," Melissa said.

"How's he going to put things' right?" Julia asked.

"He needs to testify in court to what he did and the facts. I'll persuade him that it's in his interest to do so. I'll suggest that I speak to the judge and get the judge to confirm that although there will be some punishment for Bones' actions, the judge will exercise leniency because he has been prepared to testify," Melissa said. "I was thinking along the lines of a sentence whereby Bones must pay money to the town council to better the town. Then at least, he'll be doing some good in making up for his criminal act."

Julia looked skeptical. "I guess we can try."

They had arrived at Bones' shop. They walked in, Bones greeted them with a smile. "Good morning, ladies. What can I do for you this morning?"

"We need a private conversation with you," Melissa said.

"That sounds serious." Bones smiled. "What's this all about?"

"We need to be somewhere private before we talk about this," Melissa said.

Bones looked worried. "We can talk in my office." He pointed the way back to his office behind him and walked toward it. Melissa and Julia followed him.

Bones sat behind the desk, indicating the two chairs in front of the desk for Julia and Melissa. "Let's hear what this top-secret matter is." Bones smiled.

"You examined Knox's body after he was shot," Melissa said.

Melissa watched Bones' expression while she talked. She saw worry in his eyes, he frowned.

"Yes, I did. That coward Matt Teeson shot him in the back." Bones said.

"How carefully did you examine the body?" Melissa asked.

Bones hesitated. "I must admit, I didn't look at it too carefully."

Melissa saw Bones shift in his chair and look away.

"Apparently, you were definite that Knox had been shot in the back," Melissa said

"Yes, I was absolutely sure he'd been shot in the back." Bones said.

"Was there not another shot that had hit Knox?" Melissa said.

Bones was silent for a while. "I didn't notice another shot that had hit him."

"Did you turn the body over and look carefully at both sides?" Melissa asked.

"No, I didn't. It was obvious that he'd been shot in the back. I didn't think it was necessary to carry out any further investigation." Bones said.

"Would you be prepared to testify in court that you never turned the body over and inspected it thoroughly on both sides?" Melissa asked.

Bones hesitated again. "No, I'm not prepared to say anything in court."

"Why is that?" Melissa asked.

"It's more than my life is worth." Bones said. Melissa noticed Bones again shifting in his chair and avoiding eye contact.

"Why is it more than your life is worth?" Melissa asked. "If it's the truth, it shouldn't be a problem."

"I've had sleepless nights over this. I should never have done it." Bones said. "But you're not going to want me to tell the truth in court."

"Why not?" Melissa asked. "My only objective is to defend Matt Teeson. I know he's innocent."

"It'll implicate your father if I tell the truth." Bones said.

"I suspected it would," Melissa said. She saw Julia out of the corner of her eye frowning at her.

"Don't look at me like that, Julia. Are you surprised that Papa is involved?" Melissa said.

"I can't believe Papa would be involved in such a thing. Knox was his favorite employee," Julia said.

"So, tell us the true story," Melissa said to Bones.

"I'm not prepared to." Bones said. "I might end up in trouble if I tell the truth, firstly with the law and secondly with your father."

"Well, from what you said so far, I think you're already too far down the line," Melissa said. "Once it's out in the open, it'll be pointless for my father to do anything to you. Everyone will know that it's him if something happens to you. What I'm prepared to do is talk to the judge and ask that he treats you leniently. I don't think he can deal with you in that court case. But maybe he and the sheriff would be happy to come to an agreement with you to deal with that out-of-court. Would you be prepared to testify on that basis?"

Bones furrowed his brow. After a minute, he replied. "I would be prepared to do that. But you need to talk to the judge beforehand without telling him what I would testify. Before I say anymore, I need confirmation that the judge would be prepared to deal with it in the way you suggest."

"All right, I'll talk to the judge, and if he agrees, I'll come back to you, and you can confirm the agreement before the trial. I'll see if I can get something in writing from the judge that you and he can sign," Melissa said.

"Thank you. As I said before, I never should've done it, and I've had sleepless nights over it. Maybe to some degree, I can redeem myself in this way." Bones said.

"The judge arrives tomorrow. The trial is only after the weekend, so I've got a few days to talk to him. I'll try and talk to him tomorrow. We'll leave you be now," Melissa said.

———

Chapter 77

"Let's get some lunch. After lunch, we can tackle Johnny Harlow," Melissa said.

"Good idea," Julia said.

Over lunch at Melissa's diner, they discussed the chances of success in defending Matt.

"Well, at least I now know Matt is innocent," Melissa said. "It's a lot easier to defend him now that I know he's innocent. Bones' testimony will certainly add weight to the defense. I'm sure we'll be able to get more evidence in support of Matt from Johnny Harlow. I'm feeling positive about this. I'll feel good if I win my first case." Melissa smiled.

After lunch, Melissa and Julia left the restaurant in search of Johnny Harlow. He didn't take much finding. He was sitting on one of the sidewalks whittling a piece of wood. They walked up to Johnny. He stood up. "Good afternoon, Mrs." he touched his hand to his hat.

"What are you whittling there, Johnny? Last time I saw you, you were making a gun," Julia said.

"I'm whittling a statue of my horse." Johnny held the piece of wood forward for them to admire his handiwork.

"That's excellent, Johnny," Julia said as she took it from him and inspected it. She handed it back to him. "We need to talk to you, Johnny." Julia detected a look of worry in his eyes.

"What about Miss Julia?" Johnny asked.

"That message I gave you the other day to deliver to Matt Teeson. You said you lost it. Is that true?" Julia said.

Johnny shifted from foot to foot and looked down at the ground. "Yes, Miss Julia."

"I don't think you did," Julia said. "I'm not going to be angry with you because I know things happen. But it's important that you tell me the truth. If you continue to not tell me the truth, then I'll be angry."

Tears filled Johnny's eyes. "On the way out to the ranch, one of your father's hands stopped me and said I must deliver the note that he gave me. He took the note that you gave to me. He said you changed your mind. And since he worked for your father, I thought it would be fine. Was I wrong to do that?"

"I can understand why you did that, Johnny. It's natural for you to trust adults, especially since you knew he worked for my father. But you should've at least told me what happened. For future, always remember to tell whoever it is you're doing the work for if something changes or the work is not carried out as that person asked," Julia said.

"Johnny, we're going to need you to testify in court as to what happened," Julia said.

"I'm scared I won't be able to do that. Will I go to jail?" Johnny asked, a couple of tears dripping down his cheeks.

"No, Johnny, you won't go to jail. All you must do is tell the truth as to exactly what happened," Julia said. "Tell me exactly what happened. Think of it as practice for telling what happened in court."

"All right, Miss Julia," Johnny said. "You gave me money to deliver a note to Mr. Teeson. I got my horse, and I started riding out to Mr. Teeson's ranch to deliver the message. I'd just left town when your father's hand galloped up behind me and stopped me. He said you changed your mind about the message and needed me to deliver a new message. He handed me the new message and took the old message. I then delivered the new message to Mr. Teeson."

"Can you describe that man to me?" Julia said.

"Yes, I can. I've seen him around town often, so I know exactly what he looks like." Johnny said.

"Describe him to me, please, Johnny. I'll also know him. I would've seen him on the ranch," Julia said.

Johnny described the man to Julia. "I know exactly who he is," Julia said. "Did you read the message that the man gave to you?"

"No, I didn't," Johnny said. "I never read messages that people give to me to give to other people."

"That's fine. You've been a big help, Johnny," Julia said.

"Why will I have to testify in court?" Johnny asked.

"Because Mr. Teeson has been accused of murdering Mr. Knox and shooting him in the back. I had wanted Mr. Teeson to come to town and meet me. But the note that you were given to give to him changed that. It said he should meet me in the alley behind the saloon at six in the morning. That was not where I wanted to meet Mr. Teeson. It was a setup. Mr. Knox met him there, and there was a gunfight. Mr. Teeson managed to shoot Mr. Knox, but it wasn't Mr. Teeson's shot that killed Knox. It was a fair gunfight. They both had an equal chance. They were facing each other. But someone else had been set up to hide in the alley and shoot Mr. Knox from behind with a rifle, and then the blame would be put on Mr. Teeson for shooting Mr. Knox in the back. So, the blame has been put on Mr. Teeson, and he was arrested and is now in jail. If they prove he's guilty, he'll hang. But we all know he's not guilty. We've got a lot of evidence to show that he's not guilty. Your evidence will help with that as well by showing that someone else set it up for him to meet Mr. Knox in the alley," Julia said. "You can see how important it is for you to testify honestly in court. It'll save an innocent man from being hung."

Johnny looked at Julia wide-eyed. "When will I have to testify in court?" He asked.

Julia smiled at him. "You'll be able to get it over and done with quickly. It'll be in the next day or two. I'll let you know. Make sure you don't go missing."

"I promise I won't go missing," Johnny said.

"Thinking about that," Julia said. "You better not tell anyone that you're going to testify or that we've had this discussion."

Johnny's eyes grew wider. "I won't tell anyone, Miss Julia. Do you think someone might kill me because they think I'm going to testify?"

Julia hesitated. "They might, Johnny. The stakes in this are high. Someone wants Matt Teeson to hang. And once the truth is known, whoever that person is, is going to be in big trouble," Julia said. "I'll let you know, Johnny. Bye."

Melissa and Julia walked away from Johnny. "I need to go back to my surgery and check there are no more patients. But that discussion with Johnny opened my mind to some not so nice possibilities," Julia said.

"The one was that someone might want to have Johnny killed to protect themselves. And then it dawned on me that, that someone might be my father. And when I said that person was going to be in big trouble, I nearly said might hang. Which is a possibility." Julia said, staring at Melissa.

"Yes, you're right," Melissa said. "Whatever Papa has done wrong, I don't want him to hang. I'm going to see if I can make some sort of a deal with the judge."

"I hope you'll be able to make a deal that saves Papa from being hung," Julia said.

"I'll leave you now to attend to your patients," Melissa said. "I need to go and see Matt."

Melissa walked down to the jail. She greeted the sheriff. "Can I see my client?" Melissa smiled at the sheriff.

"Yes, sure. Same as last time. You need to stay out of reach of him. I'll give you some privacy as well." The sheriff said. "I'll bring a chair for you to sit on."

"Thanks, sheriff," Melissa said.

Melissa walked to the cell and sat on the chair the sheriff had placed for her. "Hello Matt, how're you doing?"

"Not too bad, I guess, under the circumstances," Matt said. "More importantly, how's my lawyer doing? Are you making progress building my case?"

"That's why I came to see you. I'm making excellent progress," Melissa said. "I'm feeling confident that I'll be able to get you released as an innocent man."

"That sounds good. Tell me about what you've found so far?" Matt said.

"We've dug up Knox's body and confirmed your story. Julia had a look at the body and identified the two bullet holes and confirmed that one was from the front and the rifle shot was from the back," Melissa said.

"How's Julia?" Matt asked. "Does she still think I'm guilty? I notice she hasn't been to see me," Matt said.

"No, she doesn't think you're guilty anymore. There's too much evidence against you being guilty for even her to believe it. She's still finding it difficult to get her head around the fact that Papa might be guilty," Melissa said.

Matt grunted.

"We had a talk to Bones. He's feeling bad about his behavior. He was not honest in his review of the body, and he admits that now. He's willing to testify in court to that effect. Provided I can get him some sort of lenient deal from the judge," Melissa said. "I'm not sure how well I'll go with that."

"That sounds positive," Matt said.

"We also had a talk to little Johnny Harlow," Melissa said. "He confirms that one of Papa's hands swapped out the note. He said he thought it would be fine because the man said Julia had changed her mind about what was in the note and had changed the note. And Johnny knew that the man worked for Papa."

"All that's good news," Matt said. "That whole part of the story was puzzling me. It almost seemed to me that Julia had set me up. And I couldn't think why she would do that."

"So far, so good," Melissa said. "I've still got a couple more things to do that I think will help you. We still need to find who fired the rifle shot. My father is going to have to testify to that. I don't think that's going to happen because that then implicates him. Even though he may be involved, I wouldn't want him to hang."

"Well, I'm afraid I've got no time for your father because of our battles. He's arrogant and wants to own everything. He doesn't know when to stop. With him, it's never enough. But I understand how you and Julia feel about it. Blood is thicker than water for everyone. So, I sympathize with you, and I wouldn't want him to hang either. I don't feel sorry for Knox. He was a cold-blooded killer," Matt said.

"So, what else have you got to do?" Matt asked.

"I want to question Jim Davies, my father's foreman. He must see who comes and goes at the ranch. One of the things I want to do is confirm the circumstances of Patrick's death and who was responsible for having Patrick killed. I was fond of Patrick, and I suspect with more time, would've loved him," Melissa said. "Depending on what happens there, I may have to question my father."

"You make an excellent lawyer," Matt said. "You're doing a fantastic job on my case. So far, you've exceeded my expectations."

"Is there anything else you think I should be doing?" Melissa smiled.

"No, I think you've got it all covered," Matt said.

"Bye, Matt, hang in there. Let me go and do the rest of my tasks," Melissa said. She thought. *I guess that wording wasn't appropriate.*

"Bye Melissa, thanks for all you're doing. I'm feeling a hundred times better than I was a short while ago. When I was put in jail, I was certain it would end in my hanging," Matt said. "Now I'm confident I'll soon be a free man."

Melissa stepped forward and squeezed his hand. "The sheriff said I mustn't get within touching distance of you." Melissa smiled at him. "Because you're a dangerous criminal."

Matt squeezed her hand back. "I'm pleased you've got the confidence in me to ignore the sheriff's opinion," Matt said.

"The sheriff doesn't believe you're guilty," Melissa said. "But he has to treat all people the same. He doesn't want to be seen to be showing favor."

———

Chapter 78

Melissa headed back to her diner and carried on working there until it was time to close. She then headed home. She joined her father, Jim, Amy, and Julia, for supper. The conversation was stilted and consisted mainly of George Hamilton discussing the ranch with Jim. Melissa felt her father constantly looking at her. She wasn't sure whether it was her imagination or whether he was looking at her suspiciously. She was deep in thought, wondering how she was going to get Jim alone to discuss what he might know that would impact the case. Toward the end of the meal, she hit upon a plan.

"Jim, won't you have a look at my horse's bridle tomorrow? It seems to be broken," Melissa said.

"Sure will," Jim said.

"What time are you going to have a look at it tomorrow? I'd like to be there when you have a look at it and show you what I mean. I need to get to the diner early in the morning," Melissa said.

"Is 7 o'clock tomorrow morning soon enough?" Jim asked.

"Yeah, seven's fine," Melissa said. She watched Jim head off to her father's study for their normal discussion and brandy and cigars. Once the door closed, she headed out to the stables. On the way across, she looked around to make sure no one was watching. All seemed quiet. When she got to the stable, she lit a lamp near where she hung her bridle. She took it off the hook and inspected it. She placed it back on the hook and went to where all the tools were kept. She rummaged around and found a file for the horses' hooves. She went back to the bridle. Then it dawned on her that she was being silly going through all this subterfuge because when Jim came to look at it, she would then start asking him what he'd seen shortly before Patrick had been shot. She realized that he would then see through the ruse of damaging the bridle and would be unimpressed with her subterfuge. She hung the bridle back on its hook, extinguished the lamp, and headed back to the house. As she reached the porch, she hesitated and checked no one was around and then headed to her room.

The next morning, she met Jim at the stables. She'd made sure she was there a few minutes before him. When Jim arrived, Melissa said. "Morning Jim, thanks for coming. I'm sorry I had to trick you into coming here to get you alone. I need to ask you some questions, but I didn't want anyone else around. There's nothing wrong with the bridle."

Jim frowned. "I can't imagine what would be so secret that you'd have to trick me into meeting."

"You'll understand," Melissa said. "You're aware, I'm sure, that I was fond of Patrick O'Hagan. His death shouldn't go unpunished. I want to find out who was responsible."

Jim's frown deepened. "I had nothing to do with Patrick O'Hagan's death," Jim said.

"I'm reasonably sure you didn't," Melissa said. "I've known you a long time. I can't imagine you would have had anything to do with it. But you see the comings and goings on the ranch, and I know you always make sure you know what's going on. The day Patrick was killed or the day before, or somewhere around that time, did you hear anything which gave you an inkling that someone might kill Patrick?"

Jim said nothing. He scraped his foot on the ground, looking down at where he was scraping his foot.

"So, you do know something," Melissa said. "I'm guessing it has something to do with my father. You need to tell me. You're going to be sucked into these things going forward in the future, and you won't be able to get out of them. You'll end up being as guilty as my father. I know you're a better man than that."

435

"If I tell you anything, what do you think that'll mean for me?" Jim asked.

"I don't know," Melissa said. "But I know things aren't going to continue as they are. People know that Matt Teeson did not shoot Knox in the back. Things are going to come out that implicate other people. I suggest you choose sides now."

"Are you saying that you're going up against your father?" Jim said. "That's brave or foolhardy."

"Brave, yes, foolhardy no," Melissa said. "The truth is going to come out one way or another, and I don't think my father is going to look good. I suggest that you choose sides now. I know in your heart you're a good man. You've been loyal to my father all these years, but that's because you're an honest, loyal person. I don't think it sits well with you doing bad things."

"What do you want from me?" Jim said.

"I want to know what you know about Patrick's death and about the shooting of Knox," Melissa said. "You see the comings and goings here and most things that go on. I don't believe you're always part of everything. But I know that you know pretty much everything that goes on."

Jim sighed. "I'll tell you what I know. But before I do that, I want you to guarantee that you won't tell George that I told you what I'm going to tell you. Or anyone else."

"I can't guarantee that," Melissa said. "I may want you to testify in court."

"I'm not prepared to do that," Jim said. "It'll be the end of my job at a minimum, but, more likely, your father will have me killed."

"You think you're going to be able to survive forever with the sort of things that go on. I think after this court case, my father won't have any power. As I said, you need to choose sides now. And I think you should choose the side of good," Melissa said.

Jim continued to look at the ground, frowning. Melissa said nothing. She watched him. After five minutes, he said. "Okay, I'll tell you what I know. I'm probably going to regret this. First, I'll talk about what I know about Patrick's death. A couple of days before his death, in fact, shortly after Patrick came to talk to you and ask you to dinner, I went to the bunkhouse with your father because there was an altercation between Adam Carter and Knox. You probably remember we were called to the bunkhouse then. After we settled them down, your father turned back to talk to Knox again. I asked him if he wanted me to come with him. He said no, it wasn't necessary. But you're right, I like to know what's going on. I followed your father without him knowing and overheard the conversation between your father and Knox." Jim stopped.

"Go on, please don't stop there," Melissa said.

Jim sighed. "Your father told Knox to deal with Patrick. He didn't say anything about killing him, but I gathered that was the unspoken message between him and Knox. Your father just said *you know what I mean,* to Knox. Knox said it would be a pleasure. He never liked Patrick."

Melissa's eyes watered, tears fell down her cheeks. "At one time, I would've never believed that of my father, but what he did, ordered for Patrick, is despicable. I promise you, Jim, you've chosen to do the right thing and picked the right side," Melissa said.

"I guess Knox purposely braced Patrick, and he knew he was quicker than Patrick, so he'd be quite safe," Melissa said.

"I heard via the grapevine that Patrick asked if he could take the loop off his Colt to give him a fighting chance. Knox said he could. As Patrick went to take the loop off his gun, Knox drew and killed him. He then went up to Patrick and unhooked the loop. When the sheriff arrived, the loop was off, and it looked like it'd been a fair fight. The only witnesses were two of your father's hands. They toed the party line. But you know what these hands are like. They can't keep their mouths shut." Jim said.

"Knox got his just desserts then," Melissa said. "But there's not enough evidence there, I guess, to back up my father

438

being part of it. That sounds like I'm defending him, but I'm not. I don't think a jury would find that sufficient evidence to convict him of anything. What do you think?"

"No, I don't think so," Jim said.

"What do you know about who shot Knox in the back?" Melissa asked.

"I don't know anything concrete about that. Again, just rumor. As I mentioned before, Knox and Adam Carter had an altercation that night we went down to the bunkhouse." Jim said. "Your father forced them to apologize to each other. Ever since then, Adam hated Knox, and in my mind, at some point in time, he was going to get his own back on Knox. The rumor has it that your father set up for Matt to meet Julia in the alley behind the saloon and sent Knox down there. Knox was happy to go down there and meet Matt with the intention of gunning him down. Knox was always super confident in his abilities and had no doubt he could beat Matt in a gunfight. He thought the previous time he came up against Matt was luck on Matt's part. But it seems Matt was much quicker and more accurate than Knox in a straight-out gunfight. Unbeknown to Knox, though, your father was getting worried about Knox. He was concerned that one day Knox would turn on him. He arranged for Adam to go down there and take Knox out. Adam was only too happy to do that because of his hatred for Knox. That's only rumor, though. I don't know for fact."

"It would be useful if we could somehow get Adam Carter to testify to that at the trial of Matt Teeson," Melissa said.

"There's not a chance he would do that," Jim said. "That would mean he would be testifying against himself and would for sure hang for shooting Knox in the back. Also, he'd be a pariah in this territory."

"I think I may have a way of doing that. I may need your help," Melissa said. "But I'll let you know. I appreciate you telling me this, Jim. You've done the right thing."

"I think it's the right thing to do. But I'm not sure I've done the right thing. If you know what I mean." Jim said.

"I do know what you mean," Melissa said.

"I'm going to head off to town now with my broken bridle." Melissa smiled.

She caught her horse and hitched it up to the buggy. She headed into town deep in thought. She went straight to the restaurant and checked everything was working as it should. Rose, her hard-working waitress, had opened up and got everything going. The judge was due in town this morning. Melissa would see the stagecoach pass the window of the diner. She guessed it was likely the judge would come to the diner for a meal as everyone recommended her diner as the only place to get a decent meal in town. Once everything was to her satisfaction, she headed off to have another discussion with Matt. She arrived at the sheriff's office, and he set her up as normal to discuss the case with Matt.

"I've made some more progress on your case Matt. But I'm not sure how I'm going to make use of it," Melissa said. "Jim Davies says that he was reasonably sure Knox shot Patrick O'Hagan on instructions from my father. But it was never an outright instruction. Jim says it was implied. At the moment, Jim is not happy about testifying to this."

"It doesn't surprise me at all," Matt said. "And it doesn't bring Patrick back. He was a big loss to this world. I think you and he would've had a great future together."

"I think so," Melissa said. "I then asked Jim if he knew anything about who might have shot Knox in the back. Again, he says he doesn't know for sure, but he picked up through rumor that it was probably Adam Carter. He thinks my father was worried Knox would turn on him one day. He was probably right. So, my father was the one who arranged the note for you to meet Knox in the alley. But then he also arranged for Adam Carter to be there and take Knox out. He thought he'd kill two birds with one stone, get rid of Knox, and have you hang for the killing of Knox."

"I'm surprised Adam Carter was prepared to do that. Although I don't know him well," Matt said.

"The day that my father implied to Knox that he should take Patrick out, my father and Jim had gone to the bunkhouse to sort out an altercation between Adam Carter and Knox. My father forced Adam to apologize to Knox, and he's hated Knox ever since that day. Jim always had the feeling that Adam was biding his time to get his own back on Knox," Melissa said.

"What I want to talk to you about is how we get all this testimony into the trial," Melissa said.

"That's going to be difficult," Matt said.

"Well, maybe not. I have an idea," Melissa said.

"You're full of ideas. I'm confident in my lawyer." Matt smiled. "What's your idea?"

"I'm going to go and see the judge today. But I want to discuss it with you first before I talk to the judge," Melissa said. "I want to lay out the full story to him and see if he can guarantee lesser sentences for getting the various people to testify."

"It sounds like a good idea," Matt said. "But I don't think you can talk to the judge. He's got to be independent. I think we need to talk to the prosecutor. The problem is all he wants is a conviction of me. It'll look good on his record."

Melissa looked disappointed. "I think you're right. I thought I had a brilliant idea, but now I'm not sure what I should do."

"Well, maybe we can still get the prosecutor to agree to recommend lesser sentences," Matt said. "We need to convince him that he's going to lose the case, and then he'll prosecute the other cases but go for lesser sentences. Then he can be sure of more wins than just one."

"Now, who's the clever lawyer?" Melissa said. "That sounds like a good idea. I was thinking of talking to the judge, which will now be the prosecutor, and asking for various sentences for those who are going to testify. For Adam Carter, if he's ever convicted of the shooting of Knox in the back, he would be hung. So, I was going to ask for a five-year jail sentence for him. With regards to my father, he must give up his ranch. That could be a problem because I'm guessing the most logical people to give the ranch to would be his family, and that maybe wouldn't be much of a punishment. We need to think about that a bit more. Maybe since he was trying to take your ranch away and grow his empire, then he should give the ranch up to you."

"Well, from my point of view, that sounds like a fantastic idea. But maybe it should be given to the town council to run, and the profits from the ranch go to the town. I would also like the Apache to get some benefit from it.

"How so and why?" Melissa said. "They've been nothing but trouble."

"I agree, they have been trouble," Matt said. "But we whites have forced it upon them. They've been hunting these grounds and traveling around them for years. Then we come along and take over and force them out. What should we expect?"

"I guess you have a point," Melissa said.

"I think we can live in peace with them. If we let them carry on the lifestyle as before. My idea is to let them hunt on our ranches but only the wild game that is there and only so much as they need for living," Matt said.

"That sounds fine. But do you think the prosecutor will go for that? I'm not sure the town council will be happy," Melissa said.

"I suspect the prosecutor won't care that much. So, if we can make a deal with him, then the town council will have to go along with it. And they'll be happy anyway because they're still getting the profits from the ranch," Matt said. "Besides, the town will be much better off living in peace with the Apache than constantly fighting them. What about Bones?"

"I think Bones' offense is much lesser than the rest of them. My suggestion was that we request that he pays money into the town council for use for the council to improve the town," Melissa said. "Then, at least he's punished in some way, and the punishment benefits the town. Johnny Harlow is just a little boy. I don't think anyone's going to want to punish him. He's happy to testify. Well, maybe not happy, but he will testify. He's repentant of what he did. All he did was trust adults. It's a good lesson to learn early in life, not to be too trusting."

"Sounds like you've got it all worked out," Matt said.

"It's lucky I spoke to you," Melissa said. "I might've messed the whole thing up by talking to the judge. I'll try and see the prosecutor this morning and then come by later and let you know how it went."

"Thanks, Melissa. I hope this is going to be a good start to a long and successful career for you," Matt said. "Particularly since it'll save my neck." Matt smiled at Melissa.

Melissa went out of the jail and thanked the sheriff for allowing her to see Matt.

"How are you going with your defense?" The sheriff asked.

"Going well, I think." Melissa smiled at him. "I'll talk to the prosecutor when he arrives and see if I can make a deal with him."

"Good luck with that." The sheriff said.

Melissa went back to her diner and carried on working, keeping an eye out for the stagecoach. She saw the stagecoach coming at about 11 o'clock. She decided to wait and see whether the prosecutor and the judge might come into her restaurant for lunch. That would save her from having to approach them at a time that maybe wasn't convenient for them.

At about 12:45, the judge walked in. Melissa went up to him. "Good afternoon, judge. I'm Melissa Hamilton. I own this diner. I hope you'll enjoy your meal here."

"I've been told it's the best place in town to get a meal." The judge said.

"You've been told correctly. I'd like a word with you about the case you're coming to try, if that's all right with you," Melissa said. "Can I sit and have a cup of coffee with you while you order your lunch?"

"I think it would be better if the prosecutor is here with us if you're going to talk about the case." The judge said. "He's also going to come here for lunch. He'll have lunch separately from me. But we can have a conference before having lunch."

"Okay, I'll wait until he joins you. I'll arrange a cup of coffee in the meantime. Here's a menu," Melissa said.

Melissa left the judge in peace while he studied the menu, and she waited for the prosecutor. She saw the prosecutor come in. He sat at the table away from the judge. She saw the judge get up and walk across to the prosecutor and sit down with the prosecutor. They had a discussion, and then the judge waved Melissa across. Melissa walked across and sat down.

"I've explained to Mr. Meyerowitz our earlier discussion, so you can go ahead with your question." The judge said.

Melissa introduced herself to the prosecutor. She then said, "I want to talk to the judge about me being the defense attorney. The problem is I'm not a qualified lawyer. In fact, I know nothing about the law."

"That does sound like a problem." The judge said.

"Yes, that's why I wanted to speak to you. To confirm that I could act as the defendant's lawyer," Melissa said. "As you probably know, there are no lawyers in this town. My ambition is to one day be a lawyer, but so far, I've had no training. I think this man deserves whatever defense he can get. I understand that if it's declared to the defendant that the person is not a trained lawyer, and he still accepts them as his defense, then that's all right. Is my understanding correct?"

"Your understanding is correct." The judge said. "But I need to be happy that you're competent to defend him."

"That makes sense. But I don't know how you're going to judge that. Also, some defense is probably better than none, don't you think?" Melissa said.

"You have a point there." The judge said. "You seem like a bright young lady. It's going to be difficult for you to become a lawyer. It's unusual for women to be lawyers."

"I know it's a disadvantage being a woman," Melissa said. "My sister is a doctor. It took a long time for her to get patients in this town. It was only when people started talking about how good she was that she got more and more patients. The first patients were because there were no other doctors in town, and they were desperate. So maybe it'll work the same for me as a lawyer. I think this town is going to grow."

"I see no problem then with you being the defendant's lawyer." The judge said. "As you say, it's better than no defense at all." The prosecutor nodded in agreement. Melissa thought she saw a smug expression cross the prosecutor's face.

"Now that that's settled, I'll let you get on with your lunch, judge," Melissa said. She turned to the prosecutor. "Mr.

Meyerowitz, I'd like to see you after lunch and discuss a deal. Maybe we can talk over coffee once you finish your lunch."

"There's going to be no deal on this." The prosecutor said.

"I think we should have a discussion first before you decide that," Melissa said.

"All right, once I've finished my lunch, we can have coffee and see what you want to talk about." The prosecutor said.

When Melissa saw the prosecutor had finished his lunch and was ordering coffee from the waitress, she wandered across. "Is now a good time to talk?" Melissa asked.

"Yes, we can talk now." The prosecutor said. Melissa ordered a cup of coffee for herself from the waitress.

"What do you want to talk about? From what I hear, this case is a certainty." The prosecutor said.

"That's why I want to talk to you," Melissa said. "I think it is a certainty. But the certainty is that Matt Teeson will be proven innocent. And I'd like to save you going down that route and losing a case. Him, being proved innocent won't be because of my brilliance either."

The Prosecutor raised his eyebrows. "You sound confident, which is contrary to what I heard."

"I first need to give you some background to this town and the area," Melissa said. "My father is George Hamilton. He's the biggest rancher in the area. But being the biggest rancher in the area is not good enough for him. He wants to own all the ranches. The man who was shot in the back was an employee of his, which you probably know. He was hired specifically for his gun skills." Melissa went on to explain what happened to Patrick O'Hagan and what happened to Knox. She then said. "I may be being naïve here, I'm giving you my whole case, but I think once you see the whole case, you'll realize that it's better if you don't have a trial." She went on to explain the exhumation of Knox's body and Julia's conclusions. She explained about Johnny Harlow and Bones. "I can bring forward two other people who will be able to back my case. But this is where I need your cooperation. I also need your cooperation regarding Bones. The man who shot Knox in the back is a man named Adam Carter." She went on to explain Adam's background and his dislike of Knox. "So, what I'd like from you is for you to confirm a lesser sentence for Adam Carter in repayment for his testimony. If he was proven guilty in court, he would no doubt hang. Knox was a bad person and was going to get shot by someone at some point. So, what I'm suggesting is to wrap this whole thing up in order to get Adam Carter's testimony. You agreed to a five-year prison sentence for him instead of hanging. It sounds lenient, but I think he can reform. So far, what's your view?"

"I'm becoming inclined to your point of view." The prosecutor said. "But go on."

"As to Bones. I suggest that he pays money to the town council which they can use to make the town a better place. Bones seems to be repentant of what he did. Which was giving false information when he examined the body of Knox," Melissa said. She looked at the prosecutor. He was nodding as she spoke. "As to my father. That's a difficult one. I obviously know him well. He's arrogant and might not admit to anything. My suggestion there is, if we can get him to admit to his part in all of this, that he gives up the ranch to be run by the town Council and the profits from the ranch to go into the town. One of the conditions to that, which I would like, is that the Apache in the area are able to hunt on the ranch for their own food."

"Why do you care about the Apache? They're just savages." The prosecutor said.

"I think the town would be better off living in peace with the Apache. My sister, Julia, has tended to their sick from time to time and got to know them. I think they could easily live in peace with the town if we give them this concession. Given that they have been hunting in this area for years and living off the land long before we came," Melissa said. "We also must banish my father from New Mexico because if he lived

451

in the area, I'm sure he'd go back to his old ways quickly. What's your conclusion on all of this?"

"There's a lot to think about. I'd like to spend the rest of today and some of tomorrow thinking about it." The prosecutor said. "In the meantime, I'll talk to the judge and tell him we've got some things to consider and that possibly it won't be necessary to have a trial. And would he indulge us by waiting a couple of days before commencing the trial? I've dealt with him a lot before. He's a reasonable man. I think he'll agree. I'll come and have breakfast here tomorrow morning and let you know if I've made up my mind by then. If not, I'll set a time to meet with you to confirm what I've decided."

"Thank you," Melissa said. "I look forward to meeting with you tomorrow." Melissa took the last mouthful of her coffee, got up, and excused herself. She left the diner and went back to the jail. She updated Matt on how far she was and said she'd let him know progress sometime tomorrow.

Supper that evening was the same as the previous night. Melissa felt her father eyeing her from time to time. She still wasn't sure whether it was her imagination or not. She realized it wasn't when he said. "I'm told you're going to defend Matt Teeson. That's a crazy idea, and I forbid it. For a lot of reasons."

"For what reasons? I'm going to do it anyway," Melissa said.

"Firstly, you're not a trained lawyer. Secondly, you're a woman, and thirdly, I forbid it," George said.

"I've already cleared it with the judge and the prosecutor. As long as Matt has confirmed, which he has, that he understands I'm not a qualified lawyer, then it's fine. It's better than no representation," Melissa said.

"Having a woman represent him is worse for him than having no representation," George said.

"That's what I'd expect from you," Melissa said. She could see out of the corner of her eye Julia smiling while she ate her supper.

"I can't imagine what your case will be," George said. "Matt Teeson is guilty and must hang."

"You know that's not true. You know he's innocent. You want to railroad this through," Melissa said.

"What do you know that I don't know?" George said.

"It's more like, I know everything that you know. That's the problem for the case," Melissa said.

"What do you mean?" George said, thumping his fist on the table.

"I don't want to discuss the case anymore at this point in time," Melissa said. "I suggest you carry on talking about ranch matters with Jim, which is normally what you do at supper."

Melissa saw George's face was flushed and his teeth gritted. He ate in silence, frowning while he ate. Eventually, his face relaxed, and he started talking about ranch matters with Jim. Melissa let a breath out, careful not to make any noise as she did so. It looked like she'd weathered that storm.

The next morning, the routine was as always. By 8 o'clock, Melissa was anxious. She hadn't seen the prosecutor. The judge was in eating breakfast at the diner. She wished him good morning. He said to her. "They were right. This is the best place to have a meal in town. If you're as good a lawyer as you are at running this diner, then the defendant has made an excellent choice in having you represent him."

"Thank you, judge, that's much appreciated coming from you," Melissa said. She carried on with the work in the restaurant, glancing up from time to time, hoping to see the prosecutor. At 9:30, she saw him walk in.

She walked over to his table. "Good morning Mr. Meyerowitz. Have you decided what you're going to do yet?" Melissa asked.

"I have decided. I hate losing cases. This looks like one I'll lose. I'm going to go along with your suggestions. I'll have to have a discussion with the judge. If he agrees, then we'll have to get written statements from the various people and a signed waiver of their rights. Then the judge can rule on their sentences." The prosecutor said.

"When do you think we'll know his ruling?" Melissa asked.

"I'll talk to him today. In fact, I'll see if I can have coffee with him after I finish my breakfast. He makes decisions quickly. So, I'm sure we'll know which way he's going before the end of today." The prosecutor said.

Melissa exhaled. "That'll be good. Will you let me know? I'll be here most of the day."

"Yes, I'll find you and let you know." The prosecutor said.

Melissa left the judge and the prosecutor in peace after that. She watched the prosecutor finish his breakfast and then walk across to the judge's table and greet him. A brief conversation ensued, and the prosecutor sat down at the judge's table. The waitress checked whether they needed more coffee. They both nodded. Melissa carried on with the work in the kitchen. From time to time, she'd poke her head out and see what was going on with the judge and the prosecutor. An hour later, they paid their bills and left together. Melissa worried. She'd hoped the prosecutor would summon her to their table and tell her they were happy with her suggestions. Once the judge and the prosecutor left, Melissa headed off down to the jail and updated Matt with the promise that she'd be back as soon as the prosecutor let her know his final decision. She updated the sheriff as well.

The judge and the prosecutor came in for lunch and sat at different tables. Melissa resisted the temptation to go across to the prosecutor and harass him for an answer. She didn't want to irritate him and get a negative response.

The waitress came into the kitchen and said to Melissa. "The prosecutor would like you to have lunch with him."

Melissa smiled at the waitress. "Thanks." She walked across to the prosecutor's table. "I believe you want to have lunch with me," Melissa said.

"Yes, I do. I've come to a conclusion. I'd like to finalize it with you and then, after that, finalize it with the judge and leave him to make his ruling." The prosecutor said.

The prosecutor read through the menu, saying nothing further. Melissa didn't need to read the menu. The prosecutor looked up for the waitress, who came across as soon as he looked up. He placed his order, and Melissa then placed her order. Once the waitress had gone, the prosecutor said, "we can start our discussion now. There's not much to discuss. I'm in agreement with your suggestions and have already bounced them off the judge, and he's in agreement. But he says he'll only make a ruling once I've discussed it with you, and he's had more time to apply his mind."

"Thank you, that's fantastic news," Melissa said. The prosecutor confirmed with her their previous discussion. He made notes as they talked and agreed. They finished confirming everything as their meals arrived. Melissa no longer felt hungry, but she forced the food down anyway.

They finished their meals. The prosecutor said. "I'll confirm what the judge says once he's come back to me. And then I guess it'll be up to you to go and get those statements. Then the judge will make his judgments based on those statements. He'll want to interview each of the people making the statements. Will you be able to arrange that?"

Melissa confirmed she would be able to and said. "Thank you for this. I'm anxious to get this over with."

"Your client's lucky to have you as his lawyer. You're better than most trained lawyers that I know, certainly more conscientious." The prosecutor said.

Melissa smiled and thanked him, and said she'd look forward to seeing him later in the day.

At about 4 o'clock that afternoon, the prosecutor came in. Melissa saw him look around for her. She walked across to him. "I hope you've got good news." She said.

"Yes, I have." The prosecutor said. "You need to arrange for you and me to meet the parties, and they sign their statements in front of me. I'll take those to the judge, and he can make his ruling."

Melissa exhaled. "I hadn't given this part of it a lot of thought. It's going to be stressful and difficult. But I'll manage it."

"I figured that might be the case." The prosecutor said. "Good luck." He turned to walk out of the diner.

Melissa sat and thought about how she was going to do this. She decided it was probably a good idea if the sheriff came with her to talk to each of the individuals. She thought about it a bit more. The sheriff didn't need to come with her for Bones, and certainly not Johnny. She'd get their statements signed in front of the prosecutor first. Then she'd get Jim's statement signed in front of the prosecutor. After that, she would take the sheriff with her to talk to, first Adam Carter and then her father. She felt better, having come up with a plan of action.

She first walked down to the general dealer, she greeted Bones. "Can I have a private word with you about the case?" Melissa said.

"Sure." Bones waved her into his office. He asked his wife to watch the store while he met with Melissa. His wife frowned at him but agreed.

Bones sat behind his desk, Melissa sat in the chair opposite the desk. "So, how's the case going?" Bones asked.

"Well, I think," Melissa said. "I've been in discussions with the prosecutor and the judge. They agree with the suggested more lenient sentences. Now, I must get the signed statements. I need you to meet with the prosecutor and sign your statement. He's agreed to recommend the sentence I suggested to you. Once he has your signed statement, he'll give it to the judge, who'll make a ruling. The judge has said he's on the side with the suggestions, but he still needs to apply his mind to it."

"Can't I get a guarantee first of the sentence? I'm worried once you and the prosecutor have my statement that, things will change." Bones said.

"I can't guarantee anything. But I've met both the judge and the prosecutor. The prosecutor extensively. I believe they'll stick to the suggestion. I think you stand a better chance than if it goes to trial and then they prosecute you in a separate trial," Melissa said.

Bones sighed. "I guess you're right. So, what's next?"

"I suggest you apply your mind to your statement and write it out, but make sure it's accurate. Then you can sign it in front of the prosecutor," Melissa said. "The prosecutor will probably want to read it and ask you a few questions and maybe ask you to change a few things here and there. And then sign it."

"All right, when do you need this by?" Bones asked.

"Can you write it out tonight and then meet us over breakfast tomorrow morning at my diner at, say, 8 o'clock?" Melissa said.

Bones said. "All right, I'll do that. Do you need to confirm with the prosecutor?"

"No, he said he'd be at breakfast at eight at my diner, and if I have any statements, then we can deal with them at that time," Melissa said. They confirmed the meeting, and then Melissa left Bones' shop. As she left Bones' shop, she looked down the street to see if she could see Johnny Harlow. She saw him walk to his normal spot and sit down.

Melissa walked across to Johnny. "I have some good news, Johnny."

Johnny stood up. "Good afternoon, Miss Hamilton. What's the good news?"

"The good news, Johnny, is that you won't have to testify in the trial," Melissa said.

"Why's that Miss Hamilton?" Johnny asked. "I've kind of got used to the idea. I was looking forward to it. I'd be famous."

Melissa laughed. "Oh, I'm sorry to let you down, Johnny. It looks like there might not be a trial anymore because of the evidence I've gathered, including your testimony. The prosecutor doesn't think he'll be able to win the case. So, he wants to take witness statements and have them signed, and then he'll decide as to whether he wants to go to court or not. From what I've told him, he thinks he won't want to go to court."

"Well, I guess that's a good thing for Mr. Teeson," Johnny said. "So, what do you need me to do?"

"Can you read and write?" Melissa asked.

"I can write a bit and read a bit, but I'm not very good," Johnny said. "Is that a problem?"

"Have you been going to school, Johnny?" Melissa asked.

Johnny looked down at the ground. "No, miss Hamilton."

"Well, Johnny, I think after this, it would be a good thing if you went to school regularly," Melissa said.

"I want to go to school. But I'm too embarrassed because I'm so far behind the other kids, and I'm older." Johnny said.

"How about if I teach you a little bit every day so that you can catch up, and then you start going to school," Melissa said.

Johnny looked up at Melissa and smiled. "I'd like that." He said.

461

"Okay, we'll arrange that for the future. In the meantime, you'll have to sit in front of the prosecutor and tell the story about the message being swapped out. The prosecutor or I will then write it down and read it back to you, and then you can sign it. Does that sound alright?"

"That sounds fine, Miss Hamilton," Johnny said. "When do you want me to do that?"

"About nine or 10 o'clock tomorrow morning. Will you be around somewhere on the streets at that time?" Melissa asked.

"Yes, I will be," Johnny said.

"I'll come and find you around about that time tomorrow morning and then take you to my diner, where the prosecutor will take your statement. I'll even give you breakfast." Melissa smiled at him.

Johnny smiled again. "That'll be swell. I've never eaten in a real restaurant."

"I'll see you tomorrow then, Johnny, and thanks in advance for giving your statement," Melissa said.

That evening when Melissa put her horse away, it so happened that Jim was also putting his horse away. She took the opportunity to talk to him. "Jim, would you be able to take some time off tomorrow morning and come and talk to the prosecutor? He wants to take down your statement.

"I don't like this," Jim said. He looked thoughtful. "I guess I don't have any choice now. All right, I'll come in tomorrow morning and sign the statement. What time and where?"

"Meet at my diner at 9:30 tomorrow morning. Will that be alright?" Melissa said. "Will my father ask questions?"

"No, that won't be a problem. He's asked me to get some ranch supplies tomorrow morning. So that works out well." Jim said.

Melissa breathed a sigh of relief.

The next morning the prosecutor was in for breakfast at 7 o'clock. Bones came in at 8 o'clock. The prosecutor was already on a cup of coffee and had finished his breakfast. Melissa greeted Bones and escorted him across to the prosecutor's table, and introduced them. She sat down at the table with them. Bones looked uncomfortable and fidgety.

The prosecutor said. "Because you could be charged with an offense. I must read you your rights." The prosecutor read Bones his rights. He then asked Bones if he understood them. Bones said he did understand them.

Bones wrote out the statement after first telling the prosecutor what he would put in it. He then signed the statement. The prosecutor thanked him.

Bones said. "I'm embarrassed by what I did. I'll never do such a thing again. Are you sure I'm going to get a light sentence?"

The prosecutor looked at Bones. "I can't guarantee anything. It's the judge's decision. But I'm reasonably sure you'll get a light sentence along the lines of what Melissa has suggested."

Bones left the diner looking more relaxed.

Melissa said to the prosecutor. "We've got time before Jim Davies comes in. I'll go and find Johnny Harlow if that's all right with you?"

"That's fine." The prosecutor said.

Melissa walked out of the diner. She didn't have to go far. Johnny was sitting on the sidewalk not far from the diner. Melissa guessed he was eager to have breakfast. "Morning Johnny, good to see you're here on time," Melissa said. "Want to come through to the diner."

"Good morning, miss Hamilton." Johnny stood and followed Melissa into the diner. Melissa introduced Johnny, who also looked nervous in the presence of the prosecutor. The prosecutor smiled at Johnny and said, "don't worry, Johnny, you've nothing to worry about. But we do need your statement to sort this business out. You won't be in trouble."

Johnny visibly relaxed.

The prosecutor asked Johnny to tell his story. Once he'd finished, the prosecutor said. "Will you write the statement for Johnny?" He looked at Melissa.

"Yes, I can do that. I'll write it out as I remember Johnny said it, and if I forget anything, I'll ask Johnny. Then I'll read it out to Johnny to confirm that it's correct," Melissa said.

Melissa wrote while the prosecutor talked with Johnny. Melissa didn't need to ask any questions. She'd heard the story enough times. "I'm done." Melissa looked up. "Can I read it to you, Johnny? You can let me know if I've got anything wrong. I don't think I have." Melissa read the statement to Johnny.

Johnny said. "That's exactly right, Miss Hamilton."

Melissa turned the statement around to Johnny, placed a finger where he must sign, and said. "Sign there, Johnny?" She handed the pen to Johnny, first dipping it in the ink bottle that she had on the table. Johnny took the pen. He hesitated a moment and then focused on the paper. His tongue poked out the corner of his mouth as he signed his name. Once he was done, he looked up at Melissa and the prosecutor.

"Well done, Johnny," Melissa said. "That's all we need from you. Let me take you over to a table and organize you some breakfast." Johnny smiled at Melissa. She stood up and led him across to a table, and sat him down. The waitress came across and asked Johnny what he wanted for breakfast. He looked uncomfortably at Melissa. Melissa suggested that maybe he would like two eggs, some bacon, and some flapjacks.

"Aah, yes, please," Johnny said. "Can I have some syrup and cream on my flapjacks?"

"That'll be fine." Melissa smiled at him. The waitress left the table to organize Johnny's order. "I'll leave you here, Johnny. I've got a few more things to attend to. When you're finished breakfast, you can leave. It's on the house."

Johnny grinned at Melissa. "Thanks, miss Hamilton."

Melissa left Johnny and went back to the prosecutor.

"Jim Davis will be in about 9:30 to make his statement. Do you need anything else?" Melissa asked.

"No thanks. I've still got some coffee here." The prosecutor said.

Jim walked into the diner at twenty to ten. He saw Melissa and walked over to her. "Sorry, I'm a bit late," Jim said.

"No problem," Melissa said. She led him across to the prosecutor and introduced him.

"I hope I'm not going to be in trouble here," Jim said.

The prosecutor smiled at Jim. "Melissa told me roughly what your statement will be. Based on what she told me, you won't be in trouble."

Jim gave his statement to the prosecutor.

The prosecutor said. "That sounds fine. Can you write it down and sign it now."

Jim wrote his statement out and signed it. "Is that it?" He looked at the prosecutor and then at Melissa.

"Yes, that's it, you're all done." The prosecutor said. "Thanks for coming in."

Melissa smiled at Jim. "Can I offer you some breakfast as a reward for your time?"

"Yes, please. The stress of talking to a prosecutor has made me hungry." Jim smiled. Melissa led him across to another table and took his order. She relayed it to the kitchen. Then she went back to the prosecutor's table and sat down opposite him.

"Well, so far, so good," Melissa said. "Now we're left with the two difficult ones, Adam Carter and my father. I'm not sure how we do this, whether it's better to bring them in here. If I can get them in here, or you come out to the ranch."

"Maybe we should collect the sheriff and go out to the ranch. I think first we talk to Adam Carter. From what you say, he'll be easier to deal with than your father. Once we have Adam Carter's statement, your father will come to realize he has no choice." The prosecutor said.

"That makes sense to me," Melissa said. "Are you done with breakfast? Shall we go and find the sheriff?"

The prosecutor stood up. "Let's go."

They walked outside and down to the sheriff's office. The sheriff was in his office. He greeted them. "I've been expecting you two." The sheriff smiled at them. "What can I do for you?"

"We've got all the statements except Adam Carter's and my father's. Those are the difficult ones. We need you to come along with us in case there's trouble," Melissa said.

The three of them went out to the ranch, Melissa in her buggy and the sheriff and the prosecutor on horses behind her. At the ranch, there was no one outside. They dismounted, and Melissa led them inside. She went to her father's study. He wasn't there. She was somewhat relieved. Maybe she could find Adam Carter get his statement, and then go and find her father. She went through to the kitchen and found Maria. "Do you know where my father is, Maria?" Melissa asked.

"No, I'm not sure exactly where he is. But he took the trail to the northern side of the ranch." Maria said.

"Do you know where Adam Carter is?" Melissa asked.

"Yes, he went with the crew to brand some cows on the eastern side of the ranch. I think you'll be able to find them easily by the cows, the noise, and the dust." Maria said.

Melissa saddled herself a horse, and then the three of them rode out to the east of the ranch. As they got closer to where the branding was happening, they could see the dust and hear the noise. They rode up to where the branding was taking place. Adam was in the process of heating the iron in the fire. He looked up at the three of them. Melissa saw worry in his eyes. He turned and branded the calf. The calf bellowed in pain. Melissa could smell the burning hair. Once it was done, Adam untied the calf, and it galloped off bucking as it went to join its mother. One of the other cowhands was bringing another calf to Adam.

The sheriff said to Adam. "We need a word with you. Ask someone else to continue with your job."

Adam glared at the sheriff. "I don't need to talk to you. I've done nothing wrong."

"If you don't talk to me now, things will be a lot worse for you later." The sheriff said.

Adam stood thinking for a couple of minutes. He then shrugged his shoulders and asked one of the other hands to take over. The other hand jumped off his horse and hitched it with a bunch of other horses that were there. He came over and took over from Adam. A hand that'd already roped a calf pulled the calf along to the hand that had taken over from Adam. Adam dragged himself toward the three of them.

"We'd like you to come with us to the ranch house. It'll be easier for us to talk there." The sheriff said.

"What's this about?" Adam stared at the sheriff.

"I don't think you want to talk in front of everybody. Let's save it until we get to the ranch house." The sheriff said.

Adam shrugged and went over to his horse. The sheriff followed him to his horse. He wasn't sure whether Adam would make a break for it. Adam glanced behind him. He was thinking of making a break for it but realized he wouldn't have a chance. The sheriff was wide awake to that possibility. Adam clambered onto his horse. The sheriff said. "You can lead the way to the ranch house."

"Am I under arrest here for something?" Adam asked.

"Not yet." The sheriff said.

Adam carried on riding. He noticed that the sheriff did not have the loop hooked over the hammer of his six-shooter. Back at the ranch, Melissa led them into the dining room.

"Before you take a seat, I'd like you to hand over your firearm." The sheriff said.

"So, I am under arrest," Adam said.

"No, not yet. It's a precaution." The sheriff said.

Adam handed his firearm to the sheriff.

"Now you can take a seat, Adam." The sheriff said.

Adam sat. Once Adam had taken a seat, everyone else sat down.

No one said anything. Adam shifted in his seat. Eventually, he said. "What's this about?"

"I think you know what this is about." The sheriff said.

"No, I don't. I've done nothing wrong, so I don't know what this is about." Adam said.

"Let me help you." The sheriff said. "You shot Knox in the back."

The color drained from Adam's face. "No, I didn't. That Matt Teeson shot him."

"Yes, Matt Teeson did shoot him. But that was in a fair fight. We've had the body exhumed, and Julia examined the body.

There was one bullet wound in the front and one from the back." The sheriff said. "We then had a talk with Bones. Bones admitted he'd been paid off to say that there was only one wound, and it was from the back. He's also signed a statement to that effect that there were two wounds, one from the front and one from the back, and that he was paid off by George Hamilton to say there was only one wound from the back." The sheriff held his hand out toward the prosecutor. The prosecutor passed Bones' signed statement across to the sheriff. The sheriff turned the statement around and held it close enough so that Adam could read it. Adam read the statement.

He looked up. "Yes, but that doesn't say that I shot Knox."

"We know you did. We're not telling you at this point the evidence and the statements that we have backing this up. But you can make it much easier on yourself. I can either arrest you, and you can stand trial. Likely you'll be convicted and will hang. Alternatively, you admit the truth here and sign a statement, and we can almost guarantee you a much lighter sentence." The sheriff said.

Adam was silent. He was looking down at the table. He looked up and said. "What sort of lighter sentence. Not that I'm admitting to anything, I'm curious."

Sheriff Gamble turned to the prosecutor. "Do you want to answer that?"

"Yes, I'll answer that." The prosecutor looked at Adam. "I'm prepared to argue with the judge for a five-year prison sentence. That's a lot better than hanging. And for murder, it's a short sentence."

"But you're not guaranteeing that?" Adam said.

"I've had a discussion with the judge. And he says he's willing to consider that. Once he has your statement, he'll consider it some more and then give his verdict. He says it's unlikely to be different from that unless something else comes to light." The prosecutor said.

Adam looked down at the table again. He said nothing for a couple of minutes. He sighed. "Okay, I'll give you my statement on the condition of the lighter sentence."

"Before you say anything, I need to read you your rights." The sheriff said. Adam looked at the sheriff. The sheriff read Adam his rights and, at the end, confirmed that Adam understood them.

"George Hamilton." As Adam said that, he looked at Melissa. "Said he'd organized for Matt Teeson to meet Knox in the alley behind the saloon the next morning. He said he no longer trusted Knox. He was worried Knox would one day turn on him. He knew I hated Knox. He was confident that I wouldn't have a problem carrying out his wishes. I've felt bad ever since. I never would've thought I'd shoot anyone in the back. But my hate for Knox was so great that I justified it to myself. To my shame, the offer of $500 from George Hamilton helped my decision. George Hamilton asked me to be there at the time when Matt Teeson and Knox would face off. He asked me to shoot Knox in the back. He said he'd arranged with Bones to confirm that there was only one shot, and it was from the back. Since Matt Teeson would be the only one in the alley, he would ensure that Matt Teeson got the blame. That's pretty much the whole story."

As Adam had been telling the story, Melissa had gone whiter and whiter. Hearing how evil her father had become shocked her.

The prosecutor passed some paper across to Adam and then a pen and ink bottle. "Please write out your statement and sign it as you told it to us." The prosecutor said. Adam took the pen, dipped it in ink, and wrote out his statement, signing it at the end.

Melissa was unsure whether she was pleased or not. This was almost the last nail in the coffin. The problem was it now confirmed how evil her father had become. She still did not want him to hang.

The sheriff said. "Adam Carter, you're under arrest for the murder of Peter Knox. Please stand, turn around, and put your hands behind your back."

Adam stood and placed his hands behind his back. The sheriff placed handcuffs on his wrists and locked them. He then checked him for any other weapons. He found a knife in one of Adam's boots, he took that. He found no other weapons. He then pushed Adam ahead of him and led him outside to his horse. He helped Adam onto his horse. He stepped away from the horse out of hearing distance of Adam while keeping an eye on him. He whispered to Melissa. "I need to place Adam in jail. And then we'll have to come back for your father. Will you wait here?"

"Yes, we'll wait here for you. On second thoughts, I think it would be better if we came to town with you. I'm worried my father might come back while you're away, which could be trouble, and I'd rather you're here when we meet with my father," Melissa said.

They all headed into town. The sheriff leading, Adam, the prosecutor, and Melissa behind. At the jail, they dismounted. The sheriff turned to Melissa and the prosecutor and said. "You should go and have a cup of coffee. I'll join you once I've locked Adam up."

The prosecutor and Melissa wandered down the street to her diner. The sheriff led Adam into his office. There were two jail cells. He placed Adam in the empty jail cell next to Matt. He said to Matt. "I brought you some company."

Matt looked at Adam. "So, what's he in for." His discussions with Melissa gave him a good idea, but he decided to act ignorant.

"It's all become a long story. I'll let your lawyer explain that to you." The sheriff said.

The sheriff left the jail office, he locked the outside door as well. It wasn't ideal leaving prisoners locked in the jail with no guard. He decided he did need a guard. He wandered down the street looking for someone whom he could trust. He saw no one that he would put faith in. He decided he would have to take the risk of not having a guard. He was sure Matt would not be a problem. And no one else knew Adam Carter was in there. He turned around and went back to Melissa's diner. He sat down with Melissa and the prosecutor. He ordered a cup of coffee. Once they'd all finished their coffee, they headed back out to the ranch. On the way out, the sheriff said. "We've got enough evidence against George now to arrest him. I think the easiest thing is going to be to arrest him. We've only got two jail cells. I'll put him in the cell with Adam. If I don't arrest him, I suspect he'll cause trouble."

The prosecutor said. "You're right, it'll be simpler to arrest him, and then we'll still get him to write out a statement for the lesser sentence, which I'm sure we'll be able to persuade him to do. It'll be the choice between hanging or giving up his ranch and moving from the territory. I know which I'd choose. But from what I hear of him, he may be too arrogant to think that he'll stand trial and be convicted and hang."

They rode on in silence. Melissa's stomach churned. She wasn't looking forward to this. As they reached the ranch house, she said. "Can I be excused from this confrontation?"

"I don't blame you, Melissa." The sheriff said. The sheriff turned to the prosecutor. "Is that alright with you?"

"Yes, that's fine. It's not necessary for you to be there, Melissa." The prosecutor said.

Melissa exhaled. "Thank you."

At the ranch house, Melissa stopped off, the others carried on. The Prosecutor said. "Do you think we should have more men? We don't know how many men are with George Hamilton."

"You have a point there. I'm not sure who I could get to help. You're right. We must get more men." The sheriff said. They turned around and headed back to the ranch house. They knocked at the door. Maria came to the door. "We'd like to see Melissa." The sheriff said.

Maria said. "You can sit on the porch here." She indicated the chairs on the porch. "I'll call Melissa for you."

Melissa came out. The sheriff noticed she was pale. "You're back quickly," Melissa said.

"We don't know how many men are with your father. We need to have more men with us." The sheriff said.

"You're right," Melissa said. "Will you be able to find enough men?"

"I'm not sure. I think we'll be able to." The sheriff said. "You keep a low profile, Melissa. We're going to head back to town and get reinforcements. We'll be back."

The prosecutor and the sheriff turned and rode back toward town. On their way back, they saw two men waiting on the road. The sheriff unhooked the loop from his Colt. They carried on riding toward the two men. As they got closer, the sheriff recognized them as Hugh and Geoff. He relaxed somewhat.

"Hello, boys. Are you waiting for me?" The sheriff said.

"We are. We've been keeping a low profile. But we want to find out what's going on. We've been watching all the goings-on and the backward and forwards," Geoff said.

"I could do with your help." The sheriff said. "I'll tell you what's going on if you come with us into town. Where's Nitis? I thought he was now your constant companion."

"He is. He's following along out of sight. We know everyone gets worried if they see an Apache," Hugh said.

"We could do with Nitis' help as well." The sheriff said. The sheriff explained to the prosecutor who Hugh, Geoff, and Nitis were. He then updated Geoff and Hugh as to what had taken place.

"That's good news," Hugh said. "So, Matt's out of jail now, is?"

"No, he's not out of jail yet." The sheriff said. "We're still busy tying all this together. As soon as it's all tied together and handed to the judge, he'll make a ruling, and then I'm sure Matt will be released."

They rode on in silence. Geoff broke the silence with a question. "So, how many more men do you think we need to take on George?"

"Well, there's five of us if we include Nitis. I think we should get another five, and then we'll be able to give a show of force to George Hamilton, and he'll surrender." The sheriff said. "I'll round up another five men in town, and then we'll head back out. You can talk to Nitis and update him and get him to join us."

"Won't that upset the other five men if Nitis joins us?" Hugh asked.

"We're all going to have to learn to live in peace with the Apache. I'll explain to the others that they're going to have to accept Nitis and that he's with us to help." The sheriff said. Hugh looked skeptical but said nothing further.

"Do you want to wait in Melissa's diner and have a cup of coffee while I round up five more people? I'll come and fetch you when I'm ready." The sheriff said. Geoff, Hugh, and the prosecutor headed to Melissa's.

The prosecutor said. "Well, all I seem to do here is drink coffee." He smiled. "Every time we come into town, the sheriff sends me to sit in Melissa's and have a cup of coffee. Or I sit in Melissa's and take statements."

Hugh and Geoff had a cup of coffee, the prosecutor ordered a sarsaparilla. He commented. "I think I'm done with coffee forever."

An hour later, the sheriff came in. "I've got five more men." He didn't comment on the quality of the men.

The posse headed out to George's ranch. The sheriff explained to the men that Nitis would be joining them, and they needed to treat him like they would any white man. There were grumblings among the five men. The sheriff said. "I want to hear you clearly say you'll treat Nitis like any other white man." There were more grumblings. The sheriff repeated himself. He said. "I want to hear clearly that you'll treat Nitis properly. The five men reluctantly agreed that they would treat Nitis properly. The sheriff waved his hand toward where he knew Nitis was trailing them. Nitis came out from behind a hill and rode up to them. He nodded to the men. There were a few halfhearted greetings.

The men arrived at the ranch. The sheriff intended to check whether George Hamilton had come back or whether he was still on the northern part of the ranch. He didn't need to check. As they arrived, he saw George Hamilton coming from the north with three of his ranch hands. The sheriff stopped and waited. He wondered if George Hamilton would make a run for it. He suspected George Hamilton would be too arrogant and think he was untouchable.

George Hamilton rode up to the group of ten men. The three men with him looked like they wanted to be somewhere else.

"So, what's this, sheriff? Is this a posse? Has Matt Teeson escaped? I'm happy to join your posse with my men and catch Matt Teeson and hang him," George said.

"No, this posse is for you." The sheriff said.

Color flooded George's face. "What d'you mean it's for me?"

"We've been busy investigating Knox's killing. We've got statements from several people. These statements implicate you in Knox's killing." The sheriff said.

"That's nonsense. I didn't kill Knox." George looked a little less confident now.

"No, you didn't kill Knox, we know who did, and we've got his statement. He says you instructed him to kill Knox." The sheriff said.

"What a load of bullshit," George said.

The sheriff said. "George Hamilton, you're under arrest as an accessory to the murder of Peter Knox."

"Now you've really put yourself out of a job." George Hamilton said.

The sheriff ignored George and read him his rights finishing off with, "do you understand your rights?"

"You're no longer sheriff. I'm firing you as sheriff." George Hamilton said.

"Do you understand these rights that I've said to you?" The sheriff said.

"No, I don't. Because you can't arrest me. I've done nothing wrong." George Hamilton said.

No one noticed the sheriff draw his gun. It was now pointed at George Hamilton. The sheriff looked at the three hands with George Hamilton. "This is not your problem. Carefully take your weapons out of the holsters and drop them on the ground. Then dismount and go and stand there next to the trough."

The three men eased their weapons out of their holsters, watching sheriff Gamble as they did so. They dropped them on the ground. They then walked across to the trough and stood there looking at the sheriff.

"You cowards," George said.

"Sensible, I think." The sheriff said. "Now you, do the same and go and stand next to them. Everyone one yard apart."

George glared at the sheriff. He didn't move for a full minute. Then he slipped his Colt out of its holster and dropped it on the ground. He dismounted and walked over to stand next to his three hands.

———

Chapter 79

The sheriff turned to the posse behind him and said. "Now cover them. I'm going to go and put handcuffs on George Hamilton."

The men in the posse drew their weapons and pointed them at the four men next to the trough. The sheriff jumped off his horse and walked across to George. He stood in front of George and said, "turn around with your hands behind your back."

"You'll shortly be out of a job and then in jail," George said as he turned around. The sheriff cuffed his hands behind his back. He then led him back to his horse. Ignoring George's comment.

The sheriff said to George. "Climb on. I'll help you." George climbed onto his horse with the help of the sheriff. His face was red. The sheriff flipped the reins of the horse over its head and led it over to his horse, and climbed onto his horse. He then turned to George's men and said. "Don't think of doing anything or following us? If you do, you'll also end up in jail and charged as accessories to murder. Which means you will also hang." The men didn't move.

The sheriff instructed three of the men in the posse to bring up the rear but keep looking back for any trouble from any of George's hands. They headed off to town, the group of horses kicking up a cloud of dust that blew away with the wind.

At the jail, the sheriff led George to Adam's cell. "I brought you some company, Adam." The sheriff said. The sheriff placed George in the cell, locking it behind him. "I'll see you boys later. I've got other work to do. I need to do my rounds." The sheriff headed off to check that all was peaceful in the town.

George turned to Adam. "I hear you're blaming me for giving you instructions to kill Knox." George jutted his chin toward Adam.

"I decided to come clean. I'm feeling bad about what I did. I should never have done it. My hate for Knox overcame my good sense." Adam said.

"You idiot," George said. He launched himself at Adam, striking him with a strong right to the nose. He caught Adam by surprise, Adam ducked his head, clutching his nose. Blood flowed out from between his hands. George went at him with two more solid punches to the face. Adam ducked away.

Matt shouted at them. "Hey cut it out. This helps neither of you. And you started it, George, back off."

George continued to go at Adam. Adam was now bobbing out the way, he had his fists up. Blood flowed down his face onto his shirt. He watched George, blocking his punches. He saw a gap and struck George with a straight left. The punch rocked George's head back. Adam followed up with a right to the jaw. George flipped back and fell on the floor. His head hit the concrete with a crack. He lay there unmoving.

Adam turned to Matt. "You saw him, he attacked me. I was minding my own business. I hope he's not dead or I'm in more trouble."

"I'll stand witness to the fact that he attacked you. Even if he is dead, which I don't think he is, I don't think it'll make things worse for you. You're protecting yourself," Matt said.

"Thanks," Adam said. He knelt beside George and checked for a pulse. "He seems to be alive. I can feel a pulse. I can also see he's breathing."

Half an hour later George groaned and eased himself to a sitting position against the wall. He sat there not saying anything for fifteen minutes. Eventually, he looked at Adam and said. "You'll pay for that."

"Hey, you attacked me, I was defending myself. If you hadn't attacked me all would've been fine." Adam said.

As Adam was saying this the sheriff walked in. He looked at George lying propped up against the wall. "What happened here?"

"Adam attacked me for no reason," George said.

"He's lying, sheriff," Adam said. "He attacked me. I was defending myself."

"Well, this is easy to sort out. Matt who's telling the truth?" The sheriff asked.

"It's as Adam told it," Matt said.

"These two are in cahoots with each other," George said. "As you know, Matt Teeson and I have always been enemies. So of course, he's going to back anyone else against me."

"Well, it's two against one." The sheriff said. "So far as I'm concerned that's settled. It looks like you need a doctor. I'll go call Julia. Although maybe you don't want her to attend to you, because she's a woman." The sheriff smiled.

George said nothing, he continued to loll against the wall and glare at the sheriff.

"I'm off to fetch Julia. Make sure you don't get in trouble while I'm away." The sheriff said as he turned and walked out.

He walked up the street to Julia's office. As always now, Julia was busy. She had one patient in with her and one waiting.

The sheriff sat in reception. A few minutes later, Julia came out. "Hello, sheriff. What can I do for you?" Julia asked.

"Can I talk to you privately? I'll only be a minute or two." The sheriff looked at the other patient waiting in reception.

Julia waved him through into her office. She closed the door behind him. "So, what's this about?" Julia asked.

"I've arrested your father for the murder of Knox." The sheriff said.

Julia looked down, the color drained from her face. "I knew you were going to. You had no choice."

"He's going to need your attention, but don't worry he's not too badly hurt." The sheriff said. "Because we only have two cells, I thought it best to put him in with Adam rather than Matt, as Adam and George are in this together, I thought that would be the safest option. Turns out it wasn't the safest option."

"Did Adam attack my father?" Julia looked wide-eyed at the sheriff.

"Your father claims that was the case, but Adam says it was the other way around. Matt confirms that." The sheriff said. "So, when you're finished with the last patient who is waiting in your reception would you come down and attend to your father? He's got a few bruises on his face and took a crack to the back of his head when he fell to the floor."

"All right, I'll be along as soon as I've attended to this patient," Julia said.

The sheriff turned to walk out. "I'll see you later then."

A half hour later Julia walked into the sheriff's office. "I'm here now sheriff."

"I'm afraid I don't trust your father, so I'll have to watch you." The sheriff said. "Do you mind if I check out your doctor's bag? Can't be too careful."

"That's fine," Julia said.

The sheriff looked through her bag. "I can't let you go in there with the scissors. Can you manage without them?" The sheriff said.

"I can attend to him next to the bars and if there is a necessity to cut anything like a bandage, you can do it through the bars," Julia said.

The sheriff led Julia down the passage to the cell. "Doctor is here." The sheriff said. He led Julia into the cell and locked it behind her. He stood at the cell door watching.

"Hello, Papa," Julia said.

George said nothing. He frowned at Julia. Julia said. "Let's see what we have here."

Julia had a look at his face and then the back of his head. George complained when she touched the back of his head. She took disinfectant from her bag and wiped the cuts and the back of his head. She then looked at his pupils. "Looks like you're not too badly hurt. You have a concussion and a few cuts and bruises. Otherwise, you're fine."

"What would you know?" George said. "He nearly killed me. It's a lot more than a concussion and cuts and bruises. But I guess that's all I could expect from a woman doctor."

Julia sighed. "Well, as a woman doctor, that's all I can do for you." She packed up her bag, and the sheriff let her out of the cell.

———

Chapter 80

The prosecutor wandered into Melissa's diner. He asked the waitress if Melissa was there. "She's in her office." The waitress said. "I'll take you through."

The waitress led the prosecutor through to Melissa's office. "Hello, Herbert," Melissa said.

"Hello Melissa, I've got an update on the case." The prosecutor said.

Melissa waved him to the seat in front of her. He said. "All we have left now to do is to get a statement from your father. The sheriff's arrested him and put him in jail." He watched Melissa for a reaction. He saw no reaction. "I'm going to ask him to tell us the truth and give us his truthful statement. In return I'll undertake to talk to the judge about a more lenient sentence. The sentence that you suggested. The judge has indicated, though, that in the case of your father he can't guarantee that he'll hand out a more lenient sentence. He's concerned that your father won't reform, and he'll seek vengeance on everyone else and then carry on with his ways."

"Are you going to warn him of the judge's thoughts?" Melissa asked.

"Yes, I will. But I still think it is worth it for him. At least he'll stand a chance of not hanging. Whereas if he goes to court without making a statement, he is almost certain to hang, given all the other evidence and statements that we have. Also, if the judge decides that he must go to trial his signed statement won't be allowed in the trial and won't be allowed to be referred to in the trial. We must rely on all the other statements, which I don't think is a problem in itself." The prosecutor said.

"Thanks for talking to me about this, Herbert. I can't defend what he's done. And I defer to your knowledge of the law. I know nothing about the law." Melissa smiled at him.

"You're learning fast. You'll make a good lawyer. This has been a good learning experience for you and will make your studies when you get down to them, more meaningful. I'll go and see your father now and see if I can get that statement. I might need to bring him back here and use your office, given there is no privacy at the jail. Would that be alright?" The prosecutor said.

"That's fine," Melissa said. "If you come back here, I'll move out of my office and work at one of the diner tables."

He left Melissa's office and headed down the street to the sheriff's office. He explained to the sheriff what he wanted to do.

"He's in a cell with Adam Carter, and there's no privacy here. We'll need to take him somewhere else for you to interview him." The sheriff said.

"I thought that would be the case." The prosecutor said. "Melissa's happy for us to use her office if that's okay with you. It means you'll have to come to her office and watch over us. If the judge rules that he must go to trial, then the statement that he gives will be inadmissible in court. And you also won't be able to quote what you heard in court."

"That seems like a good solution." The sheriff said.

The sheriff collected George Hamilton from the cell. He explained that the prosecutor wanted to question him. George, per normal, made a fuss about it and said he had nothing to say to the prosecutor. The sheriff said that he needed to see the prosecutor regardless of his thoughts. He led the moaning George down the street with the prosecutor to Melissa's office.

In Melissa's office, the prosecutor said. "Thank you for coming down here to discuss your case."

"I didn't come down here willingly. The sheriff forced me. None of this will have any weight in court," George said.

"It's your right not to say anything further. But before you make that decision, let me put you fully in the picture." The prosecutor said. "Our interest is getting to the truth in this case. We have the truth anyway without a statement from you, as we have everyone else's statements that implicate you. It's not necessary that we have a statement from you."

"Then why bother?" George said.

"We prefer to have everything that we can get. And given your relationship as a family man, we prefer you don't hang, and that you reform." The prosecutor said. "If you're prepared to give us a written statement of the truth, then I'll argue to the judge for a more lenient sentence for you. If you're not prepared to do that. Then it's certain that you'll go to trial and hang for the murder of Knox."

"I won't hang for the murder of Knox. I didn't murder him. Adam Carter did," George said.

"But you gave the order." The prosecutor said.

"It's still my word against Adam Carter," George said. "You'll have difficulty proving in court that I gave the order."

"It's possible. But I think the likelihood is, with all the surrounding evidence, that the jury will convict you. Then you'll hang." The prosecutor said. "What I'm giving you is an opportunity to avoid being hung. It certainly is not a guarantee because the judge will still have to consider everything, and he may decide that you must go to court. If you do go to court, the statement that you give now will not be admissible. All you are doing by giving your statement is adding another string to your bow."

George said nothing. He sat frowning. Two minutes later, he said, "You guarantee that this statement that I give now won't be admissible in court if it goes to court?"

"That's correct." The prosecutor said.

"All right, I'll do it," George said.

"Before you write it out, I'd like to hear what you're going to say." The prosecutor said.

George told the prosecutor what he was going to say. The statement was vague and didn't say exactly what the prosecutor thought it should say. They argued back and forth about it, eventually settling on a statement that the prosecutor could live with. The prosecutor pushed a pad of paper across to George together with a pen and ink bottle. George wrote out his statement and signed and dated it. The prosecutor reached across and pulled the statement to him, turning it around to read it.

When he'd read it, he said. "Thank you. I'll take this to the judge and argue for the more lenient sentence."

The sheriff led George back to his cell and locked him in.

The prosecutor updated Melissa that he now had George's statement and was ready to talk to the judge.

———

Chapter 81

The sheriff went back to his desk, sat down, and put his feet on the desk with a sigh. It'd been an exhausting day for him. He hoped the rest of the day would be peaceful. That hope was short-lived. One of the barmen from the saloon arrived in his office red-faced and sweaty, breathing heavily. "Sheriff, you're needed urgently at the saloon."

The sheriff sighed. "What now?"

The barman said. "Paul O'Brien is drunk and is attacking one of the other patrons."

Sheriff Gamble stood up, took his hat off its hook, placed it on his head, adjusted his gun belt, and said. "I'll be along now."

The barman raced off ahead of the sheriff. The sheriff followed, frowning. When he pushed his way into the bar, he saw there weren't many people there. He saw two men being held by groups of other patrons. The men didn't look like they were too damaged. The sheriff walked up to them and asked what was going on. Even though he knew pretty much what was going on. Paul O'Brien was the town drunk and was always getting into fights after a few drinks. Normally the sheriff would lock him up for the night and let him go in the morning. But today, he couldn't do that. The jail was already full. He walked up to Paul O'Brien and said. "Paul, I'm tired of you causing trouble. Unfortunately, I can't lock you up. But I can't do nothing either. I'm tired of you always causing trouble. So, what I'm going to do is handcuff you to the rails outside the saloon. I have no doubt the customers coming and going will have a few things to say to you as they come in and go out."

"You can't do that." Paul O'Brien said. The men had relaxed their grips on the two men now that the sheriff was in charge. Paul O'Brien broke away from the group of men holding him and swung his fist at the sheriff, catching him on his cheekbone under the left eye. The sheriff was slow to react. He hadn't expected Paul O'Brien, in his drunken state, to move so quickly. Paul O'Brien swung another punch at the sheriff. This time the sheriff was able to duck, and Paul O'Brien's follow through carried him through to fall flat on the floor. The sheriff knelt on O' Brien's back, stuck a handcuff round O'Brien's right wrist, and then snapped the other wrist into the handcuff. He pulled O'Brien off the floor and marched him out amidst a profane torrent of words from the man. The sheriff then undid the handcuff from O'Brien's left wrist and hitched it to the rail outside the saloon. He wasn't far from the horses hitched to the rail. The horses didn't seem to be too fussed about the human company.

Chapter 82

Melissa walked down to the sheriff's office for the umpteenth time. The office was locked. Melissa sat on the bench outside his office, thinking. *At least there's a bench to sit on now. That's an improvement.*

Half an hour later, she saw the sheriff walking down the street from the saloon. His shoulders drooped, his stride slower than normal.

As the sheriff walked up to her, she stood up. "What's wrong, sheriff? You look like you're carrying the weight of the world on your shoulders?"

The sheriff smiled at Melissa. "It feels like it. With all the goings on with your father, it's exhausting me. But I guess I shouldn't complain. You're carrying more weight than me. I had to go to the saloon and deal with Paul O'Brien. He's always causing trouble down there. Because I've got no space in the jail, I've hitched him to the horse rail outside the saloon."

"He can't be too happy about that," Melissa said.

The sheriff unlocked his door. "Are you here to see Matt?"

"I am. I want to update him. We're now at the stage where we have all the statements and can talk to the judge. I'd like to talk to Matt on his own. Is that possible?" Melissa asked.

The sheriff slumped his shoulders and said, "yes, that's possible. I'll come with you, and you can meet him in your office at your diner."

"Sorry, sheriff, I'm adding to your exhausting day." Melissa smiled.

"That's fine. The walking does me good," he patted his stomach. There was a small roll there, not that big, though, given his age.

The sheriff walked down the passage to the cell. "Matt, you have a visitor." He saw Matt's face brighten. When Melissa appeared behind him, the sheriff thought he saw Matt's face drop. He wondered who Matt had been expecting. *Julia maybe.* The sheriff smiled. He opened Matt's cell door. "Come, Matt, your lawyer wants to brief you."

They headed off down the street to Melissa's office. She put Matt in the picture of where everything was. He said, "that sounds good. Looks like you've got it all tied up. Does that mean I'll be released soon?"

"I think so," Melissa said. "The only unknown is what the judge will decide on my father. He says he is not decided yet. He's concerned that if my father is released and even if he is out of the territory, he'll come back and cause trouble, or he'll cause trouble wherever he is. So, he may say that my father will have to go to trial. Despite all the bad he's done, I don't relish that. But even if that is the case, I'm sure you'll be released."

"Where's your sister? I thought she might at least pay me a visit. Does she still think I'm guilty?" Matt said.

Melissa smiled. "I'm not sure. Not surprisingly, this business with our father has put her out of sorts. So, you've taken a fancy to my sister, have you?" Melissa saw the sheriff smiling out of the corner of her eye.

"No, that's not it. I thought she might come and visit me. I thought we were getting on quite well." Matt blushed.

Melissa smiled again. "I'm afraid your face is giving you away."

Matt frowned. "Well, as my lawyer, you need to get on and get me released."

"I'll do that," Melissa said.

The sheriff took Matt back to his cell, leaving Melissa at her diner. The prosecutor was still there at one of the tables.

She walked up to the prosecutor. "Are you ready to put the cases to the judge?" Melissa asked.

"Yes, I am. I'll track him down and arrange for us to meet after breakfast tomorrow. I'm sure he'll want to have breakfast here. I certainly will. Then we can maybe meet at 9 o'clock. I'm happy for you to be there with me." The prosecutor said.

"That sounds good," Melissa said. "Will you let me know when it's confirmed? I'll be here for about another hour. Otherwise, you can let me know tomorrow morning. But I'll plan for 9 o'clock."

Three quarters of an hour later, the prosecutor walked back into her diner. He saw she wasn't out front, so he walked back to her office. She was sitting behind the desk.

"It's confirmed for 9 o'clock tomorrow morning." The prosecutor said. "But I'll be here for breakfast at 7:30. Will you have breakfast with me?"

"Yes, I will." Melissa wondered whether this was a working breakfast or something else.

———

Chapter 83

The next morning Melissa met the prosecutor for breakfast. They went over the various statements at breakfast and confirmed what the prosecutor would say to the judge. Melissa guessed that this was a working breakfast.

The judge walked in at 7:45. He walked over to their table and greeted them. He confirmed that they would meet after breakfast at 9 o'clock in the diner. He then wandered across to his normal table in the corner overlooking the street.

They finished their breakfast before nine, so they had a cup of coffee while they waited for the judge. They saw the judge was still finishing off his breakfast. The judge finished his breakfast and waved them across.

"Are you ready to update me?" The judge asked.

"We are. I'll do the updating. Melissa will interrupt if I get anything wrong." The prosecutor said.

He summarized everything for the judge. He said that Knox had been shot in the back by Adam Carter, and he had Adam Carter's statement confirming that. Matt Teeson had also shot Knox, but that was from the front, and Knox had braced him and pushed him into drawing. Bones had been paid off by George Hamilton to say that there was only one wound, and it was in the back, to imply that Knox had been shot in the back by Matt Teeson. Since, at that point in time, no one knew about Adam Carter, the blame was put on Matt Teeson. The prosecutor confirmed he also got a statement from George Hamilton. That George Hamilton ordered Adam Carter to shoot Knox in the back. The prosecutor mentioned there was also another case tied up here. A suitor of Melissa's, Patrick O'Hagan, was shot on the instructions of George Hamilton. He said they had a statement from Jim Davies, George Hamilton's foreman, that he heard George Hamilton giving an indirect instruction to Knox to kill Patrick O'Hagan. Jim Davies also confirmed that the two hands that were there at that time and witnessed it saw Patrick O'Hagan ask if he could remove the loop from his gun before Knox drew. Knox confirmed that he could, but as Patrick O'Hagan moved carefully to remove the loop, Knox drew and shot him. He then walked up to Patrick O'Hagan and removed the loop from his gun so that it looked like it was already off. That, though, the prosecutor said, was a different case. All the statements were obtained on the promise that he, the prosecutor, would ask the judge to be lenient on the sentences in return for their statements. That included George Hamilton's statement. The prosecutor then outlined the sentences that he was requesting. Bones would pay whatever money the judge felt fit into the town Council for the betterment of the town in the future. Adam Carter appeared remorseful, and it was suggested that he be given a five-year prison sentence. The prosecutor believed that Adam Carter could reform and was regretful of his actions. George Hamilton, he suggested should give up his ranch either to his two daughters or to the town to be run by the town council and the profits from the ranch to be used for the betterment of the town, whatever the judge deemed fit, and that George Hamilton be banished from the territory.

The judge interrupted from time to time to clarify points.

The prosecutor passed the pile of statements across to the judge.

The judge said. "I think I've got all I need now to decide. How about we meet tomorrow morning here at nine again. I'll let you know my decision then."

The prosecutor said, "that suits me fine." He looked at Melissa.

"That's good for me," Melissa said.

The next morning, they met again in the diner at 9 o'clock.

After the greeting pleasantries, the judge came to the point at hand. "I've made my decision. I concur with your recommendations on Adam Carter and Bones Chapman. In the case of George Hamilton, after much deliberation, I can't go with your recommendation. From my review of your submissions, it appears to me that George Hamilton is unlikely to reform. He is likely to be a repeat criminal, in my opinion, whether he be in this territory or elsewhere. So, in the case of George Hamilton, he will still have to stand trial. Bones will have to pay $1000 to the town Council. It's going to be a hardship for him, but I'm sure he won't do something similar in the future. Adam Carter will spend five years in jail. He has a lucky break there.

"I expected you to go with that." The prosecutor said. He looked at Melissa. Melissa's eyes were watering, but she said nothing.

"Melissa, I can understand you not wanting to comment." The judge said.

Melissa nodded.

"I'll relay the message to the various parties. Melissa, your father is going to need representation. I'm not sure whether he'll ask you. But if you don't take on his representation, I'm not sure who he'll get. He'll probably want to bring someone in from outside. You need to think about what you want to do if he asks you to represent him. It's unusual to represent family because of the emotions involved, but it is allowed in law." The prosecutor said.

They finished off the meeting, and Melissa went back to running the diner. She was having difficulty focusing on the task and was using it, unsuccessfully, as a distraction from the fate of her father. The prosecutor headed off toward the general dealer.

———

Chapter 84

When the prosecutor arrived at the general dealer, Bones was serving a customer. The Prosecutor waited until the customer left the shop. He then said to Bones, "can we meet in your office to discuss the judge's ruling?"

Bones stared at the prosecutor, wide-eyed, the color drained from his face. He called his wife to fill in for him at the front desk while he consulted with the prosecutor. His wife came out of the office and greeted the prosecutor. The prosecutor and Bones went into the office. The prosecutor closed the door behind him.

"The judge has made a ruling on the various parties involved in this case with Matt Teeson. Obviously, there is not going to be a trial of Matt Teeson now, given it is clear he is innocent. If you're happy to sign an admission of guilt, then we can deal with your sanction without a trial. If it goes to trial, your sentence is most likely to be significantly worse. I'll let you know what the sanction is now. You can then decide by this afternoon or now whether to accept or not." The prosecutor said.

Bones slumped his shoulders. "Let me have it." He said.

"You'll pay $1000 to the town Council. They'll use this to the benefit of the town. Are you prepared to accept this?" The prosecutor said.

Bones sat for a minute, looking down at his desk. "I have no choice but to accept it. I guess I deserve this. That's a lot of money. My wife's going to be unhappy with me. I'll sign the acknowledgment of guilt." Bones held his hand out for the document.

The prosecutor passed the document across to him. Bones read it, picked up his pen, dipped it in the ink bottle, and signed.

"Thank you." The prosecutor said as he took the document from Bones. "I'll be on my way." He stood up and headed out the door. Bones remain slumped in his chair, looking down at the desk.

The prosecutor made his way to the jail. He greeted the sheriff and said, "I need to have a private word with Adam Carter. It'll be short."

"We can do it outside the office here at the bench that I've put in." The sheriff said. "Is that alright?"

"That'll be fine." The prosecutor said.

The sheriff went down the passage and said, "you have a visitor, Adam."

"Who is it?" Adam asked.

"It's the prosecutor." The sheriff said.

Adam frowned. The sheriff opened his cell door, placed handcuffs on Adam, and led him down the passage and outside to the bench. The prosecutor followed the sheriff out and stood facing Adam.

"The judge has made a ruling on the various parties involved in the Matt Teeson case. You can either consider it until this afternoon, or you can decide now. It's up to you. If you decide to accept his ruling, you'll need to sign an admission of guilt, which has the sentence included." The prosecutor waived the admission of guilt form in front of Adam.

"I'm listening," Adam said.

"The judge has ruled that you'll serve five years in jail. If you don't accept that, then the matter can go to trial." The prosecutor said.

"I'll sign the admission of guilt. I got off lucky." Adam said.

"I think so." The prosecutor said as he handed the admission of guilt to Adam. "You better come inside and sign it at the sheriff's desk."

They walked inside. Adam sat at the sheriff's desk and signed the admission of guilt. He handed it to the prosecutor. The prosecutor thanked Adam and tucked the form into the folder he was carrying. The sheriff led Adam back to the cell and locked him in, removing the handcuffs.

The sheriff came back down the passage to the prosecutor.

"I now need a private word with George Hamilton. But this will be a lot longer. How do you want to deal with this?" The prosecutor said.

"I think the safest thing is for you to consult with George through the bars. Don't go within reach of him. I'll take Adam Carter and Matt Teeson for coffee at Melissa's." The sheriff said.

"That'll be fine." The prosecutor said.

The sheriff took a chair down the passage and placed it facing George's cell but out of reach. The prosecutor sat in the chair and greeted George. Meanwhile, the sheriff took Adam and Matt out of the cells after cuffing them and said, "we're going for a cup of coffee at Melissa's diner."

The prosecutor waited until the sheriff left with his prisoners. He then spoke to George. "The judge considered all the parties involved in the Matt Teeson case. He's come up with sanctions and sentences for all parties, provided they sign an admission of guilt, except for you. He considers your crime too great to give a reduced sentence.

"So, you tricked me into signing the admission of guilt."

"Not at all." The prosecutor said. "I mentioned at the time that the judge would have to consider it and, in your case, might not be prepared to give a lighter sentence. If that was the route he went and said you had to go to trial, then the admission of guilt form that you signed previously would not be allowed in court."

"But now everyone knows what's in the admission of guilt. So that helps nothing," George said.

"It does help. The jury won't know anything about the admission of guilt. They're the ones that will decide whether you're guilty or not." The prosecutor said. He then read George Hamilton his rights again. He finished by saying. "You'll need to get some representation in court. Do you know who you are going to get?"

"How am I going to get someone to represent me?" George said. "There aren't any lawyers in this town."

"We'll give you time to find a lawyer from another town. You'll have to get someone to act as a liaison for you." The prosecutor said. "I'll give you a week to find a lawyer."

"I think I'll choose Melissa as my lawyer," George said.

"You think that's wise? She's obviously going to have a conflict of interest, and she's not a qualified lawyer." The prosecutor said.

"She seemed to do an okay job for Matt Teeson, got him off. So, she can do the same for me," George said.

"It's one thing getting a person who's not guilty off, but totally another getting a guilty person off." The prosecutor said.

"My decision's made. Melissa must represent me," George said.

"You still have to get her to agree to that." The prosecutor said. "I'd be surprised if she'll agree."

"She agreed for Matt Teeson, so it's more likely she'll agree to me. I'm family," George said.

"You want me to talk to Melissa and send her down to talk to you?" The prosecutor said.

"Yes," George said.

"I'll do that." The prosecutor said as he turned and walked away. He continued up the street to Melissa's diner. He walked up to the table where the sheriff, Adam, and Matt were sitting. "I'm done with George." He said.

"Thanks." The sheriff said. "We'll finish our coffee and head back."

Matt said to the prosecutor. "And when am I going to be released?"

"Shortly. I'll need authorization from the judge."

Matt grunted.

The prosecutor looked around for Melissa. He couldn't see her. He sat at the table, waiting for the waitress to come and offer him a cup of coffee or whatever he wanted. The waitress saw him and came over. "Can you organize a cup of coffee and then ask Melissa if she can come here to talk to me. Is she in?" The prosecutor asked.

"One coffee coming up. Yes, Melissa is in. I'll tell her you're waiting for her." The waitress said.

Melissa came out with his cup of coffee and greeted him. "I believe you want to talk to me."

"Yes. About your father. You better sit." The prosecutor said. Melissa sat.

"I relayed the judge's message to your father." The prosecutor said. "He was, of course, none too happy. I pointed out to him he needs to get representation for the court case. I've given him a week to get representation. I was anticipating him having to find someone from out of town. He said that he wants you to represent him." The prosecutor looked at Melissa and raised his eyebrows.

"That's ridiculous," Melissa said. "Surely I can't represent my father."

"You can." The prosecutor said. "You need to get him to sign an acknowledgment that you're not a lawyer. Other than that, you can represent him. I'll give you what he must sign. We don't want him to use that as an excuse at the end of the trial to say he was inadequately represented and therefore must go to trial again."

"I'm not happy about this," Melissa said. "I'll need to talk him out of it."

"I hope you're successful. I think your father is going to bully you into it." The prosecutor said.

"He's always so scathing about women doing what he calls men's work. I'm surprised that he's now asking for me to represent him. He's obviously got some trick up his sleeve," Melissa said.

"That's the reason I'm saying I'll draft the acknowledgment that you're not a lawyer for him to sign." The prosecutor said.

"I need to get this over and done with. Otherwise, I'm going to be permanently stressed," Melissa said. "I'm going to head down to the jail now and talk to him."

"Good luck." The prosecutor said. "You'll need it." He smiled at Melissa.

Melissa headed away from the prosecutor's table, head down, a frown etched on her forehead. She walked down the street to the sheriff's office. "Morning, Sheriff. I'm here to see my father. I believe he wants me to represent him."

"I don't envy you." The sheriff said. "I'll put handcuffs on him, and you can sit on the bench outside and talk to him."

The sheriff set them up and wandered down the street and leaned against a wall where he could keep an eye on them. "How're you doing, Papa?" Melissa asked.

"How do you think I'm doing?" George said.

"Dumb question, I guess," Melissa said. "I believe you want me to represent you. My answer is no, I can't."

"Typical woman. Can't do the job properly," George said. "I gather you say you want to be a lawyer. Well, lawyers must defend all sorts of people. It doesn't matter whether they think the person is guilty or not. Every person is entitled to a competent defense. So, if you want to become a lawyer, you can't be picking and choosing based on who you think is innocent or guilty."

Melissa didn't answer. She frowned. She thought. *He has a point. Maybe I need to take this on to see whether I can be a proper lawyer.*

"That's made you think, hasn't it?" George said.

"Why do you want me to represent you? You've always been of the view that women can't do these types of jobs," Melissa said.

"Well, even if I lose the case, at least I'll have proved one thing. That I'm right, women can't do these jobs," George said.

"I think you have an ulterior motive. You think if you lose the case that you'll be able to declare that you did not have competent defense and therefore the trial needs to be declared a mistrial, and you go to trial again," Melissa said.

George said nothing. He stared at her. Melissa guessed she'd hit the point. She continued. "If I did take the case on, it would be on condition that you sign an acknowledgment that you're aware I'm not a qualified lawyer and that you accept that my defense will be competent, and you may not later claim mistrial on the basis of my competence. The prosecutor will draft the document for you to sign."

"Would you be prepared to sign that?" Melissa asked.

"I might. I'll have to read it first," George said.

"I'll bring you the document to read. I'll have to fetch it from the prosecutor. I'll leave it with the sheriff, and he can give it to you. If you sign it before the end of today, then I'll act as your lawyer," Melissa said. "If it's not signed by the end of today, then I'll assume that you don't want me to represent you, and that will be that. The sheriff can bring me the signed document once you're done."

"I'm happy with that," George said.

Melissa stood up. "Bye, Papa. I'll be hearing from you."

"You will," George said.

Melissa waved the sheriff across. The sheriff said, "that was quick. So, you managed to turn him down without an argument."

She explained to the sheriff what was happening and her reasoning. The sheriff looked at her, skepticism written over his face. "I don't envy you. But for sure, it'll be a good test of whether you'll be able to hack it being a lawyer."

Melissa went back to the prosecutor and updated him.

He said, "I drafted the document anyway. Here it is." He handed the document to her.

"Everything is happening a lot quicker than I thought. I feel like I'm being railroaded." Melissa smiled, the smile not reaching her eyes. She took the document from the prosecutor and headed back down the street, and left the document with the sheriff.

An hour later, the sheriff walked into the restaurant with the signed document.

"Oh dear," Melissa said. "I'd hoped that document would put him off."

"Good luck with your task." The sheriff said as he turned to leave.

At supper that evening, Melissa gave the signed document to the prosecutor and said, "he signed the document, much to my surprise. What happens next?"

"I'll take it to the judge and see if he accepts you being appointed as defense. I don't think he'll have a problem, unfortunately for you. Then I'll come back and let you know whether you can act as your father's lawyer. If you can, then you need to consult with him and build your case. I'll check with the judge how long he'll give you to prepare your case. I don't think it'll be long, maybe three days. I'm guessing the court case will be on Monday." The prosecutor said.

"Well, this'll be a good test of my character," Melissa said.

The next morning at breakfast, the prosecutor confirmed to Melissa that she could act as her father's lawyer. After receiving the confirmation, she headed off down to the sheriff's office to consult with her father and build the case. The sheriff asked how long she'd need with her father. He said he could give her an hour.

After consulting with her father for an hour, she felt she had a good case along the lines of the law had been circumvented somewhat by the judge handing out various sanctions without trial. Also, she would argue that since he already signed an admission of guilt on the proposal that he would get a more lenient sentence, that the judge would be influenced by this. That the judge in court would, in any dispute during the court case, rule in favor of the prosecutor.

George was beginning to think his daughter might make a good lawyer. "I think you've built an excellent case. I can't see how we can lose."

"You shouldn't get too excited. I know nothing about the law, and the case I've built might be a load of nonsense in terms of the law. We'll have to wait and see," Melissa said.

She walked back to her diner, deep in thought. She was having difficulty reconciling to the fact that she could well get her father off even though she knew he was guilty. She was conflicted. On the one hand, she didn't want her father to hang whatever he'd done. On the other hand, she knew she'd be getting him off on technicalities. When she got to the restaurant, she saw Julia at one of the tables. "It's unusual for you to be here at this time of day," Melissa said.

"Yes, it is. I gather you're going to represent Papa at his trial. I wanted to talk to you about that and see how you're feeling," Julia said.

Melissa sat down at the table. She exhaled and said. "To be honest, not great. I'm conflicted. I think I've got a good case, and I can get him off or, rather, a not-guilty verdict. I don't want him to hang, so that's a plus. On the other hand, it doesn't seem right that someone should get away with murder, even if they are family, on a technicality. The reason I took the case on was, originally, I said I wouldn't take it on, but Papa and the prosecutor pointed out to me that if I want to be a lawyer, then it doesn't matter really what I think about whether someone's guilty or not. Everyone has a right to a competent defense. So, my thought was that this is a good test of whether I really want to be a lawyer."

"I was going to say that you shouldn't take on his case. Now, having heard what you said, it makes sense," Julia said.

Melissa smiled at Julia. "I was hoping you'd find a good reason for me to turn it down."

"What's happening about Matt? Shouldn't he be released now?" Julia asked.

"Yes, he should. I'll hunt out the prosecutor and see what's happening," Melissa said.

As she said that, Matt's voice came from behind her. "Hello, beautiful ladies."

They both turned around. "I was asking Melissa when you'd be released. She was going to go and check up with the prosecutor," Julia said.

"I thought you'd be missing me." Matt smiled and looked into Julia's eyes.

"I don't know about that. It was a random thought that crossed my mind," Julia said.

"Hah, I know different. Can I join you, ladies? Now that I'm out of jail, I feel like choosing my own meals rather than relying on sheriff Gamble to choose my meals," Matt said.

"You're welcome to join us," Melissa said. Julia frowned at him.

Matt sat down. He turned to Julia. "That frown doesn't fool me."

Julia smiled. Melissa waved the waitress across. "Can you bring a menu for Matt?" The waitress placed a menu in front of Matt.

"I'll start with a cup of coffee to drink while I study the menu." Matt smiled at the waitress.

Chapter 85

Monday morning arrived. The judge had said Monday is the date for the trial starting at 10 o'clock. The town hall was full of almost every resident from the town and around. Melissa was at a table that had been placed for the defense. Sheriff Gamble would bring George in shortly. The prosecutor was seated at the table placed across the aisle from Melissa. The judge's table had been placed on a platform at the front of the town hall. Currently, the desk was empty.

Sheriff Gamble unlocked George's cell. George held his hands out in front of him for the handcuffs. Sheriff Gamble locked the handcuffs onto George's wrists. As he did that, he thought, *I should've put his hands behind his back. I don't suppose it matters.*

He walked George down the street. As he got to the town hall, he walked between two columns of people who wanted a better view of the prisoner and to pass comment as he went. As they were passing between the columns of people, the sheriff saw Paul O'Brien and thought, *drunk as usual.* He noticed Matt Teeson was about to walk in the door and had turned at the commotion. As the sheriff and George Hamilton came next to Paul O'Brien, Paul O'Brien leaped out at George and said, "you're going to get what's coming to you, murderer."

Sheriff Gamble was to George's right. He went to push Paul O'Brien away. George grabbed Paul O'Brien's gun from his holster and turned to sheriff Gamble. There was a shot. George fell to the ground. The sheriff glanced at George, saw he would be no further danger, and looked around as he drew his weapon. He saw Matt Teeson standing there, his gun now by his side. There was a puff of smoke lingering in front of him.

The sheriff walked up to Matt. "You saved my life there." The sheriff said. "He was turning to shoot me."

The sheriff turned back toward Paul O'Brien. He glared at Paul O'Brien and said. "Hands behind your back." Paul O'Brien turned and put his hands behind his back. He was too stunned to do anything else. The sheriff placed the handcuffs that he had on his belt onto Paul O'Brien's wrists. "Paul O'Brien, you're charged with public nuisance and causing danger to the public." The sheriff asked one of the bystanders, who he knew well, to keep an eye on Paul O'Brien. He knelt beside George Hamilton and felt for his pulse. There was none. As the sheriff looked up, he saw Melissa, Julia, and the prosecutor pushing through the Crowd toward them. Immediately Julia and Melissa saw their father on the ground and rushed forward. Julia checked her father for a pulse, even though she'd seen the sheriff had already checked. She turned to Melissa and shook her head. Tears ran down her cheeks. "He's dead."

Melissa burst into tears. Melissa knelt beside her father and put her hands on his chest. Oblivious to the blood. The sheriff moved everyone back. He saw Bones in the crowd. "Bones, you'll need to remove the body and do what you normally do."

"Will do, sheriff." Bones said.

"Everyone stay where they are. I need to take statements from everyone on what they saw." The sheriff said.

"Who shot him?" Julia asked. A number of fingers pointed toward Matt and said. "He did."

Julia looked accusingly at Matt. "Looks like you shouldn't have been let out of jail."

No one else said anything, Matt didn't answer her.

The sheriff explained to the prosecutor what had happened and suggested he should tell the judge what had happened. He said he'd get statements from everyone to confirm or to make sure that his understanding was correct. The prosecutor headed off to tell the judge that there was no longer going to be a trial. After the consultation with the prosecutor, the judge turned to the crowd in the hall and announced that there would be no trial and that those that were going to stand for jury duty were excused.

Melissa and Julia went back to Julia's surgery. Once they were sitting down in Julia's office, Julia said. "So that Matt Teeson never should've been released. He's a murderer."

"I'm as upset as you," Melissa said. "But I don't believe that Matt Teeson it's a murderer. From what I hear, Papa grabbed Paul O'Brien's firearm when Paul O'Brien, who was drunk as normal, pushed his way to Papa and shouted insults at him. Papa saw an opportunity to escape, grabbed Paul O'Brien's firearm, and was turning to shoot sheriff Gamble. As I understand it, if Matt Teeson hadn't been so quick, Papa would've shot sheriff Gamble. Let's wait and see what the sheriff concludes after his investigation."

"You may be right. I'm upset. But if I look at it rationally, it's a better way for Papa to go than being hung. And it would've been worse if he shot the sheriff. I still don't know whether I'll be able to forgive Matt Teeson. I know there's no logic in it," Julia said.

Chapter 86

The next day the sheriff reported back to the prosecutor and the judge on his findings from all interviews. There were no conflicting views on what had happened. Amazingly the stories from the witnesses were all similar. Had Matt Teeson not been so quick, he, the sheriff, would be dead.

The judge looked at the prosecutor. "Do we need to stay on, or are you happy with the sheriff's conclusion?"

The prosecutor said. "We don't need to stay on. I'm happy with the sheriff's conclusion."

The prosecutor turned to the sheriff. "Will you ensure that Bones pays his fine and Adam Carter is safely transported to his permanent prison?"

"Yes, I'll make sure that all happens." The sheriff said.

"So, what happens about George Hamilton's ranch?" The prosecutor asked the judge.

"Let's meet with his daughters and debate with them what to do." The judge said. "Do you know if the girls are in town now, sheriff? You always seem to know what's going on and who's where."

"Yes, they're both in town at the moment at their places of work. Do you need me to fetch them?" The sheriff said.

"Yes, that would be good." The judge said.

The sheriff headed off to find Julia and Melissa. He came back in half an hour and said. "They'll be here shortly."

The three waited around for Melissa and Julia to arrive. When they arrived, the judge said. "Thanks for coming, ladies. I want to discuss what will happen to your father's ranch, given all the discussion we had around it."

Julia and Melissa looked at each other. Julia said. "We have discussed it. Theoretically, in terms of the law, as far as we know, the ranch should pass to our mother. Or whatever other dispensation my father's will makes. We also had a discussion with our mother on the topic last night. We've had a look at the will, which leaves it first to our mother, and if she dies, it comes to us. We agreed that it would be owned by the three of us, my mother, Melissa, and I. The profits from the ranch would be used to finance Melissa's law school and further training for me as a doctor. We would always leave enough funds in the ranch to maintain and develop the ranch further. We would like to provide a scholarship for one of the Apache to become a doctor. We would also like to go along with Matt Teeson's thoughts that the Apache should be able to hunt wild game on our ranches. We will, after all of this, try and ensure that a quarter of the profits get paid to the town Council to develop the town further. Whatever our father did, we would like to see that some good has come out of it."

The judge and the prosecutor looked at each other. The judge spoke. "Well, that sounds like a good conclusion to this mess. I like your ideas. I'm not so sure about the scholarship for an Apache to be a doctor. Firstly, I don't know whether they will have the brains or command of English to pass medical school. Secondly, I don't think they'll be accepted at medical school, firstly by the school and secondly by the students there."

"We have taken that into account," Julia said. "That would be our goal, to try and ensure that happens. If it's not possible, well, so be it."

"Well, I'm not sure what to say. It's been a tough time for you two." The judge said. "We'll be on our way tomorrow. Good luck for the future."

The prosecutor echoed the judge's words, and they split up. The judge and the prosecutor left on the stagecoach the next day.

————

Chapter 87

Julia had not seen Matt since the shooting of her father on the steps of the town hall. She was in two minds about whether she wanted to see him. She was having difficulty getting her mind around the fact that he'd shot her father. She knew she was being unreasonable but somehow couldn't change her feelings. She focused on running the practice, which was growing. She decided to avoid Matt. That was easier than trying to figure out what to say to him.

Jim Davies continued to run the ranch. Julia and Melissa knew this couldn't be a permanent solution. Jim was a good foreman but would need some guidance in running the ranch. Jim still had supper with the family as previously. After supper one evening, when Jim had left, Julia said to her mother and Melissa. "We need to talk about the future and the running of the ranch."

"Yes, I've been thinking the same," Melissa said. "We haven't had time until now." They sat around the dining room table and discussed the matter.

Julia opened. "Jim's a good ranch foreman, but I don't think he's up to running the ranch on his own. I don't know how we're going to deal with that. We don't necessarily need someone full time above him. But we need an experienced rancher to guide us in the bigger things. Anyone got any suggestions?"

"I've been thinking exactly the same thing," Melissa said. "I was thinking that we should see if Matt Teeson could run his ranch and ours together. What do you both think?"

"I'm having a problem getting my mind around what Matt did," Julia said. "So, I can't see it working, him running the ranch. I'm not sure that I trust him."

Melissa was about to respond and then bit her tongue. "What do you think, Mama?" Melissa said.

"This is all a bit foreign to me. Your father was a dominating personality, which is what I guess attracted me to him. I wanted someone who made all the decisions. As a result, I don't have any clear thoughts on it. I'll leave it up to you two girls to decide. You seem to have inherited your father's good traits."

Melissa turned to Julia. "We've had this discussion before about Matt, and you know you're not being logical."

"I know," Julia said. "Maybe we need to give it time for me to come around."

"We can do that. But we can't give it too much time," Melissa said. "I'm convinced that would be the best arrangement. But let's leave the decision for a couple weeks. Is everyone okay with that?"

Julia and Amy both said that seemed like a sensible suggestion. Everyone headed off to bed. It took Julia a long time to go to sleep. Her mind churned over her feelings for Matt Teeson. At the moment, confusion still reigned. Eventually, she fell asleep.

———

Chapter 88

Matt Teeson went back to running his ranch. He now had Geoff, Hugh, and Nitis as his ranch hands. He was happy to wake up on his own ranch. Geoff was already up making breakfast.

"Morning, Geoff. It'll be good to have one of your breakfasts again. Not that the breakfasts from Melissa's diner were bad. It's good to be back," Matt said.

"It's good to have you back. We were worried we'd have no jobs. That's, of course, not all we were worried about. We were worried about your neck as well. The law doesn't always work the way it should," Geoff said.

Nitis and Hugh came up from the stream. They looked fresh and clean but cold.

"Morning, boys. Good to see you and be back to normal," Matt said. Over breakfast, Matt issued instructions for the day. Once he'd issued the instructions, he said, "I'm going to go and see your chief, chief Mescal." Matt looked at Nitis.

"Why are you going to do that?" Nitis asked. "He's going to stake you out and torture you again and then kill you."

"I said I was going to allow him to hunt on my ranch. I want to go and arrange that with him and live up to my word," Matt said.

"It's good you want to live up to your word," Nitis said. "But I don't think it's worth it at the expense of your life. I'd have a better chance of surviving if I went to talk to him."

"I don't think so. Chief Mescal will be angry with you for releasing me and leaving the tribe. He'll treat you much worse than me," Matt said.

Nitis was silent for a while. "You're probably right. I don't think any of us should go and see him. We'll play it by ear, and if we bump into him and the opportunity arises, then we make this suggestion to him."

"Nope, I made a promise, and I'm going to keep it. I want this to happen as soon as possible," Matt said.

Both Hugh and Geoff put in their objections. Geoff said, "we've just seen off a whole lot of trouble and are getting back to normal. Now you want to go put yourself back in trouble again. Doesn't make sense to me."

"You're not going to dissuade me. You need to focus on the ranch work. I'll be back, don't you worry," Matt said.

Nitis realized there was no changing Matt's mind. "Well, if you're so determined to go, you might as well do something useful. Check on Nascha for me and see if I still have a chance with her, but don't let her know my feelings for her. Also, let her know I'm alive."

"I was going to do that anyway. I saw how you and she were together," Matt said.

———————

Chapter 89

Geoff, Hugh, and Nitis rode out to the ranch to carry out their chores. As they left, they wished Matt luck and said, "I hope you come back."

"I will don't you worry," Matt said as he rode off.

Matt camped next to a spring overnight, shooting a jackrabbit for supper. The next morning, he finished the jackrabbit at breakfast and rode on toward the Apache camp. He scanned the horizon and close by for any sign of the Apache. He didn't want to be ambushed. He wanted to go into the camp of his own accord. That way, he felt chief Mescal would realize his intentions were good and listen to him. Around noon he was close to the Apache camp. He hobbled his horse near some water on good grass. He walked to the hill overlooking the camp, moving silently between rocks and bushes to avoid detection. He waited, watching over the camp until he saw his best opportunity to get into the camp before being detected. He moved down toward the camp keeping behind boulders and bushes. He moved up a gully to the edge of the camp. He stopped there and watched further. He hid his weapons in the gully. He moved into the camp when he thought it was safe to do so. When he walked into the camp, he walked in with his hands in the air. Two warriors spotted him, ran toward him, and grabbed him, pulling his hands behind his back. They dragged him to chief Mescal's wikiup.

Chief Mescal was sitting outside his wikiup talking to two of his warriors. He looked up. "Well, look who we have here." He said. "So, you've been caught sneaking around the camp."

"No, I walked into your camp with no weapons and my hands up. I come in peace. I have a proposal for you." Matt indicated his lack of weapons. "You can check with these warriors."

Chief Mescal questioned the warriors in Apache. They answered him.

"It seems like you're telling the truth," Chief Mescal said. He spoke to his warriors again in Apache. They sat him down in front of the chief and stepped back. "So, what is it you want to talk about?"

"I said to you before I want to live in peace with you. I want to open my ranch up to you and your warriors to hunt on. You could hunt the wild game on the ranch, and I could continue running my cattle there. We could even bring more wild game on to the ranch, maybe drive some bison there. We need to make sure that the land is not overgrazed, though. I also want to talk to the Hamiltons about the same arrangement on their ranch."

Matt told chief Mescal about the goings-on over the last few weeks and the death of George Hamilton. He said, "I assume Mrs. Hamilton will be the new owner of the ranch, or it may be Mrs. Hamilton and her two daughters. I think they would agree with me and be happy to allow the same arrangement. They also want to live in peace with you. It was only George Hamilton. He wanted to own everything and keep everything to himself."

"What happened to Nitis?" Chief Mescal asked.

"He saved me because he knew my intentions were to live in peace with you. The other reason he saved me was that when you attacked me, I could have killed him, but I spared his life. He felt he owed me a debt. He's an honorable man," Matt said. "He's now working for me on my ranch. But he would like to mend fences with you. I think he would like to marry Nascha. Do you think you'll be able to forgive him?"

"Given what you say, if I see it in action, I can forgive him," Chief Mescal said. "How're you going to ensure that we are not attacked by the rest of the townsfolk?"

"I can persuade them that it's in their interest to live in peace with you. Also, they'll see that I'm allowing my ranch to be used for hunting by you, which doesn't affect them other than ensuring they can live in peace with you. I'll come back and let you know when I've cleared it with everyone," Matt said.

"All right. I'll let you go. Where are your weapons and horse?" Chief Mescal asked.

"I hid my weapons in the gully next to the camp. My horse is tethered further back. I wanted to show you that I came in peace. So, I had to sneak in and ensure that none of your warriors captured me while I still had my weapons," Matt said. "Could I see Nascha before I go? I promised Nitis I would check in with her and let her know that he is alive and would like to come and see her."

The chief spoke to the two Apache warriors who had brought Matt to him. He then turned to Matt. "They'll take you to Nascha. After that, you can be on your way, and I'll see you when you bring back the message that you've cleared the arrangement with the townsfolk."

The warriors led Matt to Nascha's wikiup. When they arrived there, one of the warriors spoke in Apache to her. She smiled at Matt. "It's good to see you again, Matt Teeson. I hear you have news of Nitis."

Matt smiled at her. "Yes, Nitis is working on my ranch. He specifically asked me to come and check on you and tell you that he's alive. He didn't ask me to say anything else to you, but between you and me, he's madly in love with you."

"Tell him I say hello. And look forward to seeing him again. That's all you must say to him. Don't go breaking my secrets to him like you did his secrets to me." Nascha smiled at him. "That will be between you and me. I need to keep him on his toes."

"I'll be on my way now. I'll tell him you look forward to seeing him and nothing else." Matt said as he turned away. The two warriors escorted him to his weapons and then to his horse. He climbed on his horse and waved goodbye to the two warriors. They stood and watched him go.

————————

Chapter 90

Julia was restless, thinking about Matt and what her real feelings for him were. Again, she couldn't get to sleep thinking about him. She was annoyed that he kept intruding on her thoughts. She decided the only way to solve the thoughts was to go and see him and see then how she felt. With that decision made, she fell asleep.

The next morning, she went into the surgery and attended to the patients. She was done by 12 o'clock. She headed down to Melissa's and had lunch there. Melissa came and talked to her while she had lunch. Julia mentioned nothing about her thoughts on Matt or what she was going to do. She didn't need Melissa advising her now that she'd made up her mind. After lunch, she climbed on her horse and headed out to Matt's ranch. She arrived at the ranch cabin. No one was there. She climbed the hill behind the cabin. At the top of the hill, she scanned the ranch land below. She saw three people moving cattle in the distance. She noted the path from the cabin that would get her there. She descended the hill and then followed the path out to the three people.

When she arrived, Geoff, Hugh, and Nitis greeted her. Geoff said. "To what do we owe this pleasure?"

"I was looking for Matt," Julia said. "Do you know where he is?"

"He went off to the Apache camp. Against our advice," Geoff said. "He wanted to talk to chief Mescal about allowing the tribe to hunt on the ranch for their food. Our concern was that chief Mescal would resume where he left off, with Matt, torture him, and then kill him. But once Matt gets something in his head, there's no stopping him. He always thinks he's right."

"Oh, dear. I'm not sure what I really wanted to see him about," Julia said. "My thoughts on him are conflicted. I'm mad at him because he shot my father, but on the other hand, before that, I had a lot of time for him. I thought maybe seeing him would clarify my thoughts. Now hearing what you said has clarified my thoughts. I'm worried that chief Mescal will do exactly what you suggest."

"I think it's unfair you being mad at him for shooting your father. I can understand it since you obviously love your father regardless of what he did. But Matt's only intention was to save sheriff Gamble," Geoff said.

"I know," Julia said. "I'm going to go to the Apache camp and see what's happening to Matt."

"I wouldn't do that at the moment," Geoff said. "You may only be compounding the problem. Matt is due back tomorrow sometime. I suggest you wait before rushing off to the Apache camp. When Matt comes back, I'll ride across and let you know."

"If he comes back," Julia said.

"Yes, there is that if he comes back," Geoff said. "I would still leave it two days."

"All right, I'll do that." Julia frowned. "It'll be an anxious wait. Thanks for the information and for offering to ride across to let me know. Don't let him know I've been looking for him. He thinks rather a lot of himself and is likely to jump to confusions."

"You're right there." Geoff smiled at her. "I won't let him know."

"I'll be seeing you." With that, Julia turned her horse and rode back to town and then on to her ranch.

———

Chapter 91

The next day Matt arrived back at the ranch at midday. There was no one at the cabin. *They must be out working on the ranch.* Matt thought. Matt made himself a cup of coffee and some lunch before doing exactly what Julia had done the day before. He climbed the hill to see where they were and then headed out to meet them.

When he arrived where the three were working, they all three greeted him, laughing, smiling, and patting his back. "Glad to see you back in one piece," Hugh said. "And not sent back in a bag and lots of little pieces by the Apache."

"So, what happened?" Nitis asked. He hoped Matt would start with Nascha.

"It went down as I expected," Matt said. "I walked into the camp and had a discussion with chief Mescal. Made my offer that he could come and hunt on my ranch. He was obviously happy, and that was that. How're things going with the ranch work?" He looked at Geoff. He saw out of the corner of his eye, Nitis frowning. He had difficulty keeping the grin off his face. He wondered how long it would take for Nitis to come straight out and ask him about Nascha.

Geoff told him of the goings-on on the ranch and that everything was going smoothly. "I think this is going to be a good year, boss." Geoff ended.

"Right, I'm back now," Matt said. "I guess it's about time I did some work as well."

Matt joined them, moving some cattle to where they were going to brand the calves that still needed branding. From time to time, he saw Nitis frowning at him. When they got the cattle to the branding spot, Nitis could contain himself no longer. He knew they'd be busy with the branding and wouldn't have time to talk. "So, did you talk to Nascha?" Nitis asked.

Matt looked at Nitis, a puzzled look on his face. "Nascha?" Matt said.

Nitis sighed. "Yes, remember, I asked you to check on Nascha and tell her I was looking forward to seeing her again. You forgot."

"Well, I had a lot on my mind," Matt said.

Nitis frowned. "I can't trust you to do anything. I should've come along with you."

Matt smiled. "Of course, I didn't forget. I went and spoke to Nascha and told her you were madly in love with her."

"That's not what you were meant to say," Nitis said.

"Well, maybe I got a bit carried away. She is well, anyway, and would like to see you," Matt said.

"Is that all she said?" Nitis asked.

"Yup, she didn't seem smitten with you. I think you're going to have to do a lot of work," Matt said. "I did clear the way for you to go back there with chief Mescal. I explained to him why you rescued me, and once I had made the deal about the hunting on the ranch, he was happy. You'll be quite safe going there now."

"Oh, so maybe you did do something right." Nitis smiled at Matt. "When can I go?"

"When we finish branding these calves, you can go. I guess it'll be the day after tomorrow," Matt said.

"Thanks, boss. I hope to be heading out then the day after tomorrow. Are you sure she didn't say anything more like she's totally in love with me?" Nitis asked.

"No, I think she has more sense than that," Matt said.

Nitis frowned. "Well, when she sees me, she'll remember how much she loves me."

"Okay, enough of this," Geoff said. "Let's get on with the work."

"Do you mind if I go into town tomorrow, boss?" Geoff asked. "I've got a few things to do."

"I think the same applies as to Nitis. Once the branding of the calves is done, then you can head to town. We'll see how it goes tomorrow. Maybe you can go the next day," Matt said.

"Thanks, boss," Geoff said.

The next day they finished branding the calves by noon. Nitis and Geoff both asked if they could be excused. Geoff said he'd be back by evening. Nitis would only be back, he said, maybe in four days or a week.

"Don't worry, Hugh, and I will keep things running here. In fact, it'll probably run smoother," Matt said. "Hugh and Geoff, you can have a day off when Nitis is back. In fact, make it two days. Nitis and I will look after the ranch for those days."

"Thanks, boss." Hugh and Geoff said together.

Geoff rode straight from where they were toward town. He would check to see if Julia was in town. If she wasn't, he would head out to her ranch. Nitis went back to the ranch cabin to gather supplies for his trip to the Apache camp. As he left the cabin, Matt said. "Good luck with Nascha. I hope she doesn't send you back here with your tail between your legs."

Nitis smiled and waved. "That'll never happen. I think she put on an act for you. She's madly in love with me."

"Well, I hope it turns out like that. I don't want you moping around here, not working hard for months because Nascha has no time for you." Matt said to Nitis' retreating back.

————

Chapter 92

Geoff rode into town and saw that Julia's horse was in the corral behind the surgery. *That'll save me a ride out to the ranch.* Geoff thought. He hitched his horse outside the surgery, dismounted, and walked into the surgery. There was one person waiting for Julia. As Geoff sat down, Julia came out. Her face lit up at the sight of Geoff. Geoff was momentarily surprised and then realized the enthusiastic look on her face was not for him. It was for the news he must be bringing.

"You mind waiting for ten or fifteen minutes while I attend to my last patient?" Julia said.

"Will you be closing up after this last patient?" Geoff asked.

"Yes, I will," Julia said.

"In that case, can I'll go and get a cup of coffee at Melissa's diner, and then you meet me there?" Geoff said.

"Okay, I'll see you at Melissa's," Julia said. She turned to the patient. "Sorry to keep you waiting. You can come through." The patient followed her through, and she closed the door. Geoff headed to Melissa's.

Twenty minutes later, Julia joined Geoff at Melissa's.

"Have you got news for me?" Julia asked.

"Yes, good news, I think. Matt is back safely. Mission accomplished," Geoff said. "Can I give him a message?"

Julia looked down at the table and frowned. After a minute, she looked up and said. "I think I'm totally doing the wrong thing here, given Matt's opinion of himself. Would you ask him if he'll have supper with me at Melissa's on Saturday night?"

"Oooh, I think that's a big mistake, but don't worry, I'll relay the message. I know he'll accept, but you might get a few comments with the acceptance," Geoff said.

Geoff was back at the ranch by evening. Matt was part way through making supper when he arrived. "Your timing's good," Matt said. "Supper will be ready shortly."

Hugh was out at the corrals attending to the horses. Matt finished cooking supper and summoned everyone to come and eat.

Over supper, Matt asked. "Did you see Julia while you were in town? She seems to be avoiding me."

"Uh, I did happen to bump into her," Geoff said.

"Did she say anything about me?" Matt asked.

"Why would she say anything about you?" Geoff said.

Matt looked disappointed. "Yeah, you're right."

Geoff smiled at Matt. "Oh, now my memory's coming back. She asked you to supper with her at Melissa's at 6 o'clock on Saturday night."

"Hah, I knew it. She's madly in love with me," Matt said. "Are you meant to relay a message back to her?"

"I said to her I would," Geoff said.

"Thanks, Geoff. Give her the following message. Despite the fact she is very forward for a woman, I understand why she would ask me to supper, so I'll come," Matt said.

"Are you crazy?" Geoff said. "You for sure will get a message back saying supper is off."

"Naah, she won't. She's too taken with me to give up this date," Matt said.

"I'll deliver the message," Geoff said. "But don't be disappointed when I come back and say supper is off and that I didn't warn you."

Matt smiled at Geoff. Geoff shook his head in wonderment.

"Well, you at least gained yourself the morning off tomorrow, Geoff," Matt said. "You can head into town when you get up and have breakfast on me at Melissa's for delivering the message." Matt handed across the money to pay for Geoff's breakfast.

"Now you're paying money and giving me time off to be disappointed," Geoff said.

Matt smiled and said nothing.

The next morning Geoff headed out to town before breakfast. He thought maybe he'd catch Julia at breakfast at Melissa's. He went straight to Melissa's. He was right. Julia and Melissa were having breakfast together.

As he walked up to the table, Julia smiled at him. "He must be eager. You've brought the message so soon."

"I have strict instructions to deliver the message as Matt told it to me. So don't shoot the messenger," Geoff said.

The smile dropped off Julia's face. "What, he had the cheek to turn me down?"

"No, not quite, but nearly as bad. He said, and I quote: Despite the fact you are very forward for a woman, he understands why you would ask him to supper, so he will come," Geoff said.

Julia's face flushed. "Why, the conceited oaf. Tell him supper is off."

"I did warn him that would be your response. But he insisted I deliver the message as is," Geoff said.

Julia clattered her coffee cup into the saucer. "I thought I might be making a mistake."

"Don't be silly, Julia. You should know him by now. You wouldn't have expected him to say anything else. But behind that façade is a gentleman," Melissa said.

"Oh, so now you've taken a shine to him, all that working closely together to get him acquitted," Julia said.

"Of course not. If that was the case, I'd be telling you to turn this date with him down," Melissa said.

Julia frowned and looked at Melissa. "I suppose there's something in that."

Julia looked at Geoff and said. "Tell him he's a conceited oaf, and the only reason I'm asking him to supper is to discuss a business transaction. He might be able to help us out. Although I'm not sure whether he has the skills."

Geoff smiled. "I'll tell him that. I'll also tell him he was lucky. My prophecy nearly came true. If it hadn't been for Melissa persuading you, it would've come true. At least you didn't shoot the messenger."

Julia and Melissa smiled at Geoff. Melissa said. "For all your good deeds, Geoff, you can have breakfast on the house."

"No, not necessary. Matt's given me some money for breakfast here. So, I suggest you take his money while the going is good," Geoff said.

After breakfast, Geoff headed back to the ranch. He rode out to where Matt was working. "What did she say?" Matt asked.

"Well, you're lucky. As predicted, she originally said there's not a chance now that she'll go to supper with you, with your conceited attitude. In fact, she said, you're a conceited oaf. It was only because she was having breakfast with Melissa that Melissa was able to dive in and persuade her that, yes, you are a conceited oaf, but don't let that get in the way of a business decision," Geoff said.

"What do you mean get in the way of a business decision?" Matt asked.

"The only reason she's asking you to supper is that she has a business proposition for you, although she's not sure you'll have the skills," Geoff said.

Matt frowned. He looked up at Geoff. "Do you think this is just a business meeting?

"Yes, I do," Geoff said. "You see, you jumped to confusions."

Matt looked thoughtful. All he said was, "huum."

"Are you going to have to go back to town and confirm with Julia that supper is on?" Matt said.

"No, she said if you don't pitch up, she'll have supper on her own. That'll then be the end of any future conversations with you," Geoff said.

"I suppose I better go then," Matt said.

"I think that would be sensible," Geoff said.

Chapter 93

Saturday arrived. Matt paced around. He then dived into the cold stream water and cleaned himself up. He hunted through his few clothes for the clothes that he thought would make him look handsomest. He only had one decent pair of jeans that looked like they were not on their last legs. That was an easy choice. He tried on three different shirts. Geoff was in the other corner of the cabin sorting out supper for himself, Hugh, and Nitis. He looked up at Matt. "You appear to be worried about something." Geoff smiled at Matt. "You're worse than a woman. I've never ever seen a man try on so many different sets of clothes. It looks to me that there was a lot of bravado going on before."

Matt looked up at Geoff and frowned but said nothing. Eventually, he settled on what he thought was his best look. He started pacing again. From time to time, looking at where the sun was in the sky. He was anxious to get going, but he didn't want to arrive early. He gave up trying to restrain himself and left, knowing he'd arrive early. He wondered if Julia would be early or late.

Matt arrived at Melissa's diner half an hour early. He wandered in and looked around. There was no Julia. He was about to duck out, but he was too late. Melissa saw him.

"You're early, Matt. It seems you're eager for this supper." Melissa smiled at him.

"Hello, Melissa." Matt could think of nothing else to say. Melissa laughed.

"Can I get you something while you wait for Julia?" Melissa asked.

"I don't know. Maybe I should just wait. I've never been on a date before," Matt said.

"Oh, I didn't know this was a date," Melissa said. "I thought this was a business meeting. Did you jump to conclusions?"

Matt was silent.

"For a business meeting, I don't think wine or beer is appropriate," Melissa said. "Can I bring you a soft drink?"

"I suppose so," Matt said.

Melissa went off to get him a soft drink and came back five minutes later with a soft drink for him.

He sat drinking the drink and watched everyone who came into the restaurant. The clock in the corner showed that it was now 6:10, and Julia still had not arrived. Matt frowned. He thought of getting up and leaving. That would teach her to be late. But he couldn't get himself to move from his chair.

At 6:15, Julia came in. She stopped and looked around and saw him. She smiled and walked over. Matt stood up. He couldn't help but stare. He hadn't seen Julia dressed up before.

Julia said. "Have you been waiting long?"

"No, I just got here." Matt regretted the words as soon as they were out of his mouth. He knew Julia would check with Melissa about what time he got to the restaurant. "Actually, that's not true. I was half an hour early."

Julia laughed. "I know. Melissa told me at the door. I guess you couldn't wait to see me."

"You're right. I couldn't. I've been like a cat on a hot tin roof this afternoon. Even though this is only a business meeting, I'm told," Matt said.

"I'm glad you understand that," Julia said.

"Is the beautiful Melissa joining this business meeting?" Matt asked.

The smile disappeared from Julia's face. "So, you've taken a shine to my clever sister who got you out of jail?"

Matt smiled at her. "Well, she is beautiful and clever."

Julia's frown deepened. Matt held the chair out for her and pushed it in as she sat. Matt sat down opposite her. "Okay, let's get down to business," Julia said.

"Beauty and brains seem to run in the family. No one can hold a candle to you. You're the smartest and most beautiful women I know," Matt said.

"I thought Melissa was the most beautiful and clever woman?" Julia frowned at Matt.

"No, that's not what I said. I said Melissa is beautiful and clever. But you're the most clever and beautiful woman I know," Matt said.

Julia tried to stop the smile appearing on her face, unsuccessfully.

"Part of the reason for me meeting you was because I've been conflicted in my feelings for you. I've been angry with you for shooting my father, but on the other hand, there are some things that I might like about you," Julia said. "Now that I'm sitting opposite you, I remember there actually are a lot of things I like about you." Julia smiled.

"So, is this a date or a business meeting?" Matt said. "I've got to know which of my games to bring to the table."

"Well, I hope it's a date. But there is business we need to discuss as well," Julia said.

"Oh well, I'll bring my date game to the table and throw my business game in as a bonus," Matt said.

"Do you drink wine?" Matt asked. "You make me nervous. I might need a sip of wine to relax me."

"Yes, I do drink wine," Julia said. "I think we should order some."

"Which do you prefer? Red, white?" Matt asked.

"I prefer red," Julia said. "I thought you cowboys' only drunk whiskey and beer."

"I'm pretending to be a little bit sophisticated," Matt said.

"Oh, are you trying to impress me?" Julia said.

"How did you guess? Now, are we on the date part of the dinner or the business part of the dinner?" Matt asked.

The waitress interrupted them and asked, "can I get you something to drink while you decide what you're going to have to eat?"

Matt ordered a bottle of red wine.

Julia continued after the waitress had left to fetch their wine. "I don't think I said anything about a date part of the dinner, so it's business."

"I guess, if you insist, we can go ahead with business," Matt said.

"Melissa and I were talking about the Hamilton ranch. My mother doesn't have the skills or really the interest to run the ranch. Melissa wants to go to law school and become a lawyer. I want to carry on with my doctoring and learn more about it. Jim Davies is good at running the day-to-day things but not beyond that." Julia paused. "So, we got to discussing how we're going to manage the ranch. We would still like to keep it, but we'd also like to do some good."

"Well, since none of you seem to be interested in running the ranch, that's a tricky problem," Matt said.

"Melissa thought that you would be the best person to run the ranch for us. We figured you'd have time since you've got three good hands on your ranch, and Geoff is capable of running the day-to-day ranch matters." Julia looked at Matt and raised her eyebrows.

Matt was silent for two minutes. He looked up at Julia. "It's a possibility. How would you pay me?"

"We thought we would pay you a monthly salary and ten percent of the profits of the ranch," Julia said. "The salary we thought would be equivalent to a foreman's full month's salary. Even though you wouldn't need to spend nearly a full month on the ranch."

"That could work," Matt said.

"The balance of the profits from the ranch would go to supporting Melissa through her lawyer training and me for further learning about being a doctor. Originally part of the sentence that was suggested for my father before the judge said that he couldn't give him a more lenient sentence was that part of the profits from the ranch get paid to the town Council. My mother, Melissa, and I would still like to do that so that some good comes from my father. We also know that you want the Apache to be integrated into this town in some way. We thought maybe we could offer a scholarship to one of the Apache to become a doctor so that he could look after the tribe. I know it's a long shot, and whoever it is will struggle because of the fact their English is not so good, and the other students would not welcome an Apache to their class."

"That all sounds good," Matt said. "Would you be amenable to the Apache hunting on your ranch for their basic needs?"

"Yes, we discussed that. I know that was one of the things you wanted to do," Julia said.

"Yes, I've already set that up with chief Mescal for my ranch," Matt said. "He'll be happy to hear that you've agreed that he can hunt on your ranch. I know he has a lot of respect for you from the times that you have attended to his warriors."

They discussed more details about the proposed arrangement.

"I'm sure we've done the business part of the dinner to completion," Matt said. "Now, can we get on with the date part of the dinner?"

"I suppose so if you insist," Julia said. "I still don't remember any discussion about there being a date part of this dinner."

"Well, we haven't eaten yet. So, if there isn't a date part, then we'll have to go hungry," Matt said.

"You make a good point," Julia said. "I guess we'll have to have a date part of the dinner. I know nothing of such matters, so I'll leave it up to you."

Matt, having now got the dinner to where he wanted, was lost for conversation.

"You're quiet now. You sounded confident that you knew how to deal with the date part of the dinner. Now it looks like you're there. You suddenly come up short," Julia said.

"Yes, it seemed easy when it was all talk, but I've had no practice at this before," Matt said. "So, you need to be patient while I learn."

"I don't like the idea that I'm an experiment for you to learn on, and then once you polish your skills, you go off and charm some other lady," Julia said. "Is that your intention? You and Melissa seemed to get quite close while she was your lawyer. Is that who you're honing your skills for?"

"Hmmm, you make a good point," Matt said. "Melissa is pretty and smart. I could do worse."

Now that Julia had suggested it, she suddenly thought that it was a strong possibility. The smile dropped off her face. She scowled at Matt.

Matt thought maybe he'd overstepped. "Have you already forgotten what I said about this before? Do I have such an effect on you?" Matt said.

Julia had difficulty not smiling. She looked at him and frowned. "I'm not sure whether to believe you or not now. You also need to come up with some more lines. I don't want a one-trick pony."

"I think I can help with that," Matt said. He got up from his chair and moved next to Julia. He got down on one knee. "Julia Hamilton, I want to spend the rest of my life with you. Will you marry me?"

Julia opened her mouth and eyes wide. "But you hardly know me. I could maybe understand if we had had a few date dinners, but this is rather sudden."

Matt stopped smiling. "I guess it is rather sudden. At least you know you'd be marrying a decisive man." He looked into her eyes and smiled. "This is a once only offer, well, maybe not. That's one of my faults. I'm persistent, so this probably isn't a once only offer. Damn, did I say that out loud?"

The restaurant had gone silent. Everyone watched, seeing Matt on one knee.

Julia was oblivious to everyone else. "I don't want you nagging me. So, my answer is yes." Julia stood up and grabbed Matt as he stood up. She wrapped her arms around him. "In spite of not knowing you for long, I know there's no one else for me."

There was a collective sigh from the restaurant. Followed by clapping and congratulations.

Matt relaxed, having got that done with. He didn't know where that had come from. He certainly hadn't planned it before. But now that he'd done it, he knew it was the right thing.

———

Epilogue

The Apache were now hunting on the two ranches. The tribe was thriving. Chief Mescal and his warriors had dealt with a bunch of rustlers that attempted to steal cattle from the Hamilton ranch.

The town looked in better condition. Some money had already come into the town council from the Hamilton ranch, and Bones had paid his fine to the town council. His wife gave him a whole bunch of angry words for being so stupid. After a week of alternating anger and silence, she said to him. "We can't be doing this forever. I know in your heart you're a good man, and you made a mistake. So, I'm now over it and have forgiven you. We can get back to where we were before."

Bones said. "Thank you, I'm sorry, and no such thing will happen again."

Adam Carter had been transferred to the territory jail. Jail did not seem to be getting him down. The other inmates realized he was one tough character, and no one messed with him. He vowed he would behave himself in jail and turn over a new leaf, never to commit another crime. Julia and Melissa had been to see him and check how he was doing. They said that he could have his job back when he eventually came out if he promised them that from then on, he was going straight.

The town grew. People were attracted to the low crime rate and the improved state of the town. All the buildings were now in good condition. Sheriff Gamble took no nonsense. As a result, the town was peaceful. People had also heard about the fact that the town was living in peace with the Apache. This attracted people to the town the fact that there was less danger than in other towns, although the white folk didn't mix with the Apache. But each seemed to tolerate the other.

Melissa had gone off to law school and confirmed to Julia and Matt that she was doing the right thing. This is exactly where she wanted to be.

Julia's practice was busy. The local men now accepted that despite her being a woman, she was a good doctor.

Two months after Julia and Matt were married, Nitis married Nascha. The wedding was held at the Apache village. Matt, Hugh, Geoff, Julia, and Melissa attended the wedding. Nitis looked like the cat that had stolen the cream. His chest was puffed out. Nascha couldn't take her eyes off him.

"That looks like a match made in heaven," Matt whispered to Julia. "Nitis looks proud of himself. Who would've imagined where we are today a few months ago?"

THE END

A list of my other books follows. Please post a review or rating on Amazon. If you are on the electronic version, page to the end, it's one more page, and the Amazon review link will come up. It's easy. Take a few seconds to post your review or rating. Also, click on the follow button, and you will be advised when my next novel comes out.

If you are on the hard copy version, go to the book on The Amazon site and post a review there and click follow.

———

Other books by AC Craft:

Follow the author for notification of new books:

Please go to my author page by clicking this link and then click follow, and you will be notified when my next book comes out, which should be every three to four months:
Author page to click follow for notification when next book comes out

Also, to see a list of all books by AC Craft and about the author.

Westerns.

A Matt Teeson Western, Book no 2 - Teeson's Creek

A Matt Teeson Western, Book no 3 - Teeson's Creek Justice

Africa, Action, Aviation, Romance Series.

Novel 1 - Cumulus Air

Novel 2 - The Phenom Quest

Novel 3 – Brutus

Novel 4 - Kate

Novel 5 - The Coffee Crucible

Made in United States
Orlando, FL
20 November 2023

39224123R00313